"Stenson fills the pages with ⟨...⟩
and memorable characters, both ⟨...⟩
NATIONAL POST

"You can practically taste the dust of the trail, smell the
blood and whiskey on the barroom floors."
CALGARY HERALD

"A delightful tour-de-force. . . . An engaging novel
that deserves a wide audience."
BORDER CROSSINGS

"Stenson displays a graceful command
of dialogue, narrative pace and detail."
THE TORONTO STAR

"This magnificent western deserves a spot next
to McMurtry and Cormac McCarthy."
FASTFORWARD (CALGARY)

"It's the depiction of the open range, amidst the natural
elements of geography and climate, that makes *Lightning* such
a literary achievement and such a damn good read."
KITCHENER-WATERLOO RECORD

"Stenson moves his narrative along with taut, muscular
writing that makes us see and feel the open range, both
the rugged and unforgiving landscape and the equally rugged
and unforgiving characters who live and die in it."
THE HAMILTON SPECTATOR

"Does what the best historical fiction should do:
deepens the reader's understanding of a
time and place while telling a compelling story."
UPTOWN MAGAZINE

LIGHT

FRED STENSON

NING

DOUGLAS & MCINTYRE
VANCOUVER/TORONTO

Douglas & McIntyre Ltd.
2323 Quebec Street, Suite 201
Vancouver, British Columbia
Canada v5T 4S7
www.douglas-mcintyre.com

National Library of Canada Cataloguing in Publication Data
Stenson, Fred, 1951–

Lightning / Fred Stenson.

ISBN 1-55365-010-7 (bound) ISBN 1-55365-030-1 (pbk.)

1. Cattle drives—Northwest, Canadian—Fiction. I. Title.

PS8587.T45L53 2003   C813'.54   C2003-910547-4
PR9199.3.S783L53 2003

Editing by Jennifer Glossop
Cover and text design by Peter Cocking
Cover illustration © Bettman/CORBIS/MAGMA
Typesetting by Lynn O'Rourke
Maps by Stuart Daniel/Starshell Maps
Printed and bound in Canada by Friesens
Printed on paper that is forest-friendly
(100% post-consumer recycled paper)
and has been processed chlorine free

We gratefully acknowledge the financial support of the
Canada Council for the Arts, the British Columbia Arts Council, and
the Government of Canada through the Book Publishing Industry
Development Program (BPIDP) for our publishing activities.

For my children, Kate and Ted

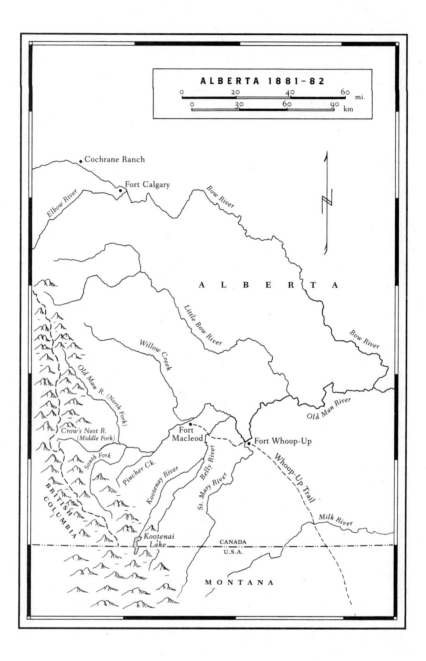

ALBERTA 1881-82

Cochrane Ranch

Fort Calgary

Elbow River

Bow River

A L B E R T A

Little Bow River

Bow River

Willow Creek

Old Man R. (North Fork)

Old Man River

Crow's Nest R.
(Middle Fork)

Fort
Macleod

Fort Whoop-Up

South Fork

Pincher Ck.

Kootenay River

St. Mary River

Belly River

Whoop-Up Trail

BRITISH
COLUMBIA

Milk River

Kootenai
Lake

CANADA
U.S.A.

MONTANA

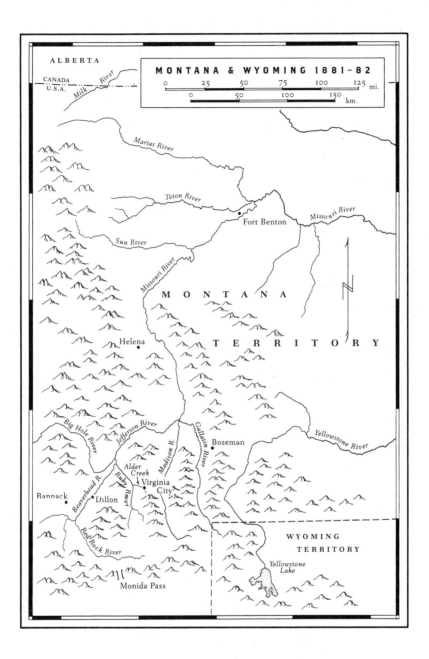

ALBERTA

CANADA
U.S.A.

Milk River

MONTANA & WYOMING 1881-82

0   25   50   75   100   125 mi.

0   50   100   150
km.

Marias River

Teton River

Fort Benton

Missouri River

Sun River

Missouri River

M O N T A N A

Helena

T E R R I T O R Y

Big Hole River

Jefferson River

Gallatin River

Bozeman

Yellowstone River

Madison R.

Alder
Creek

Ruby River

Virginia
City

Bannack

Beaverhead R.

Dillon

Red Rock River

WYOMING
TERRITORY

Yellowstone
Lake

Monida Pass

MONTANA

THE GATHER

When the last blizzard rolls in so you'd swear the wind is blowing from four directions, when the air is so full of snow that it breathes like feathers, when your cattle drift with the whirlwind looking for a place to pile and die, when inside your cabin watching a flame panic and dance, you surmise that no one ever guessed the world would end in a blizzard . . .

. . . just then, dawn sets fire to a morning and pours hot light on the quilted earth. The brilliance reflects so evenly that the inside of your nose and your eyelids burn red. The roof shingles dance with lacy water off their curled edges.

Your cowboys ride down the drifts, release the mass of avalanched cattle, who once they believe in life renewed pour back down the trail to the river's edge and drink.

For all your fears, only one cow dies. At the water's edge, she reaches her nose across the ice fringe, is horn-bowled into the fast-moving current, and drowns.

All in all, you rejoice.

DILLON, MONTANA

April 1881

OVER THE RUBY MOUNTAINS, the sun rose inside a winter halo and ignited the flat, snowy valley of the Beaverhead. A crooked line of cottonwood stags marked the river and led to town. Dillon was an afternoon town, and its one-sided main street glowered in the morning, while across the boardwalk and the mud, the tracks of the Utah and Northern Railroad beamed light. Up that line, prosperity had come, and for the moment, Dillon was the end-of-steel and the logical centre of everything in southwest Montana. The boosters were happy.

Across the tracks to the west, the town stopped and a scrubby flat began. It stretched to a row of dry hills. There, in the angle between flat and closest hill, stood a soddy, old enough for grass to have grown on its roof. There were no windows, not even paper ones, and the dawn arrived inside through the cracks between door boards and down one moted beam that augured through a knothole.

STEPPING OVER BODIES and through the dusty streams of light, Doc Windham made his way to the stove and felt its side. There were still hot coals in the bottom, and when he threw in a handful of kindling, it flamed. Though not the frigid mornings of a month ago, this wasn't springtime either. It was that time of advent when summer's wages are a distant memory and spring round-up but a prediction, a time when Doc and his wintering partners, Dog Eye and Lippy, along with all the other out-of-work cowboys on the Beaverhead, had begun to starve. If a prairie chicken or a rabbit did not die on your bullet each day, you ate beans or went hungry.

The problems of this season had been forecast in the fall, when Doc and his partners were let go by Poindexter and Orr, the biggest ranch in the region. Laid off, there was nothing for the cowboys to do except head for town, and because the P & O surrounded the town of Dillon, that meant Dillon. Or rather they had come to this deserted soddy on Dillon's outskirts, and moved in before they knew its story:

how the squatter who built it had gone broke and hanged himself from the first tree in any direction tall enough to get him off the ground.

As winter came on strong, they had learned to get out and clean the roof, lest the weight of the snow push the sods between the pole beams some night and crush them. If the form of falling weather was rain, it arrived inside as a dark slurry that they dodged with their plates of beans and cups of coffee. The soddy's purpose was to retain heat through the coldest hour, and theirs had done so, barely.

Doc pushed more deadwood into the stove and closed the door. Through several holes in the rotten metal, he could see the dancing yellow. On the stove-top was the coffee can. Doc threw in the last of the grounds.

While he waited for the coffee to boil, Doc considered his companions by the yellowy light. Lippy Mann, twenty-one and keen as scissors, was sitting up in his blankets now, raking at his curly mop of blond hair. Not one to lie in bed full of woe, Lippy rose and pulled on his clothes, snapped his suspenders, which he liked to wear tight. As far as Doc could remember, Lippy had not spoken in two days. That was his nature: to be quiet and quieter. During times of adversity, he was all but wordless.

Dog Eye French, a skinny Texan of twenty-five, was another matter. He was never quiet if awake and had been tiresome through complaint for months. At present, he was stretched luxuriantly from wall to wall, probably only pretending to sleep, which he would do sometimes for an hour, waiting to make sure all the work was done.

By nature, Doc was the most talkative of the three but did not believe in bellyaching. Not doing so when times were hard was an enjoyable challenge. At thirty-seven, Doc was old for a cowboy, but he believed experience had given him a resource of philosophy most cowboys lacked. For example, in the present instance, Doc looked beyond the hungry moment and saw spring. Come spring, ranchers hired round-up crews. It was inevitable. A law. If the Bible had been written in Montana, it would be a biblical law.

While the stove smoked out its many holes and the coffee can began to rattle, Doc thought more about the spring round-up. He thought in particular about Poindexter and Orr, who had reliably hired him in the past. He wondered, as he had almost every day this cold winter, why the P & O foreman had passed on him and his partners in the fall.

Doc turned his gaze on Dog Eye, who was finally sitting up. He stared at him cruelly while the noise in the can escalated. Dog Eye, who got his name from having eyes sad as a hound's, looked very much like a hound this morning upon seeing Doc's expression.

"Dog Eye, let's go over this again, before I bow down to Poindexter and Orr's cow boss. What did you do to annoy the man?"

The hound's eyes looked away.

"I did nothing. If you don't believe me, don't."

Doc was about to argue when it occurred to him that Dog Eye was correct. Doc was being annoying and unfair, just the way Dog Eye was most days and would become again as soon as he was awake enough. Even though Lippy never spoke, Doc knew his thoughts and they were tiresome too. All three of them had spent too long in this soddy staring at the oil-can stove, wondering if this was the day its side would fall off, arguing whose turn it was to fiddle with the coffee-can stovepipe collars when they began to smoke.

Too long around their rude table by the light of a homely bitch lamp, playing poker and three-card monte and stook and rummy and whatever else anyone could remember. They had chased bills and coins around the table's crooked surface until, by virtue of trips to town for flour and beans and never enough whisky, the pile of money had all but disappeared.

And the only relief from these tiresome rituals was to go to town again.

The true measure of today's desperation was that Lippy agreed to come when Doc proposed it. Lippy Mann, who hated town because he hated to be seen.

BY EARLY AFTERNOON, the three cowboys were in chairs in the most unpopular saloon in Dillon. Here, there were none of the lurid paintings or Indian souvenirs that decorated most saloons. There was nothing at all to look at except the odd mouse trotting along the foot of the grey walls. Even though the place was empty, Lippy sat in shadow, with his hat brim low and his coat collar high.

"This is the worst saloon I've ever seen," said Dog Eye, his voice booming. "I thought we come to town to see other human beings. This saloon doesn't even have a whore."

Fat, the owner and bartender, listened from behind his bar. He showed his hurt by turning his mouth down into his many chins. Even the motion by which he smoothed his soft hands over rivulets of egg yolk and bacon fat on his aproned belly was sad.

Doc leaned close to Dog Eye. "There is no call to insult Fat. This saloon has the cheapest shots in town. It has no people, and that's how Lippy likes it. Lippy has a right to come to town too."

Out of the dark coat collar, Lippy said, "I'll go to the livery barn. I want to look at horses anyway."

This was the truest thing said in an hour. Since they had no horses among them, Lippy was pining. Horses were Lippy's closest friends. But true or not, in the growing disturbance of Doc's mood, he would not hear of it.

"You stay put and drink your drink, Lippy."

"It's gone."

"Dog Eye does not have two bits to rub. All his talk about popular saloons and whores is nonsense. A better saloon would throw him out. As for whores, Dog Eye couldn't buy a dance with the plainest buffalo whore in Montana."

There was a little bead of amber in the foot of Dog Eye's glass. He rolled it back and forth, rendered silent for the moment.

Dog Eye did not have many good features. Most of what was good in him were his cowboy skills, so that he became a worse person the longer he was on foot or in town. It was a good question why Doc kept company with him and had done for two years, and the answer was that Doc had not chosen it. Though it was not much in evidence today, Dog Eye French had burred onto Doc, seeking in Doc a replacement for the father he'd lost in the Civil War. Because Doc was in favour of people doing what they wanted, Dog Eye remained. Lippy had been with Doc longer, and Doc liked him better, but he reasoned that even a real father doesn't like his offspring all the same.

The saloon's door stood open, and Doc looked through it to where a sickly sun was trying to warm a dingy afternoon. After a promising start to the day, a wind from the north had blown a mess of cloud over the valley. Twice since they'd come, little snow flurries had filled the air and disappeared into the mud. The street outside was so empty that when a wagon passed, Doc jumped. The mules in harness had to suck each hoof out of gluey depth.

Just then, out of the darkness above them, a fly fell and landed among their glasses and beside the buckled deck of Civil War playing cards. It narrowly missed the coal-oil lamp that Doc had coaxed Fat to light for them, and perhaps in its winter crack above had mistaken the lantern's rising heat for summer. A big greasy green-reflecting fly, its luck in life was to fall on its back. Round it spun, and depending on the pattern of grain or knot or carved initials, it propelled itself this way and that.

"Four bits next time I have money says that fly falls off the table closest to Lippy," Doc said.

Dog Eye and Lippy both leaned forward, a quickness of interest where gloom and fatigue had been. The fly hit a piece of petrifying bacon fat and threw left.

"I'll take your money, Doc," said Dog Eye. "I say it falls on you."

"Com'mon, Lip. In or out? You can't wait 'til it's teetering."

"The empty chair," said Lippy.

They watched the fly and were better entertained than they had been. They cheered and jeered as the fly buzzed close to any edge, and chided each other for breathing hard or making any motion that might produce an influential fan of air. The fly was more or less back in the middle, beside the lantern's metal base and stuck on the shoal of the card pile, when Len Spikes made a silhouette in the door.

Len wandered over with half a yard of light winking between his bony knees. A southern waddie, Len had been one of the oldest men on the cattle drive that had brought Doc to Montana. Back then, Len had been on the far edge of his prime, and now, in Dillon, he was near his trail's end. A job as cook's helper last summer hadn't paid enough to last the winter. That, coupled with his weakness for whisky, had turned this season of cold into a mortal threat. Len looked as though he hadn't eaten for a week and probably couldn't stomach it if you gave him a beefsteak. What he needed was a drink.

Doc stood and greeted his friend. Len's hand shook violently until Doc got it clamped. He gestured toward the open chair and Len fell into it, rubbing his leg hard. Dog Eye gave Len a dirty look, disappointed at the game's interruption and not liking to share his table with a drunk.

Len sat nodding and grinning, while Doc felt in his pockets. In a far corner were a couple of coins, all that remained.

"Fat!" Doc called out. "Would I be right in thinking that a dollar will stretch to a round of whisky for my friend here and the rest of us?"

Fat looked worried. A creature of complaint, no deal ever struck him as good. At the same time, he was unlikely to let their dollar leave his saloon. When he brought the bottle and an extra shot glass, Doc nudged his elbow.

"Don't be cheap, Fat. You're getting the last of our summer's wages, and you've had your share of the rest. Bear in mind that the river of money refreshes come spring."

To his credit, Fat poured their glasses full.

"Let's drink to spring and summer—boys, Len. To the warm sun on our full bellies. To the bronc twisters who are right now civilizing the next horses of our lives."

It was a cruelty to Len to toast so long. When Doc was finished, Len lowered his mouth to the glass and, under the stained broom of his moustache, sucked at the skin of whisky that was hugging the shot-glass rim. Then he tried to lift the glass but set it down quick when the shake in his hand cost him a drop. He was at a loss, needing that drink so badly and not having the steadiness to get it where he needed it to go.

"Lippy, Dog Eye, go take a piss."

Dog Eye wanted to argue, but Lippy got him by the shoulder and towed him. When they were out the back door, Doc said, "If you don't mind, Len, I'll help you with that."

Len Spikes's watery blue eyes gleamed gratitude and fear. Doc hoisted Len's glass and held his own empty one underneath. He tipped the full one carefully to the quivering mouth. Between them, in two tries, they got it done.

"Thanks, Doc," said Len, rubbing his wrist across his wet mouth, licking the wrist as an afterthought.

Then Lippy and Dog Eye returned and sat down, and Dog Eye yelled a curse that made them jump. "Goddamn fly's gone!" He looked around, pointed at one of the legs of Doc's chair. "There he is!"

"How can you tell, Dog Eye? You mark its ear?"

That caused Lippy to laugh inside his collar. You couldn't move a foot in any direction without scrunching a fly that had lost his winter's perch in the ceiling.

"Never mind, Dog Eye. It killed half an hour and no one got hurt." Doc turned to Len Spikes. "Now, old friend, I know you came to tell us something."

"You best get over to the Corinne Hotel, Doc."

"Why so?"

"There's this fella? Says he's a Canadian Mountie. Name of Walker? He was waiting for the stage, but he told somebody he was looking to buy cattle. A bunch of ranchers got him waylaid. The Beaverhead's overstocked. Plenty want out."

"How many head's he after?"

"Plenty. It's to start a ranch in the British Possessions, for a man named Cochrane."

"Damn it, Len. That's a good tip and none of us has money to buy you a drink for it."

"That's okay, Doc. You already give me more than most would give old Len."

Doc could tell Len was about to blubber. He stood, put his hand in the old fellow's armpit, and hauled him up.

"Come on, Len. Up and at 'em."

Dog Eye turned in his chair, stared up at Len Spikes with a look of disgust, and said, "This ain't no use. I bet half what he said is made up."

Dog Eye was tipped back on his chair. Then he was on the floor on his back. Doc had hooked the toe of his riding boot around the front chair leg and yanked.

"Dog Eye, abuse this good man again and there will be trouble between us."

"I just meant . . ."

"I hate an excuse more than I hate a lie."

Doc stepped back and Dog Eye did not move. Doc guided Len to
the door.

AFTER PARTING WAYS with Len Spikes on the street, Doc made his
way down the boardwalk to the Corinne Hotel. Maybe a dozen cowboys sat on benches outside the barbershop and another two saloons,
with their legs out long and their decaying boots crossed at the ankles.
They were a hungry-looking bunch, most of whom had disposed of
their earnings in more exciting towns before crawling home. As Doc
walked around them and over them, tipping his hat and saying good
day, he tried to keep his optimism to himself. In the bid for employment, they were his competition. But thanks to Len Spikes, Doc had
the edge. Len had told him in parting that Lowell Ferris was among
the ranchers seeking to sell. Not long ago, Lowell had been a cowboy
and Doc's compadre. Lowell would help Doc if he could.

Next door to the hotel, Doc crossed the path of a homesteader
slumping sacks on the tail of a wagon in front of Poindexter's store. A
sad-looking woman with a baby waited for him on the seat. The two
horses asleep in the traces had red sores under their gaping harness
leathers. Pilgrims depressed Doc. There was no spring round-up for
them, no summer wages, no grub pile. Just porridge and the odd
prairie chicken, and the constant turning upside down of what God
had seen fit to put the other way. That it had to be better than what
they came from was frequently said, but Doc didn't believe it. What
could be worse than this?

Besides depressing him, there was nothing like the sight of a
pilgrim to make Doc glad he was a cowboy. He hurried on to the
Corinne Hotel.

The Corinne was a sturdy two-storey building, made to seem larger
by a tall false front. Under the overhang of the upstairs balcony, a
young giant, seemingly hairless under a big hat, stood in the hotel

doorway. His buffalo coat was long and a shotgun barrel showed out the front flap by his knee. Somebody's bodyguard, and as such, he represented an obstacle. Doc's plan had been to sit on the bench beside the hotel door and wait for Lowell Ferris to come out. What seemed predictable was that the young ape would feel it in his jurisdiction to move Doc on. Just imagining that made Doc angry.

Two of Doc's most pronounced traits did not fit well together. One was a wish not to die a stupid death. The other was an urgent need to push back in situations of injustice. He met bad behaviour with the same, reckless and sudden, even when it placed him in the peril his careful side went so far to avoid.

"Excuse me, young fella. You're in my way."

The boy's eyebrows stood out white against his sunburned forehead. He looked Doc up and down.

"Come back later," he said.

"Now why would I come back later when I'm here now?"

"Walk on, mister."

Doc stared at the guard's enormous boots until the boy bent down and looked at them too. Then Doc kicked his shin. When the young bully brought up the barrel of his shotgun, Doc was waiting. With his free hand, he accelerated its rise into the boy's face. On impact, one side of his nose started to bleed. Right then, unexpected to all including himself, the young guard pulled the trigger and blew his own hat off. A few pellets caught his brow and grazed up more blood. Doc felt a shower of relief that the bully boy had not shot himself worse. Such was the law in Montana that Doc could have been blamed. While the guard held his face and cursed in a whiny tone, Doc ran inside and stood for nervous seconds in the dark.

When his eyes finally adjusted, there were two men standing and a third farther back in a leather chair. All three had their pistols pointing at him. Still, it was a pleasing sight, for Doc knew two of them. One of the standing men was Lowell Ferris, and the seated one was William Orr. The third man Doc didn't know. A city man in a well-cut suit, he stood closest and looked agitated. The way he pointed his gun made Doc's belly twinge.

"Whoa, gentlemen. I am unarmed."

"Explain that gunshot, sir, and do so quickly!" The city man's wood-coloured eyes were jigging in his head.

"Hold on now, Darnell. Hold on."

That was Lowell, who took a step and pushed the nose of the man's six-shooter down. Though it was early in the day, Lowell had drinks aboard. His big meaty face was red, and he was smiling under his walrus moustache as though the fracas was over and he was already telling it as a story to his friends.

"This is Doc Windham. You remember Doc, don't you, Mr. Orr?"

"What's the shooting about, Doc?" Orr asked peacefully, as though he were inquiring about the weather. "Darnell's man try to kill you?"

This was a swipe at the agitated man. Poindexter and Orr was one of the biggest ranches in the whole northwest, but neither William Orr nor Philip Poindexter felt it necessary to travel with a guard.

Just then the guard himself ran in, face still bloody and his bit of hair twisted up. He shoved his shotgun into Doc's ribs from behind, enough to bruise the bone. Doc watched Lowell bring his gun up and point it at the boy's chest.

"Darnell? Call off your dog if you value him."

Darnell reached around Doc and gave his bully a backwards shove. "Dwight! Outside!"

That the boy was named Dwight struck Doc as funny. That, and being sure he was saved, made him laugh. Doc's laughing made Lowell laugh. Darnell sank onto his chair, disgusted. His gun pointed at the floor like a droopy willy.

William Orr struck a match and held it to a cigar. Puffing, he said, "That was quite an entrance."

As briefly as possible, Doc explained. He admitted responsibility for the guard's bloody face but not the gunshot.

"I'm surprised you go unarmed in town, Doc." This was Orr, letting Doc know he was no fool.

"I exaggerated on that point." Doc's pistol was tucked in the back of his pants where he usually kept it.

Lowell told the man at the hotel desk to give Doc a drink. He also asked him to sit, but Doc declined. "I only came to ask you a question."

"We're celebrating that I sold my cows—conditional on the man upstairs seeing them," said Lowell.

As Doc had the whisky in his hand, he raised it: "To your sale." He threw it back and returned the glass to the counter. "I'll wait outside."

In the street, a few people were gawking, drawn by the gunfire. They were studying Dwight, who sat on the bench dabbing blood from his face with a gory handkerchief. His shotgun leaned against the wall. Doc looked at him long enough to verify that the young man hated him and was thinking about revenge.

"So, Doc, what's your question?"

Doc jumped. Instead of making him wait, Lowell had followed him out.

"Let's walk. This fella might shoot me."

Rather than buck the wind, they walked south to where tall houses poked above the cottonwoods, spawn of the recent railroad boom. Doc came to the point. He told Lowell he knew about the cow sale and wondered if it meant he needed cowboys.

"That was good thinking. Who you got?"

"Lippy Mann and Dog Eye French."

"I guess I know those boys. Lippy's . . ." He gestured at his face. "Thing is, Doc, the Mountie bought a lot more than mine. This Senator Cochrane he's buying for is after seven thousand. As I'm suddenly out of the ranching business, Major Walker hired me to be his trail boss to Canada."

Lowell reached in his pocket and brought out a roll of bills, peeled some off.

"I think you need horses. Should be enough left over for food and so on." Lowell winked.

Doc pocketed the money and they shook on it.

WHILE THE HUNGRY cowboys of the town got the news and composed a mob in front of the Corinne Hotel, Doc's crew stayed at Fat's, drinking immoderately and eating beefsteaks. Dog Eye nagged about going elsewhere until Doc gave him the price of a whore. When Dog Eye left, practically running, Doc gave Lippy most of the rest to buy horses. This was such good news that Lippy leaned out of his collar and grinned. He did not seem to notice or mind how his harelip fanned in the light.

The first crowd Fat had seen in months was building, drawn by the sudden show of money. Because these others were not his friends, Doc got lonesome after Dog Eye and Lippy left, but then Len Spikes arrived. Doc fetched him a chair and a glass, and served him from the bottle. They drank and reminisced about the Bozeman Trail and the Sioux who almost killed them, about Uncle Jack and the sorry way it had ended for him. Then Len's eyes went funny. Doc guided his head onto the table and let him sleep.

With no more familiar company, Doc obliged two fellows who wanted a card game. The three played draw poker, with Len's head on the table like a humorous fourth. Luck follows luck and Doc won more hands than he lost.

Doc would often think back on that night, and it was always the same four things he remembered. Lippy's harelip grin. Len Spikes's daffy peacefulness, having outdrunk his pursuers. Fat staring like an emperor across a sea of full chairs. And Dog Eye returning with his hands in his empty pockets, wearing the wistful look of one reminded, however briefly, that God put two kinds of people on this world, not one.

It was Doc's last night of drinking in the town of Dillon.

BOZEMAN TRAIL

Summer 1866

THE FIRST SIXTEEN YEARS of Doc Windham's life were spent in a Texas town, a dusty place whittled small by repeated Indian attacks. Most of the people had left before Doc was born, and taking over abandoned houses was as close to a trade as his father had.

Out of this childhood, Doc's best memories were the occasional visits of his father's youngest brother. Jack Windham was a cowboy, sharp and agile, whose first action on any visit was to beat up Doc's father and lock him in the woodshed, away from drink. Billy Windham was thus prevented from bullying his wife or beating his children as he dried out.

While the imprisoned drunkard cursed and roared, Jack took the boys and gave them training their father had neglected. He took special pains with Doc, because Doc was the youngest and the least damaged by his father's excesses. Most of the skills Jack imparted were cowboy ones, because that was what he knew. Though few and far between, the lessons were the basis of Doc's future trade, the slender know-how that enabled him to escape his home when he finally did.

The occasion of Doc's freedom was the outbreak of war between South and North. Doc's four brothers, two of whom were already apprentice drunkards, went to fight, eager to escape the stagnation of their lives. Doc felt differently. Not raised to any patriotic feelings, except perhaps that Texas was good, he went the other direction into westernmost Texas, where, in a seam between the main trails of commerce and battle, he found a ranch that had lost all its help to the war and would hire him.

There, far beyond the fields of slaughter, Doc practised his roping and riding, learned the hundred and one other skills that make a cowboy. He did not think much about the war, except to hope that his favourite uncle would survive it and see some day that his nephew had become a cowboy.

In time, it would be known that half of Doc's brothers did die in the Civil War. Doc's father was another casualty, in the sense that he died while begging a returning Confederate soldier for a drink. The man was nursing a bottle as he rode through town. First Doc's father had run beside the man's stirrup. When the man ignored his begging, Billy reached and grabbed the bridle beside the bit. The tattered soldier reached for his pistol and shot Billy Windham as you would a dog.

But Uncle Jack survived, and when he came to his brother's home to see what had happened to that branch of the family, he found his brother dead, and the family dispersed. He collected enough information to track Doc westward, to find him in his distant hideout.

During their visit, the first in five years, Doc assumed Jack would approve of him, because he was by now an able cowboy. But what Jack saw was a young man living casually, working as required for whatever was offered, showing no ambition or restraint. He told Doc he feared he was becoming "a frivolous man," and the statement landed like a punch. Doc had heard Jack say the same of his father.

The remedy, as Jack saw it, was a dangerous adventure, an experience that would take some of the silliness out of Doc and render him tougher, more like a veteran of war. Doc wasn't sure he wanted to be like the crippled, defeated men that Texas was now so full of, but he was of an age when the words "dangerous adventure" were appealing.

What Uncle Jack offered was a cattle drive, a chance to take a thousand longhorns from Texas to Missouri. The cattle belonged to Nelson Story, a man who had already made a fortune in the gold fields of Montana and was about to wager those profits on an attempt to put Texas beef on eastern tables. Uncle Jack was very high on Nelson Story and felt Doc would learn much from any experience shared with the man. The trick would be getting Story to take Doc, for he wanted only trail-hardened cowboys who could shoot straight and stay calm. Whereas Doc could handle the cowboying, he fit no other part of the description. Jack's ace was that Nelson Story wanted him as his second in command, his *segundo*, perhaps badly enough to take Doc too.

And so it came to pass.

FOR MOST OF THE WAY to Missouri, that summer of 1866, the problems of the drive were routine. Many thirsty stretches, one bad stampede that killed a horse and mangled a man, high water in the rivers, Indians making threats and trying to charge tolls. But at the Missouri border, they ran into a kind of trouble that could not be out-run, out-waited, fought, or bribed.

The Missourians on the far side of the Missouri River were claiming that Texas cattle had ticks that carried Spanish fever. To keep tick fever out, they had blockaded the river. Likely the Missourians didn't want Texas cattle cheapening their own, but they had convinced the public of the Spanish-fever threat. An even larger herd had already been turned back, so Story and Jack knew the blockaders were serious.

Those earlier Texans had given up and sold their cattle on the south side of the river at a huge loss. It was that or lose them off the bed ground to thieves at night. But Nelson Story would not be so cheated. Taking only a day to make up his mind, he turned halfway around and pointed his cattle up the Missouri River's western shore toward Fort Leavenworth. Once there, he bought a mountain of goods and several wagons, and enough oxen to pull them. Quite a few cowboys quit rather than accept the change, and the replacements were younger and greener men, similar in experience to Doc.

They were headed for Montana now, was what Story told the boys. They would sell their longhorns in the gold fields and make an even bigger success.

NELSON STORY'S CHOICE of route was straight north until they intersected the Oregon Trail, then west up the Platte River. They would cross from Fort Laramie to the new Bozeman Trail that would lead them to the Montana towns of Bozeman and Virginia City, the latter being a famous gold-digging site.

This was another language to Doc, who was out of Texas for the first time, but Uncle Jack appeared to understand it. Jack told him the change of plan would put even more hair on his chest, because the Sioux Indians up that way had not been beat and did not believe in the inevitability of their doom.

"Platte means flat" was another of Jack's pearls of wisdom, and the river of that name certainly was, braided all over the bottom of a spread-out valley. As in many slow rivers, there was quicksand.

Along the Platte, on both sides, were immigrant roads, the means of getting from the East to places like Oregon and California. Many a wagon train crawled beside the cattle drive. If the hollow-eyed travellers weren't silent, they were singing religious songs. The drovers passed many graves of pilgrims whose dream of free land had ended short.

Where the Platte branched into two forks, they took the northern river. In time, the trail brought them opposite Fort Laramie, where soldiers crossed the river and told Nelson Story to stop. When he told them he was planning to branch off north for the Bozeman, the soldiers said Colonel Henry B. Carrington of the U.S. Cavalry was up that way, either garrisoned at Fort Reno or already at work on a new fort called Phil Kearny. The plan was to build forts even beyond that, right up into Montana, to prevent Sioux interference with prospectors and settlers. But in the sequence of things, Nelson Story was too early. At the moment, Colonel Carrington was facing stiff resistance from the Indians and having trouble protecting himself and his men. He could not defend a herd of longhorns and cowboys on top of that.

The young officer who passed on this message was a Yankee. They were all Yankees as far as Doc could see, and the officer, though younger than Mr. Story, was not respectful. He stood close to their boss to make himself seem taller. He held his chin so high he could barely see past it.

To Mr. Story, this wasn't much different from the Missouri blockade, and he treated it the same. That night, he broke open a long wooden box in one of his wagons and presented each cowboy with a breech-loading Remington rifle, oily and new. Leaving by night, they passed Fort Laramie. Where the immigrant road met the Bozeman Trail, they branched northwest onto the latter.

They had been told by the soldiers at Laramie that the Sioux were very dangerous around Powder River. When they were near it, just a few miles short of Fort Reno, the Sioux attacked. Doc had often imagined what an Indian attack would be like, and of course it looked like none of what he had foreseen. It happened more quickly than in his imagination, and his view was much more limited. What he saw most of was the wagon he was hiding behind. Inside it, where a rope was loose and the canvas pulled back, he kept seeing the round face of a clock and wondering why they needed it. Then he looked up. High above him, an Indian on horseback held up some kind of bludgeoning stick with a rock in the end. Doc ducked and the rock smashed the top edge of the wagon box just above his head. He felt cowardly doing so but shot underneath the wagon at the horse's legs. When the horse went down, somebody else shot the Indian.

The raid didn't last long. When the Indians rode off chasing a number of Mr. Story's cattle, Doc looked around, elated at having survived. The first face he saw was pasty pale and cinched in pain. It was

Eric Schauerte, and there was an arrow shaft buried up to its feathered end in his shoulder. The man's jaw jittered, and he had his fist around the shaft. Blood welled from his hand.

Doc felt bad for Eric, but he still felt lucky about himself. With the Indians gone, Doc assumed they would go to Fort Reno and ask for shelter. Instead, Nelson Story chose a few men to stay with the cattle and the wounded, and told the rest to mount fresh horses.

"Com'mon, boys," he yelled, as if inviting them to town for a booze.

The wide track left by cattle and unshod horses was easy enough to follow into the badland hills. There were a good places of ambush every hundred yards, but the Indians were so confident they had kept on and left no snipers or sentries behind them. Mr. Story and his men rode right up to the Indian camp and, from a position above, poured lead down on the Indians until they ran for their horses and left the cattle behind.

In this battle, Doc fired until his Remington was red hot, but felt greatly fearful of an arrow coming back at him through the smoke.

There was a lot of whooping and yelling on the ride back but Doc was silent. He had a tickle on his shoulder where the arrow had gone into Eric Schauerte. All that day and often afterwards, he would feel that tickle and be frightened.

Upon their return to the site of the original attack, Nelson Story chose Doc and Uncle Jack to ride the back trail and check on an old Frenchman they had passed earlier in the day. He had been camped by a little stream, alone except for a boy of twelve. Mr. Story had told the Frenchman he could come with them, but the scrawny-bearded man refused, saying the cowboys frightened him more than the Indians did.

Doc and Uncle Jack found the old man and the boy dead. Both were scalped, the angry red of their fleshless heads bright in the sagebrush and dust. They were the first scalped people Doc had seen, and Uncle Jack made him angry by laughing at whatever came on his face at the sight of them.

At the same time, Mr. Story sent other men to Fort Reno. They returned with an ambulance, into which their two wounded men were lifted. Doc never saw Eric Schauerte again. The rest got back to driving cows, moving them up the trail toward Fort Phil Kearny.

Three miles short of that fort, six blue cavalrymen came and told them to stop. From here on, the grass was reserved for the army, they said. The soldiers told Nelson Story to come with them. Mr. Story asked Uncle Jack to accompany him, and at the last minute, Jack waved Doc over and he went too. The three cowboys rode behind the cavalrymen.

The fort was a novelty for Doc, something he would never forget. They were still building it, and heavily armed, well-guarded wagon trains were going out empty and others were coming back from the mountains loaded high with stockade poles. The work was being done as fast as possible because there were still gaps in the outer wall. Doc had never been inside a place that smelled so green.

Mr. Story, Jack, and Doc were escorted into the biggest cabin, oc-cupied not just by Colonel Carrington but by his family and a coloured maid. Doc saw other children out a glass window, playing with a pet antelope. When the three men were led into Carrington's office just before the meeting, Doc saw a Bible open on the colonel's desk. It wasn't even in English.

Carrington entered, and Doc liked the looks of him. He was straight backed and haughty like the officer at Laramie, but looked as though he might have earned it. Doc kept liking him even when he got angry at Mr. Story.

Colonel Carrington told them how he had lost horses on his sec-ond day at Phil Kearny. He had seen right away that seven hundred men were not enough for the four forts planned, and had asked to be reinforced, but the ears of officialdom were closed. His wood wagons were in constant peril in the black forests to the west. The Indians showed aggression every time the soldiers went for wood. Same with the haying detail. One minute the men worked with scythes. The next they had to take up their guns. Behind the colonel's back, the men were calling this "Fort Perilous." They didn't know he knew.

It was a red-faced talk, supposedly a description of the predica-ment that Nelson Story and his cowboys shared. The colonel would become short of breath, have to stop, then start again. The upshot was that he wanted to send them packing back to Fort Laramie, right across the main channel of the Powder River near where the Indians had attacked them, where the Frenchman and the boy had been scalped.

Mr. Story gave the colonel every impression that he was sorry he had pressed on so far and become a nuisance. He would certainly go no farther. Back in camp, he was in a different mood. Furious, he gave orders to build trail corrals, one for oxen, one for longhorns. How could they wait? he roared. Wait for what? It was almost October. Even if they did turn back, they'd run into snow. The logical way to go was forward, if the confounded army would let them pass.

They waited two weeks. One day, an Indian snuck in close and killed one of the men. Dick Bastien. Soon after, Mr. Story gathered them together and made a proposition. If the men were with him, they would leave in the night with the cattle, not for the south but for the north. If they could get as far as a day away, Mr. Story doubted the army would follow. But he wasn't going to force the men. They would put it to a vote.

Doc was in favour of going no direction at all. He was in favour of going into the fort with the women and children, and playing with the pet antelope. But forward or back was the question, and Doc waited until his uncle's hand went up, and he put his hand up right after. There was only one man who voted against Mr. Story—and somewhat against the rules of voting, Doc thought, Mr. Story pulled a heavy navy pistol and said he would hold the cowboy prisoner. He had to, he said, or the man might run back and tell the soldiers.

They left that night. For more than a week, they drove by night and grazed the cattle under guard by day. That they could do so was a testament to how well trail-broken the longhorns had become. For Doc, it was a nightmare. He could not get the idea out of his head that the big Indian with the stone war club was behind him. Given this way of driving, there was no time to sleep except an hour or two in twenty-four, which added to Doc's fear, made it more lively. Sometimes he saw the Indian with the stone club appearing and disappearing along the murky edges of night, and in the shimmers of day when it was his turn to guard the cows.

Then, there was another skirmish, this one in daylight. The men were close-herding the grazing cattle, and had cover. They fired on the attacking Indians to the full capacity of their guns. There were no losses this time on the cowboy side, except for a couple of wounded cows, which they butchered and ate.

A couple of days later, still another attack was repulsed, and after that, nothing. When the cowboys considered the Sioux country to be behind them, they became jolly. But the tickle in Doc's shoulder would not go away.

Beyond the site of the fourth fort, C.F. Smith, they went back to driving by day until they passed through Emigrant Gulch and came to Bozeman City. This humble accumulation of shacks was the end of the line for Mr. Story and his cows. Here, he would sell his cattle and open a store (which explained the clock). He thanked the boys and paid them out in drafts payable in Virginia City.

BETWEEN BOZEMAN CITY and Virginia City, Doc crossed the beautiful Madison Valley for the first time. He and the other cowboys rode through its chasm bottom, then rose out of that valley and through a notch on the far side, following a wagon road. They entered the Alder Gulch and saw Virginia City at its near end. Uncle Jack went ahead to warn the trading company at which they would cash their drafts. When Doc and the others arrived, Jack was standing outside the store, and he told them to pack away their guns in their saddlebags so it was clear they were not there to commit robbery.

Once the banking was done, Jack led the way down to the livery corral, a place called the Elephant Corral, where they put their horses, brushed them well, and left them. They were Mr. Story's horses and were at the corral on his account, but there was an offer that each cowboy could buy his horse for sixteen dollars, which was reasonable.

As segundo, Jack gathered them together beside the corral gate and made a speech.

"I will not tell you how to spend your wages, even though it's a shame to see boys lose it all and not even get a clean suit of clothes out of months of hardship and danger. Whores, the same. Couple of things to remember. This is a mining town, in case you haven't seen one. Life is cheap and everything else expensive. Remember everyone you deal with is drunk."

Mr. Story had given Jack enough money for a few rounds, and they went to the first saloon they came to for that purpose. The only stipulation was that the barroom have a woman, and the saloon, a hurdy-gurdy house by night, did. The woman who served them sashayed about and made light conversation with everyone. She wore a dress cut low on her bosom and a skirt big as a church bell. Her hair was piled up and hanging down in black ringlets. She had something red rubbed into her pale cheeks and kept her lips closed most of the time, even when she smiled. When she talked, they saw her teeth were black. The boys agreed her best feature was her eyes, which were the colour of wet sand and kind. She told them she hoped they would come back in the evening and buy some dances with her.

On the first and second drinks, they toasted Mr. Story. He had been a hell of a ramrod and had led them through by never being weak in the face of trouble. He had hoodwinked the cavalry whom no one liked—Yankee bastards—and had shown them a thing or two about fighting Indians.

Talk of cavalry reminded Jack of a local danger. He reminded the boys, mostly Texans, that many in this town were bound to be Yankees. Trouble could arise out of that. Avoid that kind of fuss, said Jack, and his having been a reb soldier, it had weight. The boys used their third whisky to toast Jack.

"Will you stay here long?" one of the boys asked him, and he shook his head. He said there was nothing here but a sinkhole for money. Mr. Story was right to bring Texas cattle in this direction. As the government fought the last hostile Indians, and as the robe hunters killed out the buffalo, a new ranching country was being uncovered. Every mother's son who hadn't done well by earlier frontiers would put his family in a wagon and head west. That meant Texas herds and more Texas herds, moving northwest. Jack reckoned he would go south and hook up with another such herd, and the boys were welcome to ride with him. Jack looked at Doc, and Doc tried not to meet his eye.

"I hate Indians," said Leo Pope, just barely on topic. He was given to stupid statements, and nobody much liked him. No one would look at him now. It bothered Doc that even when a fool like Leo said it, the word "Indian" made him see Eric Schauerte clutching the arrow in his shoulder, or the Indian with the stone club towering above him, or the old Frenchman and the boy scalpless in the dust.

Jack's speech suggested that the drinks in that saloon were the end of their shared trail. But when they stepped out blinking from dark into light, they did not disperse. They hung together as the months of campfires had trained them. They continued to walk up Wallace Street in a tight group.

When they met a young man in cowboy dress, they stopped him. It turned out he was Kentucky born, a freckle-faced youngster who was more than happy to tell what he knew. The gulch went west for miles, he said, with gold diggings all the way and a bunch of what you might call towns. Virginia City at this end was the biggest. Nevada City, farther on, was also considerable. Pointing back down Wallace Street, the freckled boy showed them where the cheapest whorehouse was, beside the Elephant Corral where they had left their horses. According to the boy, the crossbeam over the corral's gate was also where the vigilantes did their hanging, when they caught a murderer or a thief. There were tents along the gulley beyond the corral and the whorehouse, and the boy said that was where the Chinamen lived. He had heard you could get an opium pipe there. He hadn't found one yet, but he hoped to.

"How often do they hang people?" asked Dolphus Gray.

"I seen one since I come," said the cowboy with pride. "Road agent. Big tall fella, or least he was by the time he'd stretched awhile." The boy laughed crazily and a couple others joined in, even though it was an old joke.

On farther, they came to a fellow standing off the boardwalk, filling his mouth from a jar. He spat or blew it out, same time as he lit it with a match. Whatever it was, whisky or coal oil, the spray burned with a flash and a roar. He had a piece of leather spread on the ground, the idea being you should throw money if you liked his trick.

Leo Pope said he wouldn't pay some greaser for lighting his mouth on fire. Ax Hanson, their big cook, pitched a coin on the hide and they moved on.

What they were really looking for were pretty women, and miners who had struck it rich. Since the latter had no insignia, it was left to argument. Some thought the mangy, long-haired men in greasy buckskins must be the ones. The other view was that newly rich men would have bought gaudy apparel by now. This opinion favoured the men with recent shaves and oiled pompadors, striped pants and boiled shirts—and was hotly contested by the men who were sure those were professional gamblers and pimps. Uncle Jack probably knew but kept quiet, enjoying their ignorance.

There were kinds of people in Virginia City that the boys had never seen before. A few in beaded buckskins had grey hair to their waists. Jack said these were leftovers from the beaver trade. The younger ones who dressed in this mode were possibly buffalo hunters.

Then there were Negroes and Chinese. They saw only one or two of the former, looking watchful for trouble. The Chinese were more numerous and shuffled along with their eyes down like dogs expecting a kick. One Chinaman, shaved bald except for a pigtail down his back, wore a kind of pantaloon or bloomer you'd expect more on a woman.

Then Doc heard a strange loud sound coming out of another saloon. The noise was bell clear, but not sweet or musical. A kind of hard crash, like coal dumped down a chute, but not that either. Doc looked up and the shingle read in dripping letters *McGinty's Bowling Saloon*. After a brief dispute, the others followed Doc inside, except for three who thought they'd rather sit on a bench outside and smoke.

Doc had read about bowling in *The Police Gazette*, a story about a San Francisco murder that had taken place in a bowling saloon. In the illustration, a man with a waxed moustache and wearing a tight suit was firing a flame out a tiny pistol into the chest of a Chinaman who looked like the devil himself. In the background, going off into the distance, was a light-coloured strip down which another man had just rolled a big ball, toward a cluster of pegs.

Now Doc was seeing it in real life: two strips of wood with triangles of close-set, flat-bottomed pegs standing at the ends. A thin man in a clerk's suit with the jacket off, bracelets holding up his balloon sleeves, danced up to the head of one strip and rolled the ball. By its sound on the wood, the ball must have been rock hard. All the boys jumped when it smacked the pegs, some of which fell skittering as others stayed standing.

Doc watched awhile and tried to summon courage. It was the one thing he'd seen in Virginia City that tempted his wages.

"It's a dollar a game," yelled an oily-headed bartender, used to reading this thought in a man's mind.

Doc jolted into motion and went to the bowling man, who had again made the pegs fall down. He was waiting on a fellow who reached out of the dark at the end of the strip and built the triangle again. Doc counted the pegs and there were ten.

"Mister?" said Doc, and the bowler turned with a look of nervous suspicion. Doc folded his arms high on his chest to emphasize his harmlessness. "I'm sorry to bother you. I just finished trailing a herd of cows from Texas, and I was wondering if I could buy you a game of this, and a whisky?"

"If both of you play, that's two dollars, plus the whisky," put in the bartender.

The stranger nodded that this arrangement would suit him. He gestured to a ball that had just rolled up a ditch beside the strip of wood.

As Doc suspected, the game was not easy. The ball was heavy and you pinched your fingers into little holes to catch hold and throw. His first few attempts flew too far in the air before landing on the strip of wood. This made the other bowler wince and the barman curse.

There were no women in this saloon, and the boys grew tired of watching Doc bowl. He offered them turns but they didn't want them. By ones and twos, they left, saying they were after rooms and shaves and new clothing. Nobody said anything about women but it was understood they would look for some later. Uncle Jack left too, to arrange a room, he said. He would come back for Doc.

So Doc bowled on, and as he'd hoped, a bit of the grace and balance of the game started to come to him. After maybe half an hour, he went to grab his ball and the stranger reached an arm in front of him and told him it was over. Doc thanked him, instructed the barman to give the stranger another whisky, paid up, and left.

When he was outside again, it was so bright Doc couldn't see anything but gold. He sat down on the deserted bench beside McGinty's door and waited. It wasn't long before Uncle Jack wandered back, carrying a brown package tied with string under his arm. The fat parcel was about the size of a saddle seat. Doc saw how carefully Jack was stepping and that was how he noticed his uncle's new boots. They were the colour of a sorrel horse.

Doc stood up to greet his uncle and began to cry. He covered his face with his hands so no one would see. Through his fingers and the blear of tears, Doc saw Jack standing beside him, holding his package, rocking heel to toe in his new riding boots. He did not look disgusted.

"Come along, young Doc," he said after awhile. "You might as well bunk with me tonight. I won't fully enjoy the day until I'm clean, and I have found a hotel that will heat us some water. I'm not so good an uncle as to let you bathe first, but I'm good enough to let you go second."

A man with no teeth, his chin curled up like an empty boot toe, came to them and opened a box of cigars. Jack bought a fistful.

THE HOTEL ROOM WAS fancy by Doc's estimations. The bed was a little sway-backed but big enough for both of them, and it had a yellow covering with a diamond design in raised thread. There was a stand against the opposite wall with a pitcher and a wash basin, and a spool across the back over which was draped a towel that had once been white. On the wall was a mirror that still had most of its silver. Doc stood before it and marvelled. His hair was longer than it had ever been, each side like a great big paintbrush. The beard he'd let grow had pushed the weak spots full and seemed almost like a real beard, but seeing Jack's shiny face made Doc want to rid his face of hair before he went back outside.

He kept going back to his eyes, which didn't seem right, even beyond the fact that he'd been crying. The black circles in the middle, the pupils, seemed smaller than they used to be, about the size of bird shot. Around his eyes the skin was all wrinkly from sun and wind. When he raised his eyebrows, the wrinkles pulled open and showed lighter skin inside. But the most uncomfortable part was how scared his eyes looked.

A tin bathtub crowded the rest of the floor, and a stubby woman with a scarf holding back her hair came every five minutes to dump in steaming water. By the time it was half full, Jack had his shirt, boots, and socks stripped off in anticipation. He told the woman that would do, and as she was closing the door behind herself, Jack peeled down naked. Instead of going straight to the tub, he went to the window he'd yanked open and propped with a stick. He stood looking out at the street and certainly didn't seem to care that the street looking back could see him naked. Then he came to the tub and, instead of dipping a toe, stepped straight in. His face did not betray if this hurt. He squatted fast and let out an ecstatic sigh when his ass hit bottom. He had a cigar clamped in his jaw and now he drew on it. Though it looked dead, it turned orange and smoked.

Jack scrubbed with the soap for not very long before he stood up again. He stepped out and told Doc to hurry and get in.

Doc did as he was told, embarrassed to be naked in front of his uncle. He felt he looked more manly clothed, because he had no scars and little hair. Jack had plenty of both. But Jack wasn't looking anyway. He had turned the room's only chair to the open window and was sitting in front of it, letting the incoming breeze cool and dry him. He mopped a bit with the towel and blew smoke.

Doc took his own cigar, which was making him feel like puking, and set it on an ash-soiled can lid by the basin and pitcher. He looked at the water which was no longer clean. Cigar ash and grass bits floated in it, and a few other things he couldn't name. He wouldn't water his horse here but didn't mind washing in it. He lowered himself in and scrubbed, then turned over onto his hands and knees and ducked his head, scrubbed his hair and scalp with soap, ducked some more.

After a while, Jack said, "Back out."

Doc stepped out beside the tub, sending a cascade of water onto the floor. It disappeared through the cracks and a man yelled from below. Jack threw the wet towel to Doc and got back in the tub.

"I want all the warm," he said. "Come winter, I'll remember. Help yourself to another cigar."

Doc went and sat down by the window, let the breeze dance in the wisps of pale hair on his damp chest. He didn't bother with a cigar, having just started to feel better in his stomach after the last one. Smoking did not always work for Doc. Cigarettes he could usually manage, but cigars never yet. He thought he must be a freak to respond so badly to things other men preferred almost to eating. But he did keep trying, hoping it was not permanent, that his body would come around as it had, to some extent, for whisky.

Doc looked back at Uncle Jack, who lay in the tub with his head on the tin lip and his white and purple knees in the air. He had his eyes closed and the cigar chomped at the dead centre of a smile.

"How come you didn't make fun of me when I cried?"

Jack opened one eye and closed it again.

"Hell, I do some crying myself sometimes. Not usually in town, though town would make me cry plenty if I stayed in one. It's more likely when I'm night-herding and sing myself a sad song. What made you cry? Homesick?"

Doc searched all over his mind for the right words. There were none for what he wanted to say.

"I been scared since the first Indian fracas. I don't think I cried because I'm scared, because I'm not right now. I think I cried because I stopped." Doc hung his head. He had failed to explain it. It seemed likely he would always fail. When he looked up, Jack had his eye on him and seemed pleased. He peeled the cigar out of his mouth, careful the leaf tobacco didn't tear his lip. He pointed the wet end at Doc.

"Fear is a thing you swallow in bad times, either because you don't want to seem like a baby, or because you don't want to lose your attention and get killed. When it's over, you give in. It's like a horse that's been strong all day will turn to butter soon as you go in the corral."

Jack stood and let the water stream off his flanks. He shook himself exactly like a horse would.

"Is it bad?" Doc asked. "That I was afraid?" Knowing Jack didn't hold his crying against him, Doc asked the second question in search of a compliment. He moved to the bed so that Jack could have the chair by the open window. Jack's cigar was just a stub now. With a lunge, he spat it out and watched it fall, then dodged back out of sight, laughing.

"Where'd it go?"

"I was trying for the top of a fella's hat. But it went in the horse trough. Horse trying to drink jumped and the fella on him nearly fell off."

"What if he shoots up here?"

"Danger can't always be avoided. Man needs a laugh."

Doc thought his question was forgotten but Jack circled back.

"When I was in the war, there were three kinds of men. Some were brave. They didn't seem to know fear. Others were so afraid that, in battle, they'd come apart. I saw a crazy old Confederate officer shoot two of his own men who were crying. Then there's the kind who were fearful but fought anyway. So, who's the bravest?"

"The first kind?" Doc sensed it was wrong but said it anyway.

"Not the first kind," said Jack. "Not in my opinion anyway. They fight as if death don't matter. If death don't matter, life don't matter, so what are you fighting for? The ones who come apart aren't brave, that's clear. Then there's the third kind, your kind. Anyway, Doc, point is you're all right. It took the drive to show you what you are. That's what I had in mind when we left Texas."

Doc must have looked puffed up, so Jack continued in a less flattering vein.

"You're all right now, but you won't necessarily stay that way. You just started in the world, really. A lot can happen. Those drunks in the street, begging for a drink, they were normal once too. They might get normal again, but the odds are against it."

Jack reached for his package and popped the string with his jackknife. Inside were two suits of clothes.

"Didn't want you putting your old clothes on after a bath. Don't reach for your money, it's a present."

Doc was tickled. The shirt was a fawn colour with a built-in bib and a round collar. The trousers had suspenders already on them.

"Shirt's new, trousers less so."

The trousers were California pants, striped, with a button fly, the newest trousers Doc had ever worn. Then came the jacket. It was a thing of beauty, like a suit coat but made of leather. It had fringes off the shoulder yoke and a patch of Indian beads on the chest. Doc was small, but Jack had guessed his size right.

Jack dressed at the same time. Though not as fancy, his suit was trimmer and had a vest. When he was done, he wiped down his Colt Dragoon with a new handkerchief, using a pointy corner to clean out the little battle scene etched on the revolver cylinder.

"You're on your own for boots," he said.

When they were both dressed, Doc started to thank his uncle and Jack raised a hand to cut him off.

"Enough talk. Here we are in Virginia City, Montana, a town full of gold and the devil's delights, and talking away like a pair of old men. You'll probably want to get drunk and do something foolish with your pecker. Who knows? If I get enough snake juice, I might too."

THEY LOOKED IN various doors until they found some of the boys in a billiards saloon next door to McGinty's Bowling Saloon. They weren't playing or even watching, but were like birds on a fence whose heads move in unison when something of interest goes by. That something was a pretty serving girl with a tray of drinks. Two of the boys were drinking foolishly fast to increase the number of her visits. She was short and nicely bosomed, with dark red hair—and quite sassy, doing them one better when they tried to get fresh.

Dolphus said, "I wish all the girls in Virginia City were pretty as you." She came back with, "I'm not sure it would do you boys any good if they were." Then she laughed so Dolphus knew she was teasing.

At the same time, the boys understood they were outclassed and stayed tame in their comments. That is, until Leo Pope, feeling his liquor, said something out of line about her being so short. Ax Hanson dragged Leo outside and shook him like a doll. Leo stayed silent for some time after that.

Around then a big awkward white man, oddly dressed and hairy as a buffalo, came out of a backroom and approached a fellow at the bar about a game. The boys had noticed the man at the bar and had been debating whether he was a Negro. He had curly hair like that but his skin was lighter. He spoke more softly than the big one, but it appeared that a bet was being made between them. There were two tables and they set up the balls on the one closest to the cowboys.

The billiards was the kind called four-ball, where there were two white balls and a couple of red ones and you were supposed to shoot one and hit the others. There was a lot more to it, but with the cute serving girl, most of the boys weren't interested.

But just as Doc had been drawn to bowling, he couldn't help but watch the billiards at least part of the time. Very soon, the big white man was losing and cursing every bad shot he made and every good shot the Negro made. A white-bearded man kept score for them with chalk on a piece of slate.

The white man's shirt and trousers were dirty with clay, probably from mining, but the black coat he wore was brushed and clean. The miner's head was the biggest Doc had ever seen, though he understood that much of it was hair. The beard was divided into three spikes, twisted and waxed.

Uncle Jack nudged Doc from the side. He had been watching the big white man too. "If that man's eyes were in a horse's head," he said, "I'd shoot it before I'd ride it."

"God's balls!" the miner roared when he missed his shot.

"God's tits!" he shouted when the other fellow made his.

The chalk slate squealed.

Another thing about the strange miner was that he wore a sidearm in a holster low on his hip even while playing, even though the ivory grip kept clacking against the wood rails when he stretched to shoot. He also had a knife in his boot, the leather-wrapped handle sticking out the muddy top. This made Doc conscious of his own ancient six-shooter, a prized possession, which was inserted under his belt at the front and stabbing him in his lower belly. It was loaded and he checked to make sure it hadn't somehow cocked itself.

Doc saw that Uncle Jack's eyes were seldom off the miner's gun. At the same time, Jack was doing something odd with one hand. It was his right hand and sometimes he cupped it in front of his ear and sometimes behind. Doc figured out Jack was imitating horse behaviour, how they heard better by pointing their ears in the direction of sounds.

Keeping the big miner in view, Uncle Jack leaned Doc's way and said in a low voice, "I hear around me that this loco miner came to town a couple of days ago with big pokes of gold dust. He's been gambling since and has lost most of it. Today, he's been in back playing poker. Now, he's taking a break at the billiards table, hoping to make his luck come back. This is a hundred-dollar game and he's all but lost."

Uncle Jack turned and stared at Doc, very sharp and concentrated.

"It seems you intend to stay in this town. If so, you better learn to think like I just did. Soon, this fellow will go bughouse. Knowing that beforehand is your edge."

Within minutes of Jack saying it, the big miner leaned to shoot, wound up unusually far, and poked Dolphus's head with the butt end of the cue. As soon as the shot was off, another miss, he bellowed, "God's tits!" louder than before. Then, instead of turning to Dolphus with an apology, he blazed him with his eye.

"Move this fucking table!" he roared. "You wrecked my shot! And if you've turned my luck to bad, I'll put a hole in your brains!"

Dolphus smiled and twiddled one moustache end between his fingers. You could tell he was trying to think up a joke.

"I'm mighty sorry that my head got in the way of your pool stick," Dolphus said finally. "Maybe later I'll spank it so it learns."

Uncle Jack got up. In an instant, he was behind the miner. Reaching softly under the man's coat, he came away with his pistol. Quick as lightning, Jack rolled out the barrel to check if it had shells, closed it up, and rammed it into the miner's armpit.

"Doc," he said sharply. "Don't watch me. Watch my back."

Doc pulled his old pistol out of his belt, cocked it, held it across his lap. He scanned the few people present, looking for someone who might be the miner's friend.

Uncle Jack spoke to the miner in a polite way. He said there was nothing wrong with where their table was, and they had nothing to do with his luck. If he aimed to start trouble on account of losing at cards and billiards, he'd be wise to pick on someone else and leave these cowboys alone. Jack gave Doc a look. He nodded at the miner's boot knife. Then he took the miner's gun to the bar and placed it there. He didn't say so, but it was understood it should stay put.

Jack came back and sat. Doc was still looking everywhere and saw how the serving girl picked up the miner's pistol and shook out the bullets. With the miner watching her, she put them in the pocket of her dress.

Jack pointed at the billiards table and made a back and forth motion that meant, "Play." But the miner had decided he was done. He conceded his loss. He went to the bar and weighed out some dust on the scale for the man who'd beat him. Then he went into the back room again, leaving his gun on the bar.

With all that, the fun had gone out of the saloon and the boys tipped back their drinks and filed out, each one touching his hat to the pretty serving girl. She gave them each a grin, while chewing some kind of gum so fast it snapped.

AFTER DARK, THE BOYS all came back to the hurdy-gurdy house where their day's drinking had begun. Enjoyment took back over as they watched what were advertised as Virginia City's prettiest women dancing with miners for fifty cents a time. Most of the cowboys were of the opinion these girls were not a scratch on the billiards saloon girl, but Henry Dagleish was in sudden disagreement. He couldn't take his eyes off a lively girl with piled-high hair and a robust bosom. She saw him looking and flashed him winks from above a fan she had spread over her current partner's shoulder.

Finally there was enough whisky in Henry that he bought a dance, and, after that, he was a goner. He poured money into dancing with that girl and seemed unable to stop. The boys tried to talk sense to him. When he seemed about to wake up and listen, the hurdy-gurdy girl turned around and pressed down on the hoop of her skirt so it pushed up in back and showed her shapely black-stockinged legs right up to the bulge of her ass. This was an amazement to all the boys, and Henry ran to buy more dances.

Ever since the billiards saloon, Uncle Jack had not appeared to have any fun. He drank whisky with a kind of steely steadiness, as if it were medicine that was keeping him right. He snapped quick looks about him, angry and uneasy. Not long after Henry's hurdy-gurdy girl flashed her legs, Jack got up. Doc looked at him for a sign he should come too.

"At ease, young Doc," Jack said, smiling but not really. "I got a bit of business. Nothing as interesting as this."

Soon after Uncle Jack was gone, the whisky started to creep above Doc's neck. The sound of the fiddle and the Jew's harp and the yawning of the floor under the dancers' feet fell together into one deep growling. Once or twice, Doc forgot to hear so entirely that the miners, cowboys, and hurdy-gurdy girls jumped up and down as if for no reason.

A gunshot outside made him hear again. The music stopped and people froze in place. Then the whole room surged for the door. Henry tried to keep hold of his hurdy-gurdy girl but she fought free and went too. The cowboys were among the last to move, being unaccustomed to this drill.

Doc went but could hardly walk. He couldn't stay on the boardwalk and even the street bounced up at him. People came out of doors, and everybody went in a mob uphill until they reached an alley between the billiards saloon and the bowling saloon. The crowd pressed into that space where a torch bobbed.

Leo Pope caught on to the idea of witnessing murder and fought his way into the crowd. People cursed him and punched at him, but he pushed through. A while later he returned, bursting to tell his story.

"It's that crazy miner. From the billiards. Somebody shot and killed him, right through the head. The girl who served us in the billiards saloon? She's all beat up. Her face is cut and her dress is torn."

"Is she dead?"

Suddenly unhappy with his story, Leo plunged back in past people who had seen enough and were going back to drink.

Hearing what Leo said made Doc feel sick. He sat down hard on the boardwalk edge and puked at the base of a water trough. He did so two more times. He scooped water into his face and let some of it into his mouth to clean out the taste.

He was sorry for the billiards saloon girl. He hoped she was alive and that the sauce wasn't knocked out of her, the way a beaten horse can become dangerous or dull. But mainly he felt sad for his own sick self.

Finally able to stand, he wandered a crooked line back to the hotel and past its empty desk, and down the swirly lamp-lit tunnel of the hall to the stairs, which groaned as he mounted. The upper hall was dark and it took him some time to decide which door handle to try. When he had it, it was locked. Uncle Jack was not back yet, so Doc slid down the wall to the floor. The wall pushed his hat brim over his face and he entered a state less pleasant than sleep.

However long later he would never know, Jack hauled him to his feet and through the door and dropped him on the bed. Jack started flopping bedrolls together. When he was finished, he dragged Doc to the sitting position and threw cold water from the pitcher into his face.

"Hell, Jack, you got the bed wet."

What came next was not reliable in Doc's memory. He thought he remembered swaying on a ladder in the frosty air while Jack grabbed his feet and planted them on the rungs. Maybe in his desire to remember the night, he had invented these things. The grass behind the hotel was crisp underfoot, and he thought he remembered his boot hitting a bottle that rang with a green, empty sound that excited a dog to bark.

Sometimes Doc remembered Jack's voice, explaining what was going on, but that made no sense. The thing he did remember for sure was a steep path and hugging his bedroll to his chest as he was hauled down by gravity in jerking puppet steps. Only when he fell did he realize he was alone.

He had a notion to climb back up the hill and look for his uncle, but even drunk, he knew that was not right. Uncle Jack had pointed him and left him. That was how Jack wanted it. Not far beyond where he'd fallen, Doc groped at his belt and found his pistol gone. He went back and patted the ground where he had fallen but could not find it.

Feeling more a fool all the time, he wandered farther down the trail that curved grey between the black.

Coming slightly more sober, Doc skirted two fires where men huddled against the cold. While the warmth would have been welcome, Doc was too spooked to join them. Acting as he thought Jack wanted him to, he kept on past the last tents of town, to where the reaching claws of trees were black against a slightly brighter sky. Pushing his bedroll ahead of him, he crawled inside some bush and kept pushing until he entered a space big enough to unroll his blankets. Taking off his boots, he slept.

DOC WOKE STIFF and cold in the grey dawn. Crawling out of his swaddle, he disliked how his new clothes were creased and unclean. Uncle Jack had wrapped his old clothes in with his blankets, and Doc changed into them. He combed his hair with his fingers, pulled on his cold, damp boots, crawled into the open. He anchored his hat and flopped the bedroll over one shoulder. Everything was white with frost, the coldest morning since Texas.

Once on his feet and moving, Doc's head ached less and he was hungry. He jogged in circles to warm himself, then made for the part of the gulch where the tents began. A few Chinese were there, up with the dawn. One woman waved to him, pointed at her cooking pot. A dog came out of a tent flap beside him, cowering and wagging its tail. He felt at his belt, remembered the lost gun.

Among the tents, Doc found Henry Dagleish, sitting on the frosty ground, pressing a finger gently into a puff of closed eye. He didn't seem to own a hat any more, and the grey-blue suit he'd bought was manured, the trousers torn across one knee.

"What the hell, Henry?" Doc said, and Henry looked up, his one visible eye red-rimmed and sorrowful. His lower lip was so swollen it showed a bloody cut that should have been on the inside of his mouth.

"They beat me up, Doc."

"Why?"

"I asked that girl to take me upstairs. I offered her more money until she did. In a room, she pulled up her dress at the back, leaned over the bed and pulled her gear down. I said, Hell no, I want you naked for all the money I'm paying. When I wouldn't give in, she took off her dress and it was like she stayed in it. Her bosom came right off and so did her hips. There were wooden things in her stockings. I'm not kidding, Doc, she took something out of her mouth, and her face went flat.

"When she was done, there was just this skinny girl there. Didn't look nothing like who I was dancing with. I said I wasn't paying, that I was going, and she pulled on a rope. I ran, but they caught me on the stairs. They got all my money, except some I had folded in a paper between my ass. I don't like this town, Doc."

They walked on farther, saying nothing, each complete in his sadness. The straggle of tents thickened around them. Some new excitement was drawing folks out the door of the little whorehouse, the men pulling up suspenders over their shoulders, the women wrapped in blankets. From up the hill, more people were descending Wallace Street, some running.

Doc's reaction was sour. He was thinking about the saucy girl and he had begun to hate what this town did for amusement. But he and Henry continued as though there was no choice.

Because they had a head start on most of the others, the crowd was not thick in front of Doc and Henry when they got to the Elephant Corral. There was no breeze to move the body or even flap the scarf below its tortured neck. An expert in these matters was standing by one post and pointing at some scratch marks. He said it meant the man hanging from the gate's crossbeam had swung himself sideways and coiled his legs around the post, scratching with his spurs to take the weight off his neck. Some did this, said the expert, though it was pointless. No one ever saved himself.

Doc looked at the strained, gelid eyes of what had been his uncle. Because Jack's clothes were not dirtied or torn like Henry's, Doc imagined a story without struggle. He imagined his uncle leaving him at the top of the trail and hurrying to the corral to his horse Rufus. Jack was probably saddling the gelding when the gunmen circled him.

Doc stood beside his uncle's dangling feet, rubbing the dust off one new boot. He moved the small rowel on the spur. He looked up at the blue hands, tied behind Jack's back. A thin branch of willow, peeled white and shaved to a point on both ends, was skewered through Jack's shirt front. It held a paper on which was printed *Murderer*.

Doc noticed too that his uncle's revolver was in its holster, maybe put back after he'd finished dying.

"Boost me up," Doc told Henry, and when he didn't move, Doc mimed knitting his hands together, palms up, as you do to help a lady or a child mount a horse. Henry did so, and Doc stepped up and leaned his hip on Henry's head so his hands were free to take Jack's Colt Dragoon out of the holster and check if it was loaded.

A hatless man in an apron came running. When he got close, he yelled in an accent that was maybe German, "Get down, you godless robber! You son of a bitch!"

Doc clicked the hammer back, smelled the gun oil, remembered the care with which the gun had been kept. He levelled it at the stranger's face.

"This is my uncle. I'm not robbing him. I'm keeping others from robbing him."

He hopped down off Henry and the two of them faced the crowd, each with one of Jack's boots in the small of his back.

The rest of the Nelson Story crew came down the hill by ones and twos. Ax Hanson and Len Spikes were the last two. They all stood at the feet of their segundo.

"Give me a lift, Axel," Len said, and the giant cook hoisted him like a child. Len took Jack's jackknife off his belt and used it to saw the noose from the rope. When they had the body on the ground, he cut the string from Jack's wrists. The hands barely came apart, would look tied forever. Doc untied his own bedroll, unrolled it. They moved Jack onto the blanket.

Around then, a man with a sheriff's star and a big belly came flopping down the hill. He forced through the crowd and came to where the boys were squatting in a circle.

"What's this then?" he asked.

"This is Jack Windham. He's my uncle."

"You shouldn't have cut him down without permission. Can you prove it's your uncle?"

Ax Hanson stood up off his haunches, towered above the sheriff. "I guess we know he's Doc's uncle."

Len Spikes moved in beside Ax and told the story, that they were a trail crew from Texas employed by Nelson Story, formerly of this town. That the hanged man was Nelson Story's segundo. Story's name made a difference. The sheriff wanted to address Len, because Len was older, but Len made him do his talking to Doc.

"You take charge of his effects then and get him buried."

"If you're the law," said Doc, "did you hang him?"

"I don't hang people. I arrest them and hold them for a judge."

Doc tore the paper off its willow stick and shoved it at the sheriff. "Who did this?"

The sheriff would not answer. He turned and split the crowd.

With the sheriff gone, a grey-bearded man came and knelt between Doc and Len, beside Jack's body. Folding his hands tight in an exaggeration of prayer, he shouted, "Dear God, please take this humble sinner into your generous home!"

"Get out," Doc told him. He was trying to decide what to do next and didn't need some crazy stranger praying.

In a voice quieter and more normal, the old man said, "I'm from Texas too, boy. Take your uncle up Boot Hill and bury him. Vigilantes have killed him. Any one of these people, that sheriff included, could have been in on it." Then he reared back and yelled, "Oh Lord Jesus, forgive us for we are all sinners before we are even born!"

"Why my uncle?"

He lowered his head, brought his clenched hands up in front of his lips. "He shot Black Elmo."

"He didn't."

"You don't know that."

The man yelled more of his prayer and Doc let him.

They rolled Jack's body inside Doc's bedroll and tied it in as many places as they had strings. Inside the Elephant Corral, Doc went to Rufus and the gelding spooked away, eyes fearful. Doc looked among the other horses and on the ground by the fence. He found parts of Jack's bedroll stomped in the muck, but one good blanket under the bottom rail was clean. Doc walked to Jack's horse with it. He spent a long time talking to Rufus and, when the gelding would accept his touch, smoothed the blanket on him.

Len convinced Doc not to bury Jack's Colt Dragoon and holster with him, nor any of his other good belongings, remembering a time when he and Jack had been on a drive inside Texas. When it came time to bury a friend who got typhus, Jack had said it was foolish and an insult to throw away things that a man liked to use. The vigilantes had not been robbers. They had even left the money in Jack's pockets and socks, and Len tucked it into Doc's shirt pocket.

Finally, they put Jack's body over the horse. It was so stiff it hardly bent. The livery man had not been here all morning, but now he was. He watched them and let them go without talk of money. Doc had to ride to steady the body. Still, it was better than carrying a horseman to his grave on foot.

The trail was steep to the top of Boot Hill, but Rufus pranced up quickly under the weight of two. The town spread out below them as did the rest of the Alder Gulch, all chewed by endless digging. The praying Texan arrived from a different direction and had a shovel that he lent them. He showed them around and told them that most of the men buried on this hill had been road agents and killers who had also been hanged, a bunch of them in 1864. Doc was angry to think of his uncle in the company of such men and chose a spot northeast of the knob, though the view was less good.

The boys took turns digging. Doc rolled his uncle out of the old blanket and into the better one, then tied it. He took care with the knots, making sure each was square and one above the other. If the tails were long, he trimmed them.

They lowered Jack into the hole when it was done, and all worked together to return the clay and little rocks, saving the biggest stones to make a cover against coyotes and wolves. A couple of the boys had gone back into town for wood and came back with two pieces nailed into a cross. Doc sat in the dirt by the grave and, using Jack's knife, carved his uncle's name. It didn't look like enough, so he carved "Texas" and the year underneath.

When he finished that, he whittled the bottom to a point and drove it tight with a stone above the head end. All the boys stood along the sides of the grave, their heads down and their hats held before them. Ax and Len stared at Doc until he understood he should say something.

"Jack Windham was my uncle. He taught me to cowboy when my own father was not good enough."

Doc stopped and steadied his voice.

"He was a good cowboy and a good segundo. I don't know if he killed the man they hanged him for. But I know the miner was a bad man and my uncle was a good man. I hope he is gone somewhere he'll like."

Ax raised his hand to let him know that was enough.

As one, they turned from the grave and walked in silence back to town. They went to the livery corral and asked to see the page where Nelson Story's debits and credits were tallied. It showed that Jack had bought Rufus for cash and owned the saddle and bridle. The senior cowboys vouched for Doc and all was delivered into his name.

After that, the boys went down the creek and drank whisky, and out of their quiet talk came a plan to leave Virginia City. Every one had lost his taste for this town, and the idea of camping elsewhere tonight appealed to them. Henry Dagleish was not the only one short of money. A collection was taken so all the boys could buy their Nelson Story horses and leave. Ax Hanson had been lucky at cards and paid triple. Doc paid a share, though he wasn't going.

When they were saddling and packing the horses, Len Spikes came and asked Doc to help him put some nails in the shoe of a skittish horse. While Doc leaned into the horse and held the hoof raised, Len asked the question he knew the answer to.

"You're planning on staying, are you, Doc?"

Doc nodded.

"You can't revenge this. There's probably a bunch, and you may not even find them. If they find you first, you could wind up like Jack."

Still Doc didn't speak.

"I'd sure leave if I was you."

After that, Len let him be.

Soon Rufus was the only Nelson Story horse in the corral. Though there were horses belonging to other people, Rufus ignored them and ran in a panicked circle, looking apt to jump the rail though it was over his head. Doc stayed as close to him as he could, saying the horse's name. The other boys were saddled and watching from outside.

Doc climbed the fence and reached over. They all took turns shaking his hand. They mumbled things but could not meet his eye. When the moment became too stiff to stand, Doc reached and slapped the ass of Henry Dagleish's skittish mare. She crow-hopped and kicked, farted and ran, and all the other horses ran after her. Doc turned his back on the picture of them leaving and tried again to calm Rufus.

After a long while, Rufus went and stood by another horse. Doc left the Elephant Corral and climbed the hill to the bowling saloon. He asked for a job setting pins.

BEAVERHEAD RANGE

Montana, May–June 1881

THE FIRST TWO WEEKS of hard riding made every one of Doc's ribs feel broken. It also addled his brain so he was slow to notice how joining Major Walker's cattle drive to the Cochrane Ranch in Canada was about to break several important promises he had made to himself.

Gathering the cattle was not the problem, for most of that was done within a hundred miles of the Beaverhead country that Doc called home. He was not terribly concerned either about going to Darnell's ranch, where he would encounter the young bodyguard whose face he'd bloodied. No doubt the boy was dreaming revenge, but Doc did not believe the fool could kill him.

The real danger would come later on the drive to Canada and in the towns and settlements along the trail, all the places where Doc would not be as safe as he was here.

Fourteen years earlier, when Doc had first entered the Beaverhead, he was at the end of his rope. He had seen a thousand Poindexter and Orr cattle grazing this tableland, each with a compass-and-square brand on its rib, and he had fallen to his knees. After a negotiation with life itself, he had decided that he was home—not home in any happy way, but more in the sense that a man is beat and knows it. In that moment he knew he would never find his girlfriend, Pearly, and it meant that there was no sense going any farther. The only benefit of that cruel decision was that the man who ardently hunted Doc probably wouldn't find him either.

On both counts, the years had proven Doc correct. The lonely sanctuary of the Beaverhead had held so well he scarcely believed his pursuer existed any more. Sometimes Pearly seemed like a fantasy as well.

But all that was suddenly behind him. Even without leaving the Beaverhead, Doc began to experience the return of all his worst dreams and fears. Each night after gathering Major Walker's cows, when Doc bedded down beside the chuckwagon in another trail camp, it was to see scalped heads in the dust or a knife dividing the face of a pretty girl. It was to feel the shattered head of a man on his shoulder like some ghoulish lover.

THAT THE TROUBLE was not all in dreams was proven soon enough. Before Major Walker arrived in Dillon, he had been west of the mountains and had purchased his first five hundred cows in Walla Walla. After the cowboys had gathered the herds closest to Dillon, the Major decided it was time to go west with a crew to take possession of this Walla Walla bunch. The job for most of these cowboys would be to get the cattle across the Hell Gate River, after which a smaller group would stay with them and push them east along the Mullan Wagon Road. In a month or two, the two herds, the Walla Walla and the main herd, would meet up, maybe in the Sun River valley or farther east toward Fort Benton.

Doc was selected for the trip through the mountains. He was one of those instructed to return to Dillon after the Hell Gate River crossing. When they got the cattle to the Hell Gate, the river was full of snowmelt and furious. On a day so hot the aroma of pine sap was sweet in their noses, they drove the cattle into the river and watched their segundo, Mose McDougall, disappear on a green horse below the boiling water. Nothing surfaced but his hat. They found Mose two days later washed up on a bar, his legs buried and his long hair full of sand. They looked for the horse another half day, wanting the saddle and bridle, but never found it.

It had been two lucky years since Doc had needed to bury anyone. He was upset digging Mose's grave and more so standing by the hole with Mose rolled in a blanket at the bottom. The only saving grace was that the Major, being a Mountie officer, spoke well at the graveside. The boys were grateful, having all seen burials made sadder by no one knowing what to say. It was while they pushed dirt onto Mose that Doc decided he would complete the gather but would not take the trail north to Canada. For the time being, he told no one of this change of plan: not Lowell, not even Dog Eye or Lippy.

WHEN DOC RETURNED from Walla Walla to the Beaverhead, two more herds had been gathered. The mass of cattle on the plain south of Dillon was becoming enormous. Harrowed up by fighting bulls, a dust cloud marked its position in the sky. Lowell had asked Doc to replace Mose, to be his new segundo, and that plus the sight of such a big herd mustering on the prairie clouded Doc's plan of quitting. He liked the look of all those cows, grazing and milling in the dust. It made him forgetful of his reasons for not wanting to leave with the drive.

The next herd on the list to gather was up in the Centennial Valley, a place that was more than a mile high. The cattle in that valley were just north of Monida Pass, where the snow was thick in the shadows and bloody-mouthed wolves strutted and stalked just out of rifle range. Frost bristled on the chuckwagon metal every morning that they were there.

When they brought those cattle down and threw them in with the others, the cowboys were told to rest their horses for two days. Then they started for the Ruby Mountains and the Darnell Ranch in the Alder Gulch. In the interval, Doc was bothered and edgy, but somehow the younger men could not see it, not even Lippy and Dog Eye who knew him best. Doc was not a good concealer of emotions—he didn't even try—but his pedigree was too well known. Doc was the one who had come up the Bozeman at the most dangerous time and had fought the hostile Sioux when they still had buffalo to eat. These things no longer existed for younger men to do, so they envied and admired it. The idea of Doc being nervous was preposterous, a joke. If he looked afraid, or talked afraid, they laughed as if he were making fun of fear itself.

Feeling his resolve turn to butter, Doc tried to find out what he could about the country the drive was aimed for, particularly Fort Benton and Canada, the former being a place he'd once been and didn't like, and the latter somewhere he had hardly contemplated.

The logical man to ask was Major Walker, whose home was Canada, but the Major had departed shortly after they buried Mose. He said he was going to Helena to await instructions from his bosses down East and to put together supplies. With the Major gone, the next best source was Lowell, who owed his present job in part to having worked in the British Possessions for a time. But for some reason, Lowell, who was talkative to a fault on most topics, shunned this one. His big meat face with the walrus moustache ends hanging below his chin became still as the moon at any mention of Canada. If Doc persisted, Lowell would get up and leave the fire.

Lowell was unlike most cowboys in several ways. While the average cowboy regards his saddle as a throne, no better place in the world to be, Lowell easily tired of riding. For part of every day, he tied his horse to the back of the chuckwagon and sat on a bag of flour beside the cook. When they started their ascent of the Ruby River, an old friend from the Nelson Story days, Dolphus Gray, joined them so he could scout for his ranch's brand among the Darnell cattle. In their first camp together, he paused while eating and said, "Why is it I feel like Lowell Ferris farted in this biscuit?"

It gave Doc an idea, and next day he sneaked up on the chuck-wagon and tied his horse beside Lowell's. He crawled in behind Lowell and the cook and started a conversation. When he bent the topic toward Canada, Lowell exploded in curses, told the cook to stop, jumped down, and demanded Doc do likewise. It seemed as if Lowell meant to fight him, but instead he led Doc in amongst the cedar and sage and gave him a scolding.

"You listen here, Doc Windham. What I was in Canada was a trader. We fed whisky to the Indians and they gave us everything they owned and whatever they could steal. Now I'd like you to tell me who is the boss of this parade."

"The Major."

"And what is he Major of?"

"The Mounties."

"And what did the Mounties come west for?"

"Subdue the Indians."

"Like hell! We'd already done that. It was the whisky traders they come against. I told him I learned the country up there working for a missionary, but if the old boy puts two and two together, I'm fired."

That was fine and good, but the Major was up north in Last Chance Gulch. Doc didn't see why Lowell couldn't tell him about Canada now, when they were alone.

Approached that way, Lowell divulged a little. "We had those Indians so drunk, they were like fool hens," he said. "A child could kill one with a stick."

"But you're saying it ain't dangerous now?"

"What the hell is with you? It's me has the bad memories of Canada. I earned them. You ain't never been there and you act as if you were headed for the pit of hell."

Doc did not care to state his reasons.

"And now you sull," said Lowell. "I suppose somehow or another it's about that girl." Back when they had been cowboys together, Doc had told Lowell about Pearly. Lowell had never forgotten.

"It isn't about Pearly," said Doc, only partly true. "It's about a man I never want to run into again. And that's not the beginning of a story. I don't tell that story." And though he had not intended to tell anyone except the Major that he was planning to quit, it was suddenly out of his mouth to Lowell. "That's why I plan to stop at Helena."

After a while of gaping silence, Lowell threw the purple fit Doc expected, digging up the ground with his heels and spurs, shouting long strings of curses.

"Damn you, Doc! You come after me for a job, I give you one. Make you segundo. And you quit?"

Put that way, it did not sound good. But Doc overpowered the urge to take it back. He boarded his horse from the wagon's gate and left Lowell scolding.

BEHIND THE RUBY MOUNTAINS, they gathered a ranch along the Ruby River. Half the crew took these cattle back to Dillon, while the other half, Doc, Dog Eye, and Lippy included, continued on and entered the Alder Gulch, where Darnell's ranch stretched along the valley's south side.

Their first camp in the gulch was near Nevada City, which was now a dying town. Virginia City, at the other end, was said to be not much better, the miners having rushed elsewhere long ago. Still, the boys were excited at the prospect of seeing that legendary town.

Beside their campfire, Lowell discussed the problem of Darnell's bodyguard. He said he trusted Doc not to do anything foolish unless this Dwight did first, but he wanted the rest of them to keep their heads too. Darnell had what was called a "gun outfit," meaning he hired men for their shooting ability.

"So don't pick no fight on behalf of Doc. If it comes to shooting, we'll lose."

Next morning, they rose early and rode to the Darnell cow camp above the gulch. Darnell's men came out of their crooked bunkhouse, rubbing and scratching. Seeing the Darnell cowboys so sleepy, and some still in their underwear, Dolphus Gray rode up between Doc and Lowell, leaned down as if to fiddle with his cinch knot, and said, "After what you said last night, Lowell, I think this is our best chance. Let's gun 'em."

When Doc and Lowell laughed, the Darnell boys didn't like it. They went back inside and didn't come out until they were dressed and armed. That was when Dwight appeared. On his over-large head was a new hat, big as a sombrero. At sight of Doc, he squinted and assumed an unnatural pose, his hand near his holstered gun.

"Damn," said Doc. "I was hoping he was too stupid to remember."

"Could be he's too stupid to forget," said Dolphus.

Lowell asked who was in charge, and a snake-thin fellow with a narrow strip of black moustache stepped forward. His eyes were sleepy and his movements slow. He told Lowell that they were to get the gather started and that Mr. Darnell would be out around noon.

The thin fellow gave his name as Bone, and Lowell signalled him to follow. They walked out of earshot, but Doc could guess what Lowell was saying: *One of your men's got a pick on one of mine. I expect you to tell your man to hold his peace and cause no trouble.*

They went to work and, when the sun was in the middle of its arc, Darnell came bouncing along in a shining buggy. The horses were a smart pair of matched blacks, more saddle than draft. This waste of good horse flesh was one more thing for Doc to dislike about him. Dressed like a lawyer, Darnell sat down to dinner at their camp as if he were doing them a favour by eating their food. He said there were more cows here than the Major was buying. When it came to the cutting, Bone would be in charge. Then Darnell said he wasn't staying beyond this meal.

They went back out after eating and gathered the rest of the day. By the time they quit, they had only a few more hills to sweep. As the Major's cowboys settled into their camp, they saw Darnell's men board their horses and gallop for town. They were no doubt going there to eat and drink while Major Walker's boys stayed with their chuckwagon and ate what Cook provided—beans and biscuits as usual. Chewing this dry fare, the boys stared in the direction of Virginia City. They looked at the smudge of town in the valley's end, then at Lowell, then at Virginia City again.

Lowell did not like the position he was in, and finally, as the sun went behind the hills, he could stand it no longer. He looked at the gathered cattle, spread along a shallow coulee and across a grassy bulge to the next draw. Most of the cows had found their calves, and the few herders held them without effort.

"Cross-eyed mule-eared hell," Lowell said. "I can't advance you wages, because I wasn't given any. But I don't see why we can't throw cash in a pile and see if we've got enough money for a drink."

When they counted the money, there was enough. Lowell divided it in half and selected the first shift to go.

"And remember, damn it: them Darnell cowboys are in town. Keep your heads."

Soon the horsemen were galloping and whooping across the hills, Dog Eye French at the front.

Lowell offered that Doc could go too, but Doc said no. Lowell chose to stay back as well. While the remaining cowboys rode with the cattle or played cards, the two older men whittled sticks into smaller sticks. Lowell assumed Doc meant to go with the second bunch and asked what Doc intended to do in Virginia City.

"I don't intend to do anything there," said Doc. "I'll go someplace when the second shift travels, but it won't be into town."

"Where else is there?"

"I have an uncle on Virginia City's Boot Hill. I'd like to visit him one more time."

"One more time? You sound like you're eighty and about to die."

"Maybe I will go to Canada after all. Maybe, if it's quiet there, I'll stay until I am eighty and about to die."

"Do as you like, but don't be a fool and wait. In case you haven't noticed, you're not doing anything."

Lippy was with the horses when Doc got to the rope corral. He had his shoeing box and was resetting a few. He helped Doc saddle Louie, a big buckskin gelding. This Louie was Doc's new war horse. He'd been part of Mose McDougall's string, and Doc had inherited him after the drowning. Doc was short in stature and did not normally select a tall horse. If you're in a low spot and can't get on, it's embarrassing. But Doc liked the horse's eye and was intrigued to see a buckskin so unusually tall. He had decided to try him for a while and was soon won over. The horse was sober and watchful, an all-arounder that could cut cows and trail them. During the month since Mose had drowned, Doc had ridden Louie as much as three days straight and never seen him bottom out. The sad part was that Mose would still be alive if he had chosen to ride Louie across Hell Gate River.

Lippy knew a little about Doc's travails in Virginia City and was acting soft with his segundo tonight. After he boosted Doc into the saddle, he stood running his hand under Louie's mane.

"Maybe I should reset that front shoe."

"It's hardly wiggling, Lippy. This horse could probably throw a shoe and not notice."

"Steer clear of them Darnells."

"I aim to."

They stood in silence.

"You should go to town, Lippy."

"You know me and towns."

"Man needs a drink, though."

"I'll get one when I do."

In truth, Doc was hoping for company. Suddenly, he did not wish to face Boot Hill alone. But Lippy was not budging. Doc slapped the reins and started away at a trot.

WHILE DOC FELT OBLIGED to go to Boot Hill, he had never been able to stay in a graveyard long, even this one which had a fine view. You could see the hills in all directions, and the Ruby Mountains to the west. Nature in its stubbornness was growing grass and trees out of the tailings piles so that even the gulch had become attractive again. Doc tried to stay to the north side of the hill, to avoid looking at the town, but there it was anyway, spread out below him.

Uncle Jack's marker was crooked and Doc straightened it and punched it in tighter with a rock. Over the fifteen years since Doc had written them, the words had grown faint. Now he darkened them with a stick of charcoal he'd been carrying in a cloth since he knew he was coming this way. Pearly's father's grave marker was gone and that was the end of that.

Looking at the rest of the graveyard, Doc wished again he had taken Jack somewhere else, instead of here with the scum of the earth.

His mood was going to hell anyway, so Doc turned and faced Virginia City head on. There was the little whorehouse at the foot of the infidel side of the street. Or at least the building was still there. Up the hill on that side was where the various saloons had been. The north side of Wallace Street was the respectable side: drummers' hotel, lawyer's office, drugstore, Masonic lodge. Doc could see only the backs of these buildings, except for inside his head.

Doc looked at everything else before he let his eyes clamp onto what had been McGinty's Bowling Saloon and the billiards saloon next door. As happened every time, his eyes filled with tears. It had not happened when he stood over Uncle Jack's grave. Something about Pearly would always be stronger, would always make Doc trembling and weak.

Using a grave stick for a step, Doc mounted Louie and rode at a gallop away from the town and the cow camp both. He kept on until he intersected the wagon road, and on again until the Madison Range reared black into summer snow. Farther on, when he could see down into the great valley, Doc jumped from the horse and sat heavily among some clumps of cedar.

Doc held the reins above his head so Louie could circle him like a picket pin. The big gelding didn't seem to mind that Doc was bawling. Whatever Doc was up to, it was an opportunity to eat, to stoke the mighty engine of his heart.

VIRGINIA CITY

December 1866

DOC WAS SETTING PINS in McGinty's Bowling Saloon when he heard the news about the Fetterman fight. Though it happened to the east, along the Bozeman Trail near Fort Phil Kearny, the news had come to the Alder Gulch by telegraph from the south.

Captain Fetterman killed on the Bozeman Trail. Eighty-one cav-
alrymen in his command, also dead.

   Fetterman and company killed by the Sioux under the com-
mand of Crazy Horse, Red Cloud's fighting chief.

The news was yelled in the door of McGinty's, and the two bowlers standing at the head of the lanes paused, considered, and then let fly.

The place Doc worked, the pit, was not quite black dark because of the light that bounced in off the pale-coloured lanes. What mattered to Doc was that it appeared dark to the bowlers and to anyone else in the bowling saloon. Doc had asked McGinty what he could see from the bar, and when McGinty said, "Nothing but your arms and hands," Doc was pleased—naked forearms jutting out of rolled sleeves, hands holding the small ends of bowling pins.

Doc would set the pins after each frame. Then he would jump onto his elevated seat and watch through a hole in the wall as the ball came sizzling, waiting for the clash of pins and the thud of the ball against canvas. Then Doc would clear the fallen pins away from the ones still standing, hoist the ball back up the track beside the gutter, and hop on the seat again right away. The customers were seldom patient: they liked to roll the instant the target was built for them.

For Doc, the pit was a haven, a place of anonymity, even beyond curiosity, for no one really cared what face went with those arms and hands.

When Doc had asked McGinty for the job, he got it instantly. McGinty's pin setter had quit that day. He'd quit because he had got things out of order. He'd hoisted back the bowling ball before he cleared the pins, and a bowler had bowled while he was still working, busting his arm. McGinty had offered Doc the job for a buck fifty a day, and Doc had amazed him by asking for less.

"I'll work for you for a dollar and two bits, if you allow me four things."

McGinty looked skeptical but listened.

"First, my name is John Smith and you won't ask me if that's my real name. Second, you let me sleep here at night. Third, I give you money and you bring me food. Last is you let me bowl for free when we're empty or closed."

McGinty could multiply two bits by the days of the month fast as any man. He agreed to the deal immediately. Doc would find out later that McGinty had been robbed a time or two, prank robberies mainly where he would lose his bowling balls or pins, and that he had been thinking about a night watchman or a dog. With Uncle Jack's pistol, Doc was one better than a dog, and at night he was free.

THE STORY ABOUT CAPTAIN FETTERMAN was talked over by every bowling pair and foursome from the day the news came to town, right through Christmas. Doc knew most of it before he saw the write-up in *The Montana Post*, the newspaper that was printed on the other side of Wallace Street. The same Colonel Carrington who had met with Nelson Story, Jack, and Doc at Fort Phil Kearney had put Fetterman in charge of a troop to relieve a detail of besieged woodcutters. One story went that Carrington was to blame for putting Fetterman in this deadly position. Another said Carrington didn't want to, but Fetterman had begged for the command.

When he galloped out to save the woodcutters, Fetterman fell for the same ruse that would go on fooling white men for years. Crazy Horse led a decoy party that Fetterman chased like the fox in an English hunt. Hot to kill Indians, the Captain led his men through the open side of a circle that the Indians closed behind them. Down went the cavalry, like tenpins, bowled by experts.

When Doc finally saw the paper, a copy left in the saloon, one line ascribed to Fetterman stood out: Give me eighty American cavalry, and I will slice through the whole Sioux nation.

After that massacre, the Bozeman Trail slammed shut. Prospectors had been pouring up it all fall, taking their chances with the Sioux in their hunger for gold. But the death of eighty-one cavalrymen had an effect that the death of a few prospectors did not. Suddenly no one wanted to challenge the Bozeman. They went the long way round.

WHEN DOC STARTED at the bowling saloon, his plan was not to leave it until he was ready to leave Virginia City. But a few things finally forced him out. First, he liked to be clean and grew to hate washing and shaving in the same bucket he used on the floors. Then there was the food situation. Doc had expected McGinty to cheat him, but the man was greedy. According to McGinty, the Fetterman massacre had gripped Virginia City in a terrible food shortage. Prices had gone sky high. The other thing was Rufus, whom Doc wanted to visit before the gelding forgot him.

Late one night, Doc went out the back door of the saloon. He pulled his hat down tight and raised his collar high. He had on Uncle Jack's Colt Dragoon and wore it loaded in all six chambers. He also had matches from the bowl McGinty kept full beside his oil lamp, and some old newspapers inside his coat.

The placer mining had turned Alder Creek into a series of gravel pools. Where a stretch of old claims was uninhabited, Doc made a fire and shaved in the ice water with his straight razor and soap. He went out most nights after that, and on a night a little warmer than the rest, stripped naked, got in the water, and scrubbed.

As for food, he started out killing rabbits by moonlight in the hills. It was slow work with a pistol. If he kept it up, he was bound to draw attention to himself. But having already cancelled the food from McGinty, he had little choice but to continue. Then he remembered the Chinese woman in the tent town who had beckoned him to her cooking fire the morning Jack was hanged. He remembered her face as he remembered everything from that morning. So he went to her tent and waited out the night. When she came out before dawn and made her fire and started heating water for people's laundry, Doc approached making sign language that he needed to eat. Without question, she brought him food and took the money he offered. He said the word "English" a few times, and she went and got her nephew who spoke a little. Doc explained that he would like to buy food on a regular basis, food he could take away. The woman agreed and they struck a deal that cost him a quarter of what McGinty had charged near the end.

As for Rufus, Doc visited him in the grey light of dawn, so he could pay the liveryman and not be mistaken for a thief.

ON NEW YEAR'S EVE, McGinty declared he would stay open all night if the drunks kept wanting to bowl. He offered Doc two dollars extra to work the shift. Somewhere, McGinty had got party things, little paper hats and paper tubes with wood whistles in them, which he put on a tray at the counter so people could look funny and make noise while they bowled.

As always happens with drinking, it started well. People were laughing more than usual, and there were fewer serious bowlers than ones who saw it as a novelty, like riding a bicycle. Everybody had a bottle wagging in his fist. Some held the bottle in one hand while bowling with the other. Some threw the ball over into the other man's lane as a joke. When one bunch got to throwing the ball up as high as they could, McGinty pointed his shotgun and kicked them out.

That happened close to midnight, when everybody was leaving anyway. Outside, people were firing guns. A display of rockets and other fireworks had been promised, and these were being readied. Soon McGinty's was empty, and McGinty himself left his precious cash register to go look at some rising fire.

Before the first rocket ignited, two of the miners McGinty had ejected came back in.

"I'll show that bastard how to bowl," said one, rocking side to side. From his pit, Doc watched the drunk pull out a long-barrelled revolver and take unsteady aim at the pins in front of Doc. The pit went below floor level and Doc threw himself flat just as the first bullets flew. He counted six shots, then dared peek up the gutter. The other son-ofabitch was just as hopelessly trying to bring his iron into line. By the time he had also emptied his gun, the canvas was like a soup strainer and two pins had been nicked. Doc looked again and they were reloading in the ponderous over-careful way of drunks. They were also creeping closer.

Outside, the fireworks had started and the firing of guns continued. McGinty would never hear what was going on in his saloon overtop of that noise. As the reloading proceeded, Doc ran out the rear door.

The bowling saloon was a long building, and the next one uphill, the billiards saloon, was shorter. They were separated by the alley where the dead miner and the serving girl had been found. Doc saw for the first time that, perhaps in civic response to that event, the street end of the alley had been closed over with wood. As the drunks were firing towards the back of the building, Doc advanced up the side wall toward the street.

He assumed he was alone, and when the next rocket whined into the sky and exploded, he was startled to see a young woman opposite him. She was beside the back door of the billiards saloon, smoking a hand-rolled cigarette. That was all Doc saw before the alley fell dark again.

The next flash turned the girl's face green. She was looking at him, steadily and without fear, and Doc saw and realized two things. She was the serving girl from the billiards saloon, the sassy one who had served them drinks, and her face was changed. She had a scar now, like a deep line drawn down from forehead to chin. Then it was dark again, and Doc felt a surge of sadness such as he had not allowed himself since Uncle Jack was hanged. He was afraid he was going to cry. He was also wondering why the saloon girl would choose to stand here, in the very place that mark on her face had been made.

There were no fireworks for a few minutes. Maybe there was a misfire or they were setting up a new batch, or possibly, so soon, it was over. Because of the wall closing off the alley, no light came in from the street, and there was no light from the moon either. Doc squinted in that dark but could not see the girl. He strained to hear but all he heard were the drunken whoops of the street revellers and the firing of their guns into the air.

Just when he had given up on fireworks, more went up. They set off three at once, and when they burst, Doc jumped because the girl's face was no more than three inches from his own. She kissed him full on the lips. He went to put his arms around her but she held up her hands and stopped him. Still, her lips were on his, soft and warm and moving.

When she stopped, Doc asked her why she had kissed him.

"It's New Year's, you Texas bonehead. People are supposed to kiss."

ALDER GULCH

June 1881

THE MORNING AFTER LOWELL FERRIS allowed them their drink
in Virginia City, the boys were cheerful over breakfast. Even
though Virginia City was dead compared to any time in its history, they'd had a few drinks, seen two girls, and hadn't had enough of
anything to hurt them. They were surprised by how many Chinamen
there were. They asked Doc why, and he told them only the Chinese
had the patience to go through diggings a second time, rewashing the
careless work of others.

The cowboys had managed to come home without injuries, and
the second shift had even drunk in the same saloon as the Darnells.
One of the boys, a noisy confident type named Tex Appleby, had even
talked to Dwight the bodyguard. "He says it's a shame that he's going
to have to kill you, Doc," said Tex, with mock sadness, "but he can't
think of a way to avoid it."

Doc noticed that several of the boys from this second shift got the
snickers every time they looked at him. He was still half heartbroken
from the night before and was in no mood for it. He got it into his
head that they had somehow learned his ancient history, about Uncle
Jack and Pearly, and had the gall to find it funny. It was a crazy notion
but he had it.

"That's enough, you greenhorns!" he stormed through a mouthful
of hotcake. "One of you tell me this minute what you're laughing at, or
I'll take a round out of all of you."

Still chuckling, though trying not to, Tex took it upon himself to explain. "Sorry, Doc, it's just funny."

"Maybe I should judge what's funny about me."

"No, Doc," said Dog Eye, "it really *is* funny."

"It is not!"

"You know then?"

"Oh, for Chrissake, what?"

"Darnell's giving us that guard Dwight as his cowboy on the
Canadian drive."

They all burst out laughing. Each outfit that sold cows to the Major had to supply cowboys to the drive as far as Canada, a man for so many cows. As Darnell was selling three hundred, he owed the Major one cowboy, and it was to be Dwight.

"That goddamn Darnell!" roared Lowell. But instead of commenting on the complications Dwight would bring to the drive, he went back to the subject of the gather and the cutting. "You watch. That sonofabitch Bone will cut out every decent cow in the bunch and claim we're square."

The boys were not about to leave the topic of Dwight.

"What you going to do, Doc?" asked Alf Tooks, a black cowboy who had only recently joined them. He was young and shy and wasn't laughing.

Lowell answered for him. "If things don't come to a head, Doc'll be watching his back all the way to Canada. None of you would like that."

"I say we get that Dwight into camp," said Dog Eye, suddenly serious. "I say we surround him at night and tell him from all of us that if he makes a move on Doc, it'll be his last."

Doc felt himself get mad again. He hawked and spat to gain attention.

"I want to ask you boys something, you in particular, Dog Eye. Would you ride my buckskin Louie without my permission?"

"Hell no," said Dog Eye, and the others looked horrified at the thought of such an intrusion on privacy.

"Then what makes you so free as to think you can fight my fights?"

Nobody had an answer. They stared into their coffee cups, swirling the grounds.

"I guess you hear me then. Now, I don't know about you, but I would like to catch a horse and go to work."

Doc got up and walked fast for the rope corral. The boys stood up in ones and twos, tossed the silt from their cups into the sagebrush, handed them to the cook.

DOC DECIDED THAT BONE resembled a blacksnake whip with eyes in the handle. That man rode over to Lowell when the Cochrane crew had finished gathering the last few hills, and while the boys were holding the cattle on one side of a dry coulee, Bone and Lowell counted them. They agreed on three hundred and sixty-two as the number of adult cattle.

"My boss instructs me to cut out everything above three hundred," said Bone. "My boss gives you all the calves under six months of age free." This was said as if it were a bonus, not common practice, which it was.

"That's awfully white of your boss," said Lowell. He peeked under Bone's charcoal stallion. "Funny, I don't see your boss anywhere."

"He left orders."

Lowell was looking particularly like a walrus today. He had cut himself a dogwood twig and shaved it skinny to pick his teeth. Currently, he was standing with the stick protruding out of the brush of his moustache like a tusk.

"I guess that means me and the boys can retire to the shade," he said.

"Go to sleep for all I care," said Bone.

Lowell was cagey. Rather than say he'd be damned if he'd stand by and let Bone choose sixty-two cows out of that herd uncontested, he said, "That sounds pleasant. I may keep one eye open while you work." Then Lowell started plunging in his mouth again with the dogwood stick.

So Bone and his men went to work and, as Lowell had suggested would happen, did not simply hive off any sixty-two cows. They painstakingly chose the best.

"Okay," said Lowell, after lounging in the juniper shade for some time, "that's enough."

The cowboys had their horses saddled and grazing beside them. They were soon mounted and following Lowell. When he got to Bone, who was about to urge his stallion back into the herd, Lowell rode in front of the charcoal's face. The stallion laid his ears back and rounded to kick. Expecting it, Lowell pulled his horse away in time.

"Sweet-tempered animal."

"Something on your mind?" Bone leaned and spat.

"Listen here, Bone, did your boss instruct you to cut out the best cows? Or is that your own curlicue?"

"Best is your opinion," said Bone.

Lowell bristled like a dog. "I hate it when people give me the lie. My boss had reason to believe that after this gather was done, you would take off the surplus in some fair manner. The nearest sixty-two, the first sixty-two. Any sixty-two *except* the best sixty-two. Since you've done it your way, we may not have a deal any more. You force me to go find my boss and tell him. That wastes everyone's time."

"What would you like better?" asked Bone.

"Throw those cows you've cut back in. Mill the works around awhile. Then your boys split off the nearest thirty-two fast as they can, while my boys cut out thirty on our side. I would not need to talk to my boss about that."

Halfway through Lowell's suggestion, Bone was shaking his head. "That's not my orders."

"Well, fuck your orders!"

Lowell turned the air blue, a dramatic fit that he concluded by throwing his quirt in a thorn bush. Bone sat back and enjoyed the show. Others in that outfit had their hands hanging close to their revolvers.

"Fine!" said Lowell at last. "Let's by all means have a time-wasting impasse! You go ahead and cut out your show herd, and then you can parade 'em down main street Virginia City if you like. Maybe the local butcher'll give you a ribbon. I'll send word to Major Walker, and until he gets here or sends word back, me and the boys will take a rest."

Bone spit tobacco juice that passed not far from Lowell's foot. He showed his black-edged teeth in a humourless grin. "I don't much care what you do."

"What *you* can do, Mr. Bone," said Lowell in parting, "is tell Darnell that when the Major comes, he better be ready to parley. The Major sure as hell won't negotiate with you."

Later, after the cowboys had retired to their respective camps, Dog Eye sat in the grass watching the Darnells try to keep the herds separate. Two men held the main herd on one side of a coulee, while a third was hard pressed to keep the sixty-two on the other side from joining them.

"Think we should help him?" Dog Eye asked Lowell. It made Doc shake his head in wonder. Dog Eye's sympathy went naturally to the worst people.

"The hell," said Lowell. "Those cattle should belong to us. But they don't because these fools are trying to steal back the best ones.

I'll be fucked if I'll herd someone else's cows when I don't even like the black-eyed bastard."

Then Lowell stood up and nodded for Doc to follow. They walked until they were behind a cedar, then Lowell asked who Doc would suggest they send after the Major. He wanted someone who could get there fast and not ball up the message.

"Lippy on Calico and Dog Eye on Louie. If I need a horse, I'll ride Pedro."

Lowell made it plain with a face that he found these choices odd.

"You shouldn't judge Lippy on appearance," said Doc. "Give him a duty, he'll wade quicksand to do it. He's got a clear head and won't mix up a message."

"Dog Eye seems not as dependable as that," said Lowell.

"I don't like sending a man alone. Dog Eye is a lot of things, but he does ride well and won't ruin a horse. I'll tell him to leave the talking to Lippy. Those boys know each other. If they squabble, it won't amount to anything."

That was good enough for Lowell, and Lippy and Dog Eye were soon gone, scooting down the hill into the gulch and west.

Lowell gathered the rest of them. He said, "I think we may have no choice but to go into Virginia City. Our wagon doesn't have enough supplies for an extended wait, and I don't see any antelope out here asking to be killed. I have money from the Major to feed us in a predicament, and it may stretch to a drink. But the Major could be back here in two days and God help any man who's sulking around sick."

Doc put in a bid for going to Nevada City, but the boys had seen it on the way in and knew Virginia City was livelier. In that case, Doc said, he would stay in camp.

"When we leave, we're taking all the horses and the wagon with us," said Lowell. "There is no camp."

MAKING A LOT OF JOYFUL NOISE, the boys rode to Virginia City and into the Elephant Corral. It was a bad way to begin for Doc, to ride under the very gate that had hanged his uncle. But it would get worse. Soon they were walking up Wallace Street, past the little whorehouse and the hurdy-gurdy dance saloon, and inevitably the side-by-side buildings once occupied by the bowling and billiards saloons. They were something else now, stores of some type, but it didn't matter to Doc. They could be torn down and just the weedy spot would break his heart.

When they sat waiting for their meal in the Miner's Café, Doc stared out the window at Paris Pfouts's old store. Behind that building, the vigilantes hanged a man named Joe Slade for no better reason than he was an unpleasant drunk. Above Pfouts's store was the space where the Masons used to have their meetings. If he bent forward and looked higher, he could see the new Masonic temple, made of stone.

Of all the goddamn bad luck, Doc was thinking, to have ridden so many valleys, in and out slick as shit through a goose, only to stick fast in the Alder Gulch.

Down at the end of the table, Pesky Boucher, a Willamette Valley cowboy who was somewhat in awe of Doc, leaned to Alf Tooks and asked in a whisper, "What's the matter with Doc? Why's he so quiet?" Alf mumbled that he did not know.

Doc imagined what the next hour would be like if he were to sit back and tell these boys all that stood behind his mood. Wouldn't they be surprised to find out what all their old segundo had done in life? But it wasn't going to happen, for those were the stories Doc only told himself.

VIRGINIA CITY

January 1867

WHEN HE WENT TO BED that New Year's night, Doc assumed that he and the girl from the billiards saloon were friends now and would see each other regularly. She would become his girlfriend, and then they would get married, and get themselves out of Virginia

City to some nicer place, where Doc would ranch cows and the girl, now a woman, would have babies. Together they would grow prosperous and then old, and whichever one outlasted the other would be so sad as to die soon after.

All of that seemed possible, even probable, at three in the morning after New Year's midnight—and completely unlikely and perhaps impossible when he woke up in the brittle cold four hours later. Doc could not quite imagine how he would ever again travel the twenty feet to where she was, and every conversation he attempted with her in his head embarrassed both of them and faltered to a stop.

About all Doc did in the coming days regarding the serving girl was to knock a knot out of the east wall, the one facing across the alley to the billiards saloon. Every time he could, he stood there looking. His heart nearly stopped in his chest when she was actually there, wrapped in a blanket against the cold, smoking. It happened twice the first week, for a total of not quite ten minutes. For these brief sightings, Doc had waited a minimum of six hours with his eye to the knothole, and had managed to freeze his eyelids and hurt the eye so it ached and he could not see right for a month.

He neglected his food and his bowling practice, and made himself gaunt and nervous. It could have gone on longer and become worse had she not yelled at him the third time she was in the alley and he was watching. It was well after midnight and freezing cold.

"I can see your damn eye," she hollered. "Get out here if you want to talk to me so bad."

So Doc put on his coat and went out to her, flapping his arms until her cigarette was spent. Then she stood looking at him in the moonlight, gave a big sigh, and said, "Com'mon inside, then. Just don't get fresh with me, or I'll never let you in again."

The first thing Doc noticed was how much warmer the empty billiards saloon was than the bowling saloon. There was a red glow in the darkness, and when he got the hang of the light, he saw it was grinning out the grill teeth of a nickel-plated pot-belly stove.

"This is the card room," she said, "and since it makes most of the money, Bobo heats it. Lucky for me, it's straight below where I sleep."

"Is Bobo your boss?"

"His name is Bob. Comstock Bob, because of selling his mine in Nevada before the whole place watered out. I just call him Bobo because I feel like it. I call him that to his face, to answer your next question."

They pulled two spool-back chairs from the poker table and sat them by the fire. She chunked in pieces of wood.

"I'm Pearly and you're I don't know."

"Doc Windham."

"What kind of name is Doc?"

"It's what I've always been called."

"I bet you've got some stupid first name you're glad not to use."

"Could be."

Doc noticed, even above the smell of the smoky pine that was burning, how much the room stank of cigar.

"How come you smoke outside?"

Pearly was in her chair by then, with her shoes off and holding her feet to the fender. She had thick knitted socks on.

"It's the only fresh air I get." When she heard what she'd said, she laughed. "I mean that. It stinks in here. I take it you don't smoke."

"Have done, but don't like it much. I don't mind if others do."

"Thanks so much," she said.

She was so prickly in everything she said that Doc was feeling downhearted. At the same time, he was giddy and pleased that she'd called him over and invited him in. He glanced sideways, just to look at her, and she was glowering.

"What?"

"If you're just going to fall all in love with me, you won't be no fun, and I won't want you around. I got boyfriends all over this town, and I don't like most of them. They can't see me without strangling their hat and looking at the floor and stuttering. I mean, who in their right mind would be flattered by that?"

"Must feel nice, having all that power over us," Doc said, irritated to be lumped in with others, also that there were others. This wasn't turning out much like the story he'd designed after she kissed him on New Year's.

Now she was grinning. "See? That's better."

"How come your teeth are like that?" Doc asked. If impulses were what she wanted, he had lots of them.

She clamped her mouth shut. "Like what?'

"One like another." He had seldom seen teeth as straight. Hers didn't stick out and weren't jumbled together or spread apart, or black.

"I don't know." She shrugged her shoulders and the blanket fell off onto the chair. She was wearing her working dress. "My mother had good teeth as far as I remember. The rest is probably that I had a mean father who never bought me candy. Didn't matter if he had money or not. By the time I had my own money, I had no sweet tooth. Still don't."

"What's he do?"

"My father?" Pearly suddenly barked a laugh. "Pushes up daisies? Provides lodgings for worms down on their luck?"

"Sorry."

"Okay, I'll be nice. He was a gambler. And he died. The end."

Doc wished that Pearly would ask him about his family, that she would be that interested. But in another way he didn't care as much as he did a minute ago. Maybe Pearly was too prickly to *be* a girlfriend. And he was enjoying what they were doing right now. Her being prickly and making him laugh wasn't so bad.

"You want to see my room?" She was already on her feet and moving in the direction of the ladder.

Doc sat like a lump of coal. Flummoxed again.

"Oh, come on," she said, coming back and grabbing his sleeve.

She climbed ahead of him, went up very quickly, and disappeared into the black. He followed, then stopped with his head above the hole. There was no window, no light.

"Boo!" she said, clamping her hands down on his shoulders. It scared him so he almost fell, but he didn't let on.

She scratched a match and lit a candle set in a can lid.

Doc took it in. The room, so called, was the back third of a long attic under the roof beam. There was a damp circle on the underside of the roof where the stovepipe went through. Beyond that, the ceiling glittered frost. Her bed was a sheet sewn double and stuffed with something, probably straw. On top of that was an old feather tick, sprouting feathers.

All this was normal, but hanging from nails in the ceiling, by strands of string, were a bunch of glass things. Doc hoisted himself so he could sit on the floor and get a closer look. Ordinary pieces of broken window glass, whole panes with spiderweb cracks. There were little ornaments—deer, horses and whatnot, fashioned in glass—and a couple of blobs of glass with loops for the string to go through. Some of these had colours in them. They turned in the stovepipe heat and the reflections were pleasing to the eye.

"It's pretty," he said.

Pearly had by now slithered in under the hanging glass onto the feather tick. There was no more than a foot and a half between her body and the lowest hanging piece.

"What happens if you sit up?"

"I don't."

"Like in the night, if you had a dream or something."

She reached up and swished her hand. She hit a couple of pieces that hit others and set up a ringing that tickled in Doc's ear.

"That's what it's for," she said.

It hadn't occurred to Doc that the glass was for anything more than ornament. When he put his mind to the idea of its having a purpose, he thought of the dead miner.

"I suppose you have a gun too."

She slid her hand under the pillow and came out with a kind of gun Doc hadn't seen before. It was a revolver, but short in the barrel, snubby-nosed. It was probably inaccurate, but Doc saw that it wasn't supposed to shoot far.

"Some girls' fathers die and leave them well off. Mine left me well armed. This is what's called a pepper box."

Doc was feeling downcast again. He hadn't expected Pearly to haul him up here and straight into her bed; it was clear she'd had some other intention. But now it seemed she might have only wanted to give him a warning.

Then he had an impulse again, one he would soon regret. One of the things he most wanted to know in the world was whether his uncle had actually shot that miner. Without thinking beyond the fact that she might know, he asked her.

Doc wasn't looking at Pearly when he said the words, so he didn't see the crash of glass coming. She'd sat straight up into all the hanging glass and ornaments, causing some to break and some to fall. She had scratched her cheek, and the pepper box was pointed at him.

"Damn you! I knew you'd talk about it! I knew you wouldn't have the sense not to! Now get out and don't come back! I'll shoot you right in your damn stupid Texas bonehead if you do!"

Doc slid down the ladder and out the way he'd entered, past the stove and out the back door. He walked across the frozen alley and through the bowling saloon's back door. It was almost as cold as outside, because McGinty was cheap and allowed no fires at night. In the dark pit, Doc wrapped himself in his blanket with his clothes on and curled up tight.

JUST BEFORE DAWN, and without having slept, Doc went out and down the hill to the Chinese town. He waited until the lady came out of her tent, then tried to explain what he wanted. She brought him inside, and her children were startled to see a white man in their tent. They fled. It took a lot of hand signs and finally the help of her nephew to figure out what Doc was after. Then a search was made all over the Chinese camp.

Doc had asked for glass, whole or broken. What came back were a solid glass paperweight with a crocus in it and a chunk broken out of one side, a tube of some material like glass which turned out to be half a broken opium pipe, and a square of glass with a fat curl at its centre. The pipe piece had a swirly colourful finish and Doc imagined it hanging over Pearly's bed, lit by candles.

He gave the Chinese lady ten dollars, and she wanted to give him back five. But he made her keep it. Then she thought of something and jumped up and rummaged in the boxes and bags that lined the tent's back wall. What she found was a piece of purple ribbon which she put in Doc's hand and wouldn't take more money for. Somehow she had divined that the glass was a gift for a girl.

That morning, Doc gave McGinty a fright by entering through the front door. When that man started to give him hell for leaving the premises unguarded, Doc said he would not be setting pins today. He took a candle and a match, a pen, some paper and ink, and retired to the pit. With his blanket wrapped around him, he wrote, *I don't want to talk about it either*. That was it. He didn't even sign his name.

When the ink was dry, he rolled the note and poked it in the knothole. He saw that it stayed there all day but was gone when he checked at midnight. By morning, it was back. Printed on the blank side was *Good*.

He took the three pieces of glass and he placed each inside a wadded page from *The Montana Post*. Then he wrapped the whole in the rest of the newspaper and tied it with the purple ribbon.

With the package in his coat, he left McGinty's through the front door and entered the billiards saloon the same way. He sat at the bar but refused when Comstock Bob offered him a drink. When Bob finally went to the poker room and started shaking ashes from the stove, Doc stepped down from his stool. He took the package out of his coat and went to the billiards table under which Pearly was sweeping. He brushed some cigar ash from the felt and set the package down.

Back in the bowling saloon, McGinty studied him as someone foreign.

"You sick?" he asked.

"I'm better," said Doc.

Doc went to the bucket at the end of the bar and broke the ice. He fished out the stiff cloth and stomped ice out of it until it was pliable. He went to the row of bowling balls and wiped each one in turn. When he finished that, he swept the lanes. When that chore was complete, he approached the counter.

"You should put a fire in that stove if you want to see another customer before spring," he said.

McGinty did not answer, and Doc retired to the pit and his blanket for a snooze. He woke to the sound of wood hitting the floor. McGinty approached the pit halfway and said, "Now on, light fires when you want 'em. But split your own wood."

VIRGINIA CITY

July 1881

T HEY HAD BEEN IN VIRGINIA CITY a week and were still waiting for the Major. Nor had Dog Eye and Lippy returned. The cowboys were back in the Miner's Café, trying to make a meal last all afternoon, when a man ran in the door and yelled that a telegram had come, that President James Garfield had been shot at the train station in the city of Washington. Everyone in the room peppered the fellow with questions, wanting to know whether the president was dead and who had shot him, but that was all he knew. Out of a long silence afterwards came a southern voice, saying, "Ain't my president anyway." A pair of Yankees looked insulted, but nothing came of it.

Finally Lowell sent Tex Appleby to stand around the telegraph office and see if more news came. After half an hour, Tex returned. President Garfield was not dead but in a bad way. They had the man who'd done it. There was no information in the telegram about the assassin other than that.

Among the cowboys, nobody seemed to know how to feel about the news, or what to say. They looked to Doc, who had something to say about everything, but he was moody again and stayed silent.

Then, without comment, Doc got up and left. He walked across the street without looking, and a wagon driver had to veer his horses to keep from running him down. Doc went into the store on the other side, and the boys debated whether he was there to buy tobacco or a magazine. But when Doc came out, he was empty-handed. A bald man in an apron, the proprietor of the store, followed him and locked up behind himself. They went up the hill and stopped before a new stone building.

"What building is that?" asked Tex.

"Don't you see the compass and square chiselled in the top?" said Lowell.

"I seen it on the P & O cows too, but I don't know what it means."

"That's the Freemason's sign. That's a Freemason temple."

"What's a Freemason anyway?"

"That's a long story and I don't know it."

The bald man in the apron pulled the ring of keys back out of his pants pocket. He looked up and down the empty street and then unlocked the door of the Masonic temple. He and Doc went inside.

"I'll be damned," said Lowell. He turned to Tex. "Looks like you can direct your questions on that topic to Doc."

VIRGINIA CITY

January 1867

BECAUSE IT WAS NOW TOO cold to stand around the alley, Doc and Pearly met nights in one or the other of the saloons. Doc would run down the hill and buy food from the Chinese woman, and they would spread it on the poker table at Comstock Bob's. After they had eaten, they would sit like an old married couple by whichever stove was lit—or else they'd bowl or play billiards.

Doc decided he would teach Pearly to bowl, and one night they did roll several games. But whatever it was about bowling, Pearly couldn't help but laugh at it. Even Doc's pin-setting struck her as amusing. Doc was a little offended, because he was practising every night. Pearly tried to make it up by saying that Doc was a fine bowler and not the original cause of her finding bowling funny. The blame for that belonged to her father, the gambler, who had introduced her to bowling and a great many other games out of a desire to find one she could make money at while he played cards.

The first thing he'd pushed on her—a game of a sort—was sleight-of-hand. He assumed a young girl, being quick, would be good at it, and he tried to teach Pearly tricks out of a book. It didn't take him long to conclude that she was never going to fool anyone in a shell game, so he moved on from there to bowling. When she proved too giddy for bowling, he switched to billiards, conscious that he was fast running out of games that were popular and available in the West.

Because her father never proposed these games as fun things, Pearly didn't see fun in them. Laughing at bowling was the closest she came. It was the artificiality of games that she never got over—proof, as far as she was concerned, that people are sheep.

"I don't think God said, 'Let's roll a ball down a strip of wood and count the pins we knock over.' I don't remember a psalm to that effect. You and me could walk out of these saloons one day and find the whole town balancing plates on a stick. It could be any damn thing."

But whether gifted with an interest in games or not, Pearly'd had a natural ability at billiards, much to her father's delight.

"I was all in love with my pa back then, just like a dog that'll do any damn fool trick its master asks. Billiards was my trick, and I learned it well so my pa would love me more. And he did."

Hearing about Pearly's billiards prowess, Doc wanted a demonstration. At two in the morning, they switched saloons and fired up two lanterns around a six-foot-by-twelve-foot billiards table. For the next hour, Doc watched transfixed as Pearly batted around one white ball and the two reds. It was a pocket table and she could shoot in the reds or make her cue ball off another ball with little effort.

The *kerthunk* of briskly hit balls hitting the back of the leather pockets came like clockwork. Then Pearly attempted to show Doc how to carom, or cannon, meaning to hit the other balls with your cue ball, which she said was the real heart of the game of billiards, but the cold beat her out.

"Bobo bought these two tables on the Comstock when it was all going broke there. He thought he had a great bargain, but there was a reason they were going cheap." Pearly pounded a shot into the opposite cushion and it hit with a dead sound, hardly rebounding. "These cushions are genuine tree rubber, which makes them lively in hot weather. When it's cold, they get hard. There's some new kind that's good year round, but Bobo didn't know. He got gulled."

If Pearly found his bowling funny, Doc found Pearly's billiards thrilling, especially when she reclined on the table with her one heel kicked up. Because she was short, she needed to jump onto the table to make several of her shots. There was another way of doing it, using a stick called a rake or a "lady's aid." The end on the stick had knuckles where you could rest your cue while you shot. But in the billiards saloon that Pearly had learned in, there had been no lady's aid. "I hate a rake," she said. "Can't use one."

"You played for money?" asked Doc.

"To quote my pa, 'Why else?' He was making so much offa me at the peak that he quit playing cards. All he did was find men to play me. That was the hardest part, especially in a new town. Men don't like losing to a little girl, but they don't like beating her bad in front of an audience either. Some were embarrassed to be seen at the same table as me. But my father had more tricks than you can imagine for coaxing people into it."

"Like what?"

"You can guess," said Pearly, stretching out across the table, "if you work your mind."

She jumped down and circled to her next shot. While she played, she never looked at Doc, only at the balls and where they stopped. She seemed to know instantly what her next shot was and where she would have to put herself to shoot it. Now, as she walked around and shot, she gave examples of how her father used to reel the suckers in.

"What? You afraid to play a little girl?"

"Please don't hurt my daughter's feelings, sir. It causes her pain to be so good yet people won't play her."

"Just play her once. If you feel she presents a challenge, we could consider a little wager."

She stopped and rubbed chalk on her cue tip.

"It was like that for the first few games in a new town. Once it was started, though, people would line up to play me. I'd beat some men ten times. Even then, they couldn't believe I was capable of doing it again."

"Is it legal to get up on the table like that? Legal in the rules of billiards, like?"

It seemed a normal question, but it made Pearly slam her cue into the frozen rail so hard it left a dent and a chalk spot. She walked out into the poker room and threw herself into a chair. Doc blew out one lamp and carried the other one after her. He sat beside her at the stove and kept quiet for a long time. Then he said he didn't mean any insult and that she was a real good billiards player, best he'd ever seen.

"For the record," she said at last, "it isn't legal. Leagues and tournaments say 'one foot on the floor.' So I could never play in nice society."

"Is that what makes you mad?"

"No. I never cared about that. I'm mad because it's how my father and me managed to get him killed."

Again, Doc didn't push for the story. He leaned forward with his elbows on his knees and his hands clasped tight. It was like his hands were his mouth, clamped shut.

When Pearly looked apt never to say anything, he said, "You don't have to tell me."

"Damn right I don't have to," she said, "but I'm gonna. Every once in a while, I need to tell it and have a good cry."

And so she proceeded.

Because of the one-foot-on-the-floor rule, Pearly's father always began the seduction of a customer by saying that any game with his daughter had to be played without that rule in force. He asked up front, around witnesses, so no one could come back on him later.

"So people got mad when you beat them?"

"Pa's rule was that one in three players is a sore loser. He always carried a gun on account of that third one. But the thing with me was, no one wanted to be a sore loser when they got whipped by a little girl. Even people who were normally real bad losers would joke and laugh and put their money down and walk away."

"So that's not what happened?"

"Don't rush me! What happened was we were in Denver. Pa heard about a four-ball billiards tournament with a thousand-dollar prize. He went and asked about it and started coaxing them to accept an under-aged girl player who couldn't keep one foot on the floor. I expect he went on about it not being fair to little people, or the whole female sex, or who knows what. Pa could really talk.

"Anyhow, I got to play and I beat everybody until I was in one of the semi-finals. What happened was the people who ran the thing didn't tell anyone else they were letting me play my way. The man I played in the semi-finals was this cold fish of a Paris Frenchman. He was proper and snobby and played in a tuxedo. Anyway, I beat him, and I did it on a long run of points that began with a carom where I'd laid on the table to shoot. After he lost, he went to the judge and said it was a forfeit because I'd made an illegal shot."

Pearly stopped. Her eyes had filled up with tears and she wiped them on the bushy sleeve of her work dress.

"Pa was such an asshole. That's what killed him. It wasn't because I was short, not really. He saw that the Frenchman was making a fuss over the rules, and nothing made my father worse than thinking he was about to lose something he thought he'd won. He was the worst loser of them all. Right in front of the whole crowd, he started making fun of the Frenchman. Putting on this funny French accent, and saying how the Frenchman didn't start complaining until he got beat, and what kind of man couldn't take losing to a little girl? What kind of *foreign* man? He never knew when to quit.

"On account of the man was a foreigner, everybody in the room was against him already. Pa didn't really have to say a thing. They booed the Frenchman and threw stuff at him, and started bumping into him, kind of tossing him from one to another and right out the door."

"Did you win the tournament?"

"No. The man I played in the final was a whiz. I missed twice and it was over."

"And the Frenchman came back and shot your father?"

"Shut up, Doc," said Pearly, crying freely. "It's my story. I tell it how I like."

"Sorry."

"Nothing happened in Denver. We never saw him again. It was right here two years ago."

"Here in Virginia City?"

"Here in this room. I was in there playing billiards and I saw that Frenchman come in. He gave me a real icy look, but I nodded to him anyway, and he nodded back. Like a fool, I thought that meant it was okay. I never did any more. I didn't run and warn Pa or anything."

Pearly sobbed so hard she had to take a break. She put her face in the sleeve of her dress and cried awhile, then sat up and wiped her face on her skirt. She snuffled back sharp and loud.

"And he walked right in here, right through that arch. And Pa was sitting in that chair there. But the thing was, Pa wasn't looking. He'd probably had too much brandy to drink. They told me later he was arguing with a drunk who said he was still in the hand when Pa said he'd folded. The Frenchman didn't even say a word. He just pulled a gun out of a holster on his shoulder and shot Pa dead." She pointed to the middle of her forehead.

Doc waited as long as he could before he asked, "Did they hang the Frenchman?"

"I knew you'd ask that. Answer's no. Goddamn Freemason vigilante bastards were asleep at the switch that night. The Frenchman had a good horse and he rode off over the Madison and the Gallatin and took Bozeman's Trail right into Indian country, where everybody was afraid to follow. He probably got scalped and I hope he got tortured first, but I won't ever know unless he's still alive and I meet him."

Pearly shivered. She jumped up and fed the fire.

"Now you know," she said.

Doc looked around him and a shiver grabbed him too, cranked his shoulders.

"How can you work here, Pearly? And sleep here?"

"That's one way of looking at it."

"Is there another?"

"My pa wasn't a very nice man, but we were a family anyway." Pearly pointed at Doc. "I know you want to ask about my mother, so don't! What I'm saying is, when I leave here, I don't plan to be back. While I am here, I might as well spend my time in the room that reminds me most of Pa."

Doc sat and thought. He mulled her story and tried to understand it all. He kept coming back to one part, and since it had to do with hanging, Doc thought for some time before asking.

"Pearly, I got a question. If you don't like it, don't get mad, all right? Just say you won't answer."

"Just ask your damn hanging question and get it over with."

"What do you mean the Freemason vigilante bastards were asleep that night? I've heard of Freemasons but I don't know really what they are."

"It's just this old club for men. Pfouts, the storekeeper, he's one. He gave them the upstairs of his store to meet in. I've been told lots of times the Masons started the vigilantes. A gang was raising hell here and at Bannack and the Masons had a meeting and decided to stop it. They hanged a bunch of people."

Doc remembered a *Police Gazette* in the bunkhouse on the Texas ranch where Uncle Jack had come and found him. The *Gazette* was everybody's favourite because it had lots of pictures and lots of shooting and featured the West quite often. In the copy they had at the bunkhouse, there was a story about Montana vigilantes hanging over twenty members of the Plummer gang. Doc had often read it aloud to the boys in the bunkhouse, most of whom could not read, so he remembered it well. The Plummers were road agents, stagecoach robbers and murderers who masqueraded as the sheriff and deputies of the town of Bannack.

"That's the Plummer gang."

"Plummer. That's right."

"I thought the hangings were in Bannack."

"And here," said Pearly. "They hanged Plummer and his deputy Buck Stinson in Bannack. Then they came here and hanged a bunch more. That store on the other side that's a drugstore now was half finished then. They hanged them from the roof beam. It was real cold and, come morning, they were laid out froze on the floor. One was called Club Foot George and somebody cut off his club foot for a souvenir."

Doc recognized most of the details but some of what Pearly said was new. She told him Buck Stinson was so mean he shot his own dog on the main street of Bannack because it wouldn't come to him. Then Stinson got morose, went into the saloon, and said next time he got drunk someone should shoot him.

"You weren't here then, Pearly. How do you know so much?"

"They did hang one fella after Pa and me got here, from a corral rail behind Pfouts's store. Guy named Joe Slade who was a real bad drunk. That's what they hanged him for—being ornery."

"You mean the Freemasons hanged him?"

"The vigilantes hanged him. I couldn't tell you if the two are always the same. Anyway, lots of people were mad at them for killing Slade, especially his wife, who threatened to kill everybody who done it. I heard about that hanging right here when it happened. The older stuff is from one of my boyfriends, Peter."

Doc felt his neck hair rise. Just the word "boyfriend" was enough to cause it. "How's he know?"

"Man who teaches school here, Mr. Dimsdale, wrote a book about it. They printed it off on the same machine that prints the newspaper. Peter reads that book about once a week."

"Does it say in there it was Freemasons?"

"Nope. That's a secret."

"Was Peter the one who told you?"

Pearly was over her tears now and beginning to enjoy Doc's jealousy.

"My, my. You've gone and cornered me into divulging Peter's deepest secret, which of course he couldn't help telling me because he loves me so. Should I tell you or should I not?"

"Com'mon, Pearly, this is important."

"Oh, all right. Peter's a Freemason. First level, or whatever they call it. It's about the most important thing in his life. Even more than me, and believe me, he's helplessly in love with me. He's the worst billiards player on earth and he comes and plays just so he can see me."

That reminded Doc of something else he wanted to know.

"Do you still play? With the customers, for money or whatever?"

"Nope. But I do play alone. For some reason, even though I think the game is a curse on my life, and got my father killed, I don't like to get out of practice."

"Did Peter say it was the Freemasons who started hanging people?"

"Calm down, would you? What Peter said was that he went to a speech by a big Montana Freemason, and that he as good as said they were behind it. He didn't say it outright, but said stuff about how the Masons were confronted by terrible wrongdoings and criminal thievery and how they had to reach deep into themselves and do things that weren't in their normal morality. Sounds like they did it to me."

Pearly told Doc that Peter was a clerk in the bank, and Doc had trouble imagining a bank clerk who played bad billiards putting a noose around Uncle Jack's neck. But they probably weren't all clerks. Or maybe they just hired hard men and kept their own hands clean.

Pearly jumped up. "Holy crow. It's almost morning."

Just then, when Doc was more or less convinced that Pearly had no interest in him as a boyfriend, she gave him a big hug and a kiss on the lips. When she pushed him away after, the tears were back in her eyes.

"I been thinking how it's not fair to keep secrets you need to know. Your uncle did kill that miner who hurt me. He shot him through the head. I fainted then. I don't know any more." She ran for the ladder and was gone.

DOC DIDN'T SLEEP MUCH that winter, and when he did, his dreams were tortured by visions. Bowling, billiards and Pearly got wrapped in with the cowboy pulling the arrow out of his shoulder and the scalped man and boy. Uncle Jack was in his dreams too, sadly never alive, just hanging in the picture somewhere.

The newest thing in Doc's dreams were Freemasons. His sleeping mind had decided to dress them in masks and hoods and big rubber boots. Sometimes they were putting a noose on Doc.

Looking for someone to blame for Uncle Jack's death, and urging along a poorly formed idea of revenge, Doc settled on the Freemasons as his probable foe. Something Pearly had said, repeated from Peter, made Doc realize there might even be Freemasons among the bowlers at McGinty's. Pearly said that the Masons had secret handshakes and signs by which they could recognize one another and pass messages. There was a secret language too: English, but in code.

Doc remembered seeing and hearing things from his pit that made no sense. Now, he started watching for it. Before too long, he witnessed a foursome of normal-looking shopkeepers and political types making signs and speaking in a strange lingo, taking care so McGinty wouldn't see or hear it. The talk had the words compass and square in it and a lot about level and square. Sometimes, it was as if they were discussing a building project, but they weren't. As pretty well always happened, the bowlers failed to consider that the hands and arms that reset their pins had ears to go with them.

When they were together, Doc could not help but pepper Pearly with questions, for she was still the most direct source of Freemason information he had. Did Peter say anything more? When would she be seeing him next?

"I hate this," Pearly said, finally. "My most ardent admirer devotes himself to *being* a Mason, and my other boyfriend wastes all our time asking questions about Masons and my first boyfriend. What I should do is get the two of you together. While you're talking Masons, I'll go find a third boyfriend who's interested in me."

While it was an improvement that Pearly now numbered Doc among her boyfriends and had reduced the total to two, it wasn't right that Doc so often infuriated her. The trouble was that Doc really was interested in Masons, and Pearly could always pry new details about "the craft" out of Peter. Even as he told her Mason secrets, Peter emphasized the solemnity of the oaths of secrecy he had sworn. That man was a complete failure as a member of a secret society.

Some of what Doc learned through Pearly was that there were many levels of being a Mason, a kind of ladder up which you moved through study and by doing what higher-up Masons asked of you. Doc's dreams were on track as far as clothing went: Masons did dress up. During their rituals, they wore some kind of leather apron. Pearly said it was made of the skin of lambs.

Peter said the Freemasons believed themselves to be descended from the stonemason who built Solomon's Temple. Pearly was of the opinion that temple was in Boston. The only Solomon Doc was aware of was the one in the Bible, the one who threatened to split a child in two. Maybe that Solomon had a temple, which must be in the same part of the world as Ali Baba's cave.

When Pearly asked Peter what the hand signs looked like, he finally maintained silence about something. He wouldn't show her, but he did say there were some for asking if a stranger was a Mason and others that said a Mason was in need of help.

As for meetings, they seemed to have two kinds. The first were regular get-togethers which any brother could attend. The second were ritual nights, which occurred as needed on the Friday before the full moon.

If he was ever going to know whether the Masons were guilty of hanging Uncle Jack, Doc decided he had to see what they did at their secret meetings. That was how he came to beg Pearly to ask Peter for the most profound illustration of his love yet.

ON THE FRIDAY NIGHT three days before the February full moon, Pearly and Doc stared out at Wallace Street through the main window of the billiards saloon. Half an hour before midnight, seven men arrived outside Pfouts's door. After Pfouts let them in, Pearly and Doc left the saloon by the back.

It was an ice-cold night: "just like the night they hanged Club Foot George," as Pearly put it. They had on every piece of clothing they owned and carried two blankets. In case anyone was watching, they went away from Wallace Street, climbed the hill a few blocks, then returned and crossed Wallace above Pfouts's store. Doc argued this was necessary because of how loud their feet scrunched on the cold snow.

When they arrived at the frozen creek behind the main street stores, they followed it down, dodging through piles of mine slag. They stopped at the back of the low stone building that held the *Montana Post* printing press. The building had wide stone sills that they could use to climb to the roof. Over this roof to its other side, it was just a short hop to the little shack next to Pfouts's store. Everything was covered in frost and slippery.

The space between the shack and the upstairs wall of Pfouts's building was no more than a foot. The window that had figured in Pearly's instructions to Peter was on that wall.

"I hope he did it," Doc said, as he was getting set to look.

"He better have," said Pearly, "or it's the last time I eat with him and listen to his nonsense."

Doc stretched himself up to the small window. It was as it should be. Peter had peeled down a corner of the thick paper the Masons used to cover it. The paper wasn't pulled down far and the view was limited, but Doc could see a third of the room, the back third closest to the alley.

"Let me look." Because Pearly was even shorter than Doc, Doc had to go on his hands and knees on the frosty shingles and let her stand on the small of his back.

"What's that on the table?"

"A Bible. And a skull with a candle in it."

Doc had just resumed looking when a man entered. He brought a tall chair and sat on it beside the small table with the Bible and the skull. Doc couldn't see his face because he had a hood over his head, but the basic costume was like a monk's habit, over which he wore a lambskin apron. The apron was snow white except for symbols written on it. He also had on fancy gloves with gauntlets that went outside the sleeves.

"Cripes almighty, it's cold out here."

"Quiet, Pearly, they'll hear."

Like most windows in Virginia City, this one was cracked. In fact, it was broken in half, and the two sides were loose enough in their putty to have shifted apart. When things started happening below, Doc and Pearly could hear most of it.

The first sound wasn't talking, but a knocking from the part of the room they couldn't see. Then a person they couldn't see either announced in a voice like a theatre actor's that there was "a report." Another voice said the man knocking was Donald Lister. Pearly started tugging on Doc's sleeve. "Friend of Peter's," she whispered.

Then there was quite a bit about how this Donald was a poor ignorant fellow, "in a state of darkness and ignorance of the light," who had come here of his own free will "to be admitted to the mysteries of Freemasonry." The talk was very repetitive, and the man on the throne, though he didn't speak, put in his two cents' worth in hand signs.

"Can you see Donald?" Pearly whispered, and Doc shushed her and shook his head no.

"We're missing all the good stuff," she said when she was standing on his back again.

"Pearly, be quiet. Try a hand sign or something."

Then she started waving in the air, all excited. She jumped off Doc's back and made quite a noise. She signalled for him to look, quick.

What Doc saw chilled him. Someone, Donald presumably, was kneeling blindfolded before the man on the throne. Around his neck was a hangman's noose, knot to the back. His clothes were peeled down and rolled up in odd ways. His right shoulder and half his chest were bare. An old slipper was on his foot and the trouser leg and shirt sleeve on that side were rolled up.

The fellow Doc couldn't see called the man on the throne his "worshipful master," and suddenly the worshipful master himself spoke in the deepest, most rumbling voice yet. He demanded to know Donald's age and if he was here of his own free will. Then he wanted to know if Donald believed in God. Doc couldn't hear Donald's answers, but he assumed he knew what they were.

Then the worshipful master made more signs, and the other men, all in hooded gowns and white aprons, came into view waving their hands and arms over Donald's head. There was talk about how Donald would have to devote his life to the secret arts of becoming a Mason.

Pearly was dragging on Doc's sleeve so he let her back up. Since she had seen the noose, she hadn't spoken, even at a whisper. Neither did she stay looking for long.

Finally, the Masons got Donald up on his feet and marched him out of sight. Doc wondered if that was the last of Donald, but the whole group appeared again on the far side of the room. The Masons walked crowded around Donald, smacking him on the shoulders from time to time.

By now Doc was over the idea they intended to hang Donald Lister, though he felt the noose was proof that hanging wasn't far from their minds. But not now, Doc believed, and not Donald. In fact, he thought they were done and would whip the blindfold off Donald at any moment. Maybe there'd be a round of applause. Maybe they'd all have a whisky.

But that wasn't the end of it. They kept Donald blindfolded and made him stand with his feet pointed in awkward ways with his hand on the Bible. That was the start of the oath-taking. Donald had to swear to keep the secrets he learned about the Freemasons. They gave him a compass to jab into the bare part of his chest, and he swore never to speak or write or draw anything he saw here.

Then they started in on what would happen if he did weaken and tell. First they would cut his throat. Then they would tear his tongue out by the root and bury it in the sand by the sea at the low-water mark. He would be known ever after as a worthless person.

They weren't making much sense any more. Why rip someone's tongue out after you've cut his throat? And, after both, who would care if they went around saying he was a worthless person? Doc also wondered about the sand of the sea at the low-water mark. He imagined someone carrying Donald's tongue in a cedar box on a stagecoach all the way to California.

Then it was over. The worshipful master said that Donald was an approved apprentice Freemason. They thumped him on the shoulders a few times and took him away.

Doc and Pearly crawled out to the front edge and waited for Pfouts's door to open. There came Donald in normal clothes, running away as if the demons of hell were on his tail.

When they got back to the window, they could hear knocking again and more business about a report. Pearly put her mouth to Doc's ear and said, "To hell with more of this."

Doc was in a quandary. Even though he guessed the whole ritual would repeat, there might be something new, something that bore on vigilantes and hanging. When Pearly saw he meant to stay, she gave him her blanket and started over the roofs. Doc followed and let her down by the wrist over the edge of the printer's building. She landed on her feet and disappeared into the darkness.

Doc returned to the window. Now that he was alone, he realized how cold it was. It must be twenty-five below. He gathered both blankets around himself and put his eye back to the peeled corner of the window. He expected to see another blindfolded pilgrim kneeling in a noose, but the worshipful master was alone, slumped a little forward and doing nothing. Doc was finding this strange when the worshipful master raised a gloved hand. He aimed a finger out of a fist and swivelled it slowly. He stopped when it was pointing at Doc.

Doc jumped away. He scampered over the roofs, threw the blankets over the edge, climbed down to the wide sill. When he landed on the ground, two men had the blankets and rushed him. They spun him and wrapped him tight and started marching him forward. He tried to fight but his arms and legs were bound.

A corral gate whined open. He could see a ray of moonlight on the high gatepost as it twisted. A horse nickered, then ran out of shadow into a far corner where she stood and quivered. She looked black in the dark, with a crooked blaze down her face. It came to Doc that this was the corral where they'd hanged the bad drunk Joe Slade. Sure he was going to die any minute, Doc wrenched and fought inside the blankets, got a hand free and punched in all directions. A hard little mouth of iron slammed him in the ribs and a voice said, "Don't!"

The store's back door opened and he was pushed inside, into a deeper dark. Their boots were loud on the floorboards of the shop. The gun was still in his ribs, and a blindfold was wrapped on him so tight he saw blue lightning. They pushed him up a set of stairs and across a floor, and he pictured everything according to what he'd seen through the window. He knew at the first scratchy touch that the noose was coming around his neck, and that next he would be on his knees. He imagined the worshipful master in front of him.

There was some time to think then, and his thoughts were peculiar. He was wondering if he was here for torture or hanging, or one then the other. Would they cut off parts of him, and if so, which ones and when? If they started cutting and torturing, he would tell everything—except about Pearly. If he told everything else, they might not notice he was leaving her out. As for his parts, they could cut off all they wanted after he was dead.

Another funny thought was about the horse nickering in the corral. He thought of how much he had enjoyed horses in his lifetime, and he had a great sadness to think he would never ride another. He was aware this was an insult to Pearly, who he had never made love to. He should have been thinking about that, and as soon as he mentioned it to himself, he was. There he was on his knees with his eyes squashed and a hard-on pressing right out the front of his pants. This made him laugh.

Now he was thinking of Uncle Jack's death, and he was thinking of it differently. He had always assumed Uncle Jack died consumed by anger and hatred. But maybe Jack also had more pleasurable thoughts when he knew the jig was up. Maybe he died with a hard-on too.

A whack on the side of the head brought Doc to the present. The Masons had been talking and such was the intensity of Doc's daydream that he had not heard them. Now the sound of their voices came as if he had pulled his fingers out of his ears.

" . . . let him go. He has seen the ritual."

"He hears."

"What difference if he hears? He cannot witness anything more damaging than he already has."

This was encouraging. If he had seen the worst, it suggested they didn't have a row of skulls in a closet, or fresh graves under the manure in the horse corral.

"Our duty is clear," said another. "We must treat him as we would a betrayer—as we will treat the betrayer when we find him."

This last didn't sound as good, for Peter or for Doc. Doc thought about the punishments mentioned in the oaths. He decided to talk while he still had the equipment.

"Gentlemen? You don't have to hang me or tear my tongue out. I can keep a . . ."

Another whack on the head and a voice by his ear. "What you'll keep is a civil tongue in your head!"

That was funny and he laughed again.

"He's addlepated!" another declared.

Then came the unmistakable voice of the worshipful master, who had not spoken since Doc entered the room.

"All of you, please be silent. Treat this as a meeting. I will chair."

There was a rumbling of feet. Being at a meeting seemed to require them to take certain positions.

"Brothers, I pose to you one question," said the worshipful master, "which I believe we must, as civilized moral men, consider before and beyond any other. We know what we could do to this young man to guarantee his silence. That is simple enough. The harder question is whether there is an alternative, something that would achieve the same end, without going beyond the normal bounds of our morality. This is not a murderer, as far as we know, not even a road agent, probably not even a creature depraved."

It was all Doc could do not to launch a testimonial.

"Well? Can anyone think of an alternative?"

The silence grew long, especially in Doc's sparking dark. Please, he pleaded, think!

"I do have an alternative," said the worshipful master, and in that moment Doc felt for him something like love.

"My alternative," he continued, "is to make of this young man a Mason. If he swears the oaths of secrecy, and lives accordingly, the fact of what he has seen will no longer matter."

"How could we believe the oath of a spy?"

"How can we believe any man's oath?" the worshipful master parried. "It is obvious tonight that those oaths are sometimes broken. If someone we trust can betray us, then perhaps another whom we don't trust can keep his oath. This man has the reason of his life to do so."

Then the worshipful master asked the others to go out so that he could interview the intruder in private.

When they were alone, the worshipful master asked if he could do anything for Doc to make him more comfortable.

"This blindfold's got my eyes the shape of eggs."

"I can't take it off, but I can loosen it. Stand up."

It would have been a simple thing, while the master stood before him working on the knot from in front, to bring up his knee. Somehow, the fact that the master took no precaution against it kept Doc from doing so. When the tension came off the blindfold, Doc felt a hundred times better and even more in the worshipful master's debt.

The master began with ordinary questions: Doc's name, where he came from, how he got to Virginia City, what he did in town.

Having heard, he said, "I know the name Windham. A man of that name was hanged last fall."

Doc saw no point in lying.

"That was my Uncle Jack Windham. A fine man and a good cowboy. He killed a miner who was molesting and carving up a girl. Whoever hanged him did wrong. I'm here in Virginia City because I want to tell whoever that was to their face how wrong they were, what a good man they killed."

"That's a strong speech. I admire your loyalty. Loyalty is something prized among Freemasons. Why are you called Doc?"

"When I was a kid, I was interested in what ails people. I splinted my brother's broken arm and it healed straight. Ever since, I've doctored people if they needed it."

"Having people come to us of their own free will is basic to our brotherhood. Establishing that in your case is impossible. Have you reasons for not wanting to be a Mason?"

"I don't know much about it."

"Presumably when you looked in the window, you wanted to know something? What was it?"

Doc swallowed hard. For some reason, he did not consider lying.

"I heard the Masons started the vigilantes. Since the vigilantes hanged my uncle, I wanted to find out about them."

"And what did you find out?"

"Nothing, except for this noose on my neck."

"I cannot answer your question directly, as I'm bound by the same oaths as any other Mason. But let me suggest a few things to you. There are many Masons. I would prefer to think they are all good people, but it stands to reason some are not. If someone who happens to be a Mason commits an evil act, is that a Freemason act?"

"If the Masons protect him."

"Good answer. How did you know to come to that window tonight?"

"I won't tell you that."

"You had somebody with you?"

"I won't tell you that."

"Good. You can keep secrets. Do you believe in a Supreme Being?"

"I'm not much for religion."

"I may not be either. The question was, do you believe in a Supreme Being?"

Doc thought for a moment. He thought of riding night herd, when the stars are pulsing and the whole sky is alive.

"I suppose. But I won't go to church. I don't see the point in that."

"No one here will ask you to. What do you say, Doc Windham? Do you want to become a Freemason?"

"I guess so."

"And you will swear the oaths in honesty?"

"If I swear 'em, they'll be honest."

"You won't tell anyone, not even your sweetheart, what went on here or what you know of us, no matter if you are here or far away?"

"No."

"Good."

Within a few hours of setting out with Pearly to spy on the Masonic ritual, Doc was himself kneeling before the worshipful master with a blindfold and a noose and his shirt peeled down and a pantleg up and the slipper on his left foot. He answered the questions and walked all around the room several times, buffeted in the blind darkness by the other Masons. Then he stood with his feet at the required angles and, hand on the Bible, swore to keep their secrets.

At last, the blindfold was lifted and the others, his brothers now, pushed back their hoods and showed their faces. When the worshipful master bared his head, Doc recognized him from a drawing in *The Montana Post* as a judge and politician and a man touted by some to be governor of Montana someday. He shook Doc's hand and welcomed him into the craft. Even the skeptical ones shook his hand and called him brother.

When Doc left Pfouts's store by the front door, he still thought the Masons had hanged his uncle. He was pretty sure the master would not have ordered it or condoned it, but maybe he was not there. Maybe things got out of hand, as they did among most everyone else. Whatever the case, Doc was now a Mason.

A savage wind had come up. Doc ran across the street, around into the alley, and up to the back door of the billiards saloon. When he knocked, Pearly said in an unsteady voice, "I got a gun pointed right where you stand, whoever you are."

"It's Doc."

"Say something that'll make me know you are alone and not being forced to get me to open the door."

"Your daddy was a gambler and he got shot in the room where you are. He's buried on Boot Hill same as my uncle. I love you. If I was being forced, I would lie in each of those statements."

Pearly shot back the bolt and opened the door. After carefully letting down the hammer on her pistol, she dropped it in her skirt pocket, then put her hands around Doc's neck. She pulled his head down and pressed her hot, wet face to his cold, dry one. She kissed him all over.

"Oh God, oh God. I thought for sure I'd lost you too. I can't stand it. I can't keep losing people. You come now."

She closed and locked the door, then grabbed his hand and towed him through the dark to the ladder. She scampered up and he followed. He sat on the edge of the floor with his feet down the hole while she lit a candle.

"You got a knife?"

He unflapped the little sheath on his belt and gave her Jack's knife. She started cutting down all the glass pieces and piling them beside the bed. Then she took off all her clothes and slid under the feather tick. With it tucked up to her chin and her eyes gleaming wet in the candlelight, she told him to come. He got out of his clothes and slid under the tick, feeling the smooth of her leg against his. She wrapped her arms around him and held tight, still crying.

"You're freezing damn cold, Doc. Now make love to me, okay, but be real slow and easy. And if I keep crying, don't worry, I'm not sad. I'm happy. I'm real happy."

So they made love, nice and slow, for a long time. The feeling in Doc's heart was much greater than his desire. Then they were neither of them slow and easy. A wild moment lit them up before it was over.

Pearly was quiet in his arms for some time, and then she asked where Doc had been and what had happened to him. He said he could not tell her and that it was important she never ask.

"Did you tell about me? And Peter?"

"Neither."

"Let's leave here, Doc. Not just because of the Masons. Whatever you were waiting for, I bet you know it now. And if I've got you for awhile, I don't need to stay here thinking about Pa."

"Where would we go?"

"San Francisco, Denver, St. Louis. Probably Denver because I already know it."

"What would we do there?"

"What we're good at."

"I'm only good at being a cowboy. You can't do that in Denver."

"You're not working your mind again, Doc."

"Pin-setting?"

"Bowling! You could gamble at that while I gambled at billiards. If we win, and I'm pretty sure we can, then we won't have to do hard jobs or be poor while we decide what to do next."

"Aren't you afraid of us gambling?"

"'Course I am."

ALDER GULCH

July 1881

WHEN MAJOR WALKER FINALLY rode up Virginia City's main street on his sweated war horse, Doc and Lowell were sitting on a bench outside the dry goods store. They got up and stepped into the street. It was more than a week since Lippy and Dog Eye had left.

"Where's Darnell?" the Major asked, before even saying hello. He had a dead calm that was more frightening than rage.

They knew Darnell's habits well by now and pointed to the hotel from which he had yet to emerge today. They asked about Dog Eye and Lippy, and the Major said they were half a day behind, resting their horses. The Major dismounted and they took his grey. Some of the other boys had gathered by now, and Lowell told Pesky Boucher to take the Major's horse down the hill, get the saddle off, water him and brush him good.

Before long, the two ranchers were facing each other across cups of coffee in the hotel's dining room, as Doc and Lowell stood out front, watching and listening through a gap between boards. Darnell started giving reasons for what he had done. The Major rose to his feet.

"If you want so badly to keep your cattle, keep them all." He walked to the door and out. In the middle of the dusty street, he stopped and waited.

It is always interesting to see a man react when his bluff is called. Doc kept looking in and saw how Darnell studied his coffee at first, then took a dainty sip. When he heard the door slap, he drummed his fingers for a few seconds, then yanked the cloth napkin off his lap and threw it on the table. His cup fell over, dumping brown in a pointed stain.

Darnell caught up to the Major in the middle of Wallace Street. With wagons and horses passing both sides of them, the deal was made as it should have been in the first place.

THAT EVENING, WHILE they did the last of their riding on the hills above the Alder Gulch, Doc felt it necessary to tell the Major what Dwight's presence among them meant. He didn't like it that Darnell was getting away with what he and his boys had fashioned as a joke and an insult.

They were sitting their horses on a steep south-facing slope. The new cut had just been completed, and the cowboys of the Cochrane drive were hazing the three hundred down the valley, while Darnell's men kept back the sixty-two.

The Major listened to about half of Doc's explanation about Dwight. Then he cut in.

"Is he dangerous, this Dwight?"

"I wouldn't think he's very dangerous."

"Then we'll keep him. He represents two horses. I'm in no mood to save Darnell money."

On a hunch, and because he didn't think the Major was giving him quite enough credit for brains, Doc replied with a Mason sign. They were far from anyone who might see.

The Major returned the sign. "I would never have guessed," he said.

"I just wanted you to know, before we started for Canada, that I was on the level."

"And on the square," said the Major. "I'm glad to have a brother in our company. It comforts me. Might I ask how you came to it?"

"Not unless we've got an hour or two."

"And how did you know about me? Or were you guessing?"

"Army officers sometimes are. I thought a Canadian Mountie might be."

Once he'd given his orders to Lowell about their return to Dillon and the start of the drive, the Major left for Helena again, where telegrams were no doubt waiting.

THREE NIGHTS LATER, in their last mountain camp before re-entering the Beaverhead, Doc took Louie and rode up a tight valley through plentiful, honey-coloured moonlight. Where the creek came glittering down through the pines, Doc stopped and sat beside it. He looked to the future down the stream's shining path.

The first thing Doc did was imagine himself as a mark on a map of Montana. Many streams like this one fed three rivers named for American politicians: Jefferson, Gallatin, and Madison. Together, they made the Missouri. The cattle drive would begin by flanking the Jefferson for awhile, then would cut north through the mountain toward Helena. After passing Last Chance Gulch and absorbing the Walla Walla cattle somewhere in the Sun River valley, the drive would come back to the Missouri River and track it east across the prairie to Fort Benton. That was where the drive and the Missouri would part company. The cattle would turn for the North Star, and somewhere farther north than Doc had ever been they would cross a line and be in the fledgling country of Canada. Above that line some distance, they would find their Cochrane ranch.

Doc thought hard about the trail north because finally he knew he was on it. When they drove Darnell's cattle out of the Alder Gulch,

Doc had come up on the chuckwagon where it was stopped to allow Lowell to tie on his horse and board. The trail boss was grinning, and he yelled out, "Your plans have changed, Windham!"

Only then did Doc understand that they had. If he quit now, or in Dillon, or anywhere on the trail up to Canada, everyone would say it was because of Dwight. A damn stupid idea that he would quit a cattle drive out of fear of such a pup, but they would think and say it, because people always take a new occurrence and march it into a stanchion where they have already milked a cow.

In order to prevent the story from becoming history, his history, Doc could do one of two things. He could battle Dwight or he could go to Canada. Young men are always ruled by passion and foolish opinion, but Doc wasn't in the habit of killing them for it. That left Canada.

When Doc weighed all this against his original reasons for not wanting to leave the Beaverhead, those reasons seemed light and chaffy, but that was only because they were not new. Sitting beside the stream, Doc forced himself to remember them and give them their due. Chief among his worries was that somewhere along the coming trail, or in some fly-blown camp or boom town, or up in Canada itself (wherever Mounties broomed their riff-raff), Doc might run into the man who had promised to kill him, a man compared to whom Dwight was a dapple-backed fawn.

Often, when Doc imagined meeting him, this broken-headed nemesis, be it in a nightmare or a daydream, he would try to flee or fight but his limbs were uncooperative. His legs would hit the ground like chunks of wood. Falling, he would go for his gun and find it wedged in its holster.

On the other side of that coin was Pearly, for it was also narrowly possible that by leaving the Beaverhead Doc might find her. But the odds of coming up Pearly were never as great as those of coming up nemesis. That was so because the murderer had expressed a desire to find and kill Doc, whereas Pearly had expressed a desire never to see him again.

All total, the final price of leaving the Beaverhead was that both Doc's hope and his fear must return. Not wanting either had kept him on this range for over fourteen years. Now something as unworthy as vanity was moving him off it. He simply could not stand the idea of Dwight puffing and bragging, saying how Doc Windham had quit as segundo rather than face him.

Louie had finished all the grass in this stony place and was starting to grumble. Doc told him to hold on for a minute.

Above the creek that folded down over its cobbles and glittered, Doc studied the northern sky. He found the dipper and the North Star, and pointing with his finger said to Louie, "There." He had hoped to talk himself out of it, to find the wisdom not to care what Dwight might say and other cowboys think, but he had failed. For better or for worse, he was on his way to Canada.

THE DRIVE

PROLOGUE

—————◦◊◦—————

Cattle or the shadow of passing thunderclouds?
Along its edge, the shadow frays. A bullied cow runs
onto bare ground, and, unable to stand the liberty, hunts
a rift, a place to reabsorb into the mass. The valley is full of
the noise of cattle.

On fresh mounts, the boys enter this cloud of beef. Point,
swing, flank, drag—they call and whistle, spin their rope
ends, urge the shape of the herd from broad to long.

An articulate horn span hurries past the rest. An old steer
moving urgently to the front where he belongs. His head sways
elaborately, balancing all the other four-legged rhythms: a
metronome for thousands.

MISSOURI RIVER

August 1881

SENATOR COCHRANE'S CATTLE HERD started down the west side of the Beaverhead, crossed the Big Hole River and met the Ruby River where its name changed to Jefferson. Well before the Jefferson threw in with the Madison and Gallatin, the cattle would turn north and rise into the mountains. But they weren't there yet.

The herd was of such a size that Doc felt compelled to look at the whole of it at least once a day. He would ride Louie or Pedro to a height of land where he could study the cattle from above. The herd was bigger in cattle than most Montana towns were in people. A cloud of yellow rose off it, joining the smoke haze of forest and prairie fires. Every vista was smudged and indefinite, flushed and bruised, as if the whole of Montana were rising in smoke or dust. Such was its immensity that ground and grass and trees remained, and always would.

From these heights, Doc could see wolves trailing and flanking the herd, running in packs where their prospects were best. Like sand through a sieve, calves dropped out and met their doom. Only far ahead or well behind the cattle did Doc allow the men to shoot wolves. To do so closer risked a stampede. And it was as if the wolves knew. Beside the herd, they would run at the hooves of a cowboy's horse, brazen, grinning. It hurt the boys not to be able to shoot, for they were trained from childhood to kill a wolf if they could.

It was not entirely the wolves' fault that they were so numerous and hungry. That was Doc's opinion, unshared. The slaughter of the buffalo encouraged huge wolf litters. They flourished on the carnage. As the buffalo feast became a memory, the wolves were unleashed on the other things that graze, or on people if the people were careless enough.

In the low country beside the rivers, Doc's climbs were also a respite from mosquitoes and flies. Bug venom had the cattle and cowboys shitting free and the horses looking gaunt and sad. Horses are surprised and a bit ashamed of illness, and also hurt by it, as if it were a prank played on them by humans.

In this stretch Doc often thought of the Major's parting instructions to Lowell. Major Walker's bosses out east were angry over the delays and wanted speed. Lowell had appealed to the Major's common sense. When the purpose is to beat winter, driving a cow fast works against you. Instead of making them more able to contend with the cold, it weakens them just before they have to endure it.

According to Lowell, the Major had listened, but in a way that said the advice would be ignored. He had his orders. He would obey them. "The gentlemen I work for are my business, not yours," he had said to Lowell in parting.

Moving beside the growing river, beset by chills and sweats and shits, neither man nor beast was permitted to rest. The cowboys put rocks in tin cans and shook them at flinching cow ears. They untied their slickers and rattled them to make another noise the cows did not like and would run from. Sick and harried, the cows did not eat, and the tallow melted off them so fast you could almost see the steam. More calves faltered. More wolves fattened.

The night camps on this stretch were bitchy, balky affairs. Silent men like Lippy withdrew further into their heads. Talkative ones like Dog Eye lamented like women at an Irish wake. Dog Eye was still not over the fact that the Major had advanced no wages for drinking and whoring the last night in Dillon. This lapse of decorum had derailed his ambition to have two girls at once at the Big Pillow. He had complained ever since and was still working himself up rather than simmering down. Lately, he had settled his blame on Canada itself, which he predicted would be dry, whoreless, and preachy. As Dog Eye was on this drive courtesy of Doc, it was Doc's duty to see he did not attract a tribe of followers.

"Did you ever hear about the coal mine canary?" Doc asked in the middle of one of Dog Eye's recitals.

"There you go," said Dog Eye, "changing the subject like we was children to be distracted."

"Not changing. Just complimenting you on being our coal-mine canary."

"Meaning what?"

"Coal miners take canaries down the mine. Hang their cages up here and there. Canary's got a small lung. Whiff of coal gas makes it swoon and drop to the bottom of the cage. Seeing that allows the miners to get out before they breathe enough to swoon too."

"This is one of your insults."

"Boys, we should all be grateful to Dog Eye for figuring out in advance every little problem we're apt to encounter. On the one hand, we're warned. On the other, we see him up and around and complaining away, and that's how we know we aren't hurting too badly."

At the same time, Doc didn't care for the management of the cattle drive either. Getting drunk at the trailhead was a tradition. All the cowboys, not just Dog Eye, were jealous of their traditions. They would risk their lives and work themselves half to death for an outfit that treated them well, but would do much less if treated indifferently. Tin-canning and slickering cattle was a sure way to coax a drive into disaster. The irrational loyalty of the men was something they might need before the drive was over. Because of the way the drive began, it might not be present when called upon.

A COUPLE OF DAYS before the herd met the trail that would take it into the mountains, thunderclouds started piling in the sky. Black-bellied billows with cauliflower tops rumbled distantly. When the herd came under it, noon turned to evening and dead still. Lowell ordered everybody but the tiredest nighthawk into the saddle, and horses and cattle stood still in the lush heavy air and the river's fishy stink, felt the occasional spit of rain, watched the growling sheets of light in the distance.

When night came and still no show, it was a worse situation. Lowell had bet all his men and his best horses on daytime trouble that hadn't come. Now, everyone was tired, but the need for vigilance was greater. He turned out three times the usual crew, and in the early part of the night, when the ground was dark but the sky still light, you could see the silhouettes of horns pricking the horizon. All the cows were standing.

Doc took his turn, riding Louie. He knew the cattle were poised to run and he tried to stay alert, to keep himself from drifting into habitual nightmares. The herd was too big to ride around, so the nighthawks rode until they met, then turned and went back until they met a different rider on the other end. After a while the cloud came in so low there was no light at all. Lowell had told every man to sing, and no excuses. The singing would settle the cows and allow the men to find each other in the dark. The voices of the cowboys came at one another as through a tunnel, and the black mass on their flank breathed and groaned, stood and shuffled.

On one end of Doc's arc of surveillance, the cowboy he met was Tex Appleby. Tex sang loud and bright as if he was on a stage in Amarillo with sixteen girls watching him from the front row. He was a born dramatist with a nice voice, and on night herd, he gave it his all, preferring laments about good young men forced to die violently and laid out in white linen, which was something Doc had yet to see.

Tex was riding his favourite horse, a showy little mare of a muddy colour that looked green in certain lights. A Texas braggart, Tex claimed she was the best horse in the whole Cochrane cavvy, and he liked to back this claim with demonstrations. While the others rested and digested after a meal, there would be Tex on his green mare, turning tight little circles right and left, or backing the mare in a straight line as far as he wanted.

She was an intelligent horse, no doubt, but Doc didn't like a horse trained to a trick. A horse was not a dog, not a pet. To Doc, it would be like taking Lippy and getting him to roll over for a carrot.

On the other end, the fellow Doc met was Dwight. There was a whiny tone to the tuneless voice, and the saddle made a too-frequent noise that, in Doc's head, made the picture of Dwight rollicking on his too-small horse. He was a terrible rider and rode small horses because they were a shorter distance to the ground. He also rode vigorously, twisting his body with every step, thinking it made him look more able.

"That you, Dwight?"

The singing broke off. The sullen voice came down the tunnel of dark. "I ain't talking to you."

"Now, don't be in a temper. You'll make the cattle run."

"I ain't talking to you."

"I heard you the first time. You just go back to singing Figaro then, or whatever that tune was."

Riding away, Doc lifted his hat and felt his hair rise. He fanned above his scalp and the fine strands bent against his skin like cobweb.

Then it came. The first sky-dividing spear. A splitting blast like dynamite. His ribs quaked. The lightning was on the river side, and as the thunder faded, Doc heard silence. Not one cow was calling. He urged Louie to a fast walk up the left side of the herd.

Two more bolts sliced the night. As if they had cut the ropes on a huge bucket, it poured rain. Then, incredibly, Doc heard a gun shot and a second one. Through his horse, he felt the tremble of the ground. Louie muscled and Doc gave him his head. When the next spear hit, the cows were in full flight, their backs like braided waves in a rough sea, their horns and tails spearing and wagging out of the mass.

In that brief light, Doc saw no cowboys. He put a steady squeeze on Louie and the gelding surged, gaining past the cattle. They were mostly English breeds, and possible to outrun. Doc wished only for the brilliance in Louie's mind to sense the coming dangers. He prayed for rattlesnakes and hawks to have eaten the prairie dogs and starved the badgers so there would be no holes.

But he also felt a tight excitement to be riding hard down the invisible, with the bugs in the wet darkness striking off his face, the carving sharpness of grasshopper wings. Dominant was the deep rumble and the shaking earth between thunder's god-like rolls.

The next white light revealed the wild eye and curly face of a labouring Hereford, the lyre horns of a Texas cow passing beside her. Then the weathered edge of a sandstone rock loomed out of a gully wall. In two bucking jumps, Louie climbed the sill to a higher level of grass.

In that phase of light, the weave of backs seemed looser and more longhorns. Doc knew that he must be near the front.

When Doc saw the leaders, Lippy was with them, riding his blue mare. In the plume of light, Doc and Lip exchanged a nod and bent their mounts to the right. Louie was a brawling horse and shouldered hard into the ribs of the nearest cow. She dodged away and into the cattle on her other flank. Lippy and Calico were doing the same and the line began to bend.

The line bent, folded, made an arc, a loop. At last, the cattle were in a mill, a tightening flower of flesh that could not but slow and still itself. The hooves and horns were a grinding wheel and Doc felt an old fear that a cowboy might be under it. Two nights ago a story was told of a cowboy so completely destroyed that his friends only knew it was him by the smashed grip of his pistol.

Eventually, the storm and rain tapered. Doc left Lippy and the others to the job of walking and soothing the herd, and he went looking in the muddy dark for Lowell. It turned out the trail boss had split the herd at a weak joint and had his own mill going farther back. Between them, they roll-called the men and came up one short. Lowell couldn't think who it was but Doc knew it was Dwight.

Morning's grey was rising now, and Doc took two boys back along the chewed ground. They passed many calves, weak, wandering, and lost, their blats hoarse and hopeless. There were dead ones too, trampled red. Far enough away from the cows to do so, Doc unsheathed his Winchester and killed a pair of red-mouthed wolves tearing at a body.

In the gully the stampede had climbed were five dead cows and more wolves gathered and snarling. Doc gave the boys permission to shoot.

Then they found Dwight—on foot, muddy down one side, limping. He wasn't injured but had blisters. Staring at the ground, he told how his horse had bucked him off at the beginning of the run. Then one of the cowboys who had come with Doc told a different story.

"Thing started because he shot his gun off twice."

Doc remembered the shots. The lightning and thunder had the cattle ready but the shots had touched it off.

"That true?"

Dwight did not look up from the ground. "Four wolves were biting at a cow right beside me."

This was logic of the stupidest kind, and the cowboy with Doc cursed and spat. Doc did nothing and said nothing. A remaining lie was that Dwight had "bucked off." More likely, his little horse had spurted from under him.

For creating a situation that killed cows and could have killed men and horses, for taking more meat off these cows, Dwight should be severely punished. But Doc had decided to leave that job to Lowell. Surprising the others, he said for the one with the strongest horse to give Dwight a ride. Doc put a wiggle into Louie and rode away.

LATER THAT DAY, DOC and Lowell took their smoking materials away from the fire. It was next to hopeless to try and count this herd, so they determined only to sweep the back trail a couple of miles. As for the horses, they had been together long enough to be as one. When the wranglers found them, they would likely find them all.

Lowell cursed the fact that now, thanks to weather and Dwight, they had a running herd. A herd that runs will run again, which adds to the problems and the danger all around. What they could not do was lose time, not with the Major up in Helena counting the minutes, and his bosses out east sending telegrams. They had to get the cows together and be ready to move the minute the cavvy was back.

Lowell had been informed about Dwight's gaffe, and now Doc asked him what he would do about it. In fact, it was already done.

"I cussed out that bastard in front of the only two boys who'll eat with him. I laid it on thick. I told him if he puts another foot wrong, I'll leave him for the wolves. He's Cook's helper until further notice."

TWO MORE DAYS and they were in the mountains, with cooler breezes wrapped round their necks and breathing lighter, sweeter air. Much of the sickness and funk was left in the low country, and the cattle, who should have been jumpy after a run, were happy too. For the first time, the stories at the fire were funny, rather than about cowboys killed in grisly ways. Doc himself felt light and joyful, except when he happened to think ahead to Helena and of the man with the stoved-in head.

CHEYENNE

February 1867

WHEN DOC AND PEARLY LEFT Virginia City, Doc was riding Uncle Jack's bay gelding, Rufus, and Pearly was in a stagecoach. When Doc could no longer stand the cold or the distance from Pearly, he tied Rufus to the stage and climbed inside. This was not popular with the driver or the crowded passengers, so Pearly and Doc started spending time on the roof, on top of the luggage, wrapped together in a buffalo robe. It was a good way to see the country, except in the highest passes where it was cold and snowed.

Doc had been wary about leaving Virginia City so soon after becoming a Mason. The day after his initiation and Pearly's decision that she wanted to go, Doc had gone to Pfouts's store and asked for a meeting with the worshipful master. The storekeeper didn't like it and Doc saw his point: like asking for an audience with the Pope the day after being baptized. But the storekeeper said he would pass on the message. As they were now brothers, he more or less had to.

Once she had made her two decisions, to become Doc's lover and to leave, Pearly was not in a waiting-around mood. They didn't fight, but it lent one vinegar note to Doc's happy days. Still, walking around town, he could not help but smile. With a smile, he told McGinty he would be going soon, and when McGinty suggested he didn't owe Doc as much as he did, on account of the wood he burned at night, Doc as cheerfully told him he would light the bowling saloon on fire before he would leave town paid less than his due.

Doc also stood firm with Pearly in the matter of leaving too suddenly. He said he would have to make it right with those people about whom he no longer spoke, and luckily, it was not a long wait. In two weeks, a message came that Doc should come to Pfouts's store that night at ten.

In the deep cold, Doc stood waiting at the store's entrance. At last, the door unlocked and he was led upstairs and admitted to the initiation and meeting room. There were candles lit, but no other theatrical properties—no Bibles, bones, or skulls. He noticed the high window in the side wall was boarded over.

At a simple table, the worshipful master sat in a well-cut suit with his lambskin apron overtop. Doc tried to get right to the point but the master would not let him. He began teaching Doc secret handshakes and other signs by which one Mason could identify another.

"The public seldom notices and never understands. It's been tested a million times."

It was like a child's game and Doc learned fast. He found it amusing until the worshipful master told him it was serious business and that he would normally not have learned these things until much farther down the road of Freemasonry. The reason the master was breaking with tradition and cutting the process short was so Doc would not go off into the world unable to identify his brothers or be known by them.

"That's what I came to tell you!" Doc said. "How did you know?"

"There are mystical aspects to the craft. This is not one of them. I didn't think you would ask for a meeting so soon without a pressing reason. I decided it must be that you are leaving, as people often do from a town like this, and that you didn't want to appear to be running away."

"That's it. I just came to let you know and to thank you, and to say goodbye."

"Freemasonry makes the world smaller. Our paths will cross again."

He asked where Doc was going and laughed when he said he didn't know. It was a nice visit, and the senior Mason said he would tell their brothers that this leaving was not an attempt to escape the solemn vows Doc had sworn. He wished him luck.

"And good luck to your woman friend, too," he said, and winked his all-seeing eye. Doc hadn't said a thing about Pearly.

The day after talking to the worshipful master, and just a couple of hours before their stagecoach was due, Pearly came running into McGinty's, where Doc was working his last few hours. She told him she had been to Peter's bank and he was not to be found. Doc shrugged as if it had nothing to do with him, but in his mind, he imagined Peter without a tongue and the tongue in a little box being buried in the sand.

RIDING ON TOP OF THE STAGECOACH, Doc and Pearly still did not know where they were headed. At the Fort Hall crossroads, they had continued east and thus eliminated San Francisco and other California towns, but the world was still wide. Denver had some good memories for Pearly and was the early front-runner. From her strange girlhood, spent mostly in saloons, Pearly's favourite place had been Denver's Elephant Corral. Doc winced at the mention, for that was the name of the livery corral where Uncle Jack had been hanged. Still, it was interesting that a business sharpie in Virginia City had named his corral after a famous one in Denver.

Denver's Elephant Corral had catered to every need and supplied every entertainment, Pearly said. It had started as a livery barn and corral, then expanded to include a hotel, a restaurant, and a few kinds of saloons. In theory, a dusty prospector could come down out of the mountains with his bag of dust, stop there, and not have to leave again until he was broke.

Pearly remembered it as a circus in which she moved with total freedom. She would visit a favourite horse in the stable, climb to the hayloft to play with a cat, come tell her father a story at the poker table, watch a little billiards, go upstairs and talk to a nice whore. Pearly was a mascot, a communal child, and no one bothered her, except to rub her hair or touch her cheek for luck.

So Pearly was thinking Denver, until a well-travelled man got on the stage at Fort Hall and told her that the Elephant Corral and much of the rest of Denver had burned. "If you haven't been to Denver since," he said, "you're in for a treat. It's rebuilt in brick." He was thinking this would please her, but it did not. The old wood-frame Denver was the place of her childhood. Hearing it was gone took away most of her desire to go there.

That opened up the whole East and the South to speculation. For awhile they talked about St. Louis, even though it scared them. It was bigger and older than the places they were used to. They imagined con men and women, who would know tricks they did not know. They imagined being taken for a ride or killed.

Though he was never homesick for Texas, Doc thought about going there too, or somewhere else down south. "Everything south of Denver smells like a bean fart," said Pearly when he suggested it, and that was that.

On board the stagecoach, a lot of the talk was about Cheyenne City, a brand new town. Most of the travellers were going there. It was the current end-of-steel on the Union Pacific Railroad and would have that honour all year. Though it was hard to want to stop at a place you had no idea of, Pearly and Doc began to be influenced. The crowd and the bustle as they entered the tent city was even more compelling. Finally, when the stagecoach stopped, they climbed down with the rest.

Cheyenne had been nothing a month or two ago. Now its boosters were calling it the country's next metropolis. Cheyenne was also proof almost anything can be done in a tent. Hotel tents, whore tents, drinking tents, food tents. Whatever there was of Cheyenne at the beginning of the day, there would be more by day's end. Each time a freighter's bull train pulled in, Cheyenne was remade.

Doc could find no bowling saloon, but there was a billiards table levelled up with shims on the dirt floor of one of the drinking tents. Stopping beside it, surrounded by dust and noise, Doc and Pearly made the decision to stay in Cheyenne for awhile. It was a river not yet panned.

Once they were on the ground, Doc found himself full of worry, something he had rarely known. Up until now, he had been the youngest in most groups and had left the worrying to others. Also up until now, he'd had no girlfriend.

But Pearly didn't want any worrying done for her. She recognized this type of place from her upbringing, the times her father would drag her into glory camps such as those in the mountains west of Denver. A deck of cards is a portable business, and her father would pick up that business and carry it anywhere, anytime.

In other words, it was ridiculous that Doc should fuss and worry over Pearly, who understood what was going on here so much better than he did. He had the sense to be quiet about his fears, but that wasn't enough. Pearly knew his thoughts as though his brain was inside out.

"According to what you told me, you went from a dirty little Texas town to a ranch, a cattle drive, and McGinty's. So don't go delving into your vast experience to protect me."

But Doc could also read Pearly's mind and knew Cheyenne worried her too.

The first night they spent in a hotel tent, and a fight started on the other side of a sheet of cotton. Before the next night, Pearly made a more detailed search for lodgings and was disgusted.

"I've had lice, thank you very much."

She led Doc into a provisioning store and bought a tent at a terrible price. They took it to the edge of town, upwind, near water, and set it up. When Doc worried about the cost, Pearly laughed at him. "We'll sell this thing for twice what it cost when we go."

Pearly did less well picking a place for them to eat that night. She was drawn to the humility of a tent that advertised rabbit stew. Fresh at least, she said, and not so tough as beef that had walked from Texas. But the rabbit must have been tainted for they spent much of the night kneeling outside their tent, trying to get rid of it.

Doc was better next day, but Pearly seemed sicker, white pale and eyes sunken. Doc said he thought he should get a doctor, but Pearly angrily dismissed this. No mushroom-city doctor was coming near her. Might as well look for help from the man with the shoe-polished eyebrows who sold elixir guaranteed to free the bowel.

"I freed my own bowel with that diseased rabbit."

Pearly groaned and cried and raged and got sick, crawled to the creek and drank. She threatened often to go back to the restaurant with her pepper-box pistol to square matters. While she was in a fevered sleep, Doc slipped out to see what doctors were available. In this way, he found something Freemasonry is good for. In front of each of the three doctors in town, he tried the words and gestures the worshipful master had taught him. When the third doctor responded in kind, he felt certain he was in the presence of a capable sawbones. It made no absolute sense, but the feeling was powerful.

When the Mason doctor recognized Doc as a brother, he did not, like the others, demand that Pearly be brought to him or that money be advanced. He asked Doc to wait while he cut the leg off a miner who had missed with his axe and waited too long in his camp. The doctor had an assistant, but when that boy wasn't strong enough to hold the miner, the doctor yelled for Doc to come and help. Doc pushed the shoulders down while the tortured man screamed obscenities and spat in his face. The man's eyeballs bulged almost right out of his purple face while the sawing went on. The request to assist was something Doc did not feel he could refuse, which showed how being a Mason worked both ways.

When the doctor came out to Pearly and Doc's tent, Pearly shrank away and told him to leave her be. But the doctor spoke to her in a forceful no-nonsense way that she finally listened to. All he gave her was boiled water he had brought in a jar. He told Doc to get busy and build a fire and boil all the water they drank for as long as they were in Cheyenne. Though bad food started her problems, the water Pearly was drinking in quantity from the creek was making her worse. It would cause her lasting trouble if she persisted.

As for why Doc was able to drink the same water and get better, the doctor shrugged. "It probably means you're from Texas."

When the doctor was leaving and Doc tried to pay him, he wouldn't take it. He made the Mason sign and left.

IN TWO DAYS, Pearly was better, and she and Doc went to the billiards saloon to watch. She had her own cue which pulled apart into two pieces wrapped in felt cloth under her arm, in case she decided to play. She doubted she would, preferring to spend this evening analyzing what went on.

What was soon clear was that a grim silent fellow was beating all comers with a never-changing precision like a train wheel going round. He looked like a top-notch player to Doc, but in whispered asides Pearly said he looked better than he was, owing to a keen eye for the table's flaws. A good billiards table needs a good floor, and the dirt one here was playing all sorts of tricks, despite an elaborate system of shims the German proprietor had driven in and was constantly adjusting.

"Rolls off right to left," said Pearly. "Left rail's a ditch."

The grim player was adept at "nursing," which was not allowed in every saloon. It was also a strength of Pearly's game. What it meant was getting the balls in a bunch so the player could tap his cue ball just a couple of inches while making a cannon, then do it again and again. A patient, controlled player, who could resist looking flashy, could exploit a pack like that for any number of points. Many regarded it as a cowardly way to play, and there were controversies over whether it should be allowed. But it wasn't outlawed in this billiards tent, not tonight, and the machine-like player continued to mow down his opponents.

Given that everybody in the tent was drunk (except Pearly, Doc, and the grim player), emotions over this unpopular way of playing were rising. A few had begun to heckle, and one drunk insisted the winning player was a "chickenshit." The man didn't seem to hear. He was craggy-faced with stand-up hair that was almost white, though he didn't look albino or old. The furrows in his cheeks ran deep and vertical so his mouth looked imprisoned between the marks. Somehow he had managed to shave clean across that rugged landscape.

Doc was wishing he and Pearly could go back to their homely tipi and cuddle up, now that Pearly was feeling better, but she surprised him by unwrapping her cue and pressing it together. Doc looked her a question and she answered with a wink.

The craggy man tried to leave when Pearly made ready to play, but seeing this, the drunken inmates jeered. A big navvy from the railroad construction crew stood in the tent door with his post-like arms folded high on his chest. The craggy player got the message. His expression unchanged, he turned and asked Pearly what she was considering as a wager.

"Before we wager," she said, "there has to be one relaxation of the rules. Because of my height, I cannot play with one foot on the floor or ground. Your choice, though. We don't have to play."

She said it loud, for all to hear, which made it a lot less his choice. What he did say was that, on account of the poor state of the floor, lying on the table was apt to make it worse.

"Couldn't be much worse," she said. "'Sides, I'm not heavy."

In fact, Pearly knew what he was saying was right, and she was counting on it. Once she'd lain on the table a few times, his knowledge of its quirks would be historical.

Then came the bet. The stranger suggested ten dollars, and Doc about choked on his tongue to hear Pearly say, "I was hoping for fifty." They settled at thirty-five, again assisted by the jeering and goading crowd.

The game was by no means a sure thing. Maybe Pearly's opponent wasn't as good as she was, but on account of her dizziness, neither was she. He took a big lead of about a hundred in a game that only went to two hundred, while Pearly got hardly any points on her first two shots. Doc was considering the world with thirty-five dollars less in it when a shot rolled off unusually far, and the man missed an easy one. It was the best lie Pearly'd had all game. She got the balls into a bunch and started nursing. She made the whole two hundred off that one cluster, much to the amusement of the crowd, who saw the craggy man as dying by the sword he had lived off.

The mob in the tent were also aware to the last dollar how much the craggy man had pulled in before Pearly came along. It was a lot more than thirty-five dollars. When he bowed to Pearly, thanked her for the game, and tried to leave, his way was again blocked by the navvy.

"Same again then?" he asked Pearly without a ripple.

Pearly didn't want to make an enemy. If there was anything her father's curtailed biography had taught her, it was this. Whereas her father was mean and would take a man's last dollar, she had learned to allow people trails of escape. In the present moment, she said, "All right, but let's call it a night after that. I'm tired."

"More than fair," he said and his lips tried to move, maybe even to smile. Win or lose, Pearly was making it so he could leave money ahead.

When Pearly shot well but did not go all the way to victory on her first sequence of shots, coming up fifty short of 200, the craggy man went to work, shooting fast, not missing, and the way the balls were sitting, he looked certain to win. Then he did miss, a shot much easier than several in his run. Pearly won after that.

The craggy man paid up and Pearly took apart her cue to a round of applause. Others wanted to play her now, but she did not waver. She thanked them and said she would likely return to this saloon tomorrow or the next day.

On the cold walk home, Pearly was pensive. Not in a bad mood or a good one, but quiet. Doc told her she had played well and he was proud. She told him he was sweet but didn't know a thing about billiards. She had not played well and should have lost the second game and come away with nothing. The craggy man had deliberately missed his last shot, handing her the win. Her silence was because she hadn't figured out why.

By the time they were in the tent, and Doc was trying to be romantic, Pearly held his head to her bosom and stroked his hair until he calmed.

At length, she said, "It has to be that he knew breaking even against me wouldn't satisfy that crowd. Those railroad men would have been at him still. So he let me win as insurance against getting a gun barrel on the head. It's too bad."

"Why?" Doc had no idea why somebody's letting you win thirty-five dollars could be bad.

"It's bad because I liked playing him. All solemn like he was. He played like a preacher in one of them religions that don't dance. And now he'll have to leave town. As long as I'm here, being the crowd favourite, he can't win."

"But you said he coulda won."

"Don't be a blockhead, Doc. *Especially* if he won, he couldn't win."

Pearly was right, as she often was. The craggy man was not in the billiards tent the next night or any other. Pearly played on, having now the perfect situation. The men who lined up to play her didn't expect to win, nor did they mind losing. She talked it all through in the tent with Doc at night, and the luckiest thing in her opinion was that not one among them seemed to be getting an obsession with her. She said you always had to look out for that one man who wanted to play you over and over, because it might mean he thought he was in love with you and wanted something.

Part of Doc's job, Pearly said, was to look out for that man, and it wouldn't be a bad idea to go up the river a few times with Jack's gun and practise hitting marks.

The only difference for Pearly, between this and other times when she had made her living at billiards, was her face. She worried aloud to Doc that having that big scar might make men more fresh with her, less respectful. Doc said all the expected things, how she was as pretty as ever, but deep in his head, he was thinking, fearing, she was right. It was a horrible instinct, among animals and humans both, to go after the wounded one. Though it put him in a rage to think it, and made him want to take Pearly out of here into some forest where they could build a cabin and be alone, he kept imagining something he'd seen long ago in Texas. Back then, he had known a parlour girl who had a wine-coloured mark like a splash on her face, something she'd had since birth. It was routine in that cat house that somebody had to listen at the door whenever she was with a new man.

Thinking like that made Doc have to get up in the night and go outside in the cold and stand with Rufus by the frozen creek. How dare he compare a whore with a birthmark to Pearly? But then he'd imagine a stranger come prowling, come thinking he could do what he wanted with Pearly because some other crazy sonofabitch had scarred her already. It was as if the mark on Pearly was a message from one insane bastard to another.

Sometimes Doc would lay his head on Rufus's neck and bawl like a baby. The only thing that could make him feel better was Pearly calling from the tent flap, "Come back to bed, you idiot. I'm freezing."

TEN DAYS INTO THEIR STAY at Cheyenne, a man showed up at the billiards tent with a lot of gold dust which he spent freely. He said he was a prospector who had until recently been in a mountain camp. After a couple of days, hanging around and playing every turn he could, his story changed. He had stayed too long in that mountain camp, he said, on account of how much gold he was pulling from his claim, and thereby got trapped by snow and almost starved. More days passed and a third variation emerged. Now there was a partner.

The miner's name was Ivan Overcross. He was big and ugly, and it was hard to isolate his ugliness in any one feature. It was not accurate to say he was ugly because his head was too big for his already big body, or that he was ugly because his forehead rolled up like flabby corduroy. His wet hanging lips, his fishy eyes. His ugliness was greater than the sum of his parts. He walked as if he were carrying buckets, crookedly, from a yoke under his skin.

After he had been in Cheyenne a week, his story changed even more. He began to say terrible things, which were terrible if you were satisfied that they came from a lunatic mind, but were even worse if you thought they might be true.

"I ate a man this winter who looked a lot like you!" he shouted at the German billiards-tent proprietor, on his knees tapping a shim under a table leg with a ball-peen hammer. Overcross opened his jaws and roared a laugh. "You think I'm joshing you," he shouted at the poor German, "but I'm not. It was in the mountains. We were trapped in there by snow. We had plenty of gold, but it ain't much use when you're starving. So I killed and ate him, before he could kill and eat me."

Pearly and Doc heard the story often after that. The mad prospector played billiards like a nervous habit. Avid, repetitive, obsessed, not very good, he played and played. Pearly raised the bet to a hundred dollars a game to see if it would scare him off. When it didn't, she lowered the bet to ten. It didn't matter. Whatever the bet, he slapped his money down.

While Pearly played him, the ghastly tales multiplied. He said that the man in the mountains was the first he had eaten, but not the first he had killed. It was his habit to kill partners, he said. That night, Doc asked Pearly if he should pull his gun on the brute and drive him off, shoot him if he had to, and Pearly said she didn't think so. She thought he would sense it coming, would feel the gun draw on him even from behind. Given his size, he could maul someone Doc's size, break his back if he got him in his grip. Pearly didn't want Doc to take the chance. Better they should wait him out, though Doc should be ready at all times.

In a more civilized place, a sheriff might have come and shut the man in jail. Maybe they would have called in the Mason doctor to confirm he was a lunatic, then sent him east to some place that dealt with lunatics. But Cheyenne had no sheriff, no jail.

Doc sat and watched Pearly and Overcross play, and his hand was always under his coat, locked on the grip of his uncle's pistol. Every night he went through the ritual of unloading and reloading the cap-and-ball gun, exercising its ramrod. He found the identical gun for sale in a store and bought it, just for the revolving chamber. He took the cylinder out, loaded it, and kept it in his pocket as a spare.

Doc imagined killing the crazy prospector a hundred times, a hundred ways.

At night Doc asked Pearly if she thought they should go, just ride out this minute, the two of them on Rufus. Pearly thought it was the right idea, but not the right time. They were making a river of money off the crazy prospector, so much that when they did leave, they could go wherever they liked and live however they pleased. Another reason for staying was that the miner didn't behave like any other obsessed man she'd met. He didn't seem interested in her in a romantic or sexual way, but only in the way of wanting her to listen to his crazy stories while they played. She supposed there was a thrill for him in that, but she didn't see how it could harm her.

BY THEN DOC AND PEARLY had learned to manage their life in Cheyenne fairly well. In the Chinese part, Doc had found a tent that would heat water for a proper bath. Since they had lots of money, Doc paid extra for privacy and fresh water. They also got their laundry done there.

But they were still sleeping on the frozen ground and that had gone beyond being tiresome. They would be leaving soon, and Pearly had decided for sure it was Denver she wanted to go to. People in Cheyenne, especially the boosters who felt themselves in competition with Denver, were always telling them how dead Denver had become. It wasn't growing, it was shrinking. Although a shrinking town was hardly a good place for a gambler, Pearly liked the sound of it. She said that with the crazy miner's money, they could set up in a good hotel and have all their meals made, and that there were probably enough rich people still in Denver to make a little money gambling, hopefully enough to pay the day-to-day and save their bankroll for the future.

The way Pearly had it imagined appealed to Doc as well. He liked the idea that they would spend more time talking and making love, or just in one another's quiet company. Here, in Cheyenne, it was pretty much strictly business.

"It's best not to moon over one another," Pearly had said, "not while we're working. I got to be sharp to play and you got to be watchful."

Pearly had been saying "just one more day" for two weeks when, in the middle of a night of heavy snow, they heard footsteps outside their tent. Doc slept with the Colt Dragoon under a rolled sweater, and he brought it out now. He could not see Pearly, but her body was hanging onto his like a spring. "We shoulda gone," she whispered.

What they were hearing was several people's footsteps, not just one. Talking as he did, the crazy miner had no friends. Doc could not imagine him coming except alone. But if it wasn't the crazy miner, then who?

Doc moved lizard slow out of the blankets and up to the tent flap. He imagined whoever it was would be watching the top part, so he budged the join down low until a crack opened. The light in the falling snow was poor, but he thought he saw the legs and feet of five men. Then came a voice.

"Sir, I doctored your wife a while ago. We would like you to help us."

Doc's worry eased. Knowing it was the Mason doctor, he pulled on his boots and put his coat on over his underwear. He stepped outside.

The doctor came forward out of the group and shook Doc's hand. Interestingly, it was not a Mason handshake. That probably meant the doctor was not here as a Mason and that Doc should not assume the other men were brothers in the craft.

"You are familiar with a man who calls himself Overcross."

"From the billiards saloon. Yes, I am."

"He brags of killing men."

"He does."

"People here are concerned. We have sent a request for information to other towns. We described what he claims to have done. We supplied a drawing. A few of those who received the letter and picture recognized him. The names he has used in other towns are similar to the one he uses here. Overton or Cross, for example. In short, we are sure there is no mistaken identity.

"What they tell us is that Ivan Overcross has in fact committed the crimes he talks about. We are confident that he is an insane killer, and that he will kill someone or several people in this town if we allow him to stay. I don't mean to frighten you, but I would say your wife and you are among those most in danger."

"What do you want me to do?" asked Doc, though he knew.

"Earlier this evening, Overcross attacked and hurt a prostitute.

Everyone has run away from that tent. He is there asleep. If we can, we will hang him."

The snow fell heavily. It was collecting in the peaks and on the brim of the doctor's hat. A chill was working its way through Doc. He sucked in hard and shook himself.

"I had an uncle who brought me to this country on a cattle drive. He was hanged by a vigilance committee for murdering a man, a man a whole lot like Ivan Overcross."

"If you refuse to help, I will accept it. It is not a light thing to kill a man. But I would remind you that Ivan Overcross is not your uncle. You say he is more like the man who caused your uncle's death."

Doc went into the tent and told Pearly he was going with them. He said the men were not going to hurt him or Pearly, that in fact they were going to do something that would protect them in future.

"Do you have to?" she said.

"No. But Overcross did all those things he says."

Pearly kissed Doc on the lips and handed him his pants and gun. He dressed and went out to join the others.

Along the way, the doctor walked beside Doc. In a low voice, he explained what they were going to do. It was a reasonable plan.

"You can't get the law to come from somewhere else and do it?" asked Doc.

"We doubt anyone would come. If someone did, it might not be in time. Overcross could kill someone tomorrow."

Now that Overcross's stories were real beyond doubt, they were vivid and horrible in Doc's mind. Doc also saw what Overcross might have done these past weeks when he was Pearly's constant billiards partner, with only Doc and the German there to stop him.

Their steps were loud as an army's on the cold snow. Before they got close to the canvas brothel, Doc proposed an amendment to the plan. Whipsawed boards were piled beside a soon-to-be hotel, and on Doc's suggestion, each pair of men picked up several. They carried them until they were fifty feet from the whore tent.

As slowly and soundlessly as they could, they laid the boards in a line. The first line went to the tent's front door. At the rear, a second path of boards was built to within a foot of the wall. From there, they could hear Overcross snoring within, though he could have been faking.

Kneeling at the back, on the end of the last board, Doc guessed by the snoring that he was no more than a few inches from that ugly head. Not knowing why he had decided to take the lead, Doc held the knife with which he would stab down through the tent. In his other hand was Uncle Jack's gun, its hammer cocked. The sound of the knife ripping the cloth was the signal for the others to come.

Doc plunged the knife. The snow muffled every other sound. He was ripping the hole bigger, when through the rent came the miner's hand. It locked on Doc's wrist. Doc yanked back with all his force and the miner came out after him. Doc slipped in the snow and Overcross landed on his chest with both knees. Unable to breathe, Doc watched the prospector bring his free hand to join the one still holding the arm. In a second, Overcross would have Doc's knife and would kill him with it.

Doc saw the others moving, their pistols waving and pointing. One held up the hangman's noose. But guns aren't worth a damn if you won't fire them. Doc brought the mouth of the Colt Dragoon to the side of Overcross's head and shot. The giant prospector slumped, the destroyed head falling over Doc's shoulder in a parody of embrace. The hands that gripped Doc's wrist spread open, fell limp as killed fish.

They rolled the body off Doc, and the Mason doctor did not hesitate. While the others stood and stared with their pistols dangling in their useless hands, he pulled Doc to his feet and ordered everyone home. He and Doc ran together. Doc holstered Jack's gun and could feel the heat on his leg. He scooped snow and scrubbed at his face and his neck. At the edge of the clearing where Cheyenne stopped, Doc held out his arm so the doctor's chest ran into it.

"I don't know what to say," said the Mason doctor. "I'm sorry."

"I'm sorry too. I never killed a man."

"I'll deal with the others. I know them."

"I imagine we'll leave."

"That could look bad."

"Bad to who? All you got to do is keep your own vigilantes from hanging me."

The snow was falling so heavily now that Doc could not see his tent. He shook the doctor's hand the Mason way and left him. When he got to where the tent should be, it wasn't there. Pearly called and stepped out of the trees leading Rufus. Rufus was saddled and everything else, including the tent, was packed and tied on. Doc boosted Pearly into the saddle and led the gelding across the frozen creek. Beyond that, Doc continued to lead him in a wide arc around the town. The snow was coming fast and they could hardly see, hardly breathe. The bonfires of Cheyenne were balls of fuzzy light through the filtering snow. Using them to locate himself, Doc kept from wandering too far or too near, and was able to pick up the Denver road on the south side.

"You cold, Pearly?"

"I'll let you know. I'll take a turn on foot when I am."

After a long time of walking the horse beside the rutted road, Pearly said, "Did you kill him?"

"Yes."

"Did you have much to do with it?"

"I shot him."

"I'm sorry I didn't let you take us out of here. I was greedy." She was crying in the saddle and Doc let her. "I won't be greedy any more, Doc. I promise."

Then, later, when Pearly asked to walk, and they were both on the ground, she hugged him hard and said, "Don't let it change your nature."

Doc hugged back but didn't speak. Whatever this killing did to his nature, he didn't imagine he'd have much to do with it. He stooped as he had a hundred times and brought up snow and rubbed it all around his face and neck. Pearly didn't ask why.

HELENA, MONTANA

August 1881

AFTER A LONG DAY of chasing the Cochrane cattle through a dry pass, a valley opened up on a wide sloping meadow. The chuckwagon was there before them, canvas luffing, its wheels close to a stream that cut through the grass and cobbles and emptied into a lake below. The aproned cook was bent over his stove, its chimney smoking horizontally in the breeze. Big Dwight was nearby, scrubbing a cast-iron skillet with sand.

The cattle had put in their fifteen miles and were tired and thirsty. They ran at the water in momentary panic. Mallards, pintails, and a lonely pelican fluttered their feet to get away. A distant dynamite explosion echoed off the rocks, and the cattle lifted their heads so the water poured out the imperfect closure of their jaws. On another day, they might have run, but now they were too tired, too intent on the water before them.

Back from the lake, Doc slid off Louie and loosed his cinch. The big gelding's eyes were already fluttering. Doc hopped around restoring feeling to his legs. Then Dog Eye rode over to talk. It pained Doc a little to see the brightness of his face. Like a bird dog attending to ducks, Dog Eye was pointing at the nearest source of whores. Helena was at most three days away, and as always, Dog Eye's mind had become rich in naked images.

When Doc wasn't interested in talking whores with him, the Texan moved on. Then came Lowell to serve notice that he and Doc must make time tonight to discuss their upcoming meeting with the Major. Doc had tried to beg off this meeting but Lowell would not have it. Since Doc had changed his plan and pledged to continue with the drive, Lowell had shared authority fifty-fifty, whether Doc wanted it or not.

Finally Doc and Louie were alone, the big gelding swelling up and snoring down beside him. Doc might have had a snooze as well, but his thoughts about Helena were too disturbing. If any of Doc's fears about this journey were correct, Helena was one of the most likely places for them to come true.

THE NIGHT, AFTER A MEAL of stew, Doc and Lowell walked away from the wagon and campfire. Lowell dropped onto the grass, popped off his hat, and proceeded to scratch every square inch of his head. "Let's keep this short," he said.

"You first, then," said Doc.

Doc leaned back on his elbows, two points against the cold ground, while Lowell calculated aloud how much time they'd lost and how far it put them behind the Major's schedule. He thought they had lost a week, and that wasn't counting the time wasted in Virginia City.

Still carving at his scalp, Lowell asked, "You got anything to ask the Major?"

"Calf wagons. I told him back in Dillon I need at least two."

"Then you'll get one. Or none."

"What about the boys going to town?"

"They sure as hell need to. I saw Slim Klippert pulling on his pecker in the saddle when he thought no one was looking. Musta had a Helena whore dancing in his brain."

"And you're for it?" asked Doc.

"I told the Major it would be wise, especially since he hurried the boys out of Dillon. He left me enough money to advance some wages."

Doc coughed up a strangle of trail dust, spat it, had a drink of gritty coffee.

"I'm against it."

Lowell stopped scratching. He made round eyes at Doc.

"I don't believe my ears."

"Well, it's true. I think it's a poor idea."

"I knew no talk with you would be short."

"I'm not against drinking or whoring. That's a man's own business. But I feel it's my duty to keep these cowboys alive."

As Lowell was clearly waiting for an explanation, Doc launched into a summary of the things he'd read about Helena in *The Montana Post* while they had been marooned in Virginia City. There had been a raft of criminal events in that town, and it had kicked off a gory vigilante response. Even given how the *Post* liked to exaggerate Helena's problems, Doc believed most of it. The vigilantes sounded like that class of men who would hang the innocent if the guilty were too elusive. Helena, in its present guise, sounded like the kind of place where an Overcross could thrive.

"These Helena vigilantes use a number," Doc continued. "It's a 3, then a 7, then a 77. When they hang a man, they write it on a paper and stick it to his back. When they warn somebody, they draw it on his cabin door."

"What's it mean?"

"They say it's part of their connection to the vigilantes of '64, the ones at Bannack and Virginia City. But I happen to know those boys had no damn number."

Doc stopped to test Lowell's interest.

"Come on, Doc. What do the numbers mean, if you know?"

"In the paper, it said three things. First was the dimensions of a grave. Three foot wide, seven long, seventy-seven inches deep. Now, who in this country is seven foot tall? Who is a tireless enough worker to dig a grave six foot deep? Why give the third dimension in inches?"

"What else?"

"Second one's no better. It's the time the doomed man has to get away. Three hours, seven minutes, seventy-seven seconds."

"Why not just say three hours? It's got a more dangerous ring."

"That's it."

"What about the third one?"

"There's an old idea that the Virginia City and Bannack Freemasons were behind the original vigilantes. The first time those Masons met was when one of theirs was dying in Bannack and asked to be buried according to their ritual."

"What ritual?"

"I wouldn't know. They probably put on aprons and hop to the graveyard on one foot. Anyway, it don't matter. First off it was *three* decided they should oblige the dying man. Second meeting, *seven* Masons showed up. Day of the funeral, *seventy-six* were there."

"You said seventy-seven."

"Dead man makes seventy-seven. That one sounds like it could be true."

Doc knew that Lowell had seen him go into the Mason temple in Virginia City. But he was either too polite to bring it up in this conversation or didn't want to prolong the talk on that account.

"I still don't see why we should keep the boys out of Helena," said Lowell, as he screwed his hat back on.

"They'll go in there and get liquored up," Doc said. "Get themselves laid and go back to drinking. Probably look for a fight. If the town's all heated up, someone'll shoot one of them or they'll shoot somebody. If it's the latter, the vigilantes could hang them for it."

"I sure as hell won't enjoy telling them."

"It's my idea. I'll do the telling."

Doc started to get up, found himself frozen at the knees. He rolled over and rose to all fours, rocked back and forth. Lowell, meanwhile, made no move, suggesting he had more to say. He leaned and spat juice in the grass. Though he greatly preferred smoking to chewing, the valleys here were too likely to catch fire.

"What about Dwight?" he asked.

"What about him?"

"Is he looking more or less likely to kill you?"

"Farther we go could mean he's weakening. Could also mean he's getting more desperate."

"Glad you're so clear."

"I don't think he's a killer. His head goes straight up in the front and the back. The ears are smack in the middle on the sides."

"What in hell are you talking about?"

"Phrenology. Science of phrenology."

"Well, in case his head ain't as safe as you think, I told him a week back we'd string him up if he kills you."

"What did he answer?"

"Nothing. He looked like he might cry."

By coincidence, when they came back to the fire, Dwight was making a show of cleaning his gun. He held it close to his eyes and made a face that Doc imagined was supposed to be frightening. Doc had seen a similar look on a man passing a kidney stone.

TWO DAYS LATER IN THE late afternoon, Lowell told the boys to throw the cattle off the trail and mill them in a flat. He pointed to a scar on the mountain and said below that was Helena. The grass and water were not plentiful, but it was enough for the length of stay the Major was apt to allow.

When the rays of the sun came long through the mountains, painting the yellows gold and the browns chocolate, turning the bit of green into Kentucky, Doc took his bar of soap to the lively stream, knelt, and washed. He flipped open his straight razor and scratched off a week of beard. He noticed Dog Eye doing the same downstream. Dog Eye combed out and slicked back his long black hair, then finished up by dabbing wax from a can onto his moustache.

Doc left the creek, returned to Cook's set-up, shook out a fawn-coloured shirt that he kept with his woollies in the bottom of the chuckwagon. It had buttons made from buffalo horn cross-cuts.

Seeing Doc and Lowell making ready to ride with no word to the rest of them, Dog Eye blew up. He kicked the dirt and stomped a clump of sage to mush. Standing with a cluster of defiant others, he yelled, "Fuck sake, Doc! Is this the cavalry or what?"

A stiff rebuke. None of them liked the cavalry. For Dog Eye it was the lead in to a colourful rant about how this drive must be some pinch-ass puritanical Canadian idea, some blue-eyed whoreless uppity English tea-granny's temperance pledge to turn a crew of red-blooded cowboys into nutless wonders. Though he had the sense not to name the Major, it was implied.

Doc waited for a pause then hit him with the truth.

"It's not the Major's idea to keep you boys out of Helena tonight. It's mine."

Dog Eye stopped and stared. The others behind him gaped at this strange betrayal. Doc and Lowell were ready to mount and did so.

"*Et tu Brutes*," Doc said.

"Damn it, Doc! Don't talk foreign at me."

"*Et tu Brutes* is what Caesar said when he saw his friend Brutus among the bunch come with knives to kill him. It's Latin."

"What the hell does it have to do with us not going to Helena?"

"It refers, Dog Eye, to what you're thinking: that my being segundo has gone to my head and that now I enjoy persecuting those of my former rank. Think about it while I'm gone."

Doc spurred up and left at a trot, Lowell's horse tight beside him. They had gone half the distance in silence when Lowell said, "I been thinking on that Brutus thing half an hour. I can't make sense of it."

"That's because it don't *make* sense. I did not want to argue the real reasons with Dog Eye, who is a tiresome sagebrush lawyer. So I sought to bewilder him with nonsense."

Lowell nodded under his tipped-back hat, face expressionless as a plate. He was still nodding when they passed between the first diggings and shacks. Some houses had coal-oil light behind paper windows, for it was almost dark.

Doc had passed through Helena in 1867, but in such a hopeless defeated condition of sadness he barely noticed it. Years later, he had chased a herd of beef steers here during the mining frenzy, but had chosen to play poker in the stockyard rather than take a look at the town. Neither memory prepared him for Helena today. It was spread all over the flank of the mountain, and some buildings down its main street were two and three storeys high. Big freight wagons pulled by six and eight yokes of mules plugged the street almost solid. Buggies trying to make time among the Murphy wagons slithered their narrow wheels in the grease.

Doc watched for the numbers 3, 7, and 77 and finally found them in sloppy red on the side of a boarded-up store. A crude skull-and-crossbones was drawn above.

When they got to the saloon part of town, a boy with a bare head and his shirt-tail hanging stood in the street with a pistol in his hand. He was drunk and took weaving aim at a circle of fighting dogs. He missed and the bullet tore up the dirt near enough to Lowell's horse to make it hop. Lowell's hat came loose and fell, and he looked comical trapping it against his shoulder while trying to keep hold of the head of his jumping horse. A thin Chinese boy wearing a blue shirt as long as a dress came carrying two buckets of water on a yoke. He was also close to where the bullet hit and flinched so hard that water splashed everywhere. He staggered trying to get his weight back under his burden. Finally, the yoke was on the ground, one bucket spilled. The boy looked in both directions, trying to decide whether to take the full bucket to his destination or spill it and go back to the pump for more.

What the young Chinese did not see was the drunken boy taking sloppy aim at him. Doc untied his rope and stabbed his spurs into Pedro. He didn't have time to make a loop so he shook out the knotted end and swung it. Coming close to the young drunk, he spun the knot and hit him in the head. The old pistol flashed. The boy flung it aside and jumped around, holding his injured thumb.

Doc pulled Pedro to a sliding stop, about-faced, and returned to the boy. Looking down at the howling fool, Doc considered the need and value of a lecture. Some angel in charge of such things had probably ruined the boy's gun, and he probably couldn't afford another. When he woke from his drunkard's swoon, he would have a sore hand, a sick headache, and a painful bump to remind him of his foolishness. It seemed taken care of.

The Chinese boy, unaware he'd almost been shot, spilled the bucket and ran with his yoke for the pump.

Coiling his rope, Doc rode to Lowell. He delivered a sermon on the now-proven dangers of Helena. If the drunk had scared the horse of one of their younger men, Pesky or Tex, there would have been an argument. The drunken boy, gun in hand, may well have tried a shot at the cowboy who was scolding him. When the gun misfired, the cowboy's gun would almost certainly not do the same. The boy would be lying in the street, wounded or dead. Meanwhile, somewhere, some vigilante sonofabitch could be watching.

Next, they went looking for a livery barn, and Doc chose one with a sign that read:

Whip Light
Drive Slow
Pay Cash
Before You Go.

The poem didn't read right but Doc approved the sentiment and thought their horses might be well treated there. They gave strict orders to the liveryman to keep the horses in stalls and not water them from the scummy barrel in the corral.

When they found the Major's place of residence, the words "preacher hotel" leapt out of Doc's past, Pearly's term for a temperance hotel of this type. The man at the desk was plainly disgusted to have cowboys under his roof and reluctantly showed them to the Major's room. It was surprisingly large and the Major sat behind a desk covered in paper. The same old iron and upright Major, but with a little pouch the size and colour of an olive under each eye.

The Major greeted them, shook hands, and made no grumbles that they were late. He pointed to a pile of telegrams, about two hundred dollars worth, and said that the owners were displeased, but they were always displeased about something. He listened carefully while Lowell described the stampede and their shortage of horses. Then the Major turned to Doc for his report. Doc started in about calf wagons and the Major raised a hand to stop him.

"I have done what I can do," he said. Then to Lowell, "I've purchased forty horses, all native. They're not pretty but they're strong and familiar with the country. I've had two young fellows riding them all week. I bought one calf wagon and two Clydesdales to pull it."

Doc held his tongue. One was better than none.

"Another thing about the calf wagon. You'll be passing places where a calf or two could be bartered. I'm not against such trade for the weaker calves, even if it's for whisky, provided it's a legitimate business of the drive. I won't have any cowboy doing it on the sly and bootlegging to the others. Will you take charge of it, Doc?"

That was all. The Major said they would meet again in three weeks at Fort Benton, on September 10. He went back to thumbing through his telegrams, and Doc and Lowell understood they should leave.

Back on the street, Lowell suggested a whisky. He found it hard to walk by all these saloons and not do that much. Doc preferred to leave town directly but didn't like to refuse his friend. Doc did insist they find a newspaper first, because he wanted to know if the president of the United States was still alive or had died by now from the assassin's bullet. They found a boy with a paper for sale, and then jingled on down the boardwalk, looking at saloons.

Doc was indifferent to which saloon they went to. They all looked about the same at night: blue with smoke, piss-yellow light. Monte and poker games were underway, played by mountain men and men in suits and Frenchmen in leathers greased to a fine mahogany sheen. There were buffalo hunters too, who had shot up the last of their prey and come to town.

Crossing an alley, they heard a woman call from above. Looking up, they saw two soiled doves with their tits resting on a balcony rail. The one who had called lifted her skirt and spread her legs and cackled as they passed below. Seated on a bench not far from this vista was the first cowboy they'd seen since the livery barn. He was too drunk to even notice them, and might as well have had his wages in his hand offering them around for all the chance he'd wake up with any.

Finally Lowell found a saloon he liked. Doc held him back and said he had to piss. In the alley, by a pencil of light through an open knothole, Doc checked the chambers of his cap-and-ball gun.

The saloon was narrow and extended a long way back. There was a crush of men in the middle that the two cowboys had to push to get by. Though the bodies and lanterns made it hot as hell, one man wore a buffalo coat, perhaps to denote his profession, and likely to make himself look bigger, the way some birds will do with their feathers when they mate or fight. When this man and Lowell were passing chest to chest, the bearded buffalo hunter looked down and said around his cigar, "Something smells like cow in here."

There was space at the end of the room where the bar ran in under a slant of stairs. Most men wouldn't fit, and it gave Lowell and Doc a private place to drink.

"What do you like about this place?" Doc asked, already tipping the front page of his newspaper to the light. There was a headline, not even the top one any more, saying President Garfield was alive.

Lowell nodded to a buffalo head nailed to a plaque amongst the bottles behind the bar. It was a bull and its beard hung low enough to brush the shiny head of the bartender as he passed back and forth.

"Ain't seen a buffalo in awhile," said Lowell.

As they waited for a drink, Doc read and Lowell kept an eye on the buffalo hunter who had insulted them. The news was that a man named Charles Guiteau was the one who'd shot President Garfield. There didn't seem to be any doubt on that point, though the trial was delayed to see if the charge would be murder. Guiteau was a lawyer, and his problem was that he'd missed out on a patronage job he felt he deserved. So he shot the country's president. As for the state of Garfield, there seemed to be some hope of him living, based on an inventor named Alexander Graham Bell trying to find the bullet with some kind of electronical device.

Doc read all this news to Lowell, and when he finished, Lowell said for him to take a long look at the buffalo hunter's mouth, the way a black stub of cigar barely showed out of his dark, foresty beard.

"Looks just like a dog taking a shit, don't it?"

Doc barked a laugh. The buffalo hunter's head jerked up. Whether or not he knew the joke was on him, he didn't like the idea of the two cowboys having any fun.

They still hadn't got a drink when the buffalo hunter started pushing through the crowd toward them. He carried his whisky glass above the heads of the other patrons, showing off his size. Lowell nodded at the room's back door, which was propped open to let the heat out. Without discussion, the two of them slipped outside into the alley. The nearest light was in a cross street ahead and they walked for it. They walked slowly and neither bothered to check behind. The buffalo hunter, even if he was drunk, was probably not fool enough to follow two men into a deadfall.

From the side street, they returned to the main one, and stood on its corner where a cold night wind chilled their shaved faces. A sign creaking back and forth to their right said *Theatre*. A sandwich board below proclaimed *Two Men, A Woman, and A Boat*, with a poor drawing of a woman kicking her bloomered leg at some musical notes. Doc had a sudden nostalgia for shows he'd seen in Dillon, for coloured lamplight and grease-painted faces. He could hear singing coming from the door.

"Let's go," he said to Lowell. "I'll pay."

"I still want a whisky," said Lowell.

INSIDE THE TINY FOYER, about the size of a billiard table except square, a young woman sat asleep behind a corner bar. Her face was on her arm, which stretched out past two unlabelled liquor bottles and a few scratched shot glasses inverted on a cloth. She startled when their boots and spurs made a racket on the hollow floor, and she sat up embarrassed. Doc asked if they had any private boxes left, and she nodded and pointed to a narrow staircase against the right wall. Three steps up, a red curtain was drawn across. The main entrance through the foyer's back wall was crossed by a curtain of the same red material. Posters from bygone plays were glued overtop of one another on the walls.

The girl charged them fifty cents apiece on account of the play was half over. Doc asked for four whiskies and that came to two dollars more. A man's deep voice from the other side of the curtain asked the girl if everything was all right. "Customers," she answered. Above this exchange, a high-voiced man and a lower-voiced woman were singing, and the sound seemed closer than it should have been.

Doc led Lowell up the narrow steps. With a whisky in each hand, he elbowed aside the curtain where the path flattened into a narrow, elevated hallway. The only light came from three doors into the theatre itself. Each led into a private box, and all the boxes were empty. Doc and Lowell took the one at the front that overhung the stage.

The theatre was miniscule. There were maybe twenty wooden chairs in skinny rows leading up to the half-moon stage. Fewer than half had people in them, the most noticeable being a porky man in a tight suit who was asleep and snoring. The man and woman on stage were inside a canoe whose ends rose high to curly tops. A picture painted across the back wall showed towers and steeples above a wharf, where more boats with curly ends were moored.

When Doc and Lowell sat down and started watching, the woman was standing in the boat, almost on top of the seated man. She was hefty and the square-cut neck on her dress meant that Doc and Lowell were looking down at her breasts. In the hot gaslight, they were yellow, wet, and gleaming. Her song was about how the skinny, spectacled man in a straw hat, sitting on the cushion beneath her, didn't love her enough. She was about twice his size and Doc imagined that was part of the joke.

It didn't take long for things to become repetitive and Doc moved his attention to the people watching, their faces like little lamps in the dark. Beside the man snoring was a family—father, mother, boy of ten. The father was watching the singing woman with great attention, while his wife gave him dirty looks over the head of their boy. The others in the crowd were single men.

Back on stage, the little man was kneeling in the bottom of the canoe. He was singing back how he really did love the woman, just needed more time to learn her ways. It didn't appear to be going anywhere, so Doc went back to studying the room and the crowd. A movement by the entrance curtain caught his eye, and he remembered the voice behind the curtain asking the girl at the bar if everything was fine.

The curtain dividing the theatre from the foyer did not close at the top because a loop was torn. This made a ribbon of light, and when the man standing there started shifting weight from foot to foot, the light crossed his shoulder back and forth. One fleshy ear poked in and out of the light.

It was a strange thing to come to a play and spend your time looking at a man in a shadow, but that's what Doc was doing. He stared so hard he almost yelped when the man lunged into the light, ran down the aisle, and jumped on stage. He grabbed the woman from behind. He slid his arm around under her bosom. The other hand had a fat flintlock pistol in it, which he raised and pointed at the woman's ear.

"Give me the money you owe me, Featherling," this villain hollered, "or she will be no one's damsel soon!" The effect was so convincing Doc started to pull his gun. Then it struck him that the man was wigged and painted and had an exaggerated German accent. He was part of the show.

The man had his back to Doc. He had huge shoulders, one higher than the other. Coils of his own reddish hair boiled from under the back of his white wig, the kind judges wear. The wig, the coiling hair, the big shoulders and stout neck—all were within a few feet of Doc and Lowell.

Then the small man jumped from the boat and ran across the water to stand among the boats pulled up at the wharf. He was a coward. All spectacled men in plays were.

Doc knew an actor wasn't supposed to turn his back on the audience, and soon the villain turned the woman in his grasp toward the glowing faces below him. Doc could see the side of the villain's head now, his nose in profile, his forehead, his ear. The ear was crisscrossed by scars. Beneath it, sweat ran tracks through the powder and Doc saw a blotched red line, a seam healed with a lump at its end, red and waxy like a boil.

When the little man in the straw hat ran behind a black partition and vanished, the crowd booed. A scrunched program flew through the air and rolled to a stop near where he'd gone. The villain spun the woman, then pushed her hard on the shoulders so she fell backwards into the canoe. She fell onto the fat cushion with a great show of white bloomers and naked ankles. The villain started a speech about how the other man loved his money more than her. Weeping, she agreed.

Then the villain turned and stared into the box at Doc.

"When I find that little man, I'm going to twist his head off his shoulders, stuff his hat in his mouth until he chokes on it. I will break each of the bones of his body in turn. I will press his head until I squash it flat."

Doc could see the woman beyond the villain's shoulder and she had stopped her weeping. She was staring at the villain with perplexity. On top of all the other feelings he was having, Doc sensed that the villain was not delivering the speech written for this moment. Whatever he was supposed to say, it would make more sense to say it to the woman or in the direction the cowardly man had fled. Doc knew he was staring into the face of Ivan Overcross.

Doc ran from the box into the hallway. He clumped and jingled to the end, pushed aside the curtain on the stairs, and jumped the last three steps, landing so hard in the foyer that the wood cracked. Outside, the wind was much stronger and colder and the sandwich board lay flat. Doc took off running in the direction of the livery barn.

Doc had Pedro saddled by the time Lowell got there. While Lowell paid the liveryman, Doc mounted. Dropping down along Pedro's neck, he galloped the horse out the door. He kept up the pace the length of main street. Beyond the last light of town, he ran the gelding another half a mile. Finally he pulled up and waited. When the two horses finally came together, both were sweated and nervy given the sudden change from sleep to hard exercise.

"Any time," said Lowell.

"I know that actor."

"I figured."

"I killed him once."

Lowell let it stand.

"I killed him and he held a grudge. He swore he'd kill me back. It's why I never left the Beaverhead all those years. I figured if I did, he'd find me or I'd find him."

"Hell, Doc, we're away and gone, probably tomorrow."

"You think he can't follow the track of seven thousand cows?"

"He don't even know about them, or that you're part of them. You're thinking crazy."

"He looked me in the face, Lowell. He saw how we were dressed. He isn't stupid."

In an hour, Doc crawled into his bedroll near Dog Eye and Lippy. Listening to the wind and the snores, he told himself not to start thinking what the events of this night meant, or reliving how it came to be. Whatever it meant could be faced more easily in the morning. He thought he was slowing down when Dog Eye's voice made him jump.

"So what did you do?"

At first Doc didn't understand the question. "Met the Major. Went to part of a show."

"And never went nowhere near a woman."

"No."

Dog Eye expelled a sigh, not so much disgusted but deeply disappointed. "Sending you to town is nothing but a waste," he said. Then came the sound of him gathering his blankets and rolling the other way. He said no more.

Doc was hurt, stabbed to the heart. The fear had stripped him naked and what Dog Eye said seemed terrible and true. If he had not devoted so much time to fearing Overcross and loving Pearly, his response to town might have been a whorehouse after all, not a show. He could have been in the arms of a woman in one place while Overcross sang his songs in another. He and his enemy could have passed in the night.

DENVER

March 1867

WHEN DOC AND PEARLY ENTERED DENVER, after the long, cold ride from Cheyenne, Pearly was behind the saddle holding Doc around his middle. It was still snowing. A mile high according to its boosters, Denver was freezing tonight. The snow sifted down onto the silent street, and Rufus's hooves marked the only path through the iron ruts and petrified dung piles. Most of old Denver was indeed gone, eaten by fire and changed to brick, but Pearly wasn't as estranged as she thought she'd be.

Through the snow and the flannel light, Pearly watched for a preacher hotel, the kind that was religious and clean, where no one very lively went. It was where you found travelling teachers, preachers, storekeepers, and rare non-drinking army officers. Another reason Pearly called these preacher hotels was that, despite their never being full, you practically had to be a preacher to get into one. They were death on whores and adulterers and had a low opinion of any woman who was not fat and still had breasts you could see. If you had both tits and colour, you were a harlot for sure. Any man entering with such a woman on his arm was either paying for her favours or cheating on his Christian wife in some other way. Preacher hotels never stopped to think that whores and adulterers wouldn't choose such a place to practise their iniquity in, not when any number of other hotels were more than cheerful to have their custom.

Pearly could picture the room already, even smell it. Grey blanket, bed like a board, metal water pitcher, window that some enemy of fresh air had painted shut. But there would be no bed bugs and no shooting. Doc needed a break from shooting right now.

When Pearly saw a sign reading *Travellers' Rest* hanging off a tawdry grey two-storey building, she thought they might be home. Closer up, she could see a sign reading *No Alcohol Consumption*, and she was certain. She reached past Doc's shoulder and gave Rufus's rein a tug in that direction. Near the hitching rail, she slid down and took the reins from Doc's crabbed hands.

"Come in with me," she said, "but don't talk."

The man behind the undecorated desk was thin and bald as an egg. He wore steel-rimmed spectacles split-keyed to the ball of his nose. Below a scrawny neck, his white shirt was long-gone yellow, tied at the neck with a lifeless tie. Over the shirt, he had a grey vest, and when he bent to look at his ledger, Pearly could see that his wife had gathered the slack at the back and pinned it.

The clerk started getting embarrassed and Pearly began her speech.

"My husband, Reverend Cox, and I will require a clean room for at least a week. Nothing fancy is needed. What is your lowest weekly rate?"

That backed him up, but soon colour rose again on his mushroom face, meaning he still felt obliged to ask the question. Pearly attacked again before he could.

"You want a marriage certificate and, while you want it for the good reason of preventing moral turpitude, we cannot supply one. Such a document is viewed as ungodly by our faith."

This perplexed the clerk so much that a word squeezed past his Adam's apple. "Why?"

"My husband would be more than happy to discuss religion with you at some other time. At present we are frozen stiff and would like to come in out of the cold. *If there is room at the inn.*"

Pearly's father had taught her all this. The last part was the clincher, a reference to Mary and Joseph denied lodging in Bethlehem, and Jesus being born among beasts—instead of in a preacher hotel where he belonged. Grudgingly, the clerk wet his pen and wrote, *Reverend and Mrs. Cox*. While he did, Pearly asked about a livery barn.

While Doc went outside to secure lodging for Rufus, Pearly mounted the creaking stairs. The hall above was narrow with not a scrap of carpet down the middle. She turned the iron key in the lock and a square bolt snapped back.

The room was just like the ones her father had taken her to whenever he needed to hide from men who had taken offence at losing or caught him in a cheat. She had forgotten the cross, though, the plain, forlorn, wooden cross above the door. There was never even a Jesus on it, the way Catholics did theirs. Pearly climbed up on the bed, took the cross down, and put it in a drawer.

Doc had barely spoken since coming back from helping kill the crazy prospector. As far as Pearly was concerned, he could stay quiet for a week. Any longer than that and she would prod him, as it wasn't healthy to stay quiet too long.

Pearly knew it was not much in Doc's nature to hurt people. That was the first thing she had liked about him. At the same time, he would not take a licking, or let her take one, and that was important too. It was a hard world, and the gun in the pocket of her dress was not for show.

What Doc did not know about Black Elmo, the man who had hurt her and who Doc's uncle had died for shooting, was that he had been nasty to her all through his gambling spree in Virginia City. He was losing at several places but always came back to Comstock Bob's to follow her around and suggest things. Pearly had made the mistake of flashing her pepper-box pistol at him, thinking that would curb his ardour. When she went for a cigarette in the alley the night she first saw Doc and his uncle, Black Elmo followed her and grabbed her. She tried to put her cigarette into his face, but he had her wrist and was too strong. With her other hand, she went for the gun in her dress pocket, but he knew about it now and was there before her.

Two very different things had happened to them, Doc and Pearly, but Pearly believed the way it left them feeling might be similar. People do things to you, things you would never choose. It changes you in some way even though you argue and vow it won't. That much was in common. Probably so was the way it kept running through your brain, no matter how you begged God to stop it.

Doc and his Uncle Jack had come to Pearly like angels: neither one in time, but neither one too late. Now it was up to her to make the world good again for Doc, just like he had for her.

From the other side of the door, she heard a creaking, and she imagined Doc walking up the stairs like he was dragging an iron ball. The Christians in this hotel had wrapped down the blanket and sheet so hard she could barely lift them. With a mighty rip she did so, resettled the covers, turned them down. She sat on the bed and waited for the door to open.

PEARLY WENT OUT THE FIRST day in Denver and bought Doc a black suit as a present. As long as he kept his coat closed over the white ruffle at the shirt's neck, he did look quite a bit like a preacher. He was certainly sad as one. But that week, every time Doc and Pearly left the Travellers' Rest of an evening, the bald clerk or his wife would eye the slender cloth wrapper under Pearly's arm and the less-than-modest dress showing under her coat.

And it didn't take the woman at the hotel long to start asking questions. Pearly said the thing in the cloth wrapper was a stick her husband used to direct singing. The first time Pearly thought Doc might be headed for recovery was when he stepped forward and took the wrapper out from under her arm. He opened it in front of the clerk's wife's face and took out the shooting half of the pool cue. He made little poking gestures with it.

"It's used for a game," he said, "a game in which sinners gamble and curse. I use it to direct godly singing, to show how evil can be turned into good."

Next time through, the woman wanted to know where Reverend Cox was preaching tonight. When Pearly said, "Way across town," it was less than convincing. The woman had that sewn lip that meant they would be seeking new accommodations soon.

"I better make some money," Pearly said when they were out on the street that night. "I don't want to go to no hotel worse than this one." Then she added, but sweetly, "How about you? You going to make some money some time?" But it was only the seeding of an idea; she knew Doc wasn't ready yet.

Denver was almost as dead as the Cheyenne boosters had claimed. There were very few wagons and buggies on the streets and few people in the stores, saloons, and restaurants. A number of businesses were boarded up, and word was that several had taken the stock off their shelves and gone to Cheyenne. But Pearly explained to Doc that there is always a low level of gaming in even the deadest town, precisely because it is dead and a person's got to do something. Because the reason for gambling is different, so is the style.

Back in Cheyenne, Pearly had presented herself to the billiards crowd as an entertainer. Like an opera singer or a magic act, she sought to amaze. Here in Denver, she made out she was just another bored person killing time. She played slow and on several occasions even surrendered the table in the middle of a winning streak. "I'm tired," she'd say. "You fellas go ahead and play." Then she'd sit and fan herself and read the paper, until one of the players politely asked if she'd like to try again.

This way of playing kept the emotions down, and hence the risk—and also the size of bets. But Pearly's view was, why get excited? She was making enough to cover their hotel and meals, which kept their previous winnings intact.

As for what she did with the saved money, Pearly was adamant it would never be put in a bank. Her system was to hide it but never in one place and never all in the same room. She had various other rules, too. "Mice'll eat paper money. Keep what you can in gold coins." Thinking of mice and pack rats, she preferred heavy canvas bags or boxes. "Never put money in the toes of your extra shoes or the lining of your coat." If she hid money under the floor or in a wall, it wasn't under "a loose board." She'd pry up a normal board and tell Doc to create a noise by coughing or slamming the door as she nailed it back down. Then she'd rub dirt in the nail holes.

As Pearly got her gambling routine established, Doc remained untalkative, but in a way that was hard to fault. Mostly, he replaced his talking with reading. He read whatever was left in the preacher's hotel: temperance pamphlets, drummer's advertisements, and such. When the local paper, the *Rocky Mountain News*, came out, he read it cover to cover. At the news agent's, he arranged for copies of *The Police Gazette* and *Harper's Monthly* to be held for him whenever they came on the stagecoach. He was a reading fool, and sometimes he would make a sound, a murmur, and his lips would move. It was a noise out of the mouth, but it wasn't talking.

Pearly tried to be understanding about this jag of reading. It was clearly what Doc needed. But she found it disturbing nonetheless, because of how much it left her out. She would ask him from time to time what was in the newspaper or magazine, and he never failed to answer, but in a mechanical way she found insulting.

"Indians killed more cavalry down the Bozeman."

"A New York fella can tell your personality by the shape of your head."

"James Gang robbed a bank in Kansas."

She noticed that if he volunteered anything, it was an update on something he'd already told her.

"Cavalry on the Bozeman weren't really killed by Indians. They froze to death."

Two weeks into their stay at the Travellers' Rest, over breakfast in a café down the street, Doc was reading the latest issue of the local paper. He turned it around on the table and pointed at a black-bordered square. The heading was LECTURE TODAY.

Professor Edward Minton, one of only Seven Graduates of the renowned American Institute of Phrenology in New York City, will address a Denver audience tonight on the mysteries of the science to which he is a devotee and of which he is an expert. To all comers,

Professor Minton will dispense practical wisdom on such matters as educating your children and choosing a marriage partner.

For a modest fee of $1, hear the master speak and perhaps win one of two free examinations. Dr. Samuel Wells' book What to Do and Why, *practical advice based on phrenological principles, will be on sale. Other books available: Dr. Orson Fowler's* A Phreno-logical Guide *and Dr. Johann Gaspar Spurzheim's* Phrenology in Connexion with the Study of Physiognomy.

"He examines your head and tells you your character," Doc sum-marized.

"I already know mine. I take it you want to go."

"Yes."

"Don't need my permission."

"No."

"Go without me. I got no bumps to read."

"I think there's more to it than bumps."

"Fine. You go and find out. I'll be working. And don't worry about the billiards saloon. If anyone dies there, it will be from boredom."

THE LECTURE HALL WAS UP a flight of stairs in a plain red building on a street devoted to dry goods and hardware. The room was about the size of the Masonic meeting hall in Virginia City, and though it had none of the signs and symbols of the craft, it did seem to belong to some other brotherhood, northern and patriotic. There was a big Union flag nailed across the front and a crude painting of George Washington looking like a simpleton.

Doc sat on a wooden chair at the edge of a row. Most of the crowd of about thirty were behind him. Several were couples and some had children. A noticeable number of the children seemed not right in their heads. Other than the children, Doc was the youngest person. He was also the only cowboy, though not dressed as one.

At the front, a suited man with a considerable beard sat low in a chair with his legs stuck out and crossed at the ankle. His socks were blue with red diamonds down the side. He never looked once at the audience as it built and chattered in front of him. His eyes were either locked on his socks or the laces of his shoes. It had to be Professor Minton.

Beside him was a table on which a white plaster head stood on its neck. All over the head were pictures and words. Though too small and far away to decipher, Doc knew what some of the words were, having read an article in *Harper's Monthly*. The pictures represented aspects of human character and the words were the names ascribed to them. Doc had memorized only *Destructiveness*, which was found above the ears. All together, they made up a road map of the brain. To see what was more or less prominent was why the phrenologists measured and felt their subjects' heads. Though people always said they were feeling for bumps, and called it "bumpology," this was just a way of making fun. The article had said distances between the parts and the general shape of the head were more important.

Something about the way the professor sat and his relation to the head on the table reminded Doc of the worshipful master with his candlelit skull. There was probably no connection between phrenology and Masons but Doc felt one right then. Being here made him feel the anxiety of when the Masons had been a threat to him, then the comfort he'd felt when the worshipful master resolved that threat by making him a brother.

While more people arrived and the addled children squealed and howled, a black-suited man with comb-grooved hair ran about the place telling everyone where to sit and urging the parents of the children to keep them quiet. Like any organ grinder's monkey, he was collecting dollars as he went around.

Well after the time when they were supposed to start, this shill went to the front and started waving his arms and asking for silence. Before he had it, he started to speak in a stumbly way about how the evening would unfold, with the professor's lecture at the start, then free examinations, then paid examinations and a chance to buy a head map and a book. He hadn't got to the end when the professor gracefully stood, tapped him on the shoulder, and nodded him away. That's all it took to create silence.

"Phrenology is a science," Professor Minton began, then he stopped.

He let that sink in for awhile. He had a whisky-amber voice that Doc liked, a loud purring that set you at your ease.

"There is a chap, Charles Darwin, who recently published a book of his scientific findings called *Origin of the Species*. Nothing overly humble about that title, is there?"

Professor Minton looked up at the audience as a prompt to laughter. When it subsided, he continued.

"Darwin travelled to the south seas and came up with a theory he calls *natural selection*. I have a little note from his book that I would like to read to you."

He tweezed a piece of paper out of a vest pocket and tipped on a pair of glasses.

"The goal is perpetuation of favourable individual differences and variations and the destruction of that which is injurious. I have called it natural selection or survival of the fittest."

Professor Minton put his glasses back in his pocket. He surveyed the crowd, looking for anybody fool enough to be impressed by that.

"You will forgive me, I hope, if I declare that phrenology had been noting these similarities and differences in humans, and providing a program for the promotion of strengths and the repression of weaknesses, decades before Mr. Darwin climbed in a boat and crossed an ocean. Mr. Darwin has noted in his studies the similarity between man and a monkey and proposes that we are all *monkey's uncles*, or more precisely that the monkey is uncle to us. I think you might forgive phrenology for having missed that interpretation."

Again, the professor stopped and smiled. Given permission, everyone laughed.

"Phrenologists do agree with Mr. Darwin that there are properties of the animal in each of us, but phrenology goes further and submits that those properties are situated in the organs of the brain. The particular organs—amativeness, love, destructiveness, self-esteem—are in the same regions of every brain, just as all our noses sprout from the middle of our faces and not from the shoulder or hip."

He began to walk back and forth behind the table and the head. He held up one hand, extended the fingers, and counted off the various parts of personality, all from memory. Some of these parts, and he told which ones, were the animal properties. Others, benevolence and such, were the human qualities. The balance among them was the measure of "one's humanity."

"The organ of benevolence or destructiveness is not the same in every man or woman—not the same size, not producing the same effect on personality. This is how people come to be different, and the phrenologist, by scientific comparison and measurement, can predict that personality, can scientifically define it."

Professor Minton talked for awhile about how phrenology could tell parents what aptitudes were strongest in their children. They could therefore know in advance how to school them, and, in the case of criminal tendencies, how to strengthen the better qualities and combat the worst. Then the professor gripped his beard and turned his back, which was the assistant's cue to bring a leather satchel.

In the satchel were skulls, which the assistant set upright, eyeholes to the front, on the table. He moved the white plaster head to the floor to make room. There were ten skulls in all. The professor turned to face the crowd and, by some gesture, caused the assistant to hold out his hands, palms up. The professor selected two of the skulls and set them on the assistant's hands. He took out a set of calipers and did measurements. He drew imaginary lines from the top (vertex) to the earhole, from the forehead to the backmost point (occiput).

As the professor worked his way through the skulls, Doc started to see what he was asked to see: how some people were very high in the head (good), prominent in the forehead (good), small in the forehead (bad), or backward-sloping above the brow (bad). Some heads were built so the majority of the brain was on top (sincipital—good) while others had their bulk at the bottom (basilar—bad). It was also better to have more brain to the front than the back.

Perhaps knowing from experience that this was when audiences started to feel too confident of their understanding, Professor Minton said that what made phrenology difficult, requiring a great deal of knowledge and sensitivity from the practitioner, was ascertaining how the various prominences and deficiencies would play out in character.

If a man had a lot of love and attachment in his brain, but also much acquisitiveness and destructiveness, he might be insanely jealous, even the kind who kills his wife out of fear of losing her. Take this same amount of love and attachment and mix it with strong benevolence and veneration and you might have a person who devotes his life to good works.

When they were down to the last two heads, Professor Minton did not compare them. He held up the first one and talked about it, how it was not just any old skull but the skull of a truly evil man. The bones of the skull bulged above and behind the ears, meaning a lot of destructiveness. There wasn't much forehead or brow to counteract it. The human qualities were pinched up in a little cupola that would have better suited a gopher.

And who was this sorry man but Lister Vance, a notorious British murderer, whose last crime before his hanging was to follow a simple pedlar boy into a bog outside the English town of Bournemouth, where he beat out his brains with the heel of his clog. Vance robbed the pedlar's pack of twenty shillings, the outrage of which fully struck the audience after the sum was converted into American money.

Then the last head was held up and displayed. Professor Minton seemed disgusted even to look at it. "Would you believe," he said finally, "that this, in life, was the head of an ordained Roman Catholic bishop?" Doc was definitely catching on. He saw in profile how the head bent back abruptly just above a puny brow. By far most of this skull's bulk was in the bottom half at the back. When the professor got to the bishop's misdeeds, they were mostly sexual: the misusing of children, girls and boys, brought to him from orphanages by evil accomplices.

For the last while, Doc had been sitting sideways in his chair so he could watch the professor and the audience. During the murderer's skull and now the bishop's, the men in the audience were one after another reaching up and pretending to smooth their hair or scratch their scalps. When they thought no one was looking, they spread their thumbs and forefingers. The women were openly feeling and measuring the heads of their children.

Doc was glad Pearly hadn't come. He knew that when the lustful bishop was being described, she would have been making little snorts and sneaking her hand up his back, tickling him in the places where the professor said the bishop's disgusting behaviours originated.

Then it was time for the examinations, and the parents of the children all had their hands up waving. Seeing this, the children got excited and waved and made noises too. Quickly, the professor pointed to one of these children, a boy, and had him brought to the front. The child wailed, but the professor went about his business as if he didn't notice. He measured, he felt, he waved for the parents to take the boy away. The boy was "a booby," Professor Minton pronounced, possessed of a very small and inert brain.

Now he asked for an adult volunteer. Doc coughed to draw attention and put up his hand. Afraid of being deemed a booby, no other man or woman was signalling. Doc knew he had a small head, for it was proportional to the rest of him, so he was taking a gamble.

After Doc was chosen, he was directed to sit at the front, facing toward the audience. Without touching him, Professor Minton walked around him three times. Then he took out his calipers and went behind. For a time he measured in silence, front to back, side to side, earholes to everywhere.

"You have all noted, I'm sure, that this gentleman's head is not large."

Oh-oh, thought Doc. Booby.

"But is it his head that is small, or is it his face?"

The audience studied Doc hard, the nearsighted ones squinting.

"It might surprise you that some of the most intelligent men of Europe, including the great Voltaire, had small faces. But look here."

Professor Minton grabbed Doc's chair at the back and reefed it around, so the audience was looking at his profile. He rubbed Doc on the brow and ran his fingers up his forehead, then smoothed his hand back and forth over the top of his round crown.

"A strong brow, a forehead almost vertical, a nicely shaped sincipital. The basilar not so absent as to prevent action. This man is keen in the senses, active and bright. If he lacks in any way, it might be in courage."

He stepped away from Doc and faced him. "Am I right, sir? Or am I wrong?"

Doc walked back to his chair in a fog. The professor's summation of his character was shockingly accurate, even down to pinpointing his native fearfulness. Doc preferred to think that, in a longer examination, the professor might have located the bolder part that could act forcefully, if cornered. For a time, Doc heard nothing and felt nothing but an echo in the nerve endings of his head from the action of Professor Minton's fingers.

When the present moment returned to Doc, all was changed. Though Doc's reading was the last of the free ones given out by Professor Minton, the positiveness of his interpretation of Doc's head had inspired an entire line-up of men now willing to risk a dollar for a reading of their own. The assistant had put the skulls back into the satchel and replaced them on the table with books and phrenological head maps for sale. There was a cheaper version of the map made of paper and a more expensive one designed on tanned calfskin.

Doc didn't hesitate. He bought the book by Spurzheim because it had lots of plates showing lots of heads of historical figures, and he bought the leather head map. Then he stood patiently beside the line of men until Professor Minton, in moving from one man to the next, saw him and met his eye. Doc nodded and said, "Thank you." The professor nodded back with a humorous twinkle.

Outside, it was snowing and blowing. Doc protected his new possessions by holding them inside his coat. When he walked into the hotel room, he brought in a cloud of snow crystals that fell glittering through the yellow candlelight. Pearly was on her back on the bed, seeming to study the ceiling. She glanced at the book and the leather map, which was rolled and tied. Doc set them on the washstand. She said nothing. Doc stayed silent as well. He stripped down, blew out the candle, and eased in on the near side of the hard bed. After awhile, Pearly reached and slid her fingers between the buttons of his underwear.

"You are cold everywhere," she said. "Goodness. I think I've just located the bump of horniness." She reached across him, pulled open the drawer, and groped for the box of Dr. Powers' French Preservatives.

Later, when they held each other and quieted down to sleep, she spoke again.

"It's a good thing your lecture was tonight, because tomorrow we'll be busy moving. A friend of the missus downstairs looked into a saloon and saw the Reverend Cox's wife reclined on a billiards table."

After awhile, when Doc thought Pearly was asleep, she asked, "Why'd you really want to go to that head bump lecture?"

"I thought if there's a kind of head that goes with evil people, we should know it."

Doc expected Pearly to make a joke, but she didn't. She stayed quiet and neither of them slept for a long time.

MULLAN WAGON ROAD

August 1881

THE DAY AFTER MEETING OVERCROSS in the theatre in Helena, Doc surprised himself by feeling better than he had in years. While he helped gather the rested herd, he felt alert and quick, sharp in his wits and senses. A lot of suspense and dread had backed up in him over time, and now that Overcross was back on his trail, those emotions flushed out. It felt so good that Doc began to wish he had never gone into hiding in the Beaverhead. If he had gone straight out and tracked Overcross instead of hiding from him, he might have felt this good all along.

After the cattle were back on the trail, Doc exchanged his saddle for the seat of the calf wagon, and drove the two huge taffy-coloured Clydesdales. Beside him was a young fellow from Ontario, Canada, who had come to the Major in Helena, wanting to work his passage to Fort Macleod. Because this Jim Adams was on foot, the calf wagon was one of few employments available to him, especially since Dwight was still cook's helper. Adams also claimed not to drink whisky, which put him above the main temptation associated with the calf job—bartering veal for liquor. Once Doc had Jim trained, he planned to leave him to work alone, but for the present, they would ride the wagon and lift the straggling calves over the steep sides together.

The only problem with Adams turned out to be his limited conversation. Beyond that he was from Ontario and had come west looking to work for a man named John Craig on a ranch in the west of Canada, Doc could get little out of him. He never spoke without a prompt and never answered with more than a yes or no if he could help it.

As they crossed the big valley north of Helena and started up into the mountains, Doc did most of the talking. His topic was Overcross and how good he felt about his own chances should a confrontation occur.

"Getting the jump is the most important thing," he told Adams more than once. "Overcross will never get the jump on me."

Part of Doc's readiness was having Louie saddled and walking beside the wagon, his reins tied loose to a stave near his hand. The Winchester was loaded in its scabbard, also within reach. Though Doc seldom wore a gun belt, he had dug Uncle Jack's holster out of the chuckwagon and wore it now. The usual reason for avoiding the holster, for carrying the old gun in the back of his pants, was to look unarmed. But Overcross wasn't likely to care if Doc was armed front or back, or not at all.

Doc asked Adams if he had a gun, and the young fellow fished an old Colt from the pocket of his coat. It was newer than Doc's but poorly kept, the kind of gun that passes through many hands but is treated kindly by none.

"If Overcross comes and you get a clear shot at him, don't hesitate any more than you would with a rabid dog." Doc then described Overcross in detail so that Jim would know him to see him. He told him to watch for any name with an "over" or a "cross" in it.

By halfway through the second day, it was clear that Adams, however verbal he wasn't, was capable. He could drive the team better than Doc could, and was already lifting calves into the wagon without assistance. Doc jumped from the wagon onto Louie, bid Adams good day, and hurried after the cloud of dust that was the cattle herd.

Part of Doc's hurry to get back with the cattle and the crew had to do with Dwight. In his new state of activeness, it bothered Doc that he'd left that feud simmer so long. Allowing a young man to go on presenting himself as a dangerous killer was at very least laziness, and possibly cowardice. Peppered up as he was, Doc wanted the thing resolved now.

He was planning to finish with Dwight within the hour, but found that Lowell, by seeking to help him, had interfered. Touched by Doc's dilemma with Overcross, and thinking that Dwight should be kept from causing Doc any additional woe, the trail boss had put the boy back with the night herders. When Doc caught up to the chuckwagon, the big oaf was asleep inside it, resting up for his night's work. The idea of stopping the chuckwagon, waking Dwight, and fetching him out seemed too public and theatrical. Doc decided to wait.

That night, during the sleeping hours, there was a commotion. An alert was sounded, and the boys were all running for their horses. It looked like another stampede, until the cattle who were running petered out of their own accord. It started and ended so quick Doc didn't make it into his saddle. He was soon back asleep and would have forgotten the whole thing if Lowell hadn't been so angry at breakfast.

All through his beans and biscuits, Lowell grumbled and cursed. He tore at his bread and mopped at his plate as though food were the enemy. He drank his coffee too quickly and burned his mouth. Afraid of being the target of his temper, the boys left for work without being told. Finally it was just Doc and Lowell, the cook, and the sleeping nighthawks.

Staring hard at Dwight, who was outside the wagon now, stretched out beside one of its wheels, Lowell snarled, "I'm going to fire that big dumb bastard. The only question is whether I set him afoot now or save him for Fort Benton. Maybe some old whisky trader could trade him to a Blackfoot for some robes."

Doc asked him what the problem was, for truly he did not know.

"Man's a disaster!" Lowell said. "First time I let him night hawk, he shot a wolf and started a stampede. Last night, I put him back on night herd, and he promptly falls off his horse and starts another run. I'm not even counting that he wants to murder you."

"I don't like to interfere with your temper, Lowell, but Dwight's my problem. Why don't you let me do as I please with him?"

Lowell stopped short, looked at Doc with new respect.

"What you aim to do?"

"Never mind. Just let me do it."

"All right. But have a good story prepared. Murder isn't acceptable, even in Montana."

When Lowell was mounted and away, Doc began by taking off his gun belt and putting it in his saddlebag. He poked his gun into the back of his pants and started toward Dwight. After approaching with great stealth, he was on one knee overtop the pink face. The boy was on his back in his bedroll. The wool sweater that was meant for his pillow had partly unrolled and was supporting only his beefy neck. This flung back his head and popped open his mouth, out whose ponderous chamber came the noise of swede saws.

Doc had seen many tricks played on a man in such a pose. A fluttering dragonfly or a wiggly worm lowered into the mouth. Or the cowboys might spit their tobacco juice in, or worse. But Doc was not here for jest. With the pointer fingers of his two hands, he measured and compared distances on Dwight's massive head. He used his palm to measure area and thus compared the sincipital zone to the basilar. He checked the areas above and behind the ears for bulge. It was as he had suspected. Unless Johann Gaspar Spurzheim was a fraud, Dwight was more human than animal, and no killer. He had more in common with Seneca the Philosopher than with Nero, the cruel Caesar.

Snake slow, Doc slid his hand under the sweater until he felt the wooden butt of Dwight's Peacemaker. He poked his finger inside the trigger guard and pulled. Into view came the pretty hardwood handle. Doc took the gun behind his own body to smother the sound and popped the cylinder. He shook the bullets into his palm, then put them in his pocket. He slid the gun back where it had been, beneath the sunburned neck.

Then Doc stood and tapped Dwight's foot inside the blanket with the toe of his riding boot.

"Come on, Dwight. Jingle jangle. Rise and shine."

Dwight awoke as from a laudanum dream. His eyelids fluttered as if some tiny practical joker had braided the lashes together. When his eyes did break open, one iris was in the middle while the other dogged it in the corner. Finally, as he got more alert, the two eyes worked in tandem. Dwight assembled his first frown of the day and slid his hand under his sweater.

"What you want?"

"I want your witty company. We have to talk."

" 'Bout what?"

"I'll tell you when we're talking."

"I told you before, I ain't talking to you."

"I'm not tingling at the prospect either. But I have been deputized by our trail boss to discuss your role in the fracas last night."

Dwight winced. Perhaps only now did he remember that on the other side of sleep he had made a foolish error. A look of sadness floated across Dwight's face before he could remake his homicidal scowl, and that fleeting look told Doc a thing of importance: Dwight did care what the other cowboys thought of him.

"I'm going over into that bunch of trees. I'm going to roll a smoke. That'll give you a chance to compose yourself. Then I'd like you to come and talk to me."

Doc turned his back and walked. Since he had his coat on against the morning chill, Dwight could not see his pistol.

When Doc got to the trees, he followed a deer trail. Twenty feet in, he found a likely spot and turned off. Through the pine cones and the needle trash, he kicked a path that passed between several close-set pines. About thirty feet along, a fallen log crossed a space about the size of a cheap hotel room. He got out a roll of high-note piano wire, the non-musical uses of which Pearly had trained him in years ago. He did what he had to, then sat on a little log. With his seldom-used makings, he twisted a smoke. All the while he faced down the scratch he'd made to the deer path and watched through the trees for motion.

Probably to show his independence, Dwight made him wait. Doc was on his second cigarette and getting dizzy by the time the big fellow lumbered up the deer path. Twice, he stopped to hoist his gun belt higher on his formless hips. When he hit the cross-roads, Doc called.

"This way, Dwight."

At the sound, Dwight flinched, crouched, grabbed his gun. He turned slowly and peered down the line between the trees. There sat Doc, framed between skinny pine trunks, one hand up near his face holding a cigarette and the other hand cupped to his knee, no weapon in evidence.

Emboldened, Dwight holstered his gun and pushed ahead through the pine branches, squinting in the shadowy light. He seemed confused to see Doc sitting so small on the log, just barely off the ground. The final pair of trees were tight to the trail so Dwight needed to turn himself sideways to get through. As he poised to do so, Doc said, "Stop there is good. I don't want you stepping on me."

"What then?" the big fellow asked, peevish.

"I hear that last night you fell off your horse and started another stampede."

"Horse spooked."

"Don't mean you have to fall off."

"Well, I did."

"Ever occur to you that if you want to make a living as a cowboy, you should learn to ride?"

"I can ride."

"Where exactly did you learn? Bean Fart, Tennessee? Square Head, Minnesota? Or some other famous horse and cattle capital I'm not familiar with?"

"I'm not taking advice from you."

"That's too bad, since I'm your segundo, and since it's advice from your trail boss."

"I got my own boss. He's back in Virginia City."

"That's like saying you can't obey your trail boss because he ain't your momma."

"Don't get me mad! You'll be sorry if you get me mad!"

"I won't be sorry if you get so mad you catch fire."

Dwight growled like a dog. He pulled his gun, then didn't seem to know what to do with it. Pointing it at the ground, he drew back the hammer until it clicked.

"Com'mon then, Dwight. Come ahead. I expect those piggy little eyes of yours don't see so good in this light. You better step closer so you don't miss."

When the hammer clicked on the first empty chamber, the gun was pointed at the ground. That was probably an accident. Dwight fanned back the hammer to shoot on purpose, but took aim at least four feet over Doc's head. When that too hit a vacant chamber, Dwight slugged the gun in his holster and squeezed himself through the pines with a bullish roar.

Hitting the piano wire with both ankles, he crashed to the ground. Doc reared his feet out of the way, having misjudged the length of Dwight when felled. The big man's head struck the log, then slid down into the moss and needles beside it. Dwight reached for his gun belt and started pressing out bullets.

Doc had by now drawn his own gun, and he nudged the barrel's mouth into the pudge at Dwight's waist. Doc's experience was that if you want to strike fear into a creature of the gut, make as though to shoot him in the belly.

"This pistola of mine is loaded. You might reconsider reloading your own."

The logic penetrated Dwight. The bullets in his hand poured out. Carefully, he lay down his gun with its cylinder hanging. Then he rolled onto his back with his hands raised, like a dog asking to be scratched. Doc reached over with his free hand and clamped Dwight's nose.

"You are the damnedest man for letting the blood outa your nose. I'm going to let go. When I do, you grab it."

After the exchange, Doc sat back and set his old gun on the ground beside him. His cigarette had gone out and he relit it. Dwight yanked a wrinkled rag out of his ass pocket and wiped and dabbed his mouth and chin, still holding his nostrils together with the fingers of his other hand.

"Good. Now we can have a more civilized conversation."

Dwight said something too muffled to hear.

"You notice by any chance how much pleasanter the company is on this drive? Compared to what you had back with Darnell in the Alder Gulch? Even avoiding our company, you must have noticed that."

Dwight unclamped his nose and bunched the bloody rag under it so that he could speak.

"I'm proud to work for Mr. Darnell. You can go to hell for insulting him."

"But why are you proud? Because he hired you? Because you came from a pig farm and never thought you'd get a job on a real ranch? I understand those reasons, except that Darnell doesn't care a hoot if you live or die. I bet if someone entered his hotel room right now and said, 'Bad news. Dwight is dead,' your famous boss would say, 'Dwight who?'"

"He sure as hell *would* know!"

"Better yet, do you think Bone cares? They ragged on you about how I had humiliated you and how you must kill me or forever wear the insult. They did, didn't they?"

Dwight's face was red and inflated. His voice had stopped on him.

"I bet they said, 'If we are ever to have any respect for you, Dwight, you gotta go on that drive and kill that old fart.' And you know what they're doing ever since? Laughing. Even when they think I've probably killed you, they're still laughing."

Dwight was straining so hard he looked like a cow about to prolapse. His nosebleed was increasing rather than abating. He seemed also to be losing his urge to argue.

"I am an old waddie, Dwight. If you insist, I can fool you every day to Canada. But I have no desire to. I would rather we end it now. In fact, I demand it. Right here and now, out of sight and earshot of everybody, I demand we quit feuding. If you'll do that, I'll make you the further promise that no one will ever know how you and me negotiated peace."

Through this appeal and the silence after, Doc paid attention to the distance between his own hand and his gun. He was assuming this would end peacefully, based on the shape of Dwight's head, but he wanted to be prepared lest the head be nature's bluff.

Dwight took the bloody rag out from under his nose, looked at it, dabbed, and looked again. Then he said, "All right."

"All right to what?"

"All right, I'll quit trying to get even."

"Good. I'll shake your hand another day when it's not so gory."

Doc stood up and poked his gun back into his trousers. He reached and tore up some moss, which he held out to Dwight.

"What you do is take a wad of this and pack it in each nostril. Same thing Indian mommas use in the bottoms of the bags they carry their babies in."

Dwight took the moss. He was still looking at it in his meaty palm when Doc cornered into the deer trail and walked briskly toward the morning yellow.

DENVER

March 1867

PEARLY HAD THEIR MOVE to Denver's Mile High Hotel planned right down to the room she wanted. When they woke up the morning after Doc's phrenology lecture, they started prying up boards and pulling bags out of rain gutters. They were out of the preacher hotel and into the new one before noon.

When Doc saw the fancy lobby and their new suite—two rooms, big bed, fluffy pillows, couch, candy jar, half of Denver laid out below the big windows—he decided to go back to work.

They slept well in the giant bed, and during a leisurely breakfast of omelets, toast, bacon, and apple juice, Doc told Pearly he was headed over to the only saloon in town where he had found bowling lanes. He had peeked in there several times and the lanes were always dark. He reckoned he would have to offer an inducement to get them lit.

"If you bring business to an empty saloon, that's enough," said Pearly. "He should pay you commission on the drinks he sells."

Fine to talk that way, but Doc had to activate the bowling lanes in the Big Dollar Saloon just to practise. He wasn't about to start gambling until he was sure he could win.

The Big Dollar was silent at one in the afternoon when Doc entered. The only sign of life was dust swirling in a beam of light. He stood at the bar, then tapped on it with his fingernails, then cleared his throat. The surprise came when the proprietor reared up in front of him. He had been lying on his back behind the bar.

"What?" said the ghastly pale man from beneath a long twirled-and-waxed moustache. He was dark haired and the black stubble on him was a week deep. He had a lot of scar damage in both eyebrows. Doc also noticed a bald place about the size of a silver dollar that he had tried and failed to cover with hair. It probably meant someone had yanked out a fistful during a fight. It probably meant he was his own bouncer.

"A whisky please, if they're half a dollar."

"You usually tell bartenders what you'll pay?"

"No. But I have a dollar and I was hoping to buy two."

"Tell you what. Rather than lower my prices, I will sell you a whisky for a dollar, then I will give you a whisky in thanks for your custom."

So the bartender poured a stiff one, and it wasn't the worst whisky, though in truth Doc didn't like hard liquor so early in the day. They stood across from each other and made small talk. In the process, Doc saw a painting of a fat nude woman on the wall and some pages out of a clothing catalogue nailed up that showed women's legs. There was a jar on the bar with some awful-looking thing floating in green murk.

"What's in the jar?"

"A foot."

"Whose foot?"

"Belonged to the murderer Club Foot George, hanged in Virginia City in 1864."

"That so?"

"Damn right."

"Well, I'll be."

Doc tipped back his first whisky, and the barman poured his second as if to get the duty over. Doc had seen Club Foot George's foot in three bars now. Nor did he like parts of dead people as decoration. It was a dismal idea of entertainment.

Having broken the ice with talk of the hanged man's foot, Doc was able to draw attention to the bowling lanes.

"Nobody wants to bowl any more," said the barman. "I guess its day is done. I think I'll rip 'em up and use the space for something else. Maybe a boxing ring."

"Maybe you just have to have some kind of special night. Say, where a good bowler meets all comers for a fee? The good bowler could put up a hundred dollars. He'll pay that hundred to anyone who can best him in three frames. All they have to do to try their luck is pay five dollars. We could put up posters all over town and maybe send some on the stage to other towns and mining camps. Get a crowd in here and lots of drinking. There wouldn't be much risk for you in such a venture."

"Fine and good," said the ghastly bartender. "But where in hell am I going to find this good bowler with a hundred dollars?"

FOR MANY NIGHTS in the new hotel, Doc and Pearly made love on the big bed that bounced wonderfully and hardly made a sound. They were happy. Pearly would sit astride Doc, wearing only a necklace of tiny pearls her daddy had given her once long ago, and she would plunge down deep, then rear back and savour. She threw her loose hair side to side, laughed and growled, looked at him with love. They were going through Dr. Powers' French Preventatives, genuine oiled silk, at an alarming rate, but Pearly told him not to worry, even at five dollars a dozen.

Doc's mind no longer contained the dead man's destroyed head. It was full of Pearly, loving and naked, and of bowling, and of how Rufus was getting on with the other horses at the livery barn. When Doc and Pearly were told to leave the Travellers' Rest, Rufus was likewise thrown out of the temperance livery barn. He was better fed in the new place, but had conceived a dislike for a big war horse that he should have had more sense than to antagonize. The new liveryman said he had to go through all sorts of shenanigans just to get them to water without one kicking the hell out of the other.

During his days, Doc was either practising his bowling or drawing leaflets advertising his bowling tournament at the Big Dollar. He had

perfected a little silhouette of what a bowler looked like from the rear after releasing the ball, and he inked that silhouette in the middle of each
page. At the top he printed:

BOWL FOR $100
AT
THE BIG DOLLAR SALOON
DENVER
APRIL 1, 1867
6 PM

At the bottom, he wrote:

$5 entry fee buys three frames
your first whisky
and a chance to win the hundred.
all you have to do is score higher than the maestro

The owner and barman at the Big Dollar was named Napoleon.
The scars around his eyes were there because he used to fight profes-
sionally. He was very impressed with what Doc was putting together.
It had reignited his interest in business, and he kept saying, "Who
could resist? What fool could resist?" Doc sure hoped no fool could,
because if this scheme failed, he was broke.

Doc bought some paste that he slathered on the backs of his signs
just before he smacked them up. He put them on poles and walls, and
for some reason got a kick out of putting them on the boards that covered the windows and doors of businesses that had moved away.

He also sent some leaflets on the stagecoach that went west to
Golden City, Central City, and Black Hawk. They were considerable
towns in their own rights, and Doc hoped to lure some people down
to Denver.

Doc and Napoleon knew the bowling scheme was going to succeed when people started coming into the Big Dollar weeks before
tournament night to ask questions. You could tell which ones were go-

ing to play because they would buy time on the lanes. Naturally, they were also buying drinks and Napoleon was making money for the first time since New Year's. Grateful to Doc for reviving his business, he offered him all the whisky he could drink, but Doc explained that was a bad gift for a man trying to settle into hitting the sweet spot between pins one and three.

Doc said there was something Napoleon *could* do for him, and that was hire a pin setter. Doc and Napoleon had been sharing the duties, and it was not a good arrangement. For Doc to do it lessened his practise time and his prestige as the maestro of bowling. For Napoleon, it meant running back and forth from the bar to the pit and being late at both ends. In the end it was Doc who found a Negro teenager named Sam, who had been hungering around the streets. Doc trained Sam late at night after the saloon was closed, and once he had some food in him, Sam was a whiz, faster than Doc had ever been in Virginia City.

Doc kept trying to get Pearly to come over from the billiards saloon to watch him play and to see how much business he was generating for Napoleon, and maybe to make some suggestions about décor, for it was still a dismal bar and Napoleon didn't seem to have any ideas for making it better. Doc thought they should have some wooden horses and maybe some Indian trappings on the walls. Get rid of that damn foot. But he was no decorator either, which was why he urged Pearly, who had a good sense of such things.

But Pearly never did come. She was too busy making money. What had changed was that a rich man had walked down the hill from his fancy home to play, and now liked to play Pearly all the time. Along the path of promoting his tournament, Doc would drop in on the billiards saloon and so had met the man. He was tall and his hair was wavy black with lines of silver. He wore a suit of good cloth that fit him well, a suit that Pearly said he'd had made special for billiards. It had room built into the jacket and trousers and vest so that it never pulled too tight when making any of the bends or stretches that billiards shots demanded. His face was always clean shaven to a shine except for little silver half-sideburns and a moustache that was so short it looked drawn on with pencil. He was one of those high-headed men that the book on phrenology loved.

The rich man's name was Smith. That was his first name. Banks was his surname. Doc told Pearly it sounded like a fake name, which made her angry. "Just because you haven't heard of something doesn't make it fake. There's lots of names out there you haven't heard."

Doc was looking for ways to belittle Smith Banks, and Pearly saw it immediately. On the other hand, she couldn't see at all how Banks liked to whittle on Doc. He was excellently polite, the kind of man who comes up with a lit match the second your Bull Durham is rolled. He was forever pulling out chairs for Pearly. But Doc had a sense that Smith Banks was not nice or polite once you got past that surface. If he excused himself and stepped out of your way, the feeling was that you were in his way but not polite enough to notice. If he smiled at what you said, it wasn't because he thought you were funny, just that he was too polite not to respond to your effort.

One time when Doc visited the billiards saloon and Banks was there, he said, "Pearly, you and Doc play. You never get a chance to play each other," and then went and sat in a chair and cut a cigar. Pearly didn't want this to happen, and Doc knew it. Though Doc didn't even like billiards and was no good at it, some perversity made him insist they play. It was only when they were at it that it became obvious to Doc what he had fallen for. The point of course was for Smith Banks to watch how bad Doc was, and to have Pearly see Smith seeing it. Doc knew it for sure when Pearly said to Banks, "You should see Doc bowl."

Banks was excellent at billiards, and Pearly did not win even two out of three games against him. It was more like seven out of ten, and the stakes were always high. Pearly was making a lot more money off Smith Banks than off the rest of Denver. Even in the fancy hotel, she was saving money again. When Doc talked against Smith, Pearly scolded him, "I hate a jealous man, Doc. You don't own me. You don't even rent me. Smith is a gentleman who has not so much as touched my arm. You better ask yourself why you're so against him."

It was a stout rebuke and Pearly might have been right to deliver it, but what she didn't explain was why she and Doc weren't as happy any more in their big hotel room, or why she wasn't putting on the little pearls for him. It wasn't all to do with Doc's being jealous. It had to do with something inside Pearly, too.

THE BIG DOLLAR WAS nearing full on the nights leading up to the tournament. So many people wanted to practise their bowling that Doc had trouble finding a time when he could practise his. Mind you, he didn't need a lot. He was smacking down the strikes and converting the spares, and had even added a shot or two to what he had learned in Montana. His cutter was breaking sharp from either side, and if he had a blow-out, all but one pin, he could mow that pin down as if it were two feet away. He could do it fast and straight, or he could do it with a big lazy curve.

In the crowd that was practising, he singled out the players who were going to be a challenge. For a long time there was only one: a straight-throwing fellow from Ohio. But Doc also knew from the start he could beat this man because he didn't have enough *body English*. Even though he could bend and cut the ball, he did not do so with enough of his body to make real round bends and sharp cuts. He tended, on account of that, to split the pins.

Then, out of nowhere, just two days before the tournament, a New York City man walked in. Such was his skinny swagger and loudness, Doc hated him immediately, but also feared him. This was a real smarty-pants who thought he was in the wilderness, teaching the Indians how to bowl. Doc hated it most when he'd say, "Rats! A little too much on the Jersey side," as if the whole world circled New York like the sun. He chattered constantly, and in his mind had won Doc's hundred a hundred times. It could happen, too. Doc had not reckoned on a player this good and felt it might come down to the New Yorker's overconfidence doing battle with Doc's jealousy and hatred.

On the last day of March, the day before the bowling tournament, Pearly showed up for the first time at the Big Dollar. When Doc turned from bowling a strike, he saw her sitting at the table she'd identified as his by his upturned hat. His heart gave a jump to see her, but the word that came to mind was "uncomfortable." Pearly was uncomfortable. When he took her hand on the way to sitting down, it was damp and that too was unusual.

"You sick, Pearly?"

"I'm all right. Look, Doc, I know you'll be jealous, and I know the timing's bad, but Smith Banks wants me to come up to his house tomorrow night and play him there. He's got a real quality table, the no-pockets kind? You play for caroms, nothing else. Three-ball, like in England. He says we'll play a couple of games for nothing first, until I know how the table plays, and then we'll play a best of ten for any wager I name. He's never beat me in a best of ten. I don't think he can."

Something explosive was rising in Doc and he didn't want Pearly to see it. He folded his bottom lip in between his teeth and bit. He knew that Pearly was not here to ask permission. He knew she was just telling him where she was going to be.

"Smith isn't one of the crazy kind. I don't exactly know what it is with him, but it's not that. He says his wife, Noella, will be at the house. I'll take my gun anyway."

Doc stayed quiet. He had only one question, and it was easier to keep it swallowed when there was just the one.

"You trust me, don't you?" Pearly asked.

Doc nodded.

"I'll see you later then." She kissed his cheek and pressed his hand. If Doc was worried by any of this, he was most worried by that ending. Pearly hated public kissing.

ON THE NIGHT OF THE TOURNAMENT, Pearly insisted on coming with Doc to the Big Dollar. First they had a small supper at their hotel, and most of Doc's food stayed on his plate. He had no appetite and wouldn't drink even a glass of wine for fear of upsetting any aspect of his balance. Then Pearly got her pool cue from the room, and they walked the short distance to the saloon. It was a warm night, with the air smelling both good and bad from things melting and other things rotting. Water streamed off the mountains and bubbled in the gutters. The saloon was brightly lit inside, the only building on the block showing any light, and when they were close enough, they saw the heads and hats of many patrons in the windows. The door to the outside was open and exhaling smoke.

Napoleon had hired extra help at the bar, a man named Jack Hill, imported for the night from the Chicago Saloon in Golden City. The proprietor there, Colonel Parker B. Cheney, was a mock-rival and friend of Napoleon's who had shut down for the night to come watch the bowling. Hill was a brilliant drink mixer, working very fast and with a lot of flashing and twirling of glasses and bottles. He was said to have invented many cocktails that had gone on to be served in bars all over the country.

Leaving Hill to it, Napoleon came and got Doc and Pearly at the door and escorted them to their reserved table near the head of the first lane.

As the number of people expressing interest in this tournament had risen, Doc and Napoleon had added new rules. First of all, to get through the list, they estimated that Doc would need to play on both lanes at once. Doc would play one game a frame ahead of the other so that if someone did beat him, the other person playing would get his five dollars back. A more likely possibility was that games would be tied after three frames. The rule here was to play another frame, and if necessary, another, until there was a winner.

At the table, Napoleon gave Doc the list of people who had signed up. It ran down the whole left side of the page, started back at the top, and went down again. There were over forty players listed and more lining up. Doc looked for only one thing and that was the New Yorker, whose name was Jackie. There was only one Jackie, and he was slated to play eleventh. Doc did the figuring in his head. If he couldn't get by the New Yorker, he would lose fifty dollars, and thirty or more people would be mad they didn't get to play. It was possible there were other ringers in the crowd, but Doc doubted it. He guessed it was him and Jackie, winner take all.

Because there was still a lineup to pay entry money and get drinks at six o'clock, that starting time came and went. When Napoleon felt he finally could begin, it was past six-thirty. The pale bartender yelled for silence and then gave a speech. He talked about fair play and hoping everyone had a good time, win or lose. He said he would tolerate no shooting in the saloon no matter how exciting things got. If anybody felt they had to fire a gun, go outside, because that's where they would wind up anyway. He thanked Jack Hill for coming from Golden City, and if anyone felt they weren't getting their drinks fast enough, they could go to hell because Jack Hill was the fastest pourer and best maker of drinks in all the Colorado Mountains.

It was very close to seven when the first challenger began to roll and everything else about the night went silent for Doc. He bowled like a Swiss clock ticks, and in very rapid order set down the challengers. In each set of three frames, Doc threw at least one strike. When he didn't make a strike, he converted the spare in solid fashion. He never split the pins once against the first ten challengers.

Jackie, the New Yorker, had begun getting vocal from the sidelines. "Clean game, clean game!" he yelled, meaning that Doc was cleaning up every pin. It was mock encouragement, obviously. The other players he harassed for their mistakes. If they rolled a gutter ball, Jackie called it a poodle. If they made a split, he had a name for every kind.

"Bed posts! Christmas tree! Snake eyes! Ooh, the big ears!"

There probably wasn't a person in the room who didn't want this Jackie to shut up.

It was bad fate that Pearly's time to go coincided with Doc's time to play the New Yorker. Just as Jackie was going to the line and hefting a ball into his hand, she pulled her watch out of her skirt and read it. She turned to Doc with a forlorn look. Doc asked her to stay just until he had played Jackie. When she nodded, Doc asked the question he had been holding back for weeks, since not long after Smith Banks had come down the hill and into their lives.

"He knows about the prospector I killed in Cheyenne, doesn't he?"

Pearly's face lost colour. She sat down and stared at the floor between her feet. "He says he'll keep our secret," she said.

"I wonder why," said Doc, "since he went to so much trouble to find it out." Smiling in a humourless way, Doc continued. "Tell you what, Pearly. This New Yorker? This Jackie? I'll bet you more than a purse of a hundred dollars he's another gift from Mr. Smith Banks."

Pearly shook her head slowly as if her neck had stiffened.

"What about it, Pearly? Does he look like a prospector to you?"

The New Yorker stood at the line, twisting his neck to look at Doc. "Com'mon, com'mon, Maestro. Don't keep us waiting."

"It's your turn," said Doc, falsely calm, "not mine."

"Don't worry about being late for Banks," Doc added, near Pearly's ear. The New Yorker rolled a strike and did a dance. "That's his buggy driver by the door."

After three frames, the New Yorker and Doc had bowled six straight strikes and were tied. The room, so loud a moment ago, was silent. Napoleon came to the head of the lanes and reminded everyone how ties were to be resolved. After that, Jackie missed his strike but converted the spare.

"Logs!" he screamed. "They never told me I'd have to bowl at logs!"

"And who would *they* be, Jackie?" asked Doc as he passed him.

"Mind your own business, Maestro."

"I am."

Then Doc missed the pocket, as Jackie had just done, but left a more difficult 3-7-10 split.

"Christmas tree! Bad luck!" shrieked Jackie, as Doc knew he would, and that was motive enough to make a fine shot, with lots of back-up and action, that spilled the pins and kept it tied.

Then Jackie threw another strike and Doc went to the line and waited for Sam to set the pins back up. They were playing on one lane at Jackie's request. Doc looked toward Pearly, and before her was Smith's buggy driver, respectfully bowed and earnestly talking. Doc stepped to the line and missed the pocket again. Two pins stayed standing. It was over.

There was pandemonium in the room. Jackie came to Doc and insisted on a big showy shaking of hands. He kept calling him Maestro. "Nice game, Maestro." "Nice run, Maestro." Jackie danced around and then he turned to the second lane and threw another strike and danced some more.

The hatred for Jackie in the room was powerful. But there was also anger at Doc, because he wasn't supposed to lose, not so soon anyway. Many had come from other towns, and now, within half an hour of the first ball bowled, it was over. They were waiting for their chance at the hundred, and they would have to go home without it.

Then Doc saw Pearly squeeze through the crowd. She didn't come to him, but to Napoleon. She reached for his shoulder and drew him down. She spoke in his ear and reached in her purse and pulled something out, which she handed him. With his bull voice, Napoleon roared the crowd quiet and held up a small but heavy bag. He shook it so they could hear the jingle of money.

"In this bag is another hundred dollar purse in gold coins. The lady here is putting up this purse on behalf of Mr. Doc Windham, so he can give you another chance to win."

There were roars of approval and applause, but then Jackie was there, dancing around, grabbing their attention in a shrieking voice. "Oh no! No, no, no! I remind you that the Maestro here is the former Maestro! If anybody is to put up another purse, it should be me. Mr. Maestro Windham can go to the end of the line and pay his five dollars like anyone else."

The crowd made various kinds of noise, not all against what Jackie said. It did make primitive sense. Those still on the list waiting to challenge probably did not care who they played. Why not this obnoxious little man from the East, who was so easy to hate?

Napoleon yelled them silent again and said there was nothing in the rules about a winner taking over. Doc Windham had created this event from scratch, and as far as Napoleon was concerned, he still called the shots. But then Pearly signalled that she wanted to speak.

"I'll tell you what Doc and I are offering," she said, "and it's probably more than this gentleman deserves." She waved a hand at Jackie. "For the right to continue to play you all, Doc will play Jackie again, for another hundred dollars. If Jackie wins, Doc goes home. If Doc wins, Jackie goes—all the way back to New York, I guess—and the rest of you can take your shot at the money after that."

The crowd was wild for this, and no one, not even Jackie, would speak against it. He came to Doc, nodded at the lane, and said, "You're the challenger this time, Maestro."

Doc stood face to face with Pearly, leaning down and putting a little grease on the sides of his fingers where they had begun to blister from so much bowling. "I don't think I can beat him, Pearly," he whispered.

"Then don't think," she said and kissed his cheek. She walked out through the crowd with the well-dressed buggy driver in tow.

AFTER MIDNIGHT, it was still warm enough to melt snow. The bottom was going out of Denver. Where the boardwalks ended, Doc's boots slurped in the mud and he could feel his trouser cuffs dragging. He walked up the long slope until he was among the biggest houses, aiming himself at the only one with a lamp burning on its porch. Doc struck the knocker three times, counted five, struck it again, and kept it up until a black man in a frilly white shirt answered.

"I'm Windham."

"I know who you are," said the butler. He looked down at Doc's muddy feet, his muddy cuffs, and sighed. He turned and led the way.

Doc followed the butler along a hall to a set of stairs leading down. The house was built on a slope and the flight of stairs brought them to ground level again. Through a bunch of windows on the lower side, Doc saw skeletal bushes and trees and the fires of the town beyond. They passed through a couple of rooms decorated with animal heads.

The door into the billiards room was open and the table was bright under a pair of hanging lamps. There was mother-of-pearl inlay on the hardwood rails and two cues were lying with their chalk ends together on the felt. Pearly and Banks were sitting in armchairs beyond the table, each with a round-bellied glass in hand and some wood-coloured liquor in its base. Between them was a round table on which stood a cut-glass decanter. Banks was smoking a cigar and so was Pearly.

Banks rose and took a step toward Doc. The black servant made some racket to which they both turned. He was stooped at a little door in a side wall, pulling out a whisk and dustpan. He started sweeping up Doc's mud and continued down the back trail to the stairs.

"Bring another snifter," Smith called after him.

Banks gestured at a third armchair beyond Pearly's, but Doc said he preferred to stand. Banks was all smiles, as if having the three of them together like this was his fondest wish.

"Where's your wife?" asked Doc.

Banks's smile cooled. "She doesn't like to come down here because I smoke. But we have all had recent adventures, haven't we?" he said, brightening. "Why don't we talk about them? Pearly here has given me another expensive lesson in the art of billiards, on my own table no less. The last of my excuses is gone. And you, Doc, how did you fare?"

Doc walked to the end of the billiards table. He started pulling coins from his pockets and spilling them on the green. His trouser pockets were round with half eagles and folding money and they took some time to empty. Next came the bag of Pearly's golden eagles and his own hundred dollars, in a mixture of currency. He was like a magician pulling scarves.

Banks smiled tolerantly. "Impressive," he said.

"I expect tonight cost you more," Doc replied.

"As a matter of fact, it did, didn't it, Pearly?" He looked at Pearly, and he patted her hand on the round table, even as it was withdrawing from him.

"I meant how much it must have cost to get Jackie here from New York."

"I have no idea what you're talking about. Ah, here's your snifter."

The servant had another big-bellied glass. He was carrying a little silver device that resembled an upside-down spur on a stand. On the base was a stub of candle, which he lit. He poured brown liquor from the decanter into the glass, set it in the ankle part of the spur. He turned it every few seconds, then presented it, warm and strong-smelling, to Doc.

Doc sniffed in the big glass as he had seen some men do. He hated the smell and set it back down. He pulled a piece of folded paper from his vest pocket and dropped it on the table.

"I guess you want me to ask what that is," Banks said around his cigar.

Doc reached and unfolded it, smoothed it. It was a small page, the kind that people with desks keep handy for messages. It had some scribbled words and numbers in black ink. It was gratifying to see a change on Bank's face. A look of slight fatigue, as though an amusement had gone sour.

"I don't know what it is, but I'm sure you're dying to tell us."

"It's the note Jackie got when he came off the stagecoach. Telling him what hotel to go to."

"Proving what?"

"It was given to him by your buggy driver, same one brought Pearly here tonight. I think those are your initials printed in the corner. I expect if we go find your desk, there'll be more of this paper."

"I suppose, being such a gentleman, you acquired it at gunpoint?"

Doc blushed.

"You didn't kill him, I hope."

"I beat your Jackie at bowling fair and square. It was exciting for everyone because it took five frames after the first three to break the tie. In the last frame, I went first and got a spare, meaning that I put the pins down in two shots. When Jackie rolled, he got a bad split that he could not convert. One pin was left standing. It teetered but would not fall."

Banks covered a yawn. "Maybe you wouldn't mind cleaning your mess off my table. I would like to go to bed. It's late."

Doc started pouring the coins back into his pockets. He gave Pearly her bag of golden eagles. Banks stood with his back to Doc, yawned again, and stretched.

"Well, well, Pearly. I hope we can do this again."

Pearly would not meet his eye. She looked afraid, and Doc hated seeing her that way.

"You got nothing to say to me then?" Doc asked Banks's back. "About how much effort and money you put into trying to make me lose? I wouldn't mind knowing why it was so important to you."

Banks turned his head, but only slightly, so Doc could see a little of his profile, the edge of one eye socket.

"What is your grievance, Mr. Windham? Has any law been broken? Except by you when you held a gun to some poor man's head? One more event in your increasingly violent career. You should be careful. Someone might tell the local vigilance committee about you. Keeping track of dangerous people is a frontier community's only defence."

He turned a bit more.

"If your point is that I wasted my money, I don't think I did. It's been worth it to see you come in here and try to impress me with a little pile of coins and watch you put on such a display of rudeness as a guest in my house."

Banks was still talking when Pearly got up out of her chair, took her coat off the stand, and left. Banks turned in the direction of her departure, took a step, and stopped. Then he and Doc shared a look that could have been an exchange of hatred but was not. What they recognized on each other's face was the pain, the worry, the loss, of love. They were mute, because there was no point in anything said or done between them if Pearly was not there to see it.

MULLAN WAGON ROAD

August 1881

THE DAY DOC AND DWIGHT MADE peace in the pines, Dwight came to Doc toward evening and asked if he would help him become a better cowboy. Dwight looked so hopeful Doc did not refuse. Before they slept that night, Doc suggested to Lowell that he let Dwight ride right flank.

"I prefer to fire the big idiot."

Lowell's assumption had been that Doc intended to either kill or maim Dwight. That they had made peace disappointed him. Doc countered with some heat that he had not gone to so much effort only to see Dwight sent away. His investment could realize profit only if the boy stayed and became something.

The following morning, Doc woke up missing the verve he'd felt every day since Helena. Something sullen was in its place. He felt bad-tempered toward the world. All that day, he pretended otherwise, in case his pepperiness returned next day. But on the second morning, he was even more out of sorts. It looked as if the energetic days had been the exception, brought on by the novelty of staring Overcross in the eye, and that this bad temper was a condition more likely to last.

Feeling as Doc now did, the idea of teaching Dwight to ride was hellish. When the big boy reminded him of the offer, and he did so every day, Doc put him off. He claimed to be sick, and it was almost true in that the thought of teaching Dwight to ride filled him with lethargy.

People imagined that cowboys were all natural saddle adepts, but that was far from true. Some, like Lippy, felt everything a horse did and balanced accordingly. Lippy rode like an intelligent burr. Dog Eye had similar athletic gifts but wasn't as good, because he never cared much about his mount. As a result, he and the horse were creatures going the same direction more than partners. Still, from the Olympian heights of Lippy and Dog Eye to the paddling depths of Dwight was a distance immeasurable.

In his mind, Doc could easily see Dwight hauling buckets of slop to pigs in some fenced-over part of the Union. Chances were he had come to horses late, long after riding seemed a normal thing to do. Size was also important, and big size was not the asset simple people thought it must be for every western activity. For starters, a big man often thought he could out-muscle a horse, which made no sense. Just about any horse could put his hoof in the ass of just about any man, and wear him like a slipper.

The other thing about size was balance. Once when Doc was a boy and whining to Uncle Jack about being small, Jack had taken two chunks of firewood and placed their flat ends on a hitching rail. One was half a foot taller than the other. He told Doc to take his pointer finger and tap one and then the other as light as he could, then gradually harder until one fell. Of course the taller chunk fell first. Then Jack told Doc to keep tapping the shorter chunk. He had to give it quite a poke before it dropped.

"There!" said Uncle Jack.

"There what?"

"You're the short wood, boy. Be thankful."

Dwight was the tall wood and ever in danger of falling off his horse. He was worse than many tall men because of how much of his height was above the legs. He compounded the problem by riding small horses, thinking that would help. His technique for staying on in a blow-up was to drive his big Mexican spurs into the strands of the cincho and cling like a baby possum in the hair of its mother.

Doc was thinking these thoughts in the afternoon as he rode down the mile of herd looking for Dwight. The herd had been on the road for five hours and a strong wind was combing them from the northwest. That meant the dust and stink were pouring onto Dwight's flank position. He finally appeared out of a yellow fog, squinting under eyebrows shaggy with dust and trying to fend off blowing grit with his hand.

"Why isn't your wiper over your face?" Doc asked him when they got close. Unable to answer in words, Dwight hauled a bloody rag from his ass pocket, the same one he had used to staunch his nose.

"Put it on. Either that or you'll cough black for a month. This dust'll enrage your lungs, cause pneumonia."

Dwight did as he was told, looking even stupider than he imagined. After riding together on the flank for half an hour, Doc said they would leave the post unmanned. They found Lippy in the drag with his dusty red silk over his face. Doc asked him to keep an eye on the right flank, and Lippy made no show of surprise that Doc and Dwight were going somewhere as partners, rather than circling each other like poisonous foes.

After the last of the cattle had passed, they sat their mounts, ass to the wind, and waited for Jim Adams and the calf wagon. When the wagon showed up, containing two lamers and a dogey, Adams returned Doc's hello but that was all. Finally, with the passing of the calf wagon, they were alone and Dwight's lesson could begin. The student was bright and eager, imagining a whole new life for himself as a top hand.

"You ride like a sack of shit," Doc told him, and the boy recoiled as if slapped. "No, that's not quite right. Not a sack of shit. More like two sacks of shit tied together in the middle."

They walked their horses for awhile in the distant wake of the herd. Doc began by giving his philosophy of the horse, a subject he normally warmed to. Today's bad mood made it come out angry. He said the part about the hoof in the ass and the slipper and how no horse could be made to do anything. Men should thank God every day for the oddity of personality that made horses allow humans to ride them. Otherwise, people would be nothing more than muckers and snarers, a race without dignity, afraid of every howl in the woods.

Then he went to the issue of size, telling Dwight he must start picking horses that fit him and stop torturing ones like the little pinto who was today's victim.

"You will think I'm a hypocrite, perched here on Louie, but Louie is a special case, a fine horse, and I can't help myself. Besides, riding too small a horse is the greater sin."

Doc slid off Louie. He hated to do it. He felt angry at Dwight for causing it and disloyal to Louie, but it had to be.

"Take Louie and give me yours. What's his name?"

"Don't have one."

"Horse has to have a name. Otherwise he don't know who you're talking to. Little horse, your name is Patches."

Dwight got off the pinto and approached Louie head-on. As he got close, he raised his hand to the gelding's nose. Louie snorted and danced back.

"Castrated mule, Dwight! If you can't imagine what it feels like to be a horse, try being human. Here comes a complete stranger. And he's a big bastard. He doesn't say a word, just reaches for your face. You're lucky Louie's a gentleman and walked away."

"I was going to pet his nose."

"In case you haven't noticed, Dwight, a horse's eyes are on the sides of his head. You marched at Louie from the front where he sees least well, and you didn't even talk. You want a horse to like you, talk to him. And mean what you say. Don't just babble. When you talk, the horse knows where you are and can make up its mind if you are civilized. As for petting, why assume Louie wants to be petted? He's not a dog."

Dwight was looking depressed about his chances as a cowboy. Doc felt that much was an accomplishment.

When it came time to mount, Dwight of course did it all wrong. He raised his boot at the stirrup from the side as if to kick the horse in the ribs. He hauled on the saddle horn so that the well-cinched saddle pulled down. He flipped the stirrup over the horn, ready to yank the cinch tighter.

"You tighten that cinch any more and Louie's going to kick you in the slats."

Doc demonstrated mounting with your shoulder to the side of the horse, so the weight goes up and down and doesn't lever. Finally both men were mounted. Little Patches, with Doc aboard, looked like he'd died and gone to heaven.

"Another thing. Don't touch my horse with those Chihuahua spurs."

As they rode along, Doc saw Louie was surging and Dwight was hauling back on him.

"Dwight, get off that horse's mouth. You're not landing a sturgeon, you're telling a smart animal where you want to go."

"He keeps trying to run. And I haven't spurred him once."

"You're squeezing the shit out of him with your legs. That says, 'Go!' So he goes. Then you haul back on his mouth, and that says 'Stop!' and he stops. I can't believe that saint of a horse isn't throwing you into the nearest prickly pear."

Dwight was looking sorrier still, but Doc noted with satisfaction that he now held the reins with some respect.

With the sun straight above and the herd stretched long where the trail narrowed to go around a mountain, Doc led Dwight down a trail through the rocks to the Dearborn River. Doc got off and slacked the cinch. He nodded for Dwight to do the same on Louie.

Doc dug a couple of biscuits and a few inches of jerky out of the saddlebag and gave Dwight half. They sat among the rocks and chewed in silence. Then Doc felt sleepy and lay back with his hat over his face.

"You think he likes me?" asked Dwight.

"Who?"

"Louie."

"Hell no!"

"You sure are grouchy."

"Yes I am. I don't apologize either."

"Just wonder why you bother."

"Bother how?"

"With me."

Still within the fragrant darkness of his hat, Doc said, "That's two different things. I am in a poor mood for reasons that have nothing to do with you. That's one thing. The other is why I decided to give you a chance to be an actual cowboy, instead of killing you. Because the two things are going on at the same time, I'm grouchy while I teach you."

"But why did you want to teach me?"

Doc yanked the hat off his face and sat up. "God *damn*, you're irritating."

Nothing further was said until they were tightening the cinches again and preparing to ride. The last of the cattle were disappearing around the mountain's corner, and it was time to rejoin them. Doc couldn't bear Dwight riding Louie any more, so they swapped back.

"I'll tell you the truth, Dwight, but it won't make any sense to you. I decided to help because of the shape of your head."

Dwight erupted laughing. Poor Patches almost jumped in the river.

"I'm not being funny. If you had bulges over your ears, you might be dead."

Dwight kept laughing, and Doc didn't have the patience for it. He pounced on Louie from a rock and trotted him away. Dwight was laughing still, and hopping on one foot, trying to poke the other into the stirrup, exactly like he'd been told not to. Patches, assuming the big man had gone mad, was doing his best to get away.

GOLDEN CITY

April 1867

THE NIGHT AFTER THE BOWLING tournament and the confrontation in Smith Banks's poolroom, Doc knew he was not welcome in Pearly's bed. He slept on the hotel room's sofa, and when he awoke in the early light, Pearly was packing their gear.

Since coming to Denver, Pearly had sold their tent and used the proceeds to buy a trunk. It stood in the middle of the floor with its lid open, and over its edges hung the hems of her dresses and the legs and arms of Doc's suit. Doc swung to a sitting position and watched as she got a chair and set it in the closet's open door. She climbed up and reached to a cubby where the bag of golden eagles was hidden. In a rare case of trust, she had placed the rest of her savings in the hotel safe.

The best thing Doc could see in the situation was that Pearly was packing his clothes along with her own.

"Where to?"

"Golden City."

Later that morning, Doc hoisted the trunk to the roof of the Wells Fargo stagecoach. A man on top grabbed its leather handles, hauled it up, and roped it down. Pearly climbed inside and Doc walked Rufus away a dozen yards to mount. Every motion was rusty, now that he was a bowler instead of a cowboy. The stage driver yelled at his team and whipped the reins on their backs. The coach jerked forward.

The road to Golden City was deeply rutted but the stage driver paid little mind. He drove wildly, and once, when a front wheel hit a rock, the whole coach rose on that side. Two unsecured bags fell from the top, and by that margin of weight, the coach fell back on four wheels again. Doc followed behind, often having to gallop Rufus to keep the stage in sight.

They rolled onto Golden City's short main street just before dark. The hitching rails were full and the street was alive with horses and wagons. There were quite a few people walking along the boardwalks. It was a smaller town than Doc had seen in a while.

Parker B. Cheney and Jack Hill were on the stagecoach with Pearly, returning to their saloon in Golden City after the bowling tournament. As a result, by the time Pearly stepped down, she had the whole town reconnoitred. She told Doc they were staying in a room above Cheney's Chicago Saloon, and that the billiards table there would be her base of operations. When Doc asked about bowling, she said there was none. She didn't seem to think it mattered, as if billiards was the real importance in their lives and bowling a frill. Even if that were true, she should have pretended otherwise.

There were hammers thumping in the twilight, most of the sound coming from next door where a hotel called the Overland was rising. Pearly said they would move there as soon as it was open.

Their room above the Chicago Saloon was comically small compared to the splendour of mere hours ago. When Pearly sat on the bed, it gave so far it nearly struck the floor. It missed mashing the chamber pot only because that china vessel with its cherub rim was tucked under the frame at the head of the bed. The bug itself did not smell clean. There wasn't even a chair to put things on, and the only place for the trunk was on its end behind the door.

Pearly was talking and Doc hardly listened once he knew it was about billiards: who played here, and how well, according to Cheney and Hill. All Doc wanted was a sign that things between them were all right. Pearly's all-business tone said everything was not all right, and that they would proceed on that basis until further notice.

THE CHICAGO SALOON had a long bar across its back wall with the billiards table centred in the open space between it and the door. Doc was now used to the quietude of the billiards saloon in Denver, and the population and wild hilarity of this bar shocked him, and perhaps Pearly, too, though she wasn't saying. At the long bar, rough and dirty prospectors stood shoulder to shoulder with suited politicians fresh from deciding matters in the Colorado territorial legislature next door. Parker B. Cheney's rule was that no territorial representative would pay for his own liquor in the Chicago Saloon, at least as long as snobby Denver was trying to steal the capital away. Doc and Pearly soon learned to talk of Denver as a hellhole and a den of hypocrites from which they were glad to have escaped.

Jack Hill was a one-man marvel of promotion, and Colonel Cheney let him run. Their first night in the saloon, Doc and Pearly were left sitting in bewilderment when Hill grabbed a bugle off a nail and let go a single sustained blast. Everyone but them surged to the bar with their glasses held out, for it was a Jack Hill tradition that the sounding of the bugle meant everyone drank free for exactly three minutes.

Hill made an outstanding array of drinks. Whisky cocktails, gin cocktails, hen-fruit cocktails, Cheney's punch, brandy punch, whisky punch, eureka punch, Roman punch, lemon flip, mint julep, gin sling. Many of his drinks were international in nature: *Chau de Goff, Pus ca Faix a la Franco Espaniola, Eau de Vie, Quien Sabe*. What's more, there was ice cream, not every day, but on weekends, when Hill's wife would turn the handle until cream and ice fused. Once made, the ice cream created a whole new set of cocktail possibilities, such as champagne à la mode and whisky ice cream. It was a well-provisioned establishment, with apples, strawberries, and a host of cigars available on most days.

Doc found the drinks and the ice cream much to his taste. While Pearly shot billiards and made money, Doc made it his business to sample every cocktail in Hill's vast repertoire.

Pearly was still not talking to Doc much, so when she came up to him on the third night, as he sipped a whisky punch, it was an occasion.

"You have decided to become a drunk, then."

Doc was offended. "That's not it at all. I like how they taste. You should try one."

"I'm working," she said, in a tone that meant he wasn't and someone had to.

Doc explained that what appeared to be inebriation was research toward the opening of their own saloon, *Doc and Pearly's*, with both bowling lanes and billiards tables, as well as ice cream and all these fine cocktails. Doc was memorizing the ingredients and measurements as he drank his way along.

Pearly scratched chalk onto the tip of her cue and looked on him without favour. "Why is it every time a man dreams up a business, it's a saloon?"

Then a fellow called for her to come take her shot and she was gone, making caroms, nursing caroms, shooting in and in-off, destroying her competition. Doc didn't even bother to watch any more, so complete she seemed without him. He used to watch every man's eyes, whether they were playing or watching from the sidelines, looking for the expression that went beyond lust to some insane ambition. But now Doc lacked the feeling that he could help her much. Instead, he waved at Hill and called for a lemon flip.

In their bed at night, Doc did nothing. In a bed so small and deeply swaled, it was acrobatic how they managed not to touch, beyond the simple kiss that Pearly bestowed on his forehead, saying, "'Night." Later, as he fell off the cliff into unconsciousness, Pearly told him not to snore, which he was doing more than usual on account of drinking. Because Doc really could not drink, every second day was given over to recovery in this dark room, with his head aching to one side and spots wheeling biliously in front of his eyes.

About a week into their stay at Golden City, Pearly was practising in the afternoon while Doc dealt with the aftershocks of his latest hangover and thought about what cocktail to choose first if he was able to begin again. Pearly came to him along the empty bar.

"You're a gambler," she said. "Why don't you do some? By my calculation, I'll be paying for your drinks inside a week."

Doc stayed silent, feeling wronged. For one thing, he had not nearly run through all the money he'd won in Denver. And how could he gamble here, a bowler in a town with no bowling alley? He began to worry that Pearly's plan was to send him away to another town while she remained here.

"What kind of gambling do you do?"

It took Doc a moment to understand the question was for him. It was Jack Hill asking, as he twisted a towel in a glass.

"Bowling. I bowl and gamble if I can find takers."

Hill looked up and down his bar and through the door at the street. The only customer besides Doc and the man Pearly was playing was a prospector, silently drunk, whose long red beard squatted on the mahogany. Hill took a whisky bottle, poured the man's glass full, then beckoned Doc to follow. They walked out of the bar into sunlight.

Along the blazing tan of main street, they continued until they came to a glowering building. Hill led Doc around to the back, where by parting through sagebrush and thistle, he entered a long strip of flat. He nodded beyond a swathe of thistle to where there were two more flats like it. It took a hazy minute for Doc to recognize the familiar measure and for his mind to intone the sound of ball on pin. Bowling lanes in their most elemental form.

"I have an interest, you might say, in this property," said Hill, "which I would appreciate you kept quiet about."

Then he led Doc to the back door, from which he pulled a cross of nailed boards. He produced a key from his waistcoat and twisted back the bolt. The door scraped open, and they walked in through the dense handiwork of spiders and over a floor scrunching with dead flies. A second key opened a large closet piled high with the stored valuables of the saloon. Shifting aside some chairs, Jack uncovered two sets of bowling pins and several bowling balls.

"I own these materials, so I have the authority to tell you to help yourself. Thing is, I might start a saloon of my own here, and Colonel Cheney would be unhappy to hear that. He might not continue to employee me, which would interfere with my savings plan. It would be better for me if you acted as though you found these things on your own and decided to borrow them."

Doc thanked Hill and asked him why he was being so generous.

"You and Pearly are a nice couple," said the barman. "You are having troubles. I thought this might help."

When Doc recovered from his latest headache, it was two days later. He found a broom in the closet of the boarded-up saloon and began sweeping tumbleweed and other clutter off the outdoor lanes. Then he repaired the divots caused by horses' hooves. He used a long board to test the lanes and was amazed at their trueness.

After cleaning and repairing two of the lanes, Doc spent a day practising. He despaired at how the spinning ball would not grab this clay surface and how the ball jittered on the tiny imperfections and hopped untrue for no seeming reason. Often the wind blew gusts of sand in his face and a really bold gust could change the motion of the ball, causing the tiny margin between a strike and a mess. Doc was not sure he could win anything here. He might even lose money and sink lower in Pearly's estimations. Though he was low as a squirrel already, he reckoned there was a place lower still, a place without Pearly, where the loneliness would be fathomless. If he didn't risk going there, he would go there for sure.

As Doc continued to practise, little groups of wastrels and bummers gathered to watch. Some Indians in town for the day came over and sat looking for some time. They had Pearly's reaction to bowling and laughed a good deal. After dark shut him down, Doc went to the Chicago Saloon and sat in a far corner writing leaflets that announced the return of bowling to Golden City. At their centre was the little silhouette of the bowler. He called his lanes the Golden Bowl and invited all to come play for fifty cents a game. Should they wish to wager, Doc Windham, resident bowler, would agree to any reasonable contest. Drinks were available at regular prices down the street in the Chicago Saloon.

Doc sent a message to Napoleon on the Wells Fargo stage. If the bowling lanes were quiet at the Big Dollar, and Napoleon could spare him, and Sam was willing, Doc could sure use some help in Golden City. Sam arrived two days later. After paying his fare, Doc took him to the Golden Bowl. Doc had dug the blown sand out of the trench at the pit end of the two lanes. He had erected a frame and bought a canvas to stop the balls and flying pins. As building materials were scarce, he'd stopped there.

Together, they cut down more thistles and giant sage, denuding a span in front of the lanes where they arranged tables and chairs from the closed saloon. Doc found a mop with which he removed the dust from the tabletops. On a normal day, it took about five minutes for them to cloud up again.

Although it was never the success the tournament in Denver had been, the Golden Bowl did a steady business. Several people worked it into their routine of activities, most not wishing to gamble but just to play. That paid Sam's wages. Every day or two a prospector would descend from the hills with a poke of gold. After getting drunk and visiting the whores, playing cards and getting beat by Pearly at billiards, he would show up at the Golden Bowl. The ones with prior bowling experience would arrive sooner and want to gamble. Some who'd never played believed they were naturals and insisted on playing for money too. This constituted Doc's wage, which, given that Jack Hill considered his money no good any more at the Chicago Saloon, meant Doc was paying his way and collecting a little extra. He would not become a weight on Pearly's purse.

From the time Doc had begun to fix up and advertise the Golden

Bowl, he had been a man restored to his former energy. He worked long hours, never thinking of anything else. He was not happy, but he was occupied, which if you aren't aspiring to be happy, is about as good.

But when it was all done and there wasn't much to do in the quiet hours but sit under his hat and occasionally wipe a table, Doc went back to planning his saloon. He was drinking again, and engraving the cocktail list of the Chicago Saloon on his brain through the rote learning of his tongue. Sam insisted on getting these drinks, and Doc's gesture in the direction of responsibility was to ask the boy to come back able to recite the ingredients. In this way, Doc was not only preparing himself for his own saloon, he was training his future barman.

The Overland Hotel opened in June and Pearly moved into it as planned. Two nights before that move, Doc had been climbing into the terrible bed when Pearly told him he was fat and a drunk. For that reason, Doc decided not to move with her. He stayed in the small room above the Chicago Saloon bar, and some nights after darkness had closed the Golden Bowl, and after he had sampled a great many cocktails, he slept on his back in the ruined bed without even removing his boots.

It was around then that he began to collect empty bottles from the Chicago Saloon. He set them in the arms of giant sagebrush and shot them to bits with his cap-and-ball Colt Dragoon. While Sam ran out and shook glass shards off the brush and set up the next groups of targets, Doc recharged the chambers with the gun's ramrod: forty-four grains of black powder, forty-four calibre slugs.

"Don't you want to quicken your draw?" asked Sam, after Doc had become adept at shooting from the sitting position.

"No, I do not. If I come up against a quick-draw man, I guess I'll just die."

"Are you sure somebody's after you?"

"A man disappointed in love holds me to blame. He wants me dead and out of the way."

"Who?"

"Don't matter who. Won't be him coming."

WHAT BROKE THE LOG-JAM between Doc and Pearly was a note delivered to Pearly's hotel. It was a message for Doc, and maybe it was sent to Pearly by mistake, maybe not. It came in the morning before anyone was awake and Pearly brought it to Doc's room in the Chicago Saloon that night. She had held the message so long, read it so often, it was soft with the moisture of her worry.

> *Windham. Leave Golden City. This peaceful town will not*
> *tolerate lawlessness of your kind.*

There was no room to pace, and while Doc lay in the U-shaped bed, Pearly stood. Her hand was balled in a fist pushed against her lips. Doc watched and was filled with love and admiration.

They had been all over what the letter meant. Doc recognized a vigilance committee letter when he saw one. His only possible hope was that they might not hang a man who had done nothing harmful in their town.

Pearly ironed that one flat. She said he himself had killed a man in Cheyenne on the assumption he was about to kill someone. *About to* was all the justification these vigilantes would need.

While Pearly turned one way, then the other, and spoke her thoughts, Doc was distracted by a structure he fancied he saw in the air around her. It wasn't like a bridge or a printing press, or anything man-made. What he decided it might be was the clockwork of history, whereby one event begets another. First a bad man hurt Pearly and was shot by Uncle Jack. Then Jack was hanged. Two deaths: a bad man's and a good man's. The system, whatever it was, was balanced and came to rest.

Something like it had begun again in Cheyenne. Again a bad man had been killed, this time by Doc, and, ever since, the system had stood unbalanced. However many cocktails Doc drank, in whatever dirt he lived, or with whatever sadness, he was still a good man. And that was too bad, for it was the death of a good man that the system wanted for its completeness and rest.

The more he studied the thing in the air, the more Doc believed in it. It rendered all the common sense with which Pearly was attacking the problem touchingly beside the point. To Doc, it was more like she was mourning his death in advance, so he could see it and be consoled. This was a bittersweet gift.

"I knew you two damn fools were going to try and kill one another," she said.

"I have no interest in killing Smith Banks."

"I know. But you practise shooting him every day."

Then Pearly started to cry and, while crying, to make sobbing speeches. This soothed Doc too, right at the heart of his greatest pain, which was not about surviving so much as knowing Pearly loved him.

"I shoulda known. I shoulda run sooner. With all his money and with my scarred face, *because of my scarred face*, he fell in love with me. That should have scared me, but I let myself be flattered instead. That was foolish. Smith has a tough mind. I don't know how to change it."

She heaved in a ragged breath.

"I'm so sorry I made you a gambler. I was so close to married with my father. He didn't touch me. I don't mean like that. But we lived together and travelled together and gambled together. It was always him and me. So when it was you and me, I went and turned you into a gambler. Took you and stuck you in his place. I couldn't help it. I'm so sorry I done that." She slumped against the wall, leaned her head on it, continued to cry. "I'm so tired right now, but we have to go. We've got to run harder than ever before."

Even though Doc felt the machine in the air was poised to drop him into a noose, he felt no desire to run. His only wish was to while away the waiting hours with Pearly.

"Can I stay in your hotel room?"

Through her tears, Pearly laughed at him.

"No, I'm serious. I'll ball up some clothes in the bed here, so it looks like I'm in it. But really, I'll be in bed with you."

"And that's going to fool anybody for more than a minute?"

But she waited while he bunched clothes under the blanket, then let him follow her out of the Chicago Saloon and in the back door of the Overland. When Doc saw how much cleaner and larger Pearly's room was, and when he smelled the new paint and the Pearly smell already there, Doc was happy. He wrapped Pearly in his arms, even as she was still coiled tight and chattering.

"I know you just want to move hotels so you can fuck me. I know that's how your silly man's brain works. You can't even be sensible about survival when half this town might be coming to kill you."

But when they lay down on the bed, the knot went out of her. She held Doc to her breasts and rubbed his hair. She told him he smelled bad and he jumped up, stripped off, and washed himself with water from the pitcher. He probably still smelled but Pearly didn't say so again. Then she got up and undressed, and they got into the bed together, under the covers against the chilly mountain night.

Against the gloss of Pearly's skin, Doc was happy beyond measure. He made love to her and wanted to soon again, laughing and giddy. So they did again and were noisy. The bed squealed and banged the wall. They cried out.

Later Pearly stroked his head and the heat between them under the covers was damp and high.

"Well, that was smart," she said. "You pretend you're in one hotel, then make such a racket there's probably nobody in Golden City doesn't know Doc fucked Pearly at the Overland Hotel tonight until she was cross-eyed."

Doc had slept poorly for weeks, since Pearly had moved next door. Now he fell into a sleep so deep it was as if he were trying to reclaim all the lost nights in one. He slept through the darkness and on through the morning. A woman with a bucket coming to clean woke him. He sat up sharply, looked around for Pearly, and saw that she was gone. So was her trunk.

He jumped to the window but could not see past the balcony. He pulled on trousers and ran down the stairs trailing suspenders. He ran through the lobby and onto the boardwalk. There was no stage. He ran inside and demanded of the clerk when the Denver stagecoach had gone.

"Two hours ago, sir. It will run again tomorrow."

Then the clerk handed Doc a letter.

Dear Doc,

*I have sent a letter like this one to Smith Banks too. To both
of you I'm saying goodbye. I told him to leave you alone because
there's no sense hanging you because it won't get him what he's
after. To you, I'm saying I'm sorry we didn't go someplace quiet
and live from the beginning instead of turning into gamblers
which leads to trouble every time. I took half the double eagles.
In this letter is a second letter for the hotel clerk. It says the rest
of the money in the safe is for you. The boy at the desk is Greg.
He's sweet on me. I told him to make sure they don't cheat you.
Don't look for me Doc because you won't find me. That's the
same promise I made to Smith Banks who for all his money won't
find me either. You know I can be smart when I have to. Best way
to forget me is find some other girl. I hope all this is in time but
you better get on Rufus and ride. I will miss you of course but
that's life, sad as hell.*

Love, Pearly

Within an hour of reading the letter, Doc had the money out of the
hotel safe and Rufus out of the livery corral. He rode Rufus down the
Denver trail at a full gallop and was slow to realize that no matter how
hard he pushed, a group of horsemen behind him were gaining. Finally, those riders caught him. He had a notion to seek cover and
shoot it out, but they were many. Instead, Doc obeyed a second instinct to drop his gun and raise his hands. If they were a vigilance
committee and not road agents, there would be some questions at
least before they hanged him.

With the men around him pointing their pistols, Doc recognized a
few. Some had imbibed Jack Hill's cocktails beside him at the Chicago
Saloon. One had bowled at the Golden Bowl.

In an attempt at legal talk, the leader said they were the vigilance
committee of Golden City, and that they had heard from a similar
committee in another town that they should be on the lookout for Doc
Windham, a hard case and gambler who had shot a man to death in a
whore tent in Cheyenne. Did he accept or deny that he was one and
the same Doc Windham, guilty as charged?

Doc imagined himself as Uncle Jack in that moment. It was as though he moved in Jack's skin. In this exact position, Uncle Jack Windham, a fine and persuasive talker, whom everyone liked, had not saved himself. Doc could not think of one way he was an improvement on Uncle Jack, could think of no skill of body or mind he could use to get a better result—until he did.

In that moment Doc poured every ounce of concentration into the memory of the worshipful master making Mason signs and gestures, the ones that were to see Doc through in the greater world. To the vigilantes around him, Doc gave a little speech about his innocence and worked into it every Mason phrase and sign he could remember. Three men in the group changed before his eyes. While the others continued to size up trees, these spoke to Doc and to one another in the secret language.

Then one of them said to the rest, "I have just realized that I know this man." The other two said they'd had a similar revelation. They asked to interview Doc alone.

Behind a tailings pile from some bygone mine, one Mason asked, "What lodge are you? And how is it that a brother in the craft has fallen so low?"

Doc did not mention Smith Banks. It was better to forget him and talk only about Cheyenne. He told them he was from the Montana Lodge, and then he named the Mason doctor in Cheyenne who could clear him beyond doubt of that of which he was accused.

"If you can stop the others from hanging me long enough to get a letter to Dr. Ingram, he'll tell you the man I shot had killed lots of people. He'll tell you I shot him when he was strangling me, on a night when I'd gone with a committee exactly like yours to see if we couldn't stop him once and for all."

The Masons decided to believe their brother. They parleyed with the others, and the result was that Doc did not hang that day. He was taken back to Golden City and locked in a feed shed without windows, where he stayed in the dark with the mice for twenty days. That was the length of time it took to find Dr. Ingram by Mason telegraph. They tracked him down, not in Cheyenne, but in St. Louis, where he had moved. It turned out he was hoping to hear from Doc

Windham so that he could tell him an important fact. It turned out to be the same fact he used to prove Doc's innocence. In his letter, Dr. Ingram told the Golden City vigilantes that Doc must not be viewed as a murderer for the most basic and unassailable reason that his victim, Ivan Overcross, was not dead. Far better that he was, but he was not. The night that Overcross had attacked Doc, and Doc had shot him in the head in self-defence, they had all fled, confident the man was dead and not sure of their own culpability before the law. Next morning, they discovered that Ivan Overcross had got on his horse and left, broken head and all.

In the whore tent where the fight with Overcross had begun, there was blood everywhere, and in amongst it, on a bloody pillow, they had found a letter. Dr. Ingram had enclosed that letter, for it was meant for Doc. It was mostly written in faint pencil, but wherever a drop of blood had fallen on the sheet, Overcross had dipped the pencil and scratched the next few letters in red.

Little Man, You have blown my skull off but you haven't killed me. Before I finish with you, you'll wish you had.

GREAT FALLS/FORT BENTON

August 1881

OTHER THAN CALVES NOT KEEPING UP, and cattle getting thin, and horses getting lame, and men threatening to mutiny, the Cochrane drive beyond Helena was without incident. The cattle threw themselves on the trail with little urging each morning, and off it whenever they saw the chuckwagon stopped. Even when they picked up the well-rested Walla Walla cows near Sun River, the two bunches did not fight much or give trouble on the trail. Well beyond the mountains now, and headed for a boundless horizon, the herd plodded forward without apparent hope or concern.

Doc's experience was that certain kinds of men can't stand things to be good. If they are not distracted by cold, rain, rough country, hard work, and continuous danger, they shine a light on their own life and find it lacking. If that breed needed a model, Dog Eye French was their man.

As the trail grew longer and less complicated, the Texan grew darker and more brooding. He would not let go of the image of a line of full whisky glasses he had been prevented from drinking, of the bevy of pretty whores he'd been kept from sporting. He no longer sought Doc out to complain, but rode, ate, and slept apart. For company he had his own little crew now, malcontents who allowed him to be their straw boss.

With plenty of time to study the situation, Doc saw the change between him and Dog Eye as having come about in two stages: both of them on the day of their arrival at Helena, the day Doc encountered Overcross in the theatre show.

Stage one was Doc's *Et tu Brutes* remark. Strange that a comment whose purpose was to have no meaning had enough to work a change, but it was so. The saying of it marked the moment when Dog Eye shifted himself out of Doc's camp and began to view Doc as part of the human multitude who took and kept things from Dog Eye French.

Stage two was Dog Eye's retaliation, coming the moment Doc laid his head down after returning that night. From his bedroll, Dog Eye had declared that sending Doc to town was nothing but a wasted opportunity.

In that single evening, each man had hurt the other, as surely as if they had stood toe to toe and exchanged blows. And afterwards, they held a grudge.

This thing that had been clouding up for so long finally broke and poured in a bug-infested camp near the Great Falls of the Missouri, a place where the Big Muddy lost its canyon appearance and spread into tangly lowland bush. Doc was sitting cross-legged in his underwear with his trousers across his knees. He was trying to see the needle in his hand. Dog Eye and three others, not the best of men, approached him, and when they were about ten feet away, Dog Eye detached and came on alone. He stood above his segundo, so close that the toes of his fancy Mexican boots almost touched Doc's knees.

Normally Doc would have criticized Dog Eye for standing too close, would have urged him to spit it out if he had something to say. Instead he went on sewing as if unaware of his presence.

When he found his voice, Dog Eye said he and the others intended to draw their pay and quit the drive at Fort Benton. Knowing it would make Dog Eye happy if his segundo cursed him and urged him to stay, or failing that if they had a nice long argument in which Dog Eye was able to detail the sources of his complaint, Doc peered up at his wintering partner and showed no emotion, not even interest. After a while, Doc shrugged and went back to mending the hole in the crotch of his corduroys. He did not look again, even as Dog Eye scuffed the ground with his tall heels and strutted off.

THE TRAIL FROM GREAT FALLS to Fort Benton crossed an austere upland, a denuded prairie that reminded Doc of Texas without the mesquite and cholla. Below and to the south, the Missouri cliffs came into and out of view, with a low range of black mountains beyond them. The country was a thirsty tan with nothing above it on most days but a pale blue through which fine, white fish-skeletons swam. On the ground the summer flowers were dead and twisted, and only the white of yarrow mottled the donkey colour.

The grass did not seem plentiful in this stretch, but when they came within the orbit of Fort Benton, where the beasts of that town were quartered, the forage was abruptly less. The tilted ground had a peeled look, like an animal who is mangy or has the hair rubbed off.

Lowell ordered the seven thousand cattle steered into the valley where a loop in the river embraced a greenish flat. Since there was no place for the chuckwagon to descend, it stopped in the head of a coulee, and Cook said he and his helper would bring the food in cans when it was ready. Cook also suggested the cowboys camp by the water and get themselves a thorough wash. An excitement rippled through the cowboy crew for they interpreted this as meaning a night in town.

Away from where the cowboys were piling their saddles, arranging their bedrolls, or already stripping off their clothes for the river, Lowell led Doc away for another meeting. Behind a curtain of young willow, sweet green fronds and copper stalks, they found a few gnarled harps of old grey wood strong enough to sit on. Lowell reached down a finger and fished it through the grass and leaves on the ground, then smiled, for it was wet enough for a man to smoke. He drew his Bull Durham sack from his shirt pocket and slid the papers from behind the bag's label. He rolled two.

When they were smoking, Lowell asked if Doc had anything for the Major. Only then did Doc tell the trail boss about Dog Eye's desertion and the three going with him. Lowell stared in some amazement. The question of why Doc had not said so before hung in the air but was never asked. Lowell cursed until he was tired. Then, as if part of the conversation had already happened, he said, "It is too important! Dog Eye is a good cowboy, even if the others aren't."

"We can do without him," said Doc.

Lowell puffed his cigarette, holding the lit end high so the dry tobacco didn't pour out.

"There is more to this," he said. "You and him had a fracas."

"Did not."

"So your partner of years ups and goes and it doesn't matter to you."

"Get this straight, Lowell. Dog Eye burred onto me two years ago in the Beaverhead, like I was his long lost daddy. Now he fancies himself grown up and independent. It was in Dog Eye's head from the start, and it is still there. I never had much to do with it."

"I hope to hell you haven't been feuding with Lippy."

"Lippy's fine."

"Well, what are we going to do? Hire more saddle bums in Fort Benton?"

"I wouldn't. I been watching Jim Adams. He knows cows and handles those Clydes like an expert. My guess is he's hiding his light under a bushel and can ride as well. I say we give him Dog Eye's string and call it square, even if it isn't. Dwight can ride as well. I held out little hope, but he's becoming almost useful. Open prairie and a trail-broke herd should take care of the rest."

In his fury, Lowell had sucked his smoke down small. He mashed the ember into his calloused palm, felt the crumb for heat, put it in his shirt pocket. The sound of the boys splashing and yelping beyond the copper stalks changed the topic.

"You going to keep the boys out of town again?" Lowell asked.

"No," said Doc. "Let them get drunk, poxed, beat up, shot, whatever they care to."

"Well, I guess it's the Major's call. I'm going to see him now. You coming?"

"Not unless I'm forced."

"I bet Overcross is nowhere near here. I bet he's still warbling to that fat woman in Helena."

"I'd take that bet. But that's not my reason."

Lowell looked like he wanted to ask but didn't. He struggled upright.

"Then you're not invited any more. Stay here and be a porcupine. I'll take Dwight to guard the pay sack, if the Major gives me one. Size is still Dwight's best quality, far as I'm concerned."

Wiping ash from his palm onto his pant leg, Lowell left Doc sitting.

IT WAS THE MIDDLE OF the next day when Lowell and Dwight returned from Fort Benton. In this valley, the cattle were independent, and the boys were mostly asleep or playing cards when three horses appeared on the hillside trail. When it was established that the third horse was the Major's grey, everyone got up and got busy. They rolled up their bedrolls, slapped dust out of their pants, slicked back their hair, screwed on their hats.

Posting up in his Mountie saddle, the Major trotted by with one glove raised and continued on to the cattle. The herd was spread evenly over the river flat, and a few of the more enterprising had gone up the coulees. For a quarter of an hour, the Major walked his horse among them, then returned and dismounted. Lowell took a heavy saddlebag off his horse and gave it to Dwight to carry. It had the heft of money, and the boys were all trying not to show their smiles. Out of his own saddlebag, the Major took a bottle of whisky, which he gave to Doc to hold.

The Major stood quietly while the men gathered. Doc thought the Major was more grave and paler than before he'd examined the herd. The cattle were neither dripping summer tallow the way they'd started out in Dillon, nor tired but fit as they'd been in Helena. Now they were clearly eating on the last of themselves.

When the last man arrived, the Major signalled Doc to start the whisky around, and as it passed he began to talk. Without any reference to the deserters, he told the men they were a good and reliable crew. He understood and appreciated how far they'd come and with how few amusements. He would not hold them back from a drink tonight, though he hoped they would not draw too large an advance and waste too much of what they'd earned on things that did not last. He said he had been in Fort Benton a couple of weeks and it was a rough town. Rather than descend to its level, he hoped the boys would behave in a way that reflected well on the Cochrane Ranch.

After the speech, the men were invited to line up in front of the Major and Lowell for their advances. As Lowell wrote the amounts in his book, Doc counted the cash from the bag. The three of them sat on slickers on the ground and each cowboy sat in front of them as his turn came. The Major asked every man how the drive had gone for him, how his health was holding up.

Dog Eye had the sense to stay out of the line, but one of his bunch did not. When that man came and sat, the Major would not look at him.

"Get up and stand aside. I'll deal with you last," he said.

Among the others in the lineup, Doc was surprised to see Lippy. Lip was famous for never drawing his pay before a job was done. It had to mean that some item of his equipment had broken.

When the last of the loyal men had passed, the Major got to his feet and beckoned the deserters. All the other men had stopped to watch, glad in their hearts that they had remained loyal. Dog Eye had the courage to come to the Major first.

"Athol French," the Major said, after a wait of painful seconds. Dog Eye's real name hit him like the tail of a whip. "I would never have thought you were the kind to shirk a duty."

Dog Eye looked as if he were standing before a powerful wind. Doc could feel how close the Texan was to begging for his job back. But, however difficult, Dog Eye stayed put.

With the paying out completed, the Major turned to Doc, to whom he had not spoken yet, and asked if he would continue into Canada. Doc had planned to reserve this decision until later, but found himself too decided to prevaricate. He said he would.

"Good then," said the Major. "And which of your men will join us?"

Doc said it was not his place to say, but he thought Lippy might, and Dwight, and maybe Pesky Boucher. But they should speak for themselves.

With that, the Major left, and the men cheered his back most of the way up the hill.

AS WAS USUAL, the men went to town in shifts, with captains elected to ensure that every man came away on time. The first bunch rode out whooping, and the four deserters followed at a more sedate pace. Lowell could have sent Dog Eye's bunch out on foot, for they did not own their horses and could not buy them, but that was an extreme punishment. Instead, he allowed them to ride to Fort Benton, where they would put the horses in a livery barn for the evening at their own expense. Then the loyal men would bring them back.

The first contingent left in daylight, and the boys remaining made a fire and played poker beside it. Inevitably, a couple of them would lose their advance and a collection would have to be taken so they could afford to drink. Doc took himself away from the others and sat on a stump. He shaved a stick into a smaller stick and wallowed in melancholy.

Cook had found a way to bring his chuckwagon down a different coulee, and the wagon was now parked by the bedrolls, its harness draped over the tongue, its tarps raised at the back. The white-top glowed inside because Lowell was in there with a lamp, trying to make sense of the numbers he'd scratched during the pay-out. Earlier, he had told Doc to take his turn in town with the first shift, and when Doc had declined, the trail boss had walked off disgusted.

Truth was, Doc was too depressed to go to town, more depressed than he had been for a long while. As was usually the case with his depressions, the reason was Pearly, whom he was missing keenly. Not long ago, a night like this would have sent him running to a whorehouse if one was near. But somewhere along the line, he had stopped visiting the soiled doves, because the thought of them appealed only for lusty seconds before dying into sorrow. Now it appeared he was even further gone, to where he wouldn't even venture to a town for whisky or cards. Giving up one of life's pleasures had cost him another two.

Doc was not entirely alone. Twenty feet away and about the same distance from the card players, Jim Adams had unrolled his bedroll and was lying on it. Adams had also refused his chance at town. Lowell thought the reason was money and offered to advance him some, but Jim had said no to that too. Being depressed, Doc recognized it in others, and across the space that separated them, he could feel Adams's pain by the way it chimed with his own. How such a young fellow had found his way into this old man's mood intrigued Doc. With most men, he would have been confident of finding out, but with Adams, he doubted he would ever know. If that boy were a well, and you threw a rock down, there might never be a splash.

It was the time of evening when there was still light in the sky but none along the ground. The sky's blue was leaching to white, and the clouds in the weakening pale were strips of ever darker ash. Into that pale glow, a hat appeared, then shoulders that Doc recognized as Lippy's. The young fellow approached without greeting and sat on the ground. He did nothing, said nothing.

After a time, Lippy cleared his throat, a seeming advent to speech, but nothing came.

"You should go win some of those greeners' money," Doc said, staring at the licking fire and the huddle of noisy men.

"Don't feel like it," said Lippy.

"They couldn't bluff a dog."

"Still don't."

Then another patch of silence before Doc said he supposed they would get along all right without Dog Eye. Lippy did not comment.

"Jim Adams is going to ride Dog Eye's string," said Doc, even though Lippy knew it. He said it loud, intending for Adams to hear so he could be included in the conversation if he cared to.

Just then, they heard the snapping of fetlocks in the dark, the approach of the first shift of drinkers returning. Even in their whisky cups, the captain had them quiet so as not to spook the cattle. The boys at the fire were up in an instant. They threw their cards in a pile and ran for the horse corral.

"You not going?" Lippy said.

"No." Doc came close to adding that it would be a waste if he did.

Lippy cleared his throat again and again said nothing.

"What is it, Lip? Spit it out."

"If we went to town, would you help me find a woman? A whore."

Doc was at once alert, respectful. "How so?"

"Other night, after you were asleep, some boys were telling stories. One said he'd heard of a town in Wyoming where the whores rode naked behind the cowboys. They'd have races like that. I bet it ain't true, but I can't get them naked whores on horses out of my head."

"I don't think I've been to that town." Doc folded his knife and put it away. He stood up. "Let's go then."

"I don't want anyone knowing," Lippy said.

They went to the horse corral and found Louie and Calico. They told the boy in charge of the cavvy they would be away for a few hours.

There was no talking for most of the ride. Doc figured he had ridden a thousand miles beside Lippy, most of them silent. Quiet at any time, Lippy was more so in the saddle. Even now in the dark, with its limited possibilities, Lippy was busy watching and listening.

Doc wanted to ask more about this new impulse but was cautious lest he spook the man. Two falls ago, a round-up crew had got it into their heads to get Lippy laid. They came at him with a rope, figuring to tie him up and throw him in a whore's room. Lippy laid the first man out and the second never came.

Above the shacks on the fringe of Fort Benton, Lippy finally spoke. "Could you find the place?" he asked. "And go in and arrange things? It's got to be dark and no kissing."

Fort Benton's Front Street was mostly bars facing over a road to the levee and river. Along it, the second shift of Cochrane drinkers was making its presence felt. Two were marching arm in arm down the dirt street wagging bottles. Tex Appleby ran out of a saloon, fired his gun in the air, and ran back. Lippy burrowed into his raised coat collar and rode from one shadow to the next.

After the first pass, Doc took Lippy off Front Street and into the darker back streets. He was looking for a certain kind of house, like a boarding house, but with something a little gaudy in the curtains, or maybe a paper lantern on the porch. The whore cribs with pianos any fool could find, but this quieter variety was not so simple.

At last Doc saw a two-storey house with a little too much welcoming light on its porch. He left his friend holding the horses and went to the door and knocked. A girl about ten answered and he thought he had made a mistake, but she stepped aside and made way for him to enter.

Inside, a flight of stairs rose and jackknifed off a landing into dark. Through an arch to the left was a sofa covered in fat rich-coloured cushions, some with gold-tasselled corners. In front of the sofa was a low oval table. In the corner of the room where a clock might have been, there was nothing, time not existing here.

From a back room, a woman appeared, a Mexican lady about Doc's age or maybe older, wearing a long dress whose hem dragged the floor. Her thick black hair was piled up and held by a comb that rose in the shape of a fan. Doc liked that she was older. He guessed that might give her a sympathy with Lippy's request.

Doc took off his hat and bowed. She asked if he would take a drink and he said he would if she would join him. He sat at the far end of the sofa. The girl of ten, maybe a whore's child and hopefully not a whore herself, came with the drinks on a tray.

"What are you looking for tonight, cowboy?" the Mexican woman asked after they had toasted each other.

Doc explained Lippy's preferences. She arched her painted eyebrows a certain way, and Doc said it was because his friend had something on his face that he didn't like people to see, and certainly not to touch.

"He's not sick, your friend?"

"It's not a sickness. It's something he was born with. What they call a harelip. Never got sewed up when he was a baby because he was abandoned. He's about the healthiest man alive, and I would guess he will sport well with a woman, though he's not much experienced in that regard."

"You have me interested," said the madam, with a smile Doc wished suddenly was for him. "Would he like me, do you think?"

Doc winked to show his approval. It was about the best thing he could think of, an older woman who was smart and able to understand how Lippy might feel; who would not tease him.

"I'll go get him."

While Doc waited downstairs, an enterprising young woman, pretty and dark-skinned, a younger version of the first woman, came and sat with him, making flirtatious small talk. She was adept at getting the word "ride" into any sentence. "You cowboys sure can ride a long time," for example.

That made Doc laugh. After a month on the trail, the boys were more likely to spend themselves and their whore money in a minute and be begging for a refund or another chance. But he imagined that Lippy might be different. He must have thought about this for a long time. He was a careful man and liked to do things right. Thinking of him up there with the Mexican madam made Doc happy. His face kept twitching into a smile which the young woman next to him kept misinterpreting.

Then the madam came down the stairs, slow and graceful. Doc looked behind but she was alone. He looked a question but she ignored him. She signalled the girl who had been pestering Doc and spoke to her for quite a while. The madam gestured to her face a couple of times and Doc understood. The young woman went upstairs.

The madam came to Doc and sat beside him, flourishing out her dress into the span of sofa between them. She opened a fan and created a breeze for herself.

"How's my friend?"

"Your friend is delightful. He asks for your patience."

So they sat together and she beckoned the child from a chair by the stairs and whispered in her ear. When she returned, the tray contained two whiskies and a deck of playing cards. Doc toasted the madam and thanked her for her help. Then he ripped his thumb down the edge of the deck.

"A few hands of draw poker, señora? You can decide what we play for."

"Let's play one hand. If you win, I take you upstairs for free. If I win, I take your five dollars and you and I go upstairs."

"Sounds like I win either way," said Doc, but the old sadness was starting.

She reached out and touched his face. "Your friend isn't the only one who's been alone too long."

AN HOUR LATER, Doc led the way into a saloon on Front Street. Lippy had decided he was concerned about Dwight, whom he did not trust the others to look out for. Doc thought Lippy might also be looking for Dog Eye. If so, he was in the money. They didn't see Dwight but spotted Dog Eye standing up to the bar in a riff-raff saloon, one boot heel hooked over the tarnished rail.

The closer Doc came, the drunker Dog Eye looked. Doc bade him good evening and the Texan's grey eyes, trying to focus, looked like mouse fur. Doc thought Dog Eye would argue with him first thing, but he only said hello then looked across Doc's shoulder with a grin.

"I'll be damned if that isn't Lippy Mann, in town and no wiper on his face."

Doc turned and it was true. Lippy was out of his coat collar and smiling his harelip wide.

"You seen Dwight?" Lippy asked.

"Yeah, I seen Doc's new boy earlier. Drunk as a pig."

"Someone take him home?"

"Wouldn't know. Not my problem."

"Where are your three?" asked Doc.

"Not my problem either."

During this conversation, an old beaver man, stinking of sweat and hot leather, pushed his face in among them. He struck Doc as the kind that can hit a pitch of drunkenness and hang there for days. Long as he was quiet, Doc saw no harm, but then he looked at Lippy and said, "What the hell's wrong with your face?"

Some clown behind them shouted, "Boy's a can't whistle. Never seen one?"

Lippy ignored both men, but the beaver man persisted. "Come on, boy, I asked you what's wrong with your face?"

Lippy looked at him, still grinning. "I'ze born with a harelip. What's wrong with yours?"

It wasn't much of a fight, and soon the three of them were outside. Dog Eye had managed to sucker-punch a bystander, so he was happy. Then he remembered that he did know where Dwight might be.

"Dwight's sick in that alley, last time I saw him."

They crossed the street and, sure enough, in the rubbish and empty bottles and worse of the alley, Dwight was laid out unconscious and smelling of vomit. Doc slapped him awake and they got him standing, and only after a considerable splashing in a horse trough could he remember where he'd put his horse. It took all three of them to get the boneless bulk in the saddle and it seemed unlikely he would stay there any distance.

Finally, it was time to go, and it felt strange to be mounting up and seeing Dog Eye still on the ground. Doc felt sorry for letting the young Texan walk to this cliff and jump off it.

"Guess that's it then, Dog Eye."

"Don't look so sorrowful, Doc. When next your eyes are full of sand and your asses are sore, you can think of Dog Eye French here in Fort Benton, full of whisky and sporting a whore."

"I'll think of you too when I'm in Canada and have some money in my pocket and can still piss straight."

Then they shook hands all around, and three rode off and one stayed.

The moon had set and the ride back was much darker, cool and damp. Far in the distance where the mountains must be were occasional pillows of sheet lightning. Just before they got to the bed ground, Doc asked into the darkness if Lippy's evening had been satisfactory.

"Fine, Doc," said Lippy. "You?"

"Fine too. You had a good idea there."

When Doc was bedded down in his soogin, he thought of Pearly for awhile, as he did every night, but it didn't last long and wasn't as sad as it sometimes was.

GOLDEN CITY

July 1867

NEVER HAD THE WORLD looked bigger to Doc than when he was released from the feed shed in Golden City. Jack Hill had taken care of Rufus during Doc's imprisonment and had fed him too many oats and apples. The gelding was sassy and spoiled. Hill had been custodian of Doc's other effects too, and while Doc strapped on his holster and loaded the chambers of the Colt .44, Hill tried to tempt him with his favourite cocktails. It was no use. Doc was soon mounted and gone.

He rode hard all the way to Denver and, once inside that town, made a beeline for the hill of fancy houses. Soon he was facing Smith Banks's butler, and the Negro stared hard at the gun in Doc's hand. He led Doc down the sequence of stairs and halls to the billiards room, where Smith Banks sat staring into space with his hand curled around a glass. He looked ten years older, gaunt and unshaved. His eyes were far back in his head, as though he'd crossed a desert without a canteen. Looking up, he did not startle.

"Oh," he said. "Mr. Windham. Leave us, please, Jones. Don't call the sheriff."

Doc felt foolish, as he always did in the face of Banks's good manners. He holstered his gun, folded his arms, leaned his ass on the rail of the billiards table. Banks stood as though to shake hands, then sank back into the chair and covered his face.

"I don't know where she is," he said. "I wish I did."

"I want to look in every damn room."

"You are such a fool, Windham. Do you honestly think this is a charade for your benefit? I heard you were about to be hanged."

"No thanks to you, I was not."

Banks removed his hands from his face. He sat up straight. He had almost succeeded in putting his dignity and superiority back together when he started to cry. Doc took no pleasure in it.

"I gambled for her," Banks wailed. "I gambled her away."

It came to Doc that if Smith Banks, with all the money in the world, had failed to find Pearly, Doc had no chance at all. He left the room, climbed the stairs, and strode past the butler, who was pointing a little derringer with a shaking hand. The man could have ended Doc's life, even with that feeble gun, but Doc decided to let him try. It didn't seem to matter much, one way or the other.

DOC BEGAN HIS SEARCH for Pearly by going east. Down the South Platte into the Platte proper. Then to the Missouri. Doc heard about a new cowtown called Abilene to the south and he rode for days only to see that it was a town just getting started without even a billiards table and no sign of Pearly. Whenever he found a stagecoach stopped, he described to the driver the scar on Pearly's face. He claimed she was his sister, for he assumed a man looking for a woman, not a relative, would seem the kind of man you should not help.

In this way, he ran with the rivers to their nexus. He arrived at the city of St. Louis.

St. Louis was as big as Doc and Pearly had feared, with more of everything than Doc had ever seen. The levee alone ran for miles and was crowded all that distance with steamboats, their stacks wisping, or blasting, or cold. The tons of cargo piled on the wharves and levee was more than Doc had imagined the world contained. Sweating stevedores, mostly Negroes, emptied the boats, then slaved in the scalding heat to wood up and load again.

Though afraid of the tall buildings and the fast rivers of people, Doc pretended affability, and asked questions of everyone who would stop for him. In every billiards saloon he found, and there were many, he put on an even more detailed show, describing Pearly to every patron. Somehow the size of St. Louis and the fruitlessness of his search made Doc think of even bigger towns, like New York, and the whole state of California, yet unexplored. Even the South was barred only by Pearly's having said once she didn't care for how it smelled. That could be her strategy now, to go where he least expected.

Thinking this way made Doc despair. For a time, in that desperation, he got as lost as he could in the bigness of St. Louis. He attempted again to become a drunkard, and when in that state, imagined that Pearly had become a whore. From brothel to brothel, he went searching. At the familiar sight of a lovesick drunk looking for a particular whore, the pimps and bouncers punched his face and threw him down the stairs. They loosened his teeth, blacked his ribs with kicks, laughed at him all the while. They would have robbed him too, but he had the sense to hide his money somewhere other than on his person, as Pearly had instructed.

Sober again, he knew Pearly was not a whore. There were too many other things she could do between trouble and starvation.

In the Chinese part of St. Louis, Doc bought an opium pipe for the first time and thought he had the answer. In his opium dream, the pain stopped and he could imagine everything turning out better than it had ever been. When he returned to normal, the loss of belief and comfort was crushing, and he saw clearly that unless he did something forceful and sudden, he would spend every cent he had left buying those pipes and that dream of contentment, no matter if it killed him.

It was in that desperate mood that he sold Rufus, his last living connection to Uncle Jack. He sold the honest gelding to the first man who met his price, even though that man had eyes like a badger. That night he denied himself the opium pipe but got drunk, and when he woke to the awful headache, he staggered forth into the nauseating light and searched for Rufus and the badger-eyed man. Exhausted, his head screaming, he sat on a bale on the levee until someone kicked him off it. Then he heard a steam whistle bark close enough to make his ears wince.

Doc ran to that boat and booked a passage to wherever it was going, which turned out to be Fort Benton, head of navigation on the Missouri River.

The boat was a sternwheeler called the *Luella*. From overheard conversations among the prospectors on deck, Doc learned that the boat was legendary. In Fort Benton a year ago, miners arrived from Confederate Gulch with a wagon entirely full of gold dust. Because the *Luella* was the best steamboat on the Fort Benton levee at the time, the gold from the wagon was brought aboard. They put the dust in iron safes, then roped empty whisky kegs to their sides in case of sinking. Along the trip, a miner fell overboard and was so weighed down by his own wealth that he drowned and was never found.

On that famous trip, the *Luella* went aground on a bar and was attacked by Sioux Indians. The attackers experienced such a fusillade of fire from the miners on deck that they fled for their lives. When the *Luella* arrived at St. Louis, it was the richest cargo of gold ever brought from Montana, and a great surge of westbound Argonauts followed.

On board, Doc was tightly surrounded by prospectors. They were pressed to the rail, waving goodbye to their friends. All had chosen to pay extra to ride this lucky golden boat except Doc, who paid the premium out of ignorance.

UP THE MUDDY MISSOURI, the famous riverboat slapped itself, leaving the smoking city for a country that soon turned to wilderness. The boilers devoured wood as fast as the black stevedores stoked it in.

On deck, rifles hung on hooks on the walls. They were for defence against Indians, but the drunkards grabbed them and blazed at anything. A deer stepping from the woods to drink. An eagle roosting in a high tree.

After two weeks of travel, they rounded a bend and surprised a hundred or more swimming buffalo. The steamboat bumped through them, and the passengers fought each other for the rifles in the racks. Others were already emptying pistols into the humped backs and lifted noses. The brown water was soon streaked red. The *Luella* was not about to stop and everyone knew it. The shooting was killing only and had no purpose beyond seeing a buffalo lose rudder and float up sideways, or thrash its limbs until it drowned.

West of Bismarck, the captain mistook a channel and the boat ground its wooden hull solid on a bar. The passengers climbed down, getting their weight off in hopes that would raise it, but it wasn't enough. They brought up the cargo and lowered it off. Finally, working iron pry bars and pulling on ropes, they scrunched the hull backwards until the boat was afloat and the paddle was free. Indians, who had probably been watching all the while, chose that moment to attack. The first arrow killed a man through the chest, not three feet from Captain Hazlett.

Shrieks and curses ripped the air. People fought each other to get through the narrow doors and behind any kind of wall. Now there were fewer men willing to fire than there were guns. Those who wanted to defend the boat found the rifles in the wall racks empty, having never been reloaded after the attack on the swimming buffalo.

Eventually, the boat churned on, and the power of steam and the iron-plated pilothouse saved them. The Indians tried to pursue them along shore but were too exposed. After two were wounded, they let the steamboat pass.

From that day onward, every scrape on the boat's bottom caused oaths, at least, and often screams and prayers. The stops to wood up lost their routine quality and became occasions of fear and hysteria. Passengers like Doc who knew their way around a gun were chosen as guards, facing the stockade walls as the cut wood was loaded.

Then came a day when the captain sounded the steam whistle a quarter-mile in advance of a woodlot wharf and got no answer. As the boat slapped closer, the slender pier stayed empty. An argument broke out on board. Passengers were trying to climb the stairs to the pilothouse, shouting, "Don't stop! Go on!" But the captain inside his steel home ignored them. Whatever this wood fort contained was better than having his boilers and engines starve silent on the river. From here to Benton was all Indian country, their uncontested domain.

Crew and passengers carried axes and saws to shore. Doc was part of the little army that flanked them, a clutch of men bristling iron as a porcupine bristles quills. One by one, they found corpses to a total of six. Four men, a woman, an infant boy. Five white, one black. All scalped and more. The Indians had burned or taken away the cut wood, but had left several logs. Captain Hazlett ordered them cut into boiler lengths. The strongest men pulled the two-handled saw, rasping spews of yellow from the logs. All the while, Doc ran his eyes along the stockade wall, tickling everywhere at once. By then, Doc was a sober man, having changed from a drunkard to a righteous foe of alcohol soon after the first Indian attack.

One of the last stops before Fort Benton was the Musselshell Stockade. The valley spread wide where the pretty Musselshell River flowed in through bluffs of poplar to meet and conjoin its big brother. Doc's eye observed the prettiness, then locked on a hanged man in the trees. Inside the stockade, no one spoke of any hanging, as if it were a private matter not to be shared with strangers.

In the stockade store, which doubled as a saloon, Doc found the murky jars he'd seen too often and didn't like. In the green alcohol fog, noses crowded like bottom-feeding fish. In another jar were ears. The labels explained that the parts had come off dead Indians, killed in a recent melee. Behind the counter on a shelf was a row of skulls, cleaned of fat and flesh and hair, polished to a shine and lacquered. The names of the Indians who had owned these skulls in life were written on pieces of paper and glued to the edge of the board that held them.

A woman with a patch of blue calico pinned strangely to her head saw Doc looking at these things and came to serve him. She told him the noses and ears cost a dollar, six for five. The skulls cost more and the price varied with the Indian. She saw him looking at the calico and explained that she had been scalped by Indians but lived. She seemed proud, and Doc left quickly for fear she meant to show him.

Less than a week later, at Fort Benton, the *Luella* anchored in the river to await a space at the crowded levee. A keel boat came by and picked up the passengers, to be united with their luggage later. On shore, Doc walked on jellied legs and looked upon the horses in the street as if they were as strange as solid ground. It was mutual, for when he tried to talk to the horses or touch them, they drew away. He no longer smelled of horse and was suspect.

On the boardwalk of Front Street, Doc saw a mad-eyed man hovering over a pail of whisky. A paper sign behind him read: $1 *a dip*. The two men at the head of the line ladled whisky into their mouths, then leaned sharply forward so the excess ran through their mottled beards back into the pail and was saved.

Doc was not tempted. He was disgusted by drunks and full of determination and certainty about most everything else. The two exceptions were his next destination and the value of his life.

Until Fort Benton, Doc had thought he was on his way to San Francisco, that he would find the eastern terminus of the Union Pacific and travel the train to the Pacific. Now the thought of a crowded rail car headed toward another clutter of humanity sickened him.

The only thing in the world that appealed was to own another horse, but his purse was slack. He spent what remained on a little skewball who was so much Rufus's inferior that Doc felt guilty mounting her. He rode out of town hollow as a reed, but that milky speckled mare was game and gave what she had every day.

On her back, he made Helena, then rode down into the Three Forks country. He chose the middle fork, the Madison. Tiny in its mammoth grasp, he continued until he saw pilgrims ascending the notch that led into the Alder Gulch.

Before he had made it once down the sloping length of Wallace Street, Doc was regretting his return to Virginia City. McGinty's was boarded over. Comstock Bob had sold to a German who couldn't understand that Pearly was a name. In the days Doc spent there, only the Mason storekeeper and the grave markers for Uncle Jack and Pearly's father kept Doc from believing his own past was a mirage.

There being no point in staying, he rode through the Chinese flumes and rockers to the west end of the Alder Gulch. He crossed the river and climbed into the Ruby Mountains. He found a pass and descended the other side into a huge flat basin hemmed on all sides by mountains. He knew by reputation that this was the Beaverhead and recognized the black bits on its vast floor as cattle.

When he finally rode among those cows, and saw the Mason sign, the square and compass branded onto every one, it was a joke so funny he slid from his saddle to the ground. Wallowing in the dirt among the small sage, he kept laughing long after he had begun to hate the dishonest sound.

In that moment he was as close to alone and without a future as a man with a horse can be. He took the Colt Dragoon and levered cap and ball into three chambers. He put the gun to the side of his skull until he remembered Overcross's awful survival. Then he tried the gun in his mouth, but hated the image and the taste. Next, he considered the moment of agony while a body was trying to die around a shattered heart.

Finally he lost interest in his death and began to dream. He did not dream about Pearly or Uncle Jack. Nor did he think of all the fine horses he had ridden, or even about himself.

What Doc thought about in that strange hour was all the reading he had done. He thought of how he had read every single thing right to its end and never considered doing otherwise, even if a book wasn't much to his liking. If life was another kind of book, not just *like* a book but an actual book, and if you did not live it to the final page, then you had set the book aside unread. If Doc was the book's character and had lost interest in the story, it did not follow that the reader side of him was ready to stop.

On that basis, Doc put his gun away. He mounted and rode. He went in search of the owner of the Mason cattle to ask for a job.

WHOOP-UP TRAIL

August 1881

T HE WHOOP-UP TRAIL BEGAN at the north end of Fort Benton's Baker Street. After leaving town, it struck a course northwest beside the Teton River. Where the Cochrane drive met it, several miles along, the trail was wider and more scarred than Doc had ever seen hooved animals and wagons make. The torn and rutted lines wove together, split apart, even cross-hatched. The sideways look was both corduroy and checkerboard. The bull and mule trains, one distantly visible, had flanked the trail so often in search of fodder and smooth running that it spread at times to half a mile.

In the last days of riding before they arrived at Fort Benton, Lowell, who was no longer afraid of being fired, had explained how the Whoop-Up Trail got its name. The Hudson's Bay fur-trading company gave up its monopoly north of the line in 1869. Canada was supposed to take over, but that country was too young and poor to act. Into the gap, Fort Benton whisky men like Lowell had poured. Their most riotous Blackfoot whisky fort was called Whoop-It-Up or Whoop Up, so the supply road took that name as well.

It was all different now, since the Mounties had come. The northbound cargo was no longer whisky, but things like beef, tea, bacon, sugar, flour, molasses, plug tobacco, tack, harness, reapers, forges, horse-shoe iron. A curious thing was how many of the old whisky traders, the ones the Mounties had come west to kill if necessary, now worked for them. The trading companies making the profit on Mountie supplies were also the same ones who had brought the whisky up the river by steamboat before.

As the Cochrane drive inched along the Whoop-Up, the only man familiar with the trail was unfit to lead them. On their last night near Fort Benton, Cook had made stew based on two antelope killed by Alf Tooks. It was eaten with gusto by all and turned to poison only inside Lowell Ferris. As the chuckwagon bumped along, the trail boss lay groaning on sacks in its bed, or hanging off the tailgate, straining at the head or rear.

Taking Lowell's place as trail boss, Doc juggled a few things. As Dwight was still green as a fish from his drinking episode in Fort Benton, Doc took him off his horse and put him on the calf wagon. He mounted Jim Adams on Dwight's little skewball Patches, rather than on any of Dog Eye's touchier stock. He also put Jim in Dog Eye's traditional driving position, left point, which offended the seniority of boys like Tex Appleby, who rode swing.

Alf Tooks, who normally scouted or rode left flank, was given the trail boss spot at the front. Doc's thinking was that Alf was the only person Jim spoke to voluntarily. From the top of the herd, Alf could see Jim. If he was having any problems, Alf could scoot back and help. That left both flanks bare, but the herd moving forward had the dumbness of a machine. Doc knew Lippy could handle the whole back end by himself.

What was left for Doc was Alf Tooks's position as scout. First thing in the day, Doc squeezed Louie to a gallop and let the gelding stretch out for a mile. At that distance, Doc hauled him in and criss-crossed, looking for rattlesnakes. Showing Louie the gun before he fired it, he dispatched a few snakes that were coiled asleep. Doc had no special hatred of snakes but knew from experience that sleepy rattlers would let the herd surround them and not know it. If they woke to the sight of all those legs, they might fly up and sink their teeth into a few.

Doc very much enjoyed scouting, even now when the wind was filled with grit. To be in front of the stink and cow dust was luxury. He supposed he could run into Overcross, but doubted it. Even if the man had managed to study the drive, he had no reason to expect Doc to be scouting when he had never done so before.

Finally, because Louie was urgent for more exercise, Doc steered him beyond the rutted edge of the trail and gave him his head. The big buckskin galloped with smooth grace all the way to where the trail left the Teton. With his legs around that working bellows, Doc stared north into a place that shone like a sheet of tin.

This spot, the Leavings of the Teton, was the drive's second northbound camp. Then, after another very long day, the exhausted herd stopped at a wet ribbon so slender they had to drive the cows off it so it could replenish above the puddles.

Underway again, they entered flat country dotted with alkalis. In the centre of one, beside a shrunken pond of orange, a lone blue heron stood like a caped messenger. Twelve miles into that day, Doc came to an alkali so big in all directions that it could not be skirted but had to be crossed.

The men pulled their wipers over their faces before they stepped on the white ground, but the cattle were on their own. Before long, the wind and the harrowing hooves had lifted a ghostly cloud that floured eyelashes and hung off eyebrows. The alkali stretched for more than a mile, and by halfway, the cattle had begun to wheeze and cough. Their straining nostrils were caked white.

When Louie coughed too, Doc took his shirt off and draped it over the horse's nose. He tied the arms behind the horse's ears. When they emerged from the alkali, the air still was not clear. Now the wind came grey and thick from the north, and they could not see into it more than a hundred yards.

Doc called for the herd to stop. He dismounted and led Louie along beside the cattle. The sound of them coughing was repeated a thousand times, each cow bunching her back to try and try again to rid herself of what was bothering her.

Though there was no water or shelter, Doc said they would stop here for the day. They had fifteen miles behind them, and he did not want to test the cattle's scorched lungs a step farther than that.

Throughout the evening, the wind continued to course cold out of Canada. Cook crossed the norther with his chuckwagon, and got the boys to help him take things out of the wagon and stuff them in the gap underneath. Behind that barrier and the popping tarps, the boys squeezed together like a family of cats. The sound of them blowing dirt out of their noses was more frequent than talk.

The worst discomfort was the lack of fire. There was not a stick of wood here, not even a buffalo chip. When darkness closed over them, there was no relieving it. The wind seemed louder, lonelier.

Out of that noisy dark, a small weird-shaped figure came. It turned out to be a boy of maybe ten wearing a bundle of sticks on his back. He pulled the tumpline from his forehead, cranked his shoulders, and shucked the load. It fell with a hollow rattle.

Cook jumped up and grabbed for the wood, but the boy pressed between and said, "Ten cents."

"Ten cents for what?" Cook asked.

"Ten cents a stick."

Cook laughed at the boy and shoved him roughly aside. He dug in his pocket and came out with two coins. "That's fifty cents. Now skedaddle."

The wood was dry and Cook soon had it burning. By the fire's light, the boy was still with them, his hand out with the coins on it.

Lippy nudged Doc with his elbow, but Doc was thinking hard on Pearly just then, on how he had failed to leave a message for her in the Fort Benton post office, how he hadn't even checked every saloon that had a billiards table. Lippy got up and put another coin on the boy's hand. The boy put the money away in a pocket. Then he looked at them all and made a sign. Later, some would say that he had crossed himself backwards, down to up, right to left. He stood awhile longer until no one was looking, then vanished.

NEXT MORNING, THEY DISCOVERED they were no more than a mile from the Marias River. Those who felt Cook had been harsh with the boy now felt he was justified. The valley was deep and wide and flat-bottomed, with ash-coloured cliffs on the far side. There was an old fort above the near shore that Lowell said was Fort Conrad, run nowadays by a man named Kipp. Old cottonwoods, huge and gnarl-barked, reached out of the thickets made of many kinds of berry bush. An oasis, but they could not stay or take it with them. The cattle watered until they were walking troughs, swell-bellied. The boys filled the barrel roped to Cook's wagon, and after that, they pushed the cattle into the stream.

North of the Marias, they took aim on a broad emptiness between a square-topped blue mesa to the northwest and a treble-humped black hill to the northeast. Lowell told them the latter was really three hills called Sweetgrass and that they were just below the Canadian border.

In the flat middle up which they travelled, the tufts of grass and little sage were even farther apart than before Fort Benton. The sandy earth was less tied down. The bone cattle walked with their eyes closed, while blowing sand peppered their noses raw. They would stop and stand sideways, pant for air. The drovers hit them with wheeling rope ends, frightened them back into motion.

After fifteen miles, they made a dry camp. Then, as if to prove that weather is not just the sucking up and pouring down of water but God's instrument after all, a change came that made no sense. The north wind that had felt like frost and snow all day was sheered off sideways by a wind from the east. The new wind smelled of rain. Barely visible piles of cloud argued in their throats.

Doc had ridden Pedro during daylight. He switched to Louie for the dark. He urged him to his longest walking stride along the cow perimeter, calling for the nighthawks to say aloud who they were and what horse was under them. His neck and the back of his head were prickling and tickling where the hair was trying to rise.

The first man he found was Dwight riding Patches. He scolded him for not singing. The big boy whined that his throat was sore. Then it was Alf Tooks, singing some Negro religious song.

Jim Adams came next. He wasn't much of a singer. He said he was riding Dog Eye's Loco, a big black gelding who was good if you could handle him.

"You all right on that old Loco, Jim?"

"I'm all right," came the voice, sad as always.

Well in advance, Doc knew that Tex Appleby was next. He was singing his heart out as usual, taking it as an opportunity to show off.

> It was once in the saddle I used to go dashing
> It was once in the saddle I used to go gay
> First to the dram house and then to the card house
> Got shot in the breast so I'm dying today
>
> Get six jolly cowboys to carry my coffin
> Get six pretty maidens to bear up my pall
> Put branches of roses all over . . .

Doc could hear the green mare too, her rapid snuffy walk snapping in the syrupy night.

Doc was moving on again when something stopped him. It was silence. Not one cow was bellering. Not one nighthawk sang. *Now it comes*, Doc thought. He jumped down from Louie and covered the gelding's eyes with his hands, and tightly closed his own. He did not open them or move when the rain came, pouring as if from a sluice in the sky.

Then the air was spanked and Doc was flying. It felt like being pulled and shoved both at once. He hit the ground with a force that drove the wind out and wouldn't let any back in. The insides of his eyelids had turned bright white. Now they popped open and fixed on something in the fading plume of light, something on the ground, fighting and splashing.

When the light died, Doc tried to crawl toward what he'd seen. All around him in the dark was the roar of falling rain. The mushy ground under his hands began to tremble, and he knew the cattle were running.

In the next crash and white light, Doc saw a body on its back in a bowl filled with steam. The head was resting on a wagon rut. Out of the swarming steam stuck naked toes. Doc saw a second man come stumbling and knew it was Jim Adams. He should have known who the man in the water was but his memory was wiped clean.

Then everything went black. When Doc saw and felt again, his cheek was pressed in mud and his mouth was full of sandy, shit-tasting earth. Another bolt lit the stage, and up ahead was Adams pulling the body from the water. He heard Adams talking, pleading. Then he heard a second voice. Doc was too weak to rise, but he was close enough to hear. The accent was young and Texan, as if from Doc's childhood. Talking in choppy bursts.

"I think I, I think I . . . "

"You *are* alive," said Jim.

"By Jesus, it hurts, though."

"Hurts where?"

"My heart. Jesus, get that out of my pocket."

"What pocket?"

"Just get the goddamn thing out!"

Doc tried again to crawl. His arm was so weak his face fell past it. He was punched by the ground. He could not move.

"Where's Grassy?" the Texan called. "Did it kill my mare?"

"Maybe you shouldn't talk so much."

"Grassy!"

It was Tex Appleby, that was sure now. Grassy was the green mare, the trick mare.

Doc used all his strength to fold his arms and prop his face. He watched into the dark, waiting for another light. When it came, it was too close. The white light and roar lasted several seconds. In it, Doc saw Jim kneeling beside Tex. He saw Alf Tooks standing over both of them. Behind the three men, not seen by any of them, the green mare was coming.

When the dark closed up, Doc heard a wet gallop, then Adams shouting. Then Doc fell out of the world again.

SOME THINGS WERE NOT known until morning. Tex Appleby was dead, beside the puddle that had boiled him. His boots were blown off; only his belt and one trouser pocket remained of his clothes. In the pocket was a knot of gold that had been his watch. On his face were red dots as if someone had dabbed him with a lit cigarette many times.

All night and morning the green mare had stood over the body, quivering. It was probable that Tex would have died anyway, but it was the mare that had killed him. Blinded by the lightning, she heard Tex call and came running. She had stepped on his chest and stopped his heart.

When the mare came, Jim Adams tried to stop her, dove out of the way at the last instant. Alf had seen it, but that was the last he saw of Jim. They called for him and he did not answer. Come morning, both he and the black gelding were gone.

Most of the cattle had raced down their back trail. Lowell showed a strange indifference to them. They would be on the Marias, he said. Before they went after them, they would dig Tex's grave.

When the hole was dug and the Texan wrapped in his often-patched soogin at the bottom, Lowell asked Doc to speak, not because he'd known Tex that well, but because they were from the same part of the world. Doc was ashamed to have to do so while sitting, but his legs were still quivery when he tried to stand. He said Tex had been one hell of a horseman, a good singer, and a considerable fancy dan. Just then he remembered Tex's song before it happened and, in his poor voice, sang what he remembered. It was the old one about Laredo and blowing the fife slowly, about a burial, and Doc left it at that. He wasn't about to say if it was a coincidence or a sign. One thing was sure, and this he did say, Texas had lost another son, like so many gone before.

They scratched Tex's name on a board that was breaking off the chuckwagon anyway. They sank it in the ground and braced it with rocks. Then the boys saddled and rode south while Doc stayed by the grave. Louie came and stood above him, sleeping on his feet with his nose lowered near Doc's shoulder. Finally, Doc found he could stand and he saddled the gelding. He mounted and rode the opposite way, into the biting north wind that had returned after the east wind had done its damage and gone.

The ground was wet and puddled. After a half a mile, Louie started whittering and straining. Doc let him go where he wanted, and they came to the black gelding, Loco. Fifty yards from the black horse was its saddle, blanket, and bridle, all neatly stacked. Loco had a rope on one leg, the far end of which was braided into a tough twist of grass. It was an old cowboy trick for bare country, done as if to leave a final message that Adams had never been as green as some had thought.

Other than that, every direction was empty.

FIVE DAYS LATER, they were moving north again when the herd met the Major coming south. His new foreman, Frank Strong from the I.G. Baker Ranch, rode beside him, and what looked like a dozen I.G. Baker cowboys were strung out behind.

The Major received the news about Tex and his face fell. Right then, Doc knew something he hadn't known before: that Major Walker was probably younger than himself. Solidity and gravity gave him a look of age, both of which failed before the story of Tex Appleby's hard death. Lowell added that Jim Adams was gone, had apparently run off in the chaos after Tex died. The Major said he had not seen the boy.

The Montana crew could have stopped right there, collected their wages, and let the I.G. Baker crew take over. But the horsemen kept on into the wind for another half a day. When they came to the place where stones had been piled to mark the border, they walked their horses round and round that cairn. It might have been funny if anything about the Cochrane drive could still be viewed that way.

Behind a tarp held up to the sooty wind, the Major paid out the rest of their wages. When done, he asked if any men would be willing to continue into Canada. Dwight and Lippy said they would. So did Pesky Boucher. The rest, even Alf Tooks, who was Pesky's close friend, looked away and wanted no part of it. There was a new chuckwagon and a new cook, so even Cook and their old wagon left. Several of the boys didn't buy their horses, but rode away in the wagon box on top of their bedrolls.

Some of those who left did not even bid their segundo farewell. Doc found it both hurtful and understandable. Something had gone wrong here, something it was best to escape and not think about for awhile. Why say falsely that you hoped to meet again soon?

Lowell Ferris did come to say goodbye. He had never wavered in his position that Canada was not for him. He reckoned he would winter in Fort Benton and then look for a ranch that needed managing. They shook hands and agreed that they would write letters and meet again.

Except for puddles, the cows had not drunk in thirty-five miles. It was time to get moving for the Milk River, which was still some distance ahead. Doc took the driving seat of the calf wagon and tied Louie alongside. When he looked in the back, two dozen sets of yearning calf eyes stared at him. He slapped the reins on the Clydesdales' hips, and they jerked the wagon into motion, into the lashing wind and Canada.

ALBERTA

THE COCHRANE LEASE

PROLOGUE

Though the sun has been sliding down the south sky for months, the season has always been summer. Now, like a magician's trick, it is morning and the mountains have turned to white. All that day, you ride the brown hills full of sadness, your heart a hole that the wind blows through.

Summer's leaving is every other kind of loss combined. You know the seasons are a cycle, but there is no consolation in that. It only stretches misery ahead of itself: invents the feeling called dread.

As for winter, what good can be said about a season when the air, the friend that keeps you alive, turns on you with a dagger?

FORT MACLEOD

September 1881

ROM THE CANADIAN BORDER north, the country rolled in low billows and long sweeps of tawny grass that stretched to distant ridges, a pattern cut by dry coulees and occasional rivers. Though it was early in September, the wind out of the north continued cold and came at the Cochrane cattle and cowboys incessantly. The long grass with so few animals to eat it seemed to advance on them, wave upon wave. The more fanciful could imagine that the elements themselves were conspiring to push them back into Montana.

When the drive had reached the Milk River, the young foreman, Frank Strong, ordered that the herd be split into dries and wets. The dries—bulls, steers, calfless cows—would go ahead, led by a teamster named Hauk. Strong himself would lead the wets—the cows with milk in their bags and calves at heel. Having taken over the calf wagon at the border, Doc had unintentionally consigned himself to the slower, more cumbersome drive. Always drawn to the hardest work, Lippy had also chosen to stay with the wets, while Dwight and Pesky jumped at the chance to move out faster with Hauk.

On the bouncing calf seat, with his bawling charges behind and his Clydes clumping ahead, Doc had a great deal of solitary time. What he found himself thinking about most was Jim Adams.

A boy so young, probably not more than twenty or twenty-one, abruptly leaving a crew who had been helpful to him was a perverse thing, and rare, especially in the young, who seldom take a step without six of their kind taking it with them. Even Dog Eye might have never left the Cochrane drive without his little tribe of allies, a thing no less true for the fact that he escaped them as soon as he could in Fort Benton.

Doc thought about Jim because of that perverse independence and because of the silent sadness that had wafted off the boy right from the first hour they had shared this wagon seat. It was Doc who had seen Adams come floundering through the wet to try to save Tex

Appleby, and Doc again who had found Loco braided to a grass tuft and Jim gone. It seemed that Doc was involved with Jim Adams by some mechanism unseen, and he kept wondering what had become of the boy or expecting him to appear, dusty and hungry, beside the trail.

The facts were that Jim had originally been going to Fort Macleod in search of a Mr. Craig. Loco's having been found north of camp rather than south suggested Jim was still headed in that direction. That he had left the horse indicated to Doc that he had not wanted to re-enter his home country a horse thief. That he had abandoned it sooner rather than later perhaps meant he wanted Cochrane men to find it rather than Indians.

All in all, it seemed likely to Doc that Jim would be found in Fort Macleod, or at least word of him would be there. As the wets neared that town, Doc became excited. When Frank Strong told the camp they would not be stopping in Fort Macleod, on account of the hurry they were in, Doc made of himself an exception. He told Strong it was necessary that he stop and barter some calves to storekeepers and citizens, that he should stop and check with the Mounties for mail.

THE NUMBER OF TIMES Doc had heard Fort Macleod mentioned since the trail turned north suggested a considerable town. As the trail began to dip into a low-relief stretch of the Old Man River valley, and he caught his first glimpses of it—a small ramshackle stockade and a cluster of little houses—he assumed he was only seeing part, that the rest must be hidden behind the taller banks to the east and west.

But there was no more. The whole town was on a dimpled flat at the head of a river curve, where the cottonwoods had already gone into walls and fires, leaving only some living scrub and berry brush for shelter. The square stockade was the upstream edge, and Doc noticed it was missing most of one wall. The posts beside the gap were charred. The rest of town was a single dusty street of mud-roofed houses and stores. To get there, Doc crossed a short rattling bridge over a sloughy creek that made of the flat an island. Doc could tell right off this was a place prone to flooding. On the outside of a river curve after a stretch of straight, the flat could hardly help but receive high water whenever some was unleashed by the mountains.

The biggest structure in town besides the fort was the Macleod Hotel, several small buildings joined and huddled behind a false front. There was a little sign wagging under its eave that showed a pistol pointed at a skull and the words *No Jawbone*, meaning no credit. Doc pulled the calf wagon to the hotel's hitching post, tied up, and went inside.

After a look at the granite basin and filthy roller towel, Doc decided against a wash. He sat on a bench at one of the long dining tables and occasionally coughed in competition with the banging of pots in the kitchen. Eventually, a red-faced, dark-bearded man emerged, wiping his hands on his dirty apron. He asked Doc what he could do for him, and Doc asked for a fried egg, preferably chicken.

The proprietor, who was English, brought Doc coffee and went back to fry the egg, leaving Doc to the company of a few late-season flies. When the stocky Englishman returned with Doc's breakfast, he sat on the other side to watch him eat it. He quizzed Doc about his outfit and got a greedy look when told that it was the wet half of the Cochrane drive. Apparently, the crew with the dries had stopped in for an evening. When Doc told him the wets were right now fording the river upstream and would not stop, he was disappointed, and in that mood, offered to sell Doc a whisky with his breakfast. Doc said it might not be too early for everyone, but it was too early for him.

The Englishman introduced himself as "Kamoose" Taylor. He said proudly that he had been a whisky trader before the Mounties came. Then he launched into an old grievance over two cartloads of buffalo robes, freshly acquired in trade, that the Mounties had relieved him of without payment.

"From here to Fort Walsh, those damn thieves are still wearing buffalo coats made from my hides."

Doc asked if he knew a rancher named John Craig.

"There is no rancher Craig," he said, shaking his hairy head with certainty. "If I don't know him, he don't exist."

About Adams, he was just as sure. If a Jim Adams ever set foot in Fort Macleod, Kamoose would know. Then he asked if this Adams was a hard case, a criminal, in case he did show up. Doc said Adams was about as far from a criminal as a boy could get.

Doc was so disturbed by the news that Jim had never been to Fort Macleod he completely forgot to barter calves or check with the Mounties for mail. He was across the Old Man River and had driven miles in the shitty wake of the herd before he remembered. By then, it was too late.

FORT MACLEOD TRAIL

September 1881

OC WAS IN THE MIDDLE OF a long section of dry between the Leavings of the Willow Creek and the Highwood River when he looked up into the wind and thought he had gone mad. Out of the dust cloud that followed the herd, a flag-flying phantasm emerged: a dozen apple-red Mounties in white hard-hats and gauntlets, flanking a dapper dan in a suit of beautiful brown. Seeing Doc, they veered toward him, then made way so the man in the brown suit and beaver hat could ride forward and address him.

The fellow was an Englishman, and he gave his whole pedigree instantly. He was the Marquis of Lorne, the Governor General of Canada, Queen Victoria's son-in-law. Doc felt he should respond in kind. He said he was Doc Windham, son of Texas, a cowboy late of the Poindexter and Orr Ranch near Dillon, Montana, delivering cows to the Cochrane Ranch.

This excited the poppet. He said he knew the Cochrane lease, having just toured it with its manager, Major James Walker. It was a wonderful ranch, the Marquis declared, with grass up to the top of the cattle's legs. Doc knew for a fact that grass that height had to do with the murder of the buffalo more than the genius of the landscape. The cattle, once assembled, wouldn't let it happen again. But he kept that thought to himself.

"I am very interested in the ranching prospects here in Alberta," the Marquis told Doc.

Doc had never heard this name. He asked when the place started being called that.

"Since I named it, on this journey," said the Marquis, "for my wife, Princess Louise Caroline Alberta." Then he leaned forward conspiratorially. "I am making a study of the ranching prospects here. The prime ministers of Canada and England are both very interested. I can tell you that my recommendation will be extremely positive."

He raised his gloved hand and drew it across the plain, then turned and drew another line across the big ridge of hills to the west. Above that ridge poked mountaintops, white with snow. "In my opinion, Mr. Windham, this may be the greatest cattle-ranching country on earth."

THE MARQUIS WAS LONG GONE, but Doc was still ruminating on his parting remark: greatest cattle country on earth. He was thinking what a hell of a thing that was to tell a Texan and that he should really have rebuked the man, regardless of his sire and dam. Doc was hauled out of these thoughts when Louie muttered and jerked enough slack in his rope to turn back his head. Doc was combed by a rough fear. He lunged for his Winchester and looked around, fully expecting to see Overcross looming behind him.

But it was Dog Eye French.

Doc pulled up the team, and immediately the strongest calves in back jumped up and walked on the weakest. They knew it was near the end of the driving day and were anticipating their chance to suckle. Dog Eye was riding a pee-yellow horse, and he circled around so as to avoid Louie's back legs and let his horse meet the gelding from the front. The two horses came nose to nose and neither seemed disgusted.

Doc looked at his one-time friend and saw that all the visible surfaces of Dog Eye's head were puffed and the colour of rotting fish.

"So, Dog Eye, you are in Canada after all."

The Texan nodded, but was not ready to speak. Doc saw that he was in pain beyond what was explainable by the visible swellings and marks. By the way he held his body, clenched between his elbows, Doc diagnosed cracked ribs. For that, it was best to lie still and not sneeze. To ride on them was painful madness. Doc thought he saw something else lurking beneath Dog Eye's grim expression. Humiliation, maybe.

As Dog Eye was not talking, Doc tried a question.

"I looked in on Fort Macleod. You?"

Dog Eye shook his head.

"There's no saloons," Doc continued, "because it's against the local law to serve liquor. Yet I traded a calf for a bottle of whisky not twenty miles south of there. And when I was in the town and had an egg at a local hotel, the proprietor offered me a drink of whisky with my breakfast. I'm thinking it might be the same with whores: that there are none, except the ones there are."

Doc left a space into which Dog Eye still did not talk.

"And if you see anything red coming, toss your gun belt in a bush. According to Frank Strong, wearing one's unlawful. You didn't happen to see Jim Adams in your travels?"

Dog Eye shook his head.

Despite the silence, Doc was flooded with forgiveness for Dog Eye. Instead of galloping past to parley with the Major's new ramrod, he had stopped with his segundo. This showed respect and manners, and Doc was proud.

"Tonight, I'll talk to Frank Strong. He's the new trail boss. He's not even as old as you. I'll talk to the Major later. Right now, you can help me pick up half-dead calves. If we're lucky we might find a played-out cow to shoot and skin."

Now it appeared that Dog Eye was going to speak. It was not very loud and was spoken more to the withers of his horse than to Doc. Doc strained to hear so he wouldn't have to ask the cowboy to repeat.

"Think it always snows here in September?"

Doc was about to say that it wasn't snowing when he realized it was. After all the days of cold, finally there was some product: a few flakes swirling in on the wind. Time would tell if they were heralds or the real thing.

Doc offered that Dog Eye could sit on the wagon seat, but Dog Eye had seen the way the vehicle banged along and preferred the familiar motion of his horse. He rode close by and Doc waited for the story of his beating. By the end of the day, when they had joined with the others in the lee of the new cook's chuckwagon, Doc still had not heard the story. Nor did he. Dog Eye French came back a changed man, capable of secrets and silence, even of letting arguable points float by. He had developed shallow depths.

COCHRANE LEASE

September 1881

TWO MILES FROM THE LONG trail's end, with the wind still blowing cold and threatening snow, the Cochrane wets fell off the world. When Doc drove his loaded calf wagon to the same edge, what he saw was a thousand-foot valley and a fat snake of river in the distant bottom. They had crossed the same river a day ago, near the Mountie fort called Calgary, but the valley there had been shallow and the river spread wide. What he saw now were spruce trees and other kinds of black climbing a south escarpment, and, above them, a series of horizons, each one higher and darker until the last black line was trumped by grey and blue. It was like the Rocky Mountains stood in the air, their peaks slathered in creamed clouds, shouldering the burden of the sky. Down below and stretching west was the one hundred thousand acres of Senator Cochrane's lease.

The wets, wearing their ribs as outside apparel, were too exhausted to walk down the hill. Surrendering to gravity, they flounced along the wagon track at a helpless trot, weaving in and out of the hill flank's brushy folds. As Doc watched, a cow was knocked off the trail and sent rolling. Her calf, heedless, swam on in the river of flesh.

THE LITTLE CAMP THAT WAS ranch headquarters could not be seen until they were in the valley's bottom and around the base of the hill. The crew that had come with the dries was closing in the roof of a small cabin, probably the Major's house until a proper big house could be raised. Pesky waved from the roof. Dwight was carrying a board from the sawpit that he lifted to the roof without a ladder.

Behind the building was a chiselled hillock that reminded Doc of Texas. Dry and brushy, with shelves of sandstone all over it, the hill was tiny compared to the one they'd ridden down, but the way it stood between two great hills, partly blocking the coulee between, meant it would give shelter to the buildings, especially during northers like the one blowing now. The creek curved around the base of this small hill and divided the Major's cabin from the camp of his cowboys. On the east side of the ribbon of water stood a white canvas wall-tent, their bunkhouse for now.

Because Frank Strong and the I.G. Baker cowboys were finished as of the last cow descending, Doc was momentarily his own boss. In that capacity he gave Lippy and himself the rest of the day off. They jumped over the creek at a narrow spot and walked to the cabin to visit with Dwight and Pesky. Both boys were excited to see them, to hear their news, and to tell their own. They were still excited about meeting the Marquis of Lorne and seemed a little let down to find out that Doc had met him too.

"Hold on now, boys," Doc said. "It don't devalue the Marquis's currency to have met me. From my point of view, it makes him better."

About then, Frank Strong came out the cabin's door, carrying what was probably a bag of money. He shook Doc's hand, and they wished each other well. Frank told Doc that the Major was inside and wanted to talk to him.

The cabin looked even smaller inside than out. The Major was hearty enough in his greeting, but by the lamplight, appeared even greyer than the last time they'd spoke. His health seemed to be tied to his cows, and probably in the last hour had declined dangerously. Doc hadn't seen the Major outside looking at the arriving wets, but he could have looked at the first few before coming back inside.

The Major invited Doc to sit on a stump that was the only extra chair. It seemed strange to start a meeting with fellows whacking with hammers on the roof. Bits of snow were still drifting with the wind, and the Major's first comment was an expressed fear of what might happen if the weather turned worse.

Doc's view was different. "I hope it does get worse, Major, so it can get better. It's a little early for winter."

That comment seemed to settle something in the Major's mind.

"Doc, I wonder if you would consider being my segundo. Unfortunately, it's probably a temporary post and not all that much of an honour." He waved at a few telegrams on his desk. "There's something about wanting to hire the permanent foreman. Someone from the East, I suppose."

Doc told him not to worry, that he wasn't insulted. He would tell the boys he was temporary segundo and so be it. That started them on a discussion of who the boys were, the crowd on the roof and any others who might be out riding with the dries.

The recital of names and histories was soon over and, for Doc, was depressing news. None of the Major's cowboys seemed to be cowboys. Two of the Major's hires were recently mustered-out Mounties of low rank. Two were beaver trappers, a father and son named Piché, who by the sounds of it were as apt to eat a horse as ride one. Another two, a German and an Irishman, had been working for the Mounties as servants until the Major hired them. They were wagon men. Doc asked if any of them could rope, and the Major said he didn't think so. Not feeling nervous any longer about the news, Doc told the Major that Dog Eye French was back, and that by the sounds of things, it was a damn good thing. As well, it seemed that Dwight had got his wish by default: by the standards of the Cochrane Ranch, he was a top hand.

"Oh, yes," said the Major, "and then we have Richard Duthie."

The description of this Duthie was elaborate. He was green about cows, the Major thought, but was an excellent horseman. He came with a considerable pedigree, like the Marquis of Lorne, and in fact knew both the governor general and his wife. He had been the princess's paddler on a fishing trip in New Brunswick. Despite what Doc had said to the other cowboys, he too was becoming less impressed with having met the Marquis of Lorne. It seemed most everyone in Canada had.

Having reviewed the manpower situation, the Major outlined what he thought should get done before winter. His first question for Doc was if he thought they should brand the cattle. Back in Montana, because of the hurry they were in, they had only put on a hair brand, a travelling brand. The owners were pressuring to have the cattle properly burned with the ranch's big C before winter.

Doc had no doubt on this question. "With all due respect, Major, leave those poor sonsabitches alone. They have suffered enough."

What Doc also suggested was that they get out and ride the lease, soon as possible. They needed to locate the best grass, shelter, and water. Then they should split the herd and take a bunch to each good place. Last thing was to build line camps for the cowboys who would be looking after the cattle in these spots.

Then the meeting was over. The Major poured Doc a whisky and thanked him for a job well done. He meant the drive. He poured a second whisky to thank him for agreeing to be the Cochrane Ranch's segundo.

THAT NIGHT WHILE THEY SLEPT, the skirmishing weather advanced. The tent started whumping, and when Doc pushed the flap at dawn, it was against a drift of snow. He stuck out his head and was attacked and stung by snow out of the north, a blizzard howling down the wooded coulee.

The tent barely slowed the wind on its way through. Little skims of white were on every cowboy's soogin and saddle. It was hard to get the boys to come out of their beds, even with the coffee pot rattling on the pot-belly stove. There was a pile of mouldy blankets in the corner, and Doc started tearing them into strips that the boys could use as scarf material or wrap around their thin leather gloves.

As for himself, Doc put on his angora woolly chaps for the first time since Dillon. He put his silk scarf over his mouth and nose and wrapped some stinky blanket around his face and ears overtop. He was thinking how it was only a week since he'd used the same wiper to strain wrigglers out of slough water when he had nothing else to drink.

At the rope corral, the horses stood with their asses to the wind and their necks bent down. Their tails were wrapped around them by the wind and their long manes blew over their lowered faces. Because of the weather and the strange look of the cowboys, most of the horses had to be roped.

In the valley, the pilgrim cattle were weak as babies and lost as hell. They were letting the wind herd them south and then east along the river, and when the cowboys caught up to a bunch just reaching the water, it was to see one young cow walk off the cutbank into the river's current. Lost.

The Major's orders were to keep the cattle on the lease at any cost. The boys rode hard, passing cows lined out along a shore path among the trees. The horses kicked through forming drifts and finally headed the column. It was as if the cows believed their brief time at the ranch had been but a respite and that they were back travelling again. The cold wind and stinging snow were their new tormentors, replacing the rock cans, slickers, and chousing rope ends.

THE BLIZZARD LASTED FIVE DAYS, and the wind blew cold and empty for another two. During that time, the cowboys' work was to thwart the cattle's seeming desire to die. Some entered a tight, brushy coulee and were followed by others until the coulee was full and snow was drifting them under. The cowboys had to rope the cows one at a time and drag them back.

Others yarded in the open, densely packed, making a form around which the snow could build. The cowboys drove their horses against these drifts, broke and rode them down. The released cattle descended toward the smell of water.

At the river, the lines of cattle had to be beaten back to keep them from pushing the front end into the swimming water.

Then, in a single night, the north wind was bullied aside by a robust westerly. When the boys rose that morning, their tent was bucking around them so wildly it seemed in danger of lifting off. But it was also warm inside. They walked out in their boots and underwear to find everything that had been frozen coming unfrozen. Water pooled at their feet, whipped in their faces off the wall tent's roof, gurgled in the oxbow stream.

A strange feature of that day was that the Major crossed the creek in the afternoon to tell them that President James Garfield had finally died of his wounds, that news having been delivered by the mail driver from Fort Calgary. The Major thought that the Americans among them might wish to know.

COCHRANE LEASE

West End Camp, November 1881

DOC AND LIPPY'S CAMP WAS ON a long flat a mile north of the Bow River. It was in the mouth of another valley that opened north and sloped upward between two sets of high black hills. Some low brush and a few poplars were something to hide behind when the west and north winds got brisk.

This line camp was near the lease's west end. Three others were arrayed elsewhere. North of Cochrane Lakes, working the lease's northern edge, were the Pichés. Doc chose them because it seemed unlikely that any cattle would climb that high. The ex-Mounties were given the territory between the Bow and its little brother the Elbow, handy to Fort Calgary so they could visit when they became lonesome. Doc left Pesky Boucher at the main ranch with the two wagon drivers, because Pesky had good horse sense for the supervision of the ranch remuda. Richard Duthie also lived in that bunkhouse. Doc thought he should be close to the Major for sherry and state decisions.

The line camp on the east end, just off the Bow River's north shore, upstream of Fort Calgary, was left to Dwight and Dog Eye. Doc had thought of putting himself with Dog Eye but decided he would only irritate him. Dwight talked less than Doc and had the added advantage of greatly admiring Dog Eye's cowboy skills. Doc thought Dog Eye could use some admiration right now, having lost some of what he used to have for himself.

As they had at the main ranch, the cowboys started their life on the winter range under canvas, until the cabin-building crew arrived. Lippy had lobbied the Major for a horse shelter, and when the wagon came, there was lumber enough for both structures. This was a "Major concession" in that the Cochrane Ranch had no sawmill yet, and the Major was buying his boards for top dollar at Fort Calgary.

Something else Lippy brought to their camp that no others had was a scythe. Shortly after he and Doc had arrived, when the blizzard's snow was still covering the ground, Lippy had insisted that Doc ride Louie in circles around their tent dragging a board. Along this bared track, Lippy went to work with his scythe.

"You must be the only man in Canada haying in November," Doc told him, the month having just turned, but Lippy ignored it as he did anything he recognized as a tease. As Doc gathered grass behind him, Lippy kept swiping the blade along the tufted ground.

Though Doc was fond of Lippy, a steady and exclusive diet of his silence was a lot to bear. While most cowboys praised isolation and decried civilization, Doc thought of himself more as a town man, the kind who sits all day in a barber shop and listens to the community's fat get chewed. Instead, here he was with Lippy, who would scythe grass in silence all day, then spend his evenings quietly braiding a horse-hair rope. When his eyes got tired, he would abruptly strip off, roll into his blankets, and go to sleep within minutes. The more Doc observed the pattern, the more he was certain he and Lippy had talked more three years ago than they did today, though that was a comparison of little to damn little.

Normally what Doc did in this situation was read, but he had arrived in this line camp with no newspapers or magazines and one book. The book was Spurzheim on phrenology, which he could more or less recite.

Finally the pressure to escape was bigger than Doc could withstand. He told Lippy he would be back in a day or two and headed west along a trail the Major said went to Morleyville, a Methodist mission for the Indians and a trading shop, run by two brothers called McDougall.

After a lengthy ride, Doc and his horse came to a river that proved deep and cold. Beyond that another few miles, about when Doc thought he must stop to build a fire and dry off, he saw a wooden steeple poking the sky. By the time he was close enough to see the whole church, he could also see several smokes from a tipi town below. A wagon trail led to and left the Bow River there, and it made sense that the settlement had been built at a popular ford.

Doc knocked on the church door and a voice called him to enter. The padre, John McDougall, was alone in the bare-walled room, wielding an axe with expressive energy. He was shaping a hand-hewn board into a part for a pew. McDougall was tall and skinny. Off his chin wagged an improbable length of dark beard, the kind that old men wear to accentuate their age and wisdom. This reverend was no older than Doc.

Doc was still wet from the river and shivering, but the missionary was sweaty himself and not inclined to notice. There was a stove in the room's middle with a crooked pipe to the ceiling. Doc had to ask if he could build a fire in it to warm up and dry his clothes. The Methodist smiled in an annoying way that suggested Doc had shown a weakness.

While Doc got his fire going, Reverend McDougall began to talk rapidly, giving a report as if Doc had asked for one. He listed his mission's many successes: number of baptisms, number of marriages, number of Stony Indian children attending the school below. He talked admiringly of his father who had started the family in this business. That story came to a sad end when the father got lost on a winter hunting expedition in '76 and froze to death.

"It happened not far from where Senator Cochrane is building his ranch."

Doc had hardly said a word and the missionary did not seem to want or need him to. He was adept at prompting and answering himself. Doc stood by the stove and, by now, his clothes were steaming, giving off a baked sweat smell that was very pleasant, being his own.

He was drowsy in that heat, and the reverend finally noticed he was losing his audience. Abruptly, he asked a few questions about Doc's origins and current job.

Hearing that Doc was a hand for the Cochrane Ranch, they compared landmarks until McDougall knew exactly where Doc and Lippy's camp was situated.

"Then you have a neighbour," he said. "Olaf Holmstrom. Have you met?"

Doc was unaware of any neighbour. The padre explained that Olaf had a bit of a farm just upriver of Doc's line camp, in some rough breaks where two coulees came close together just before they spilled into the Bow. Holmstrom lived there with his Stony wife and the woman's two children from a first marriage. Her first husband, also a white man, had been drowned moving cut timber down the Ghost River, the one Doc had crossed and got wet in. Reverend McDougall had married Olaf Holmstrom to his bride right here in the church.

"You should visit Olaf," McDougall said at the end of the story, and Doc agreed. With the excuse of wanting to visit Olaf today, Doc got away from the talkative Methodist and the echoing church.

After buying some tobacco and papers at the other McDougall's trading shop, Doc rode back east and recrossed the Ghost River. He did so closer to the river's mouth, where it was more spread and shallow, and he got less wet. Then, as instructed, he rode along the steep-sided breaks of the two wooded coulees. At first he found nothing, but on another pass, he saw some tramped snow where stock had recently been fed hay. Only by coming right to the coulee's edge could he see down to a house and a barn, both so small they could have been from a European fairy tale.

As Doc started Louie down the bank, a slab-chested man came out of the barn. He wore a shapeless hat scrunched so low his broad spade beard seemed to grow out of it. He wore moccasins to the knee and a rough-out moosehide coat, sewn the Indian way.

Doc dismounted at the bottom of the cliff, so as to look more harmless, and Olaf Holmstrom approached with a grin. In a spot of snow-bright sunshine, they smoked and talked. In his lilty accent, the

Swede told Doc much of what he already knew from the Methodist. But Doc hadn't understood that the children weren't little children. They were mostly grown. The teenaged daughter was in the house with her mother, and the son was at the Cochrane Ranch, working as a carpenter's helper on Major Walker's big house.

When Doc asked about animals, Olaf whistled with his fingers and cattle came running out of the bush. When they saw Doc, they put on a theatrical pantomime of horror and receded back into cover. It was enough time to see they were fifteen young cows, all Herefords, and bred. They were also in better flesh than Doc had seen any animals since the summer in Montana. Olaf told him he had bred the cows to another squatter's Angus bull because that would promise smaller calves, easier for his "girls," all heifers, to bear. The progeny would be black white-faces. Their black bags would not sunburn, even on snow.

All through this conversation, Doc was thinking how much Lippy would have liked it. For Lippy, horses and cows were the only topics worth talking about. That Doc liked conversations about humans as well or better was one of the sources of their silence.

About that time, Olaf's wife brought out a hot bannock in a cloth. She was a confident Indian woman, not much younger than Doc. The bannock was so fresh it was steaming. Serviceberries had bled purple all through it. There was no sign of the daughter, and reading the thought out of Doc's head, Olaf said his daughter was shy and would stay inside.

Then Olaf laughed and asked if Doc had come to turn him off the lease. Senator Cochrane and Duncan McEachran, the owners of the Cochrane Ranch, had come in the summer and told him he would have to move because he was on their lease. He had told them maybe the lease should move since he was here first, but they were rich men and Olaf knew that would not be the end of it.

Doc told him it was not his reason for coming. If the ranch thought that way, they'd forgotten to tell him. But Doc had noticed that Olaf's cattle were not branded, and he could imagine problems if the Cochrane cows and his were ever to mix.

"Why haven't you branded?"

"Don't have one," said Olaf.

"Someone could rustle your cows or claim them, and you couldn't prove otherwise."

"They come when I call. They wouldn't come if you called."

"You don't usually get to call your cows in court." But Doc left it at that. He knew Olaf couldn't bear to touch his "girls" with a hot iron, a feeling against which there is no point arguing. After eating a big chunk of tasty bannock, Doc thanked Olaf's wife and said he'd like to visit again. Then he rode the short distance home.

NOT MANY DAYS LATER, when they were out checking cattle, Doc led Lippy within sight of Olaf's place. Soon they were arguing. Doc said to come on and meet another human being for a change. Lippy said he'd go home and Doc was welcome to visit long as he liked. Then Olaf surprised them both, coming out of the trees on foot.

Since Fort Benton, Lippy hadn't been hiding his harelip in company. At the same time, he didn't seek out people any more than he ever had. With Olaf, Lippy kept his face in the open and, after awhile, began to warm to what Olaf was saying about cows. Olaf had no reaction to Lippy's appearance that Doc could see.

Pretty soon, Olaf and Lippy were in avid conversation, Lippy talking as easily and as much as Doc had ever seen him do. Doc couldn't deny it made him jealous that Lippy could talk to a stranger more easily than to him.

When Olaf asked them to come in and eat, that was another matter. Lippy reverted to shyness and said he wasn't hungry. Olaf had already mentioned his wife and daughter, and Doc knew it was the thought of not one but two women staring at him across a table that made Lippy balk.

"My daughter will sit behind a cotton sheet while we eat. Don't be offended as it's only shyness."

For some reason, Olaf's saying that made Lippy less certain about not eating. It was as if Lippy understood for the first time that refusing invitations is not polite. This got Lippy as far as Olaf's yard, before he stopped again and said he'd prefer to eat his meal outside with the horses.

"We'll all eat outside, for it is beautiful today," said Olaf. "Except my daughter, like I told you."

They hauled out a home-built table and some chairs, though it really wasn't that warm, and there was Lippy sitting straight across from Mrs. Olaf (whom Olaf called Inge). They ate venison and more bannock, and it was fine. Inge had the same good manners about Lippy's face as Olaf did, and soon Lippy was talking to her too.

It was an amazing day, the only mystery being the daughter. Though they never saw a hair of her, Doc had the tickle that suggested she was watching out a window. Riding away through the dark, Doc tried to engage Lippy on this topic.

"She prefers not to be seen," said Lippy, from his saddle, and the tone was sharp. It was rude to speculate about Olaf's daughter was Lippy's message, and no more of it would be allowed.

COCHRANE LEASE

West End Camp, December 1881

BECAUSE WINTER HAS NO CHOICE but to happen, things got cold again in December. In the middle of the month, a speck appeared on the snow to the east. Doc and Lippy were tacking up Louie and Calico, about to check on some Cochrane cows that had gone up the north valley.

The speck was a rider, and Doc hoped it was a delivery of provisions because they were running low. It would be odd to come on horseback, but maybe the wagon road was drifted. Doc was thinking that he and Lippy could make a game out of the identity of the rider when Lippy said, "Dwight."

"Damn it, Lippy, that man and horse together are no bigger than a match head. How could you know?"

"Man's bigger than his horse. Off kilter."

That he was almost certainly right was irritating. Doc had never convinced Dwight a man should fit his horse, and he did have the annoying habit of riding on one haunch at a time.

Doc got a little of his own back when Dwight was closer.

"He don't have a saddlebag or a bedroll, so he's expecting to ride straight back. Means he's got news, not just come to visit."

"Horse is favouring her left front," said Lippy, not to be outdone.

Close up, Dwight kicked off Patches and fell on his hands and knees in the snow. He jumped up and ran toward them.

"He's gone! With Pete."

Pete was the yellow gelding Dog Eye had bought in Fort Benton. Though he was a bad colour, Dog Eye preferred him, even to Loco.

"How long?"

"Three days."

"And you don't think he's just quit again?"

"He left his gear."

"He's not in a poker game over at the I.G. Baker store?"

Dwight shook his head. "He didn't dress very warm, Doc."

"Neither did you, you big fool."

Lippy gave Dwight's horse a bundle of hay and got his shoeing box. Doc led Dwight inside. They were out of firewood but had a pile of coal. Doc had made some jumpy matches by soaking pine needles in coal oil, and those and some coal made a fire in the stove. As Dwight had white spots on his cheeks, Doc made him rub his face with snow and put a blanket over his shoulders.

Dwight tried to tell the story, but it kept jamming on his tongue.

"Slow down, Dwight, or you'll never get it said."

"It's a girl."

Though ambiguous, it was a start.

"What's a girl?"

"When we trailed in, we crossed that river called the Elbow?"

"Yes."

"When we crossed it, some half-breeds come to watch."

"So?"

"And there was a girl."

"What girl?"

"That's her. Dog Eye said right then she was the prettiest he'd seen, and how he was going to cross back some time and visit her."

"That family are probably fort hunters."

"It's two families. In two houses anyway."

"And Dog Eye went calling?"

"Sundays. Then he started staying two days at a time."

"With her family?"

"No. He stayed with a freighter in a camp near the fort. That's the thing, Doc. Her family don't like him. The mother even come at him with a knife."

"I'm going to hate the answer, but how old is this girl?"

"I'm not sure. Fourteen?"

"Boiled owl! Egg suckin' dog!"

Doc marched around the narrow space of the cabin for a moment, thinking.

"Now, Dwight, you didn't come all this way to tell me Dog Eye's in love, or that he's a day later than usual. You got reason to think he's in trouble. What is that reason?"

"He's got no friends over there, Doc. The freighter's mean and don't like him. He ain't been eating. He hardly took a bedroll. He's got Pete and that's about all. And it's awful cold." Dwight was wringing his big hands, looking sorrowful.

"Okay, Dwight. We'll ride out now. You got grub at your camp?"

"I shot two cows that were dying. I took off the hides and butchered 'em."

Lippy was inside by now. Doc told Dwight to take the blanket he was wrapped in. They would leave Patches and take Pedro, Doc's spare. Doc dug out his emergency whisky bottle, half full, and put it in a saddlebag. He got his Winchester and its scabbard down from a nail, checked that his old cap-and-ball pistol was loaded and strapped it on. He noticed then that Lippy wasn't doing anything.

"I'm not going," he said.

Doc was silenced.

"I saddled Pedro for Dwight already. I reset Patches' shoe. She's fine to run behind. I promised Olaf I'd help him cut slabs. It's a two-man saw."

"I thought you'd come," said Doc. It sounded pitiful.

"If Dog Eye's in a fix, you and Dwight are enough."

ON THE RIDE DOWN the open valley, the glittering beauty of the day kept contradicting the idea that there was trouble. It was also hard to believe in the depth of the cold with the sun so bright. As they rode, Dwight harped on the idea that the Halfbreed girl's giant brothers and father might have caved in Dog Eye's head with an axe.

"They hunt meat for the Mounties, Dwight. How's that apt to work if they start killing white people? Same with the freighter."

What that left was the cold and Doc had no answer for that.

The shortness of the day and the late start meant they came to the ranch buildings in the merest remnant light. It was enough for Doc to the see the form of the Major's big house, still unoccupied but closed in at the top. In normal circumstances, he would have sought out Mrs. Olaf's son from the carpentry crew to say hello, but as it was, he and Dwight made for the cowboys' new bunkhouse, where they found Pesky Boucher and Richard Duthie keeping the stove warm and heating some stew.

Doc told Dwight's story and asked both men to keep it dark until they knew the truth—in case Dog Eye was found safe in a whore tent or drunk.

Then Dwight and Doc were back in cold hard saddles under a crescent moon. It was much colder in the dark. They left Patches behind with Pesky.

Though they hadn't spoken of it, both Doc and Dwight hoped to find Dog Eye at the line camp. A little light through a crack, some sparks flying from the chimney, and the whole matter would be resolved. But as soon as they could see the shack's glower on the snow-lit ground, that hope was gone and their mood fell through it.

"You need a warm up, Dwight?"

The big fellow didn't answer but Doc saw how his shoulders shook at just the mention of warmth.

"I'm cold enough," Doc said, trying to bend his stiff legs to get one over the saddle.

There was coal heaped in a corner and Doc got it burning with a couple of his jumpy matches. Dwight lit the lamp and by its light Doc saw he was frostbit, again.

"You got to gather that blanket tighter to your face, Dwight. Put more snow on your cheeks until they aren't so stiff and waxy."

While Dwight was thawing the spots on his face, Doc noticed angora chaps on a nail.

"Christ, Dwight, Dog Eye doesn't even have his woollies?"

Both men were impatient with the process of getting warm. As soon as Dwight started to howl and jump from the pain of coming thawed, Doc wrapped the big face with a strip of blanket he'd been warming at the fire. He tied it tight below the eyes and tucked the tails in at Dwight's neck. It made a bag that his breath would go into and spread against his cheeks. Then they set out again.

It wasn't long before they were at the black Bow River, where wagon tracks entered. Downriver, they could see the foggy light from behind the Fort Calgary palisade.

Doc studied what he could of Dwight by moonlight, saw how his boots were dangling below Pedro's belly. He ordered him down and told him to take off his chaps, pants, and boots. "Roll your underwear up above your knees."

When he was on the ground, Dwight saw that Doc hadn't budged.

"How come you ain't?"

"I'm a short man on a tall horse. I crossed this river in September and didn't get a boot wet. I'll take your chaps, your pants, and your blanket. Put your socks in your boots and hold them up with your free hand."

The horses didn't care to enter the black water. Ice-cold fog rose off it like veils. The fog kept the moonglow from penetrating, and Doc could tell by Louie's jumpiness that plates of floating ice were hitting his legs. Doc leaned ahead and talked, told him he was a fine horse and not to be afraid. He yelled for Dwight to talk to Pedro, but most of what Dwight did was yelp and whinny over his parts that were in the water.

When they walked out the other side, Doc told Dwight to get down and rub himself dry with the blanket before he dressed. With his own blanket, Doc rubbed the frost off the horses' legs.

"If this don't teach you to ride a taller horse, nothing will."

Doc was in too much of a hurry to make a fire. Nor did he go to the fort. The only way that the fort would know about Dog Eye was if his trouble wasn't serious or was over. There were only two places it made sense to look: at the freighter's camp and where the Halfbreeds lived. Dwight had been to neither but was sure the freighter's place was close to the ford.

Doc's preference was for the freighter to be away, but such was not the case. When they came to the camp, the moonlight showed two high-wheeled wagons beside a rectangle tent and a shabby corral full of oxen. The tent had a stove, probably buried in the ground, and the pipe out the canvas ceiling was smoking and sparking. The oxen were on their feet, and as the horsemen moved toward them across the snow, they shrank back, their eyes like carriage lamps when the moon's light fell into them.

Doc turned back and walked the horses slowly into a patch of trees a hundred yards away. He tied the horses tight. Given Dwight's opinion that the freighter was a hard case, Doc thought it best to approach with caution. He handed Dwight the Winchester and kept his own hand on the grip of his Colt. They walked slowly forward to the side of the corral away from the tent.

Leaving Dwight crouched by the poles, Doc crept closer. He dusted snow off a patch in front of the tent flap and built a little heap of his jumpy matches there. He struck a lucifer and dropped it on the pile. As soon as the match left his hand, he ran to Dwight.

The little explosion followed by fire and the snap and jump of the last pine needles to ignite was modest but effective. Within a minute, the freighter came boiling out of the tent flap in his underwear with his buffalo gun poised. A skinny youth came after him uncurling a bullwhip. The boy had been sleeping fully dressed.

"Freighter!" Doc called from behind the fence. The little pine-needle fire was still burning and the freighter squatted beside it. Doc could still see him between the rails and kept a bead on him. The old tickle started on his back. "Damn it, Dwight, lower that rifle."

The freighter swivelled his buffalo gun at Doc's voice.

"No, sir," said Doc. "You cannot see me, but I am aiming at your head. The smartest thing would be to set that rifle down and raise your hands away from it. Now."

The freighter saw the sense and did so. The boy yanked the bull-whip back and cracked it. The end snaked around the closest corner-post, wrapped, released. The oxen surged away.

"Freighter, tell that boy to drop the whip."

The freighter spoke sharply and the boy threw the whip down in anger.

Doc stood and approached them. He picked up the freighter's rifle, then pulled the whip along the ground until the handle was closer to him than to the boy. The last yellow tongue of fire went out, and Doc recalled what he had seen by its light. A sour-faced man, who seemed unable to open his eyes. A boy with a starved face and sunken eyes. It was the boy's proneness to heroics that made Doc keep his weapon levelled.

"This is crude of us, Freighter, but we are not thieves or murderers. We are friends of Dog Eye French. We hope to save him from trouble."

The freighter made a strange noise. He was only clearing his throat but it made a high piping sound. When he spoke, his voice was tight and difficult.

"Don't know no French."

Dwight spoke behind. "He calls himself Brutus."

"Oh, for Chrissake. Brutus then."

"Brutus ain't here," croaked the freighter.

"He up at the Halfbreed camp, maybe?"

"Could be. Clive? You know?"

The boy shook his head.

"Do we know the girl's name, Dwight? Or the father's? The ones *Brutus* is annoying?"

"Madeleine," said Dwight.

"Nap Taureau," said the freighter. "Her father."

"Freighter, how much trouble is Brutus in, would you say?"

The sour-faced man only grunted. Doc could tell the conversation had become too long and philosophical for him.

"Mind my asking what your name is, so I can call upon you in a more civilized way another time?"

"Tesk."

"I'm Doc Windham. This here's Dwight."

"Windham?"

"Yes?"

"Don't visit. Tell Brutus, don't visit either."

Tesk bent into his tent and the boy followed. Doc laid the old buffalo rifle on the ground outside the flap.

"One more question, Mr. Tesk? Where would I find Nap Taureau's camp?"

"South to the Elbow. Then west."

Departing, Doc asked Dwight if he was all right, if his face was numb again. Probably lying, Dwight said he was good. There was a trail to follow now. Once they were beyond the confusion of bull and wagon tracks, a single horse trail led off. After a few minutes of riding, Doc got down. He told Dwight to do the same. If they kept their feet working, instead of just hanging in the stirrups, they'd be better off.

After half an hour's walk through mainly stumps and a few patches of brush and trees, they came to the Elbow River. Tesk had said to go west from there and Doc hoped it wasn't far.

Silhouetted by the declining moon, a big hill rose in front of them on the right. A more shadowy hill to the left was probably on the Elbow's far side. Here on the river's north bank, they walked in trees that had yet escaped the fort's axemen. Then they entered a natural clearing. In it were two cabins, both dark except for sparks out the rock chimneys. In a snake fence between, four horses stood watching, their breath pulsing in the moonlight.

The cabins were beyond the hill's shadow. Where Doc and Dwight were, on the clearing's edge, was darker. The snow brightened things a little, but it was still hard to see.

"Dog Eye!" Doc yelled.

"Hell, Doc. They'll hear."

"Then maybe they'll help us find him."

They led their horses along the edge of the clearing toward the hill, a dense bluff of poplars to his right. Doc was trying to see a trail in the whitish murk. Louie started to murmur. Doc could see his ears and they weren't pointed at Taureau's corral. They were forward.

He led the gelding farther. When Louie started looking sideways, Doc followed that look into the trees. Standing among the thin poplar trunks, Pete was tied short to a branch, his head hanging.

Doc knelt and felt the ground. He found a packed place and, feeling in an arc, another. That gave him a direction. He was just a few feet from Taureau's clearing again when he tripped over Dog Eye's legs.

The Texan was curled in the snow. He had his hands pushed inside his clothes and his face on his hat. Beside him was a black smudge that had been a fire. Doc pulled off his glove and plunged his hand down Dog Eye's neck. It felt stone cold in there. Doc put his fingers before Dog Eye's mouth and nose and felt nothing.

"Goddamn you, Dog Eye! Don't be dead!"

Then he thought to touch the fire. He put his bare hand in the black and, though he felt no heat, he felt something. The spot was not ice cold. It meant Dog Eye had been beside a fire today.

Doc stood and looked in all directions, started off in two. Then stopped still and controlled himself.

"Is he dead?" asked Dwight.

"I don't know. Pick him up and follow me."

Doc entered the clearing, yelling. He ran to the door of the first cabin and banged with his fist. The door rattled but otherwise nothing. He beat on the door some more and heard some French said on the other side.

"Mr. Taureau, I don't speak French. I have a frozen man here needs to warm at your fire. If he don't, he's dead. Do you understand me?"

The door squawked open, showing black inside. The business end of a Sharps rifle poked out. Doc unbuckled his gun belt and handed it into the dark.

There was a conversation in French and Cree, a man and a woman. A match popped and lit a candle.

"Come."

Inside, Doc saw by the meagre light that the space was mostly empty. There were buffalo robes on the dirt floor in front of the stone fireplace. The coals in that hearth were red hot and waves of heat came off them into the room. The man who must be Nap Taureau stood in his underwear and looked at Dog Eye in Dwight's arms. Taureau pulled a buffalo robe in front of the fire and pointed there. Dwight laid Dog Eye down.

Taureau's wife came with a second robe. She pushed Dog Eye over from his back to his side, so he faced the heat. She tucked the second robe around his back and over his side. As Doc's eyes grew more accustomed, he saw the girl, Madeleine, as a pair of black eyes looking over the edge of a robe.

Dwight was whimpering, saying that Dog Eye carried stiff like a dead man.

"Well, he's frozen stiff, Dwight. Don't mean he's dead." But he certainly seemed to be. His face was serene, as it never was in life, like he was having a good sleep. He was pale blue.

"What do you think?" Doc asked Taureau, who had squatted down on his heels beside Dog Eye, studying his head. He did the same as Doc had, felt down Dog Eye's shirt and frowned. He talked to his wife in a mixture of French and Cree.

Taureau turned to Doc. "Dead from cold is different than dead from other thing. Mebbe come back."

The woman spoke some more. All Cree as far as Doc could decipher.

"She say best thing is lie beside him no clothes on."

Doc was pretty sure she wasn't volunteering. He looked at Dwight and decided it wasn't his duty either. Doc started with his woolly chaps.

"Listen to me, Dwight. I know it's vanity in a solemn moment, but I don't want this story all over this range come summer."

"Yessir."

While Doc got out of his clothes, Taureau and his wife stripped down Dog Eye. The boots wouldn't come and Taureau asked Doc if he could cut them. Doc said yes, and Taureau produced a big dagger. He slid the double-edged blade between Dog Eye's ankle and the tight-fitting leather.

As Doc was about to get out of his underwear, he looked at both women. They were still looking at Dog Eye. Doc's nakedness didn't impress them much.

Doc crawled in the robes and hugged Dog Eye from the back. His flesh was exactly like ice. If it weren't that his friend was probably dead, Doc would have laughed from embarrassment. He knew it was what a lot of folks thought cowboys were up to all the time.

It took forever to make any impression on Dog Eye's temperature. If he was warming Dog Eye at all, it was much slower than he was cooling himself. Finally, he decided Dog Eye's back had warmed a little. He rolled him over and tried the front. The fact that the front was as ice cold as the back had been was not encouraging.

While this performance went on, the family from the other cabin entered: Taureau's two giant sons and a young woman. She had a baby and let it suck her breast once they had sat down. They spoke quietly in French and Cree, while they watched one naked white man hug another who was probably dead inside the buffalo robe.

"His eyelid moved! I swear, Doc!"

Doc didn't tell Dwight, but he thought that even if Dog Eye were stone dead, he would eventually come unfrozen enough for things to move. But then he also felt something. He would decide later it was the second Dog Eye's heart began to beat.

In about an hour, it was clear that Dog Eye French was alive. Now the question was for how long, and whether there would be much point in his being so.

As Dog Eye was nearing the same temperature as Doc, Doc got out of the robes and put his clothes back on. Madeleine had come closer to watch the revival, and she was very pretty. Fourteen was probably high as an estimate of her age. It was not unheard of to marry a girl that age, but Doc could not imagine her choosing it. Probably what she felt about the Texan was frightened, and maybe a little flattered that a grown man, not too ugly, was helplessly fond of her.

Doc turned his attention to the Taureaus. Nap Taureau was sitting back from the fire between his sons, smoking a little clay pipe. His wife had boiled up some stout tea and passed cups around. Doc's cup was gouged out of a cross-cut that gave the tea a piney flavour that was the best thing about it.

"It is very nice of you people to help this man back to life. I know he's been a nuisance."

"What's nuisance?" asked the son's wife, the one with the baby. She had good English.

"Pain in the ass," Doc translated, pointing at his bony own. Everyone laughed—except for the girl Madeleine, who was still too frightened.

Nap asked for Doc's attention and pulled the robe off Dog Eye's feet. Doc had not looked since Taureau cut off the boots. Now he saw that the toes were twice their normal size and black as coal. Even the nails were black. Dwight, who had come over to see, gagged at the sight.

Taureau was staring hard at Doc's face to see if he understood. Doc nodded.

Unfortunately, when Dog Eye came to his senses—it must have been after midnight—he did so cursing most profanely. All the thawed out frostbites on his face and ears and fingers were paining more than he could stand. Doc could not imagine what the feet would feel like, if not numb. It was also possible that Dog Eye had frozen himself into the core of his body. That might feel like you were burning from the inside out.

Doc put his mouth to the Texan's ear. "Listen here, Dog Eye. I know you are hurt, but there are ladies present."

Doc sent Dwight out to get the bottle out of the saddlebag on Louie. The whisky was so cold it had to be heated before they dared put any into him. After the chill was off, Dog Eye drank it all in gulps.

Because the fort was only a fifteen-minute ride away, because Dog Eye was thawed out, and because his fate was more the Mounties' business than this family's, Doc dressed Dog Eye and wrapped his feet in a blanket. Last thing, he went around the room shaking hands. The girl was last and she touched Doc's hand as if it were on fire. She did not look at his face.

Outside, while Dwight and Doc tied Dog Eye onto Pete's back, the Texan started cursing again. He said Doc shouldn't have sucked up so much to the Taureau family. Then to Dwight: "Doc always has been a suck-up. He'll be in politics before it's over."

"It was damn near over for you, Dog Eye. Don't be so impertinent."

"Now there's a five-dollar word."

Though Doc pretended to mind, the return of Dog Eye's obnox-iousness pleased him. Not knowing what was to come, the normalcy of Dog Eye's behaviour helped him believe in a tomorrow that would be the same as any other day.

AT FORT CALGARY IN THE middle of the night, Doc sat beside Dog Eye, who was good and drunk from another infusion of whisky. To-gether they stared at his black toes.

"I sure never thought I'd have feet like that."

"I'm sorry you do."

"I know what it looks like now. Once, when I was in San Fran-cisco . . . "

"You were only in San Francisco once."

"That's what I said. Don't in-rupt. I went to a place where they had a real gorilla in a cage. I went right up and that gorilla reached out and grabbed my shirt. Gorilla's fingers looked 'zactly like my toes do now. 'Zactly!" Dog Eye flopped back. "The cold has turned me into a gorilla."

Doc looked at his bright red cheeks and ears, the weeping nose swelled twice its size and apple red.

No, he thought. It's not the cold. It's love did. Let's just hope love didn't turn you into a dead gorilla.

"I really do love her, Doc."

"I can see that, Dog Eye. That is plain."

FORT CALGARY

December 1881

THE FOG FROM THE RIVER was thick and white over Fort Calgary the day the Irish doctor cut off Dog Eye's toes. Doc had the young Texan as full of whisky as the doctor would allow, and he made Dwight stay not only outside the door, but outside the whole fort. Doc was pretty sure Dwight would come to pieces at the same time

Dog Eye did, and he didn't want that interfering with anybody's concentration, especially his own.

At the knife's first bite, Dog Eye screamed. Not long after, he passed out. The Irish doctor, who looked way too young to be doing what he was doing, said, "This is a terrible mess."

Doc agreed, but the Irish doctor seemed angry, said the blood was not what he meant.

"I could take all the small toes off and he would be able to walk normally again. But he's frozen his feet too deeply for that. I have to take the big toes too." He pointed at the discoloured front pad on the bottom of each foot. "Most people don't know this is part of their big toe. The third joint. When I take it off, and I have to take off both of his, your man has half his feet. He'll never walk right again."

In the bright light of several lanterns, the Irish doctor kept carving. There was blood everywhere. Doc could feel spots drying on his face.

"There is a silver lining," he said to the Irish doctor. "Dog Eye French never liked walking much anyways."

In the slaughterhouse gore, lit bright with lamps and candles, the doctor laughed. Doc laughed too. It didn't much matter what you did. Laugh, cry, bark like a dog.

FOR TWO HELLISH DAYS, Dog Eye screamed when awake, sweated and chilled in a laudanum drowse the rest of the time. Strange nonsense fluttered off his tongue, about his beloved, about whores, about horses, never about his feet. Doc worried that he was too weak to keep off infection, but in some die-hard, bean-eating Texan way, Dog Eye kept that evil away. After three nights of fever his body cooled. He was still rigid with pain but it looked possible for him to live.

That was when Doc sent Dwight to the ranch. He had kept him back until he knew what the news was, whether they were preparing for a healing or a wake. He told Dwight to go easy on the details, to say only that Dog Eye got in a serious mix-up with the weather and froze some parts.

Thinking of ways to get Dog Eye home, Doc thought of a cariole. In a Halfbreed wintering camp in Montana, Doc had seen dog teams and elegant sleighs, sometimes with a child or a sweetheart bundled inside, face peeping out. Now he imagined Dog Eye's face being the one in the cariole. He imagined a silken passage compared to the gait of the smoothest horse.

Doc left Dog Eye at the fort and went to the Taureau camp. The men were out hunting but the mother and girl were home. The girl sat cross-legged with her dress spread in front. She was fitting gut strings to a child-size snowshoe frame.

Mrs. Taureau asked after Brutus, and Doc said the cowboy was still alive and that what they needed now was a dog team and cariole sleigh that could carry him to the Cochrane Ranch. Mrs. Taureau told Doc how to get to the camp of a man named Fleury, who lived on the Fish Creek. He had what Doc needed.

"Brutus lives then," said Mrs. Taureau when Doc was in the doorway, though he had told her as much minutes before.

"Yes," said Doc. "Who knows for how long, but he lives now."

He looked at the girl and found her staring. A string was clenched between her teeth. Her hands were motionless.

"Tell Brutus not to come here," said Mrs. Taureau. Doc saw on her face what Dog Eye probably saw plenty of: the cool set edge of something boiling.

"You mean ever."

"Never."

The girl began to cry, and Doc left wondering what might have passed here. Maybe, after watching Dog Eye return from the dead, the girl believed he had returned for her. That was a powerful story. Who knew what furies Mrs. Taureau had come up with to remove that fairy tale from her daughter's heart?

AS AGREED BETWEEN THEM, Fleury came to Fort Calgary next morning driving his dogs. He had red ribands on the handles for it was Christmas Day. He knew a man downstream who had a raft, and that fellow was also bribed away from his Christmas drowse by the contents of Doc's purse.

The cariole, Dog Eye, the barking dogs—the whole works went on the big raft at once. Fleury and the raft man poled across the Bow at the fording place, while Doc followed on Louie, leading Pete. On the other side, after straightening out the harness, cracking his whip, and cursing a good deal in French, Fleury drove the dogs up the wagon trail toward Morleyville. The little French Halfbreed ran behind the sleigh and hardly ever stood on it. He and his dogs went at a pace that was hard for Louie and Pete to match on the slippery surface.

As Doc had asked him to, Dwight had gone to the east end line camp after alerting the ranch of Dog Eye's trouble. Arriving there in the glittering afternoon, Doc found the shack smoking out its stovepipe and surrounded by horses. When the sound of the barking dogs carried inside, a stream of cowboys poured out, more than you'd dream the small building could hold. They had been waiting with Dwight for Dog Eye, and now they crowded around the cariole, staring at the Texan, whose eyes were fogged and face chalk white.

A moment both joyful and awkward. Doc could smell whisky on everybody. He broke it up, saying they must hurry. Pesky Boucher had the fastest horse, and Doc sent him ahead to alert the Major. The rest rode behind Fleury's ribboned sleigh.

The tableau of men and horses escorting the sleigh reminded Doc of meeting the Marquis of Lorne, with flags flying and all the white-helmeted Mounties on matched horses. The Marquis had no little French Metis, cursing his dogs in three languages, no drunken cowboys whooping it up to hear their echoes bang off the frozen air. Doc was with his own and felt it keenly.

COCHRANE RANCH

December 1881

THE MAJOR'S BIG HOUSE WAS WALLED and roofed, but none of the plastering or painting had been done inside. Dwight carried Dog Eye through the back door and into the first room, which was a servant's room behind the cast-iron stove. Joe Mah, the Chinese cook, was pulling a goose and two ducks out of his oven, and the black top was covered with steaming pots full of potatoes and vegetables. The house smelled of roasting fowl and wood smoke.

It was going to be a tight squeeze but Doc asked Dwight and Pesky Boucher to fetch him a bed from the bunkhouse so he could keep an eye on Dog Eye through the night. As an afterthought, he asked for a shirt, if anyone had a clean spare.

While Doc waited for the bed and shirt, the Major brought his wife back. She was a very pleasant white woman. She shook Doc's hand, and the Major took her back to the other guests. Doc was just getting over that meeting when another white woman came down the hall. She was tall, slim and reddish-blond. She wore an elegant dress and a glittery necklace. He could see her jewellery plainly because her hair was tied up on her head, and her dress had no shoulder on one side. She had brought some kind of red berry mixture in a jar and was explaining to Joe Mah that it went with the birds. Then she turned to Doc, acknowledged him with a nod, and looked beyond him into Dog Eye's room.

"How is he?"

"I don't think he'll be eating Christmas dinner, but he's fair. Trip from Fort Calgary doesn't seem to have hurt him."

"His eyes look strange."

"That's laudanum, ma'am. He's been stewed as a prune for days."

She said she was Esther Prieston and very pleased to meet him. Doc bowed and stood grinning like a fool until she asked him for his name.

"Doc Windham."

"Are you a doctor?"

"Cowboy, ma'am."

"What's your real name?"

"Doc's what I go by."

"And what about Dog Eye? I doubt that's his Christian name."

"Athol, ma'am, though he doesn't much like being called that."

Then the Major was back. He said that while the other boys would be served their Christmas dinner down at the bunkhouse, he and his wife hoped Doc would join them here at the big house. Doc was about to refuse, saying the bunkhouse was more his style, when Esther

Prieston said she would be delighted to have dinner with a real cow-boy for a change. Doc's loyalty to his own fell apart.

After Esther and the Major left, Doc stood still with little birds singing in his forehead. Then the Major returned and was handing him a coat.

"Sorry. This sort of occasion . . ."

"Don't worry, Major. I know there's times people dress up."

Left alone, Doc tried on the jacket in front of a little mirror above the washstand in his room. It was big, big as the Major. About then, Pesky and Dwight returned with the bed which they squeezed down between Dog Eye's bed and the outer wall. On it was a boiled shirt from Richard Duthie. Pesky dug in his pocket and gave Doc a crum-pled strip of black cloth, a strip of stiff white cloth with holes in the ends, and a bunch of black studs and cufflinks.

"You know how this thing works? Richard says the tie's got a bow already in it, if you're careful."

The boys left and Doc tried on the shirt. He was staring in the mir-ror when Dog Eye spoke up behind him.

"You look like a boy in his daddy's clothes."

"Thank you, Dog Eye. That helps my confidence greatly."

Doc looked back and saw that Dog Eye was having a rare moment of brightness, a clear window between pain and opium.

"You need a shave," he said.

"Boiled owl! I forgot."

Doc poked his head out and asked Joe Mah if he had a straight razor. Mah's answer was to gesture at all the food and steaming pots, meaning he was too busy. Doc ran out the back door and through the frigid air to the bunkhouse. There was much hilarity at seeing him with Duthie's long shirt flapping, but they only withheld the razor a moment.

Back in the kitchen, Doc dipped hot water from the stove reservoir into his washstand basin. The razor wasn't much for sharp but his beard came off.

"Anything you need, Dog Eye?"

"I'm hungry."

Doc towelled off and ran into the kitchen again. He opened his jackknife and stabbed a couple of pieces of goose off the platter. Joe Mah tried to wave him off, to explain that the goose wasn't for the cowboys. Doc took it anyway.

Dog Eye picked up a slice of bird and nibbled on the edge.

"It's goose," said Doc.

"I know it's goose. I lost my toes, not my mind."

Doc unbuttoned his corduroy trousers and started pushing the shirt tail in. There was an impossible amount of tail on Duthie's boiled shirt. Dog Eye started to laugh.

"What's so damn funny?"

"Keep tuckin'."

"I'll look like I got a swollen ass."

"You'll look like you *have* an ass."

Doc finally got the collar and cuffs studded. He pulled on the tie and snugged it up. Then he put on the coat. There was a hairbrush by the basin and he ripped at his unclean locks. One thing about hair this dirty, he thought, it has its own pomade. The only problem were the dirty trousers and the boots that were months from their last shining. It could not be helped.

Knowing it was only to invite ridicule, Doc asked Dog Eye how he looked. There came no answer. The cowboy was asleep with the goose slices hardly touched on his chest.

THE DINING ROOM WAS BIGGER, the table longer, and the number of people more than Doc had imagined. Somebody had whacked down a sizeable evergreen that glowered without decoration in the dark beyond. As Doc had feared, his entrance caused silence. Everyone stared at him, each with a wine glass in hand. He expected them to burst out laughing, but instead, a woman put her drink down and started to clap. The others had to put down their wine and clap too.

"Our hero," she said, and as he sat in the open chair beside her, Doc's face was sizzling.

For a time, Doc could not seem to pry his eyes out of his lap. When he finally did, he was staring straight into the ice-blue glitter of Esther Prieston's eyes. Her face was hollowed under strong cheekbones and, while the other women were powdered and rouged, her face was freckled brown from the sun. So were her neck and her naked shoulder. Thinking about how the sun got there long enough to brown it, Doc turned red again.

"Doc," the Major said sharply. "I'll make some introductions."

To the Major's left was his wife, whom Doc had already met in the kitchen. Continuing down the side across from Doc were Mrs. Winder, Victor Prieston, and Esther Prieston. On the near side, the Major's right, he introduced Captain Winder, who was a Mountie, and Mr. and Mrs. Enright (the woman who clapped and called Doc a hero). On Doc's right, at the foot of the table, was Allan Patrick, a neighbour from Ghost River way. Doc had already heard of Patrick, who had brought a small herd of cattle all the way from Ontario. Doc would have liked to ask him questions, but the Major was now filling in the introductions with information.

The Enrights and Priestons were new to the country, he said. Both couples were about to get into ranching. The Enrights already had a lease near High River. The Priestons weren't as far along. They had decided they liked the country near Crow's Nest Pass far to the south and would try to locate a lease there that suited them.

The Major then turned his attention to the Mountie, a big man whose mutton-chop whiskers were an enormous red froth on each cheek.

"We ranchers owe Captain Winder a great debt," said the Major, and the Mountie waved off the compliment. The Major went on to tell how it was Winder who went to Ottawa and urged Senator Cochrane to pass the bill that got the ranch frontier rolling. The one-hundred-thousand-acre leases, and so on. Winder got one of the first leases for his trouble, close to Fort Macleod. Winder's brother-in-law, Fred Stimson, was managing a newer lease west of High River called the North West Cattle Company.

Something that was hard for Doc not to notice in all this introducing was that he was the shortest person present, with the possible exception of Mrs. Enright. All the men had a foot on him and Esther Prieston was half a head taller as well. His oversized clothes further dwarfed him so he must look to the company like some runty bunkhouse breed thrown in with the purebreds.

What didn't daunt him was the cutlery. He had got that awkwardness over with long ago, in the fancy hotel in Denver when he'd stayed there with Pearly. Back then, he thought all the forks must be spares in case you threw a few on the floor. He remembered putting the napkin, big as a towel, in the neck of his shirt only to have Pearly snatch it out and stuff it on his lap.

Doc tried his hardest not to stare at Esther Prieston, using as a technique staring at her husband instead. He was the tallest of the men, possibly as tall sitting as Doc was standing. Doc decided Victor Prieston was a pointless height, a height that would get you thrown from a horse and shot first in a war. When Prieston grinned, he had a lot of teeth, like gravestones in a tight row. Of course, Doc was jealous of Prieston. Not that he wanted to be the man, but he certainly did want his wife.

About then, Mrs. Enright, at Doc's elbow, asked about Dog Eye. She called him Athol, so Esther had already supplied that piece of information. Doc said Athol was not doing badly for a man without a toe to his name. Victor Prieston was grinning again, and Doc longed to ask him what the hell was funny about that.

Talk of Dog Eye stalled the conversation. Nobody wanted to be the one to move on. The Major figured a way out of it by yelling a toast. "To Athol! Good health!" It was supposed to carry back to Dog Eye's room. Doc went along with it, yelling too, his glass of red wine raised, even though he knew Dog Eye was out cold and dreaming opium dreams.

They were by now into the main course. Joe Mah circled with platters off which the guests served themselves. Between dishes, the wine glasses were replenished. They were fine big-bellied glasses and Doc wondered how you got such things across the country in one piece. He'd heard it said that some rich folk sunk them in molasses.

With the topic of Dog Eye concluded, the conversation turned to ranches and cattle. The Enrights were asked to describe their lease and how they aimed to stock it. Then Winder talked about his lease and the one Fred Stimson was managing. Prieston was primed when his turn came.

"Pasturage and good cattle are certainly the keys to success, but in such a wide open place as this, why sacrifice good hunting and scenery? That's why Esther and I prefer a location close to the Rocky Mountains."

There was silence after that one, for it implied an insult to those who had chosen to ranch outside the mountains. Winder changed topic, asking the Major what summer would bring for the Cochrane Ranch. A lot of dead cows and calves was Doc's thought, and the Major did allude to the bad winter they were having. The upshot was that Senator Cochrane wanted him to buy another herd of cattle in Montana and get them here as soon as possible. Four thousand more.

"I haven't had a chance to discuss it with Doc here, but I'm hoping he will be my trail boss."

Doc had a mouth full of goose and was watching the glitter of Esther Prieston's earring. At mention of his name, Esther turned and looked at him. His reflex was to grab the napkin and mop his face. That made her smile all the more.

"I guess we'll talk about that later," said the Major when Doc seemed incapable of reply.

Thanks probably to the wine—several bottles having been consumed—the talk became more energetic. Victor Prieston seemed to be the most inspired, and Doc noticed how many of his sentences began with "In England." Once he had launched an England statement, the Enrights chimed in with, "Indeed, in England." Because Doc was inclined to notice everything about Esther, he saw the colour climbing her throat. Unless he was mistaken, she was getting angry.

Now Prieston was on about how superior English cattle were and how it was "imperative" they bring some west before the Canadian frontier was ruined by American cows and bulls. Suddenly, Doc found he was mad too. He suspected it was less about what Prieston had said than it was to keep in harmony with Esther.

"You could do with more American cattle up here, not less," said Doc, and he hated that he had a little quaver in his voice, like he was moved by strong emotion.

"That leaves me wondering what you think quality is in a cow, Mr. . . . ? I'm sorry I've forgotten your name." Prieston opened his mouth and showed Doc the whole white array.

"I consider it good to have cattle that can live through winter. If you've got one can win a ribbon out east or in England but can't rustle and dies out west, I would regard that as not a good one."

"Bravo, Mr. Windham!" It was Esther, clapping her hands together in front of her face.

"What kind of cattle would you choose, Doc, if it was up to you?" This was the Major and the question was more than casual. Doc was talking about the poor condition of the Cochrane cattle, and both the Major and he knew it.

"Some of our Anguses and Herefords are doing all right. They'll make the winter and produce a calf. The shorthorns are less good. We're going to lose a bunch of them. I think if you bred in some long-horn, they'd still be fancy, but they'd be tough enough to live here."

Prieston used his height to lean halfway across the table toward Doc. He was cutting across Esther and forcing her to sit back.

"You can't be serious. Are you saying that a shorthorn is not a good cow?"

"That's not what I said. I said they're not doing well here. I wouldn't know how they do in England, nor does it matter."

"And you think we should take our good English cattle and cross-breed them with American mongrels?"

"Only if you want to see them live."

Allan Patrick laughed. "I think he's got you, Prieston."

Next time Doc dared to look at Esther, she was regarding him differently. When she saw him look, she spoke to him, not a whisper but still a message not meant for others. "Victor believes anything from England must trump anything from anywhere else."

"Aren't you from England?"

"Goodness, no. I'm from Ontario."

After that, Joe Mah started to bring the dessert and coffee, and Doc got up to help. Even though it was nice to sit across from Esther, Doc's emotions were too fussed to stay put. They all sounded English to him, the men and the women. They all had manners that made him feel awkward. The dessert was a pie made with serviceberries, and as Doc watched, not one elbow was on the table, not one fork was heap-ing or dropping food.

"Don't you want your pie?" Esther asked, seeing how Doc had not touched it.

"I'm thinking I'll take it back and see if Dog Eye wants any."

This was a lie of the worst kind, the sort of thing Dog Eye would say to a woman to impress her with how sweet he was. Doc was ashamed to have stooped to it.

"It's been a pleasure, Mr. Windham. I hope we meet again."

Doc gave up trying not to look into her lovely eyes.

Victor Prieston stood to his full height and flung his arm across the table. "Yes, indeed. A pleasure." Before anyone else could make a fuss over him, Doc grabbed his pie, fork, and coffee, and fled.

Dog Eye was exactly as sound asleep as Doc knew he would be. Flat on his back, mouth open, twitching. He looked like he was chasing rabbits in his sleep. Doc climbed on his own bed and started eating the pie. Every bite turned on a new lantern picture of Esther. When the pie was gone, he drank his coffee, resting his head on a frosty log. Now Pearly's face was in the lantern show too, scowling.

There was a desk in the front corner of the room next to the washstand. Doc got up and checked the drawer. There was a pen, plus a couple of nibs and paper. After a struggle, he got the lid off the ink pot and found a bit of liquid moving in the bottom. Doc sat and wrote a note.

Pearly. I am at Ft. Calgary, Canada.
Either there or Ft. Macleod. Doc

Doc had written this kind of note before and stuck it up in post offices as he came to them, but the feeling behind it tonight was different. Usually he wrote it while pining, but tonight he did so from guilt. He felt unfaithful. He spent a long time thinking whether it was a mistake to include both forts like that. It meant he could never be sure she hadn't written until he had checked for mail at both. But he was also afraid Fort Calgary was too small a place for the mail to find. Finally, he left it the way it was.

Having finished the note to Pearly, he set a new page in front of himself.

Cochrane Ranch,
Christmas Night, 1881

Friend Lowell Ferris,

One of the boys from the bunkhouse here told me you were coming to Canada. I couldn't let that one pass. But if the Circle Ranch at Macleod gets you for a foreman, they are getting a good one. Wish I had some better news but Dog Eye French froze his toes and had to have them cut off, every one. Doctor said he will be a cripple. He never did like to be on foot and now has an excuse. The Cochrane cows we pushed so hard are starting to die, quite a few. Calving will be no good either. Lippy is good and has made friends with some squatters. Big Dwight is fine and a better cowboy than I thought possible but still disappointed he is no dazzler with a rope. I may be passing you on the trail because the Major has just told me we're getting four thousand more cows out of Montana. Says I should trail boss.

I have a favour to ask. In this letter is a message for Pearly. I hope you will put it up in the Ft. Benton post office before you leave down there. I got no special reason for thinking she's there, but I leave the message where and when I can. Pearly is on my mind tonight because I met a woman about as nice, probably nicer, as nice wasn't Pearly's best feature. But this woman is married to an Englishman, the one who all the jokes are about. She has me feeling lonely and regretful of my bachelor life. I'll be looking for you up in Canada.

If you write, tell me any news you have of the Beaverhead.

Your friend,
Doc

COCHRANE RANCH

East End Camp, February–March 1882

THE COLD WEATHER HUNG ON THROUGH January and part of February, followed by a chinook of such warmth, with so much trickle thaw, that most of the green cowboys proclaimed winter's back was broken. About then, Arctic cold shouldered the chinook aside. Every drop in every stream, every sodden drift and pool, froze hard. The cattle tried to muzzle through and could not. Their tender noses shone red, but the grass was entombed in crust.

If the cattle had been allowed to drift, they would have come to where the hard shell ended. But the eastern ranch owners were determined to make their own bad luck. Keep them on the lease was their law, and the Major enforced it. The boys turned the cows away from salvation, forced them back toward doom.

BY THEN, DOG EYE was back in the eastern line shack, but now his wintering partner was Doc. This was Doc's idea. He had sent Dwight the other way to live with Lippy.

All the years that Doc and Dog Eye had spent arguing provided the content for a yawning silence now. Without anything said, Doc knew that Dog Eye would have preferred Dwight, on the assumption that Doc would talk too much, would deliver homilies on why Dog Eye must forget Madeleine and how he should set his mind to deal with his infirmity. He probably assumed Doc would come at him with baking soda foot baths and poultices.

Knowing his partner's mind, Doc resisted these urges and observed the same silence as Dog Eye did. By day, Doc rode Louie up and down the river turning eastbound cattle. By night, he read books he'd borrowed from the Major.

While Doc was at the big house looking after Dog Eye, he had mentioned his fondness for reading to the Major. The Major led him to his office immediately, pointed at a couple of shelves of books. "Help yourself."

Doc picked out *Great Expectations* by Charles Dickens. Doc had read two other books by the Englishman and liked them. As he was about to go, the Major reached and plucked another from the shelf: *Leaves of Grass* by Walt Whitman.

"You might like this," he said. "Poems by your countryman."

According to writing on the back of the book, Whitman was a Yankee from New York, but Doc guessed he knew what the Major meant: that Whitman was more his countryman than Charles Dickens was.

At the eastern line shack with Doc Eye, Doc soon had both books read. *Great Expectations* was a cracking good yarn, the kind Doc liked best. Plenty of close calls, ups and downs, victories that came out of almost certain defeat. As for *Leaves of Grass*, Doc had never read an entire book of poems before, just verses in the newspaper. His hopes were not high, but once he was into it, the Whitman book gave him a type of experience he'd never had before. Good as it was, once Doc had read *Great Expectations*, he could never again be surprised by how Pip's adventure ended. With Whitman's poems, he could read them over and over and find something new every time.

In fact, Doc started believing that there was a Whitman verse for every occasion. For instance, one of Doc's concerns was that Dog Eye never doctored his feet. Only after the lamp was snuffed did he remove the boots that Doc had bought him at the I.G. Baker store. When Doc heard the sound of the boots coming off, he sniffed the air rapidly like a dog, but never smelled anything but hot leather.

> *Back on his pillow, the soldier bends with curv'd neck and*
> *side falling head,*
> *His eyes are closed, his face is pale, he dares not look on the*
> *bloody stump,*
> *And has not yet look'd on it.*

There was the truth. Dog Eye could not bear to have his damaged feet looked at, not even, or perhaps especially, by himself. But Doc knew better than to read any of this to Dog Eye, who was even less likely to take the truth from a Yankee poet than from Doc.

Not every aspect of Whitman pleased Doc. The back of the book proclaimed that the book gathered together the whole of American experience, and that was wrong. There wasn't a single mention of cowboys. But the most troubling thing was a verse Doc found about evil:

> *I make the poem of evil also, I commemorate that part also;*
> *I am myself just as much evil as good, and my nation is—*
> *And I say there is in fact no evil . . .*

Whitman struck Doc as an honest poet, but this smacked of a flimsy excuse for the waste and mess of the North's war on the South. It also ignored those like Overcross who do evil for evil's sake. Still, because Doc admired Whitman, he couldn't leave it at that. He continued to roll the words around in his head, waiting for a new understanding to come.

Often when Doc was doing this rethinking, it would link up somehow to the latest news about President Garfield's killer. During his stay at the Cochrane big house, Doc had found a *Fort Benton Record* from November that featured news of Guiteau's trial. Guiteau was doing his best to seem crazy, yelling out how God had asked him to kill Garfield, and chasing his own lawyer around the courtroom. Meanwhile, his lawyer was contending that Guiteau, so obviously crazy, hadn't known what he was doing when he killed Garfield. Was it right to hang a man too crazy to understand his crime? It was the first time anyone had tried this strategy in a murder trial, and Doc dubbed it the "crack-brain defence." He also didn't buy it. If Whitman was right and there was no evil, and if murder was craziness, then swing the jail door wide and burn up all the nooses. Everyone was innocent, and look out.

AS FOR WHAT DOG EYE did in the evenings while Doc read, it was about the same as he did by day. He lay on his bed and stared at nothing. Well-addicted now, he often took nips of laudanum. Doc knew for sure he was on his second bottle, and maybe it was more. If he switched empty for full in the dark, Doc would never know.

Then came a day when Dog Eye broke his silence to say, "You're out of makings."

"I don't feel like smoking right now."

"Well, maybe I do."

"You don't smoke."

"I think I'll take it up."

Dog Eye reached into the gaping front pocket of his trousers, produced some folding money, and tossed it across onto Doc's stomach.

"Instead of staring at me or that book, why don't you go to I.G. Baker and buy us tobacco? Maybe that long lost woman wrote you a letter."

It was more than Dog Eye had said in two weeks. Now he lapsed into a drowse, his eyelids fluttering.

Doc would have liked to rebuff Dog Eye's suggestion, but it was exactly what he wanted to do. There was stew on the stove and chopped wood in the corner. Doc had cut Dog Eye a crutch so he could get outside and take a crap if need be. As for the cattle, some might try to go east, but if Doc was only half a day in town, he could get in front of them opposite Fort Calgary and herd them back on his way home.

Doc slicked himself up, melting snow on the stove for a bath of his upper parts. Then he saddled Louie and bid Dog Eye farewell. In the cabin doorway, Dog Eye leaned on the frame and watched Doc go. After a few minutes, Doc turned to look back and Dog Eye was still watching.

From across the river, Fort Calgary and the collection of cabins around it looked as cold as any place on earth. Every chimney had a twist of smoke pasted to the whitish blue above it. From the amount of smoke coming from behind the Fort Calgary palisade, the whole place might have been on fire. Sound carried far on the icy air, and Doc could hear axes striking in several directions, the tedious work of staying warm and fed come winter. Closer to hand, the chimney on Tesk's tent was cold and his ox corral empty.

Enough traffic had used the ford to keep the ice from the edges, and Doc coaxed Louie in. Coming out the other side, Doc untied a blanket from behind the saddle and brought it to the ground. He rubbed Louie's legs to knock off the ice and warm them a bit. The big horse shuddered and snorted plumes of white. After all the trouble-free work of this horse, Louie's left front leg had become prone to swelling. Doc had poulticed and wrapped him until he was blue in the face, and would buy more Green Flag liniment at the I.G. Baker store today, but it didn't seem to be doing much good. Doc did not know what he would do if this fine horse broke down on him. It was the kind of thing that kicks the heart out of you, the prospect of which makes you want to quit cowboying altogether.

As he approached the fort, Doc's mood changed and he began to anticipate. The mail was what caused it. No matter how many times he had come to a post office and been disappointed, the feeling never went away. As there was no such anticipation associated with the I.G. Baker store, Doc entered Fort Calgary first. He had become familiar here because of Dog Eye's feet. As he passed through the open gate and around beside the parade square, he nodded to several redcoats and other folks, and most of them nodded back.

The young constable behind the desk in the orderly room was one Doc did not know. On a pillow of curly dark hair, his little pillbox hat sat askew. He had it strapped from the back of his head to the hollow below his lip, a thing that looked silly and uncomfortable. The constable's reddy-brown moustache was so long and gracefully elaborated that Doc could imagine it flapping and taking off. The moustache also had the unwanted effect of making the man's other features seem bland. His blue eyes, round like a doll's, contained a hurt look, as if they knew they were too close together and were embarrassed. Having shaved well today, he was pink-cheeked as a girl.

Because Doc liked to know people's names, he stuck his hand out and said, "Windham, Doc Windham."

"Constable Ned Cort."

When Doc let go the hand, Cort made a fist and set it on a green blotter between an open ink pad and two wood-handled stamps. He asked if it was mail Mr. Windham was after. Doc said it was, and Cort turned and pulled envelopes out of a grid of pigeonholes. There wasn't much for W and none for Windham.

"I wasn't really expecting any," said Doc, when the fellow gave him a sorrowful look.

Then Doc put his elbow on the counter to signify he was willing to gossip. To engage the man, Doc asked him questions and showed flattering interest in whatever he said. Conversation was not difficult, for Cort came well primed with complaints, chief among them that he had been transferred from Fort Macleod in July.

Doc asked if Cort liked Macleod so very much then.

"No, no," said the young man. It was more that he had hoped to be out of the Mounties by now. He had hoped to purchase his discharge so he could devote all his time to business. "And then out of the blue, they tell us in June there'll be no more buying of discharges, or substitutes either."

Cort had lowered his voice for this seditious talk. What rankled, he went on, beyond being stuck longer in the Mounties, was that he had opened a bowling alley in Fort Macleod's St. Martin's Hall, at a rental of fifteen dollars a month. "And three months later comes the rule about discharges. I was still managing to run the bowling in my spare time, but that's when they transferred me. I had to sell and take a loss."

Doc asked how the Mountie work compared, Fort Macleod to here.

"Calgary's quieter," said Cort with certainty. "Much less rowdiness and drinking."

"How does the public get all this liquor?"

"I don't mean the public. I mean the Mounties. They're notorious drunks at Macleod. Have you been there?"

Doc said he had stopped in briefly on his way through with the Cochrane drive.

"Did you see the part of the fort that's burned?"

Doc said he had.

"Bunch of the boys were drunk at the fort. Commanding officer was away. One of the corporals took a squaw into the shoe shop. She was drunk already and he'd promised her a bottle. But, in the shop, all he showed her was his peter. Next thing, they're in a fight and knock the stovepipe off. Big fire. Burned up the shoe shop, the saddle room, and the stables. We got the horses out but a lot of saddles and shoe leather were lost. Typical instance."

"And you don't have that here?" Doc asked.

"Not nearly as much. Dead boring, actually." Cort squinted his doll eyes, trying to think of something. "Brown went into his room to clean his pistol. Thought it wasn't loaded and shot the wall. And somebody killed old Lilly, a C Troop mare we all liked."

"No drinking?"

"Oh, there's some. We arrested two gents for eighty gallons of whisky. Big fine. More money than I've seen. We've got an Indian, Yellow Horse, in the guardroom right now, along with the fellow who sold him the liquor to get drunk on. Pace was the bootlegger, he's from Macleod. Trying to branch out."

"You get a lot of news still from Macleod?" Doc suggested.

"Oh yes," said Cort with a wink. "Still have friends there. Write me letters."

"Anyone mention a rancher named Craig or a young Ontario fella named Jim Adams?"

Doc was expecting the usual negative replies, but Cort said yes to both.

"I used to work in the orderly room at Macleod," he said. "I remember there was mail waiting for a Mr. Craig for the longest time. He never did pick it up while I was there. Adams was after my time. But friends tell me he worked at the fort, mucking out the stable. He turned out to be such a drunk they put him in the guardroom. They fired him after that."

"Can't be the same Adams," said Doc. "Mine doesn't touch a drop."

Cort sulled. He had filled Doc's bill and got no credit for it. He started shifting through a stack of envelopes. Doc thanked him and left.

A FEW DAYS AFTER this visit to Fort Calgary, Doc began to have trouble with a section of the river he called "the glacier." Half a mile west of the line shack was a place where no trees or brush grew to the edge of the river. It was an old gravel fan that had been receiving the debris from a big coulee for a thousand years. Besides being treeless, the area sloped to the river and was attractive to cattle as a place to water.

All winter long, through the melts and freeze-ups, ice had been building on this fan. When the last big chinook had come, followed by the deepest freeze, the fan had gone from streaming wet to solid ice. Before, there had always been seams between the ice to the river, but now the ice was continuous: eighty yards of it along the bank. The ice in some places was rutted and rough, in other parts smooth. From the river to the inland edge, it ranged from ten yards wide all the way to thirty.

For the first while after the hard freeze, the cattle had done their east-west travelling higher up, past the line shack where the wagon trail ran. But after Doc's trip to Fort Calgary, about three hundred cows found the glacier and started trying to water there.

For the first few days, Doc worked alone against the tide of cows pressing to the river. He would get them off the ice in one place, look back, and see that others had passed him farther up or down. Usually, they would go a ways onto the ice before they noticed the slippery feel. The lucky ones would catch enough bumps and edges to scamper out. But an unlucky few tired themselves out and "spread," meaning their four legs slid apart until the weight at the centre came crashing through. Beneath a cow's tail is a delicate bone that bends to allow the birth of her calves. The *coup de grace* on the ice sheet was the sound of that H-bone snapping.

On the fourth morning after Doc's trip to Fort Calgary, he explained this state of affairs to Dog Eye. To his credit, the cowboy didn't make Doc ask for help more than once.

Doc saddled and bridled both Pete and Louie in the little pine-pole corral Dwight and Dog Eye had built in the eastern lee of the shack. They had closed the north side with frozen cowhides. Doc lined Pete up in front of the door and led Dog Eye out. Once he'd given him a leg up into the saddle, a semblance of the old Dog Eye appeared. Straight and arrogant.

In case Dog Eye thought Doc was exaggerating, a cow, spread and broken, was waiting for them on the ice sheet. Doc dismounted and crossed to her, trailing the rope that Dog Eye held ready to dally on his saddle horn. Spreading didn't usually kill a cow, just ruined her, and the first thing Doc had to do was draw his Colt and shoot her. Then he looped her hind legs and Dog Eye and Pete skidded her off. Doc peeled the hide off before it froze. The sad thing was the cow had a calf, and it came up and suckled while he skinned her.

Every day, they went to the ice sheet and, while they saved most of the cows, they had failures too. One cow made it all the way to the lip of the ice shelf, without seeming to notice anything. Then she saw that the water was too far down to drink and, turning, was unable to move without sliding backwards. If she had panicked, the ice shelf could have broken under her or she might have slipped off. Instead she stood stock still, as if willing to wait for spring.

She happened to be where the ice sheet was widest, and Doc ran out of rope before he got to her. Dog Eye let go his end and Doc carried the lasso farther. From a few steps away, he flipped a loop over the cow's horns. When he gave a little tug, the calm erupted. The cow dove off the shelf into the current and went bobbing off, head up among the ice cakes.

Doc ran alongside her. Finally he was off the ice and in among the poplars. With almost no rope left, he wound what little he had on a trunk, the bark peeling as the rope bit. The rope tightened on her neck, the cow swapped ends and held, facing upstream. Dog Eye rode over, ducking branches, and as Doc hauled the cow through the water, Dog Eye took over the rope end and dallied it on his saddle horn. When the cow finally came out, flanks running water, Doc pulled the rope off her and was rewarded by a hook in the ribs from her horn. It wasn't enough to stab him but plenty hard enough to leave a bruise. He kicked at her on the way by, and she kicked him back, went running off indignant.

That night, Doc gave Dog Eye both ropes and asked him to plait two ends together to make one. It would be a hell of a thing to throw but at least it would reach across the ice.

The ice sheet's last secret was what Doc called "the funnel." On the east side, where the coulee's watercourse ran in summer, was where the ice sheet had built up first. The ice above the water channel obeyed the contour, wedging down. Twenty yards down that wedge and a few feet short of the shelf's edge, the various thaws of winter had spiralled out a hole. The funnel's mouth was three feet wide and went right down to the river. Doc worried that a cow who stepped in the top of the wedge would easily wind up down the hole.

Dog Eye said this was nonsense, and Doc said, "You wait." In fact, Doc thought it had already happened, because on the rough ice at the funnel's mouth, red and white hairs were trapped in the fissures.

The more cattle who killed themselves on the ice or had to be killed, the more carcasses there were. Doc got Dog Eye to drag the bodies to the top of the slope where they formed a kind of fence, in the hope that the cattle would shy away from it. But they did not seem to recognize their kind without the hair on. During the day, the cowboys would drive the pilgrim cattle west, away from the glacier, and put a scare into them, but every morning they were back.

While Doc did this work, he often recited some Whitman. When he approached a cow on the ice, the poem he used most went this way:

> Divine am I inside and out, and I make holy whatever I touch or
> am touch'd from;
> The scent of these arm-pits aroma sweeter than prayer;
> This head more than churches, bibles, and all the creeds.

> If I worship one thing more than another, it shall be the spread of
> my own body, or any part of it,

> Translucent mould of me, it shall be you!
> Shaded ledges and rests, it shall be you!

In truth, Doc often told the cow the parts he most wanted to tell Dog Eye.

One morning while Doc and Dog Eye were patrolling the ice sheet, a family of Indians came out of the trees from the west. They had two horses among them, each pulling a travois. One travois held their rolled-up tent. The other held some children and an old woman smoking a pipe. A younger woman walked beside. The horses were of the cayuse type, the long hair on their faces frosty on the tips. Riding one horse was an old white-haired man, and on the other was a younger fellow. The cavalcade stopped beside the fence of skinned beef and stared longingly. They were plainly hungry. The skin on their faces was sucked on tight.

The old man kicked his leg over the high withers of his horse, slid off, and landed with a bounce. He walked past the carcasses toward Doc. Doc dismounted to greet him. Doc got out his sack of makings and offered it. The old man pulled a pipe out of the robe he was wrapped in and pointed in the bowl with a scant-toothed smile. He had pin pokes on his chin and in his forehead from the smallpox, the last epidemic of which had been in 1870.

They smoked and began a parley that was mostly signs. The old Indian had a few words of English and understood Doc's pet phrases in Sioux. What came out was that they were not local Indians, not Stony, but Blackfoot. There was a Blackfoot reserve down the Bow beyond Fort Calgary. The family had gone hunting but had little success. Now they were trying to get home, but thought they should inquire about all this meat that seemed to be left for the eaters of carrion.

A little more sign talk and the old man understood what Doc wanted back. They could butcher and eat the frozen cattle, so long as they helped keep cattle off the ice and took the hide off any that died from this day forward. The women were confident enough about the deal that they started standing up the tipi poles.

THE TIME SPENT WORKING on the ice span had been good for Dog Eye. Now that the Indians were doing such a good job of clearing cattle off the ice, there was nothing left for the cowboys to do. Liberated from improving work, Dog Eye went back to bed and to his laudanum.

After a few days, Doc began scribbling a plan on a sheet of paper. When done, he showed it to Dog Eye: a schedule of riding by which the two of them could investigate this part of the lease in under one week.

"You go ahead then," said Dog Eye from his bed, cuddling his laudanum.

Doc pretended to get heated. "The Reverend McDougall's father had a whole lifetime of Canadian winters and still froze to death near here. I refuse to do likewise just so you can sit around peacefully stoned."

This was poor logic, but when Doc saddled the horses next morning, Dog Eye hobbled out, not bothering with his crutch. It was the first time since losing his toes that he mounted Pete without assistance.

For the first hour, Doc let the scenery pass in silence. Moving slow, they ascended coulees and crossed benches on a sinuous upward path. The sun was out and the wind was in the north, going over their heads as long as they were climbing. Then everything sloped the other way and the wind was full in their faces.

Doc was riding first and he stopped and let Louie swap ends, tail to the wind. As Dog Eye came close, Doc addressed him.

"Dog Eye, I'm not going to dodge around. We need to talk about what has happened and what is likely to happen."

Dog Eye squinted into the wind, at the racing snow-snakes all over the crusted expanse. He let Pete turn as well. Facing south, the chiselled blue mountains were to their right, a blur of ice fog and smoke marked the river and the town to their left.

"No," he said.

"What do you mean, no?"

"You don't need to know. You want to know because you're nosey. You could have talked me to death by now. I appreciate you didn't. But now you're starting, I want you to stop."

"Preaching Jesus, Dog Eye! You can't go around in total silence the rest of your life."

"Says who? Besides you."

"That's no way for a man to live."

"You're right that far."

"What's right? What did I say?"

Doc took a breath on which to float another speech, but Dog Eye released the rein to Pete's light mouth, and the gelding started down. Louie pulled to follow. Over his shoulder, Dog Eye spoke.

"You don't have the pull on me you think you do. You did once, but I grew up."

"Dog Eye, use your damn head . . ."

"Shut up, Doc. Your horse is limping. Take him home."

THAT NIGHT, AS THEY SAT by the stove in the wavering light of the bitch lamp, the mood in the shack had changed. Dog Eye had lanced two swellings: his own resentment and Doc's urge to give advice. Beyond that, speech was possible.

In a mood that bordered cheerful, Dog Eye took his drops of opium and alcohol and began to reminisce. He told Doc things he'd never told before.

In his early days in Texas, Dog Eye had been the youngest son of a family picked clean of men by war. He had been raised and praised by a widowed mother and several unmarried and widowed sisters and aunts. He never questioned all their female love and grief. Instead of taking any responsibility for them in return, he started riding for local ranches. When he had the skill to go farther, he did. Finally, he left on a cattle drive headed north. To his weeping womenfolk, he promised money and his eventual return.

Several times, Dog Eye came back in the general direction of his family, but always stopped short. Like a bird in a series of updrafts, his way south was always met by another herd of cows coming north. Because he spent money freely and foolishly, being broke was enough to get him floating back north again. The head and tail of these trails moved northward too, until he hit Montana, and now Canada.

"The shameful thing," he said to Doc, looking not the least ashamed, "is that when I had a friend going back to Texas, I'd make him promise to visit my mother and sisters, and to tell them how I loved and missed them. I sent money too. But I never once visited myself."

The better mood in Dog Eye held for a second day. That second night, Doc dared ask questions, even ones about Madeleine Taureau. It turned out she wasn't the first woman Dog Eye had lost his heart to. Back in his hometown in eastern Texas, where his childhood had convinced him it was all women's lot to love and admire him, a young girl of the town had hooked up with him, fucked him silly, made him murderously jealous by dancing with other men, then left him suddenly, literally in the middle of the dance floor. A fellow cut in during a waltz, a big brute, and as Dog Eye was deciding whether to hit him now or later, his girl made a face at him, jumped in the other fellow's arms, and went whirling away. Forever.

Embittered, Dog Eye took pride in not loving the women who came after that. He had been cruellest to the ones who loved him most. He took an evil pride in riding off, even imagining how he must look through their tear-blurred eyes.

"Then Madeleine," he said, the first time Doc had heard the girl's name from his mouth. He let it stand alone in the air awhile, vibrating. "I never thought I'd be so took. I just was. The funny part is she barely knew I was alive."

"So it's harder than the girl back home?"

Dog Eye studied the little bottle in his hands. "In Texas, I was jealous like a child of his toy. I'd die for Madeleine."

"Still?"

Dog Eye studied the bottle, his oracle. "I guess not. It wouldn't make sense to die for someone who doesn't know or care. If I die, it will be for me."

THE DAYS AND NIGHTS that followed were not pleasant. When a laudanum bottle ran empty, Dog Eye reached into his saddlebag for another. He took the drug often now, and when Doc warned him you could die of too much, Dog Eye found it funny.

Now when he sat on the side of his bed staring at the stove, Dog Eye didn't want to talk about himself. He regarded that story as finished and wanted Doc's life in return. Normally, Doc liked to tell about himself, had devised his life story into a series of entertaining set pieces, but Dog Eye wouldn't allow any of that.

"I told my life fair. Don't be cheap with yours."

One of Doc's stories was how he had shot Overcross at close range but not killed him, and how that began the crumbling of his life with Pearly.

"Christ, Doc, only you could shoot a man in the head an inch away and miss."

"I didn't miss. I had bits of his goddamn head all over me. A normal man would have died."

When Doc told the rest of the story about Pearly, Dog Eye laughed.

"You are the biggest fool I ever met. You always made out you were better than us, and all along you were just lovesick for a girl you ain't seen since 1867."

"To hell with you, Dog Eye."

"You like advice, Doc. Here's some. Give up trying to be everybody's boss. Pretty soon, not even the likes of Dwight will follow you."

This stung. Many things Dog Eye said did. Like the bulldog fly, he took a chunk every time he bit.

"So what happened to you in Fort Benton?" asked Doc, wanting to cause pain in return. "How'd you get your cracked ribs and bruises?"

The Texan's eyelids pulled apart. He took another sip. He laughed to show his contempt for the question.

"That's the spirit," he slurred. "Let me see, now. Did a disappointed whore take a hammer to me while I slept? Was I corn-holed by a crazy miner? Or maybe I was passed out drunk when some cowboys tied my ankles under an outlaw horse. What difference does it make?"

"If I pined my life away on Pearly, isn't that what you're about to do?"

Eyes closing, words smearing, Dog Eye said, "You don't know what I'm about to do."

A FRESH STORM BLOWING in from the northeast brought a white man with it. He wore a buffalo coat and rode a stout muscled bay that was almost black in the smothered light. Doc opened the door when he heard the horses calling. The man who came in was one of the few Doc had seen in Canada with no hair on his face. When he stamped his moccasins inside their door, ice in the hair of his buffalo coat rang like chimes.

In an English accent, or maybe one from down East, the man identified himself as Earnest Worthy, Indian agent for the Blackfoot reserve. He had come in search of a family he believed was living near here.

The man annoyed Doc from the start. He hated people who wouldn't say what they'd come to say.

"You know damn well they're here. What of it?"

"They told me they were going to hunt. They were permitted off the reserve for a fixed time, which has elapsed. They are illegally at large. I wanted to ask you to tell your employer that I am removing them today and to apologize for the inconvenience."

Doc could have cheerfully pistol-whipped this man. He knew his anger was not in proportion but made little effort to head it off. At the same time, he did pretend politeness.

"Why don't you take off that coat and let some warm in? That's coffee on the stove."

"I don't care for coffee boiled. I don't know how you cowboys drink it."

"I blow on mine, then sip it, then swallow it. I thought my method was conventional."

Though he was slower than many would be, Worthy began to take offence.

"You seem determined to be unpleasant. I didn't catch your name."

"I didn't throw it."

"I have come to relieve you of a burden. I have no idea why I'm so uncivilly received."

"I had not noticed a burden."

"The Indians!" said Worthy, finally getting hot.

"You should ride back where you came from then, because they are no burden. I don't wish to be relieved of them."

"I am here to do my job, sir, and believe me, *I will do it.*"

"The Indians have a job too. They're skinning our dead cattle."

"They are not entitled to work for anyone without my knowledge or consent. They are illegally at large. They are trespassing."

Doc stood close in front of the man, staring up into his hairy nostrils. God knows what size he really was inside all those clothes, but in them he looked a colossus.

"*You* are the only one trespassing on this lease. So why don't you get the hell off it?"

"I have had enough, sir. I will report your conduct, and your language, to Major Walker, who is well known to us."

Doc noticed an extra sound in the room. He turned and saw Dog Eye clapping his hands very slowly. The combatants left off and stared at the glass-eyed cowboy, lying on his bed, staring up at his thumping hands.

Two hours later, the Indians, following their agent, came to the cabin. Worthy kept riding but the Indians stopped and the old one dismounted. He took a few steps toward the cabin, then waited. Doc went outside and shook the old man's hand. They did not have the words they needed now, but maybe that was better, more dignified. Two old waddies bidding farewell, voiceless but moved. Then the little caravan started up again, swallowed by the whirling snow, as if it had never been.

DOC AWOKE SEVERAL times that night, the first time when the cabin wall was hit broadside by a heavy wind. The long overdue chinook. It shook the walls all night, and whenever it woke him, Doc would grin in the dark, imagining the dripping morning, the snow crust dissolving, the top of the ice sheet glistening with thaw that would hopefully eat it fast and end their troubles.

When he woke with the dawn, the room was barely cold, though no fire had been lit overnight. He rolled over to see what Dog Eye was making of the change and saw his bed was empty.

Doc pulled on his boots with the spurs already on them. He ran out and found Louie alone and only mildly agitated in his corral. That Louie wasn't more excited told Doc that Pete could not be far and was probably upwind. Doc crawled on Louie's bare back and rode him west, until they could see Pete standing at the ice sheet, reins dangling, and no rider in sight. Doc pushed Louie until the horses were nose to nose. He scanned the ice and couldn't see Dog Eye, and then he did. The cowboy was standing at the eastern edge where the wedge began to lower. He was watching down it, and following that line of sight, Doc saw a horn tip just above the edge of the funnel.

Doc got down, tied the bulky rope off to Pete's saddle horn, checked the cinch, then walked and paid out rope until he stood with Dog Eye.

"Think we can get her?" Doc asked.

"Almost in the other world already," said the Texan, his voice blurry. "Maybe I can get her out of there."

He took the coil of rope from Doc's hand. "I feel good today," he said and started into the top of the wedge. Then he ran, dancing down the bright wet ice, the loop end of the rope still trailing from his hand. The wind took off his hat, flapped his vest. He let himself fall, boots forward, so that he slid along the fluting on his skinny ass.

Doc was running too by then. He saw Dog Eye hit the funnel, saw his boots hit the cow's head and knock her through. Dog Eye's skinny hip hit the hole's far edge. Then, still holding the rope, he dropped from sight.

Doc was still running when the rope along the ice beside him sprang tight, jumped off the ice and spiralled, made a singing sound.

"Hang on, Dog Eye! Goddamn it, hang on!"

The rope fell slack.

When Doc hit the funnel hole, he was no longer on his feet. His boot heels hit the far side. He clawed with his spurs until they stuck and held him above the hole. It was glowing space and flowing black beneath that. He pulled the rope out of the black river, pried his fingers into its dripping end, yanked the loop wide and put it over himself. He pulled his arms out and fell.

A blur of white. Cold that burned. The glowing underside of ice turned green, receded. His boots hit the rocks on the river's bottom and he bounced. When he was back under the ice, the current was dragging him downstream by his wet clothes. Face sometimes in, sometimes out of the water, he clawed at the ice from underneath, his fingers feeling so cold they could snap off.

He had forgotten the rope, until it bit so hard he couldn't breathe. In the grip of an awesome power, he was yanked upstream, skidding upside-down along the underside of the ice. When he came to the hole, he was jerked into it, up it, into the brilliance of light.

Now he was sliding along the top of the glacier, and the knobs and flutes were punching his face and bruising his body. He twisted his neck enough to see Pete's yellow legs braced and marching. Doc yelled at the gelding to stop, but Pete had a job to do. He kept on until Doc lay exactly between two skinned carcasses.

In the red chiselled gut of one of these cows, a raven stood and eyed him with scorn. After staring a while at Doc's eyes, the bird made a knocking sound, spread its wings, and rose.

FORT CALGARY/COCHRANE RANCH

March 1882

THE CHINOOK WAS BLOWING WHEN Dog Eye French drowned. It was still blowing when they found him three days later. His body made it past Fort Calgary and washed out on a bend farther on. He was found by the raft man who had carried him across the river on Christmas Day.

The body was taken to Fort Calgary, and that was where Doc went with a wagon to fetch him home. For all his fondness for boom towns and whorehouses, Dog Eye had spent more time on ranches than anywhere. Doc decided he should be buried on the last ranch of his life.

The Mounties had taken up a collection and hired a carpenter to build a pine box. It seemed a good one to Doc, who'd seen many cowboys go to the promised land in only their bedrolls. He got some help lifting the coffin into the wagon and more crossing the river. Neither Doc nor the Mounties wanted Dog Eye floating off a second time.

Doc got the wagon and the corpse as far as the line camp and stopped. He half expected the place to be full of cowboys again, as it had been on Christmas Day. Then he knew his mission. It was to pull off Dog Eye's boots and look at his feet.

Doc went in and got the hammer Dwight and Dog Eye had used to build their horse corral. It had ears for pulling nails and Doc levered with them until the lid came off. He had looked at Dog Eye's dead face already and tried not to look at it again. He prised off one boot and peeled down the grey sock. It was still damp.

It was a sunny day, warm and intensely bright, and right there in the gaudy sparkle, Dog Eye's foot rested pale in Doc's hand. Beyond lacking toes and having purple seams where the skin had been over-lapped and sewn, besides that and being dead, it was a normal foot, a healthy foot. He almost pulled off the other boot, but stopped himself; asked what it was he was trying to prove.

That Dog Eye French had a reason.

That was what he wanted all right: a reason he could understand and tell the others. If Dog Eye's foot had been swollen and putrified, a reason would have existed. Pale and cool, the foot had nothing to say.

FOR THREE DAYS, they burned coal on the gravesite, on a bench be-tween the big house and the river. They dug until the shovel hit frozen ground and the bits came off like hoof trimmings. They kept adding coal, and burning, until they got beneath the frost.

As the only witness to Dog Eye's death, Doc was in charge of the story. He painted a picture of duty done a little too well. Seeing the horned cow stuck in the funnel, Dog Eye had hurried on the ice and lost his footing. He fell, slid, knocked the cow through, went through himself. Somewhere along the line, he had lost hold of the tow rope.

Why wasn't the rope around Dog Eye, the cowboys wanted to know. Why was Dog Eye doing the work on the ice in the first place, given the state of his feet? Doc replied that mistakes had been made. In a month of trouble, it was the only time Dog Eye had worked other than on his horse. He had wanted to, maybe because he was bored of sitting his horse all day with little to do. As for the rope, that was probably Doc's fault, for setting an example of walking on the ice with the rope only in hand. The boys seemed to accept the story, and so did the Major.

On the day of Dog Eye's funeral, they put the coffin on the Major's buckboard and let Pete trail behind. The Major drove. Doc rode Louie alongside Pete so the yellow gelding wouldn't be lone-some. Lippy had fetched Reverend McDougall from Morleyville to say the words. Among the men, Doc was selected to speak what the Rev-erend called a "eulogy," a kind of story of Dog Eye's life. Doc had done this for several men before but had not known it was called a eulogy. At the same time the word wasn't brand new, so he must have encountered it in his reading. *Doc Windham gave the eulogy*, he kept thinking, a satisfactory echo of something.

Doc spoke with candour of the good and bad of Athol Dog Eye French. He told what Dog Eye had just finished telling him the other night of how he'd grown up in a Texas family, after the Civil War had killed all its older menfolk, how badly he'd been spoiled by all those widowed and unmarried women, which perhaps accounted for Dog Eye's being forgetful of his manners sometimes. It almost certainly accounted for him thinking women would always love him, which many did.

The Major cleared his throat, so Doc skipped over the trouble with the Halfbreed girl, and concentrated more on Dog Eye's cowboy skills, which were among the best Doc had ever seen. He could throw a hoolihan with so little effort that horses wouldn't move as the rope sailed over their heads. He never caught just one heel of any animal he roped. His bunkhouse and town skills may have been less, but a man can't have everything.

Without going into unnecessary detail, Doc suggested Dog Eye had lost his toes in the process of becoming a better man, and that he probably lost his balance on the ice because he had no toes, so that ironically becoming a good man had killed him. At that, the Major cleared his throat again, and Doc understood he was to stop.

There were tears in a few eyes, Doc saw with satisfaction. Surely that was what a eulogy was for.

The sides of the hole into which the pine box lowered were blackened from the coal fire. A lump swelled in Doc's throat as the box hit bottom and the ropes slid out. He took his turn on the shovel until they had Dog Eye covered. For the last couple of nights, while the grave was burning, the boys had fashioned a marker that read *Athol French*, and his dates. It didn't look like enough, so Doc had carved *Texas Cowboy* below the other words. He thought of other things like "died in Canada," or "died saving a cow," but each sounded stupid seconds after the inspiration. Finally, he let it be.

When he saw the marker pounded into the ground, he was glad he
hadn't added anything. "Texas Cowboy" had a ring to it. He would enjoy such a phrase on his own grave, if the dead can enjoy.

Doc was about ready to cry, so he left the grave, leading Louie and
Pete. His grief seemed excessive, even to him, given how often Dog
Eye had tried his patience. But when all was said and done, Dog Eye
was like a son to Doc, however wayward or how often Doc had refused
the idea. Dog Eye had been like a son just as surely as Lippy was and
Dwight was becoming. Family the cowboy way, among people whose
real families were too far away or too far in the past to matter. If Doc
did not grieve for Dog Eye French, who would?

In some other way, grief is always for the self, and as Doc led the
horses up the slope toward the ranch house, dabbing at his eyes with
the tail of his clean wiper, he knew he was crying in part because of
the last chunk Dog Eye had bitten out of him. What if he was too old
to boss young cowboys? In the absence of them, what else could Doc
do? How lonely might life get?

Then Lippy caught up with him.

"Doc, hold up. Something."

Doc had noticed that Lippy went through the funeral without his
face covered. His whole manner seemed changed. He was more
confident, even physically stouter. The cooking of Olaf's wife and
daughter.

"Not more bad news, Lip. I've had enough."

"It's good."

"You got my hopes up. Let's hear."

"I'm getting married."

Doc hoped his face didn't show what his mind had just done:
flopped over and wailed. Doc had never considered this: that Lippy
could get married. A great cascade of loss hit bottom.

"Olaf's daughter," Doc said.

Lippy nodded and looked proud. Then his face darkened. He had
read out of Doc's mind something he didn't care for.

"She isn't . . ." He pointed at his mouth. "Her name is Lilly and she
ain't got nothing like me." Then he smiled. "She's pretty. Just shy of
people."

"Will I meet her?"

"Not right away."

At the ranch house, there was a lunch. The boys sat around the edge of a sitting room, trying to balance cups and plates on their wide-apart knees. Lippy was in the chair beside Doc, talking about how he and Olaf were going to raise cattle together.

"I hope he's going to get a brand."

Lippy said he had one, that they had registered it at Fort Calgary yesterday. Then Lippy suggested Doc come in with them. Olaf believed there'd be a homestead law soon and free land.

Doc smiled at the notion.

"I'm not as mature as you, Lippy," he finally said. "Probably never will be. I don't think I could settle down the way you mean."

He said it as a joke, but it was true.

THE CROW'S NEST

PROLOGUE

Burned hair on every breeze. Cow sound continuous. An armada lost in a fog of dust and smoke.

The roper's horse comes walking, dragging a double-heeled calf. Near the fire, a boy grabs a kicking leg and sits down hard. The branding iron comes running. Dabs a message in hot iron through hair on hide. Sizzle of sudden grease. Roll of yellow smoke into the brander's face.

It's a bull, so you kneel in the angle of his flank. Stretch the scrotum and cut the bottom. An elfin cap, lined in pink. You reach into the blood with two fingers, find the first ball, pull it into the air. Scrape the cord until it falls apart. Flick it away. Massage the white belly hair, find the shape of the second ball under the skin and delve for it.

Set free, the calf jumps up, totters, runs. Tries for distance from the pain. The cow flares her nostrils, receives the smell of her calf, finds something evil mixed with it. Blows hard, smells again, looks for someone to blame.

COCHRANE RANCH

April 1882

SPRINGTIME IN ALBERTA was not a sudden burst into flower, not any more than anywhere else in Doc's West. Though not as dry as Texas, the big hill above the Cochrane Ranch house appeared from under the snow in a state of brown and dust, and stayed that way for some time.

The first soaking melts and sudden rivers stank of death. Even though they dragged the bodies out of the water, not a stream or lake on the Cochrane Lease was fit to drink without boiling.

The cows started calving, and every man was kept busy pulling. To push a calf out was more than the exhausted cows could do.

But spring has ways of masking disaster. When the hills came green, tinged with crocus blue, when the calves bucked and ran, sweetly stung by a spark of joy, it made up for a lot that wasn't right.

AFTER MOST OF THE CALVES were on the ground, it was time for round-up. The cowboys from the line camps came to the main ranch and filled its bunkhouse, ate big meals put up by the Major's Chinese cook and his helpers. What extra men could be found were hired on, and several ranchers from around the community came to volunteer. Even some squatters came.

The day before round-up, it was time for Doc to give everyone their orders. He asked the new hires and volunteers to leave the bunkhouse. He closed the door behind the last one, then told the others who had worked through the winter how they shouldn't think too much about the dead cattle lying around. The cowboys were entrusted with keeping the cattle alive, that was true. But it wasn't anything they'd done or not done that had killed them. The fate of those cows had been foretold long ago, by eastern men who decided to bring them late and rush them every step. They were the ones who should clean up this mess, the ones who never did.

From this assignment of blame, Doc exempted the Major, but he did so less in his own mind. He believed the Major obeyed his orders too well, that he had obeyed some he should not have. In this, he could have taken some advice from Walt Whitman: *Resist much, obey little.*

Now Doc called the new hires and the volunteers back in and began a second speech about how the gather and branding would go. They had two wagons. One would gather the west end. The second would gather the east and across the river. A third crew would be gathering and branding steady up north over the hill at Cochrane Lakes. The Major had designed and built a fancy squeeze gate there for holding and branding the adult stock.

As for dividing the crews, there was scant talent to divvy up. He and Lippy would take charge of the west wagon. He'd make a crew out of new hires and volunteers that could help them. Pesky would boss the second wagon, with Dwight and the ex-Mounties, and some new hires from Fort Calgary, as his help. At Cochrane Lakes, the Major and Richard Duthie could boss the ex–Mountie servants and the Pichés, and make up the balance with the Major's friends and their hired hands.

More than once, Doc almost said Dog Eye's name. We need ropers, he would think, and automatically Dog Eye would come to mind, riding quietly into a herd, not seeming to move a muscle, but coming out with a calf double-heeled.

Then he'd remember: there is no Dog Eye. For all the cows and grown steers, he and Lippy would have to team rope for the west wagon, and neither one of them caught heels worth a damn. Across the river, Pesky could do most of the roping, but when it came to the grown animals, Dwight was going to have to help. Dwight!

Doc was finished his speeches. He asked the boys to stick around in the bunkhouse for the Major, who also wanted to talk to them. To kill the time, card games started, as many as there were decks. Everybody seemed to be smoking and it was hard to breathe, even with the door open.

When the Major crossed the creek from the big house, Doc saw that his manner was grim. He had seen his boss displeased before, but never like this. Doc called everyone to order but noticed that the visitors didn't stop their card game.

The Major stood inside the door, popped his gloves three times, then spoke.

"The Cochrane Ranch lost many cattle this winter," he began, and Doc assumed that was the problem. It had occurred to the Major that round-up meant finding out the exact number of dead. The thought of sending that number east was eating him. "Because the cattle were in poor condition at the start of winter, the number that died doesn't tell us much about ranching at this location. We are going to try again. I will bring a second herd from Montana this summer, enough to make up for the winter's losses and more. In other words, there will be more pressure on the grass of the Cochrane Lease next winter, not less. Which brings me to my main point."

The Major swept his gaze over the room. Doc figured out what was coming by the way he looked from squatter to squatter. He also eyed the small ranchers who lived along the perimeter.

"Because we did not have time to brand on the trail last summer, or here on the ranch in the fall, we absolutely must brand now. As soon as possible, the Cochrane C must go on every animal found on this lease. Those are my orders: to brand every cow, bull, steer, heifer, and calf found on this lease."

"Now hold on!" One of the visitors was standing. He still had three playing cards in his left hand. He was an American, dressed with Californio flare, one of those who lived along the edge of the lease. "You mean to say, if you found mine wandering with yours, you'd brand them?"

"If they're on this lease, yes."

"The hell!" The American threw down his cards, picked up his hat, slapped it against his leg, and screwed it on. "That's damn thievery! You're supposed to round up yours, not rustle mine."

"What about stealing grass?" asked the Major, staring the man down.

"You got grass galore. If your cows hadn't been too tired to climb a hill, they'd've found plenty." The American started toward the door, pushing men out of his way. "Lemme out of this robbers' roost."

Most of the squatters and ranchers followed. Watching them go, Doc's sympathy was with them. What the Major had just said went against everything he knew.

When the Major went back to the big house, Doc told the remaining men that he'd had a new thought. Though the two wagons would still go out first thing in the morning, maybe a couple of scouts should get started tonight. He told Pesky to saddle up and go east: to see where the cows were and the best places to brand them. Lippy should do the same in the west. He told them to get a move on to make use of the remaining light.

Doc felt fondness and sadness as he watched Lippy bounce up and head out. He would miss this partner who could divine a meaning, no matter how coded. Doc said "scout" and Lippy heard "Olaf." He knew Lippy would meet them tomorrow at midday and tell them he'd swept the southwest corner and there was no need to go there.

What Doc also knew was that the Major's pronouncement about branding other people's cows meant he himself must soon leave. As soon as this gather and branding were done, Doc would fire himself, draw his pay, and go.

MACLEOD TRAIL

July 1882

I CAN'T WORK FOR THIS RANCH any more. I'm not loyal to it."

For six weeks of gathering and branding, Doc rehearsed those words in his head. Finally, a few hours after the last calf was branded, he spoke his piece to the Major. Instead of being angry, Major Walker asked for a reason and listened quietly while Doc gave it: his scruples about branding other people's cows. While Doc explained, the Major ran one hand over his short hair to the back of his neck, which he squeezed and rubbed. Doc thought of what he would do in the Major's place, and decided he would at least try to make himself feel guilty for reneging on his promise to be the trail boss on the next drive from Montana.

"Are you taking any others with you?" was the Major's next question.

"No. I speak for myself."

Doc knew Pesky and Lippy were staying, and he was pretty sure Dwight would leave with him. Still, it was accurate to say that he didn't speak for Dwight either.

When they got to the matter of horses, Doc said he was hoping to buy Louie. The Major reminded him that Louie was a fine horse. Doc agreed, but noted Louie's bad leg. The gelding was less valuable than he had been. This was a horse trade after all.

The Major had already paid Doc by then, and Doc counted out and shoved some money back across the dark-veined oak.

"That's too much," the Major said.

"It's for Pete too."

The two horses were buddied up to an extent Doc had seldom seen. He also believed that to ride Louie away, with no second horse to spell him off, would destroy the big buckskin.

The Major pushed half the money back and Doc assumed the proposition was rejected, that the Major was punishing him after all. But what he said was, "Pete belonged to Dog Eye French. If anyone has a right to him, it's you."

On his lap, Doc had the two books he'd borrowed: *Great Expectations* and *Leaves of Grass*. He raised them, set them on the desk, thanked the Major for their use.

"Which did you like best?" the Major asked.

"The Dickens was a good story, but Whitman meant more to me."

The Major picked up *Leaves of Grass*, studied the cover a few seconds, and handed it to him. "Then have it."

Doc was feeling pretty low. The gift drove him the rest of the way to the ground. After shaking the Major's hand the Mason way, he slunk away contrite.

THAT WAS TWO DAYS AGO, and now Doc rode Pete and led Louie through the big hills south of Fort Calgary, on a road that cut through spruce on the northern slopes and emerged into hot July light on the southern descents. Rippling tides of grass swirled around brown warts of low brush. The crocuses were long blown but the summer flowers stood bright. Wild rose sweetly signalling its thorn. Old man's whiskers nodding three heads the colour of plum pits. Buffalo beans in sprays of butter yellow.

Doc went very slow, in honour of Louie, and they made their first night's camp on Fish Creek. It was the same place he'd come on Christmas Eve, when he hired Fleury's cariole. There was a big freighters' camp there now, two bull trains having met going opposite directions. Crew tents were pitched and a big fire was roaring. The men were making a lot of hilarious noise and firing guns, and Doc steered away. Nothing would depress him faster than hearty company. He picketed his horses where the brush was thick and the freighters' noise muffled. What he did that night beside his own fire, before sleep would come, was relive the rest of what had happened as he readied himself to leave the Cochrane Ranch.

Though he had made it his policy not to badmouth the Major or try to sell others on his complaint, Doc's leaving was a thing known to everyone on the lease. Men he barely knew stood around with long faces watching him pack his gear. Lippy was no doubt anxious to get back to Lilly, but steadfastly refused to go until Doc was gone.

On his tarp and bedroll, Doc had assembled his woollies, his extra clothes, his phrenology book, the new Whitman, his leather head map, so old and soiled you could hardly see anything on the leather but dirt, his roll of piano wire. He flapped in the ends, rolled it tight, tied it. Into his saddlebag, he put mainly weaponry: the Colt Dragoon, its holster belt, plenty of ammunition, the extra cylinder coated in bee's wax. Because he didn't like the way it lay in a corner, Doc picked up Dog Eye's bedroll too and made a second turkey with it. He put the biggest outfit behind Pete's saddle and the lighter load on Louie.

Then he stood before Lippy, the two of them facing the fact that it might be the end of the trail for them. A man never really knows, once he leaves a place, if he'll ever return. Lippy asked if Doc would come to the wedding and be his best man, probably in the fall after beef round-up, and Doc said that nothing in the world would please him more, but that he couldn't promise because he did not know where fall would find him.

Lippy nodded. "I guess you'll be back sometime, though," he said. "Maybe we'll have kids by then." For some reason, those children of

Lippy and Lilly, who didn't even exist yet, cut Doc the deepest and prompted his eyes to water. He reached and shook Lippy's hand. "This is all the farewell I can take," he said.

All through the packing he had looked for Dwight, and when he was ready to mount, he still hadn't seen the big fool. He imagined that he was settling up with the Major, but why had he been so damn slow to start? Here was Doc at the peak of a wrenching scene of farewell, and Dwight wasn't packed, nor was his horse caught.

Guessing what Doc was after, Lippy nodded to the bunkhouse corner, round which the trail led to the outhouse. Lippy nodded a second time and more emphatically to mean that Dwight was there for reasons beyond taking a crap. Doc strutted back. In the bunkhouse shadow, on the shallow bank of Big Hill Creek, Dwight was sitting on the ground, his shoulder against the smooth bark of a young aspen and his rounded back eloquent with grief.

"Boiled owl, Dwight! If you're coming, come!"

"Can't go," the wet voice came.

"What you mean, you can't? I see no Oregon Boot on your foot. No captor's gun to your head."

"I won't!"

"Okay, that's different."

Doc waited. He would not make this easy for Dwight. Dwight was going to have to get this stone off his tongue by himself.

"I like my job, Doc. It's good and I've kept it. When I go, I want to be able to get on other places."

He turned his wet pie of a face toward Doc. His head was bare, and his funny little sprigs of hair stuck up. It was hard for him to meet Doc's eye, but he did.

"I can get you on anywhere we go," said Doc.

"That's not what I mean. I mean go myself. Not just take a job that's a favour to you."

Doc had an awful urge to hit Dwight. He had been mean to this boy since they met, right from the moment he'd made him shoot off his own hat and bloody his face. Then he'd tripped him with piano wire and broke his nose on a root. He had ridiculed him and showed no patience when he taught him to ride. Every statement he made to

Dwight seemed to begin with a curse. And, right now, he wanted to curse him more, make a fist, beat him to a stump.

Doc walked back the way he'd come. He waved off several people who advanced to help him board his horse, made a mighty leap, and hit Pete's stirrup first try. He leaned down and untied Louie's halter rope from the porch pole. He looked at each person for a second or two, then looked at the bunkhouse corner where he knew Dwight was about to appear.

"Dwight, come on."

Dwight crept out from beside the building, came forward as if expecting to be quirted.

"I been thinking," said Doc. "What you should learn next is how to twist steers."

Dwight lifted his big head.

"It's something only a big man can do. You grab the head. You bite the lip. You twist him down, fast! You're laughing, Dwight, but I'm serious. It's a prized skill. In all my time as a cowboy, I knew only one man who could do it."

A grudging smile came to Dwight's face.

"You need a decent saddle too, so you better take that one off Louie. It's Dog Eye's. He's not needing it any more."

Then Doc was gone. The horses seemed to want to run up the giant hill, even Louie on his bad leg. Doc let them run until they were out of sight, then proceeded at a walk. All the while, he did not look back. There is never much sense in looking back. He was crying and laughing at the same time, because he was sad and because he had never known anyone who could twist down a steer. He had heard that a Negro cowboy did it in shows, but Doc had always thought it was a lie.

THE NEXT DAY, LOUIE'S LEG was swollen and hot, so Doc rode Pete again and took it just as slow. The Sheep River was raging with runoff, and after they'd bucked through it, Doc made his horses stay standing in an eddy for most of an hour, thinking it would cool the big gelding and do Pete no harm.

While they stood, he watched a caravan of wagons come to the river and cross it from the south. The families appeared to be moving everything they owned, and when the current heaved the wagons, bits and pieces fell off. A rocking chair fell and rocked away down the river. A big two-handled saw sank into the froth while its owner cursed from the wagon seat.

Doc assumed they were from Fort Macleod and headed for Fort Calgary. When he had stopped at Calgary to check for mail, he had been amazed to find a mushroom town. The railroad was due to arrive later this year, and the few shacks of old Calgary were now the centre of a canvas city. Huckster, chancer, and booster were all present, sitting outside tents on nail kegs, looking smug, smoking fat cigars. Doc asked a couple of men he recognized what was going on and found that a goodly number of the pilgrims were from Fort Macleod. Heart of the country just a month ago, Macleod was, according to these men, in full eclipse. Fort Calgary was the place to be.

As Doc rode between the Sheep and Highwood Rivers, more and more of the sky was blotted out by cloud. It was spitting rain by the time Doc came to the Highwood and made his camp by a bluff of aspens, not fifty yards from a stopping house. He ran around and gathered an armload of sticks, started a fire in an old firepit, and sat with his tarp bridged over his hat brim, watching rain spit and hiss into the flames.

Sitting there, not wet but damp and chilly, Doc felt woeful and alone, and waited for thoughts of Pearly to show up and make him feel worse. To ward her off, he imagined an ugly husband and four brats, three with ringworm. The ruse succeeded and his reward was Dog Eye.

Over and over, as Doc wallowed in the rain, Dog Eye fell through the ice funnel into the other world. Over and over, Doc let him slip. Dog Eye was too young to know for sure he wanted to throw his life away, that nothing better awaited him around the bend. The only person whose job it was to convince him, who could have done anything at all to delay him by force or trickery, was Doc.

Dog Eye told Doc that no more cowboys would follow him now that he was old. He said not even Dwight would, and it had come to pass. Now, Doc made the cut a little deeper by telling himself he deserved no more. Dog Eye French, drowned in the river, was proof.

Doc hated being alone more than anything. He was always quick to critique poor company, but the truth was he would not leave even the worst company, if the alternative was himself. As long as he had other people, he liked himself fine, felt fortunate to be himself. But, alone, as tonight, all that pride dissolved and could not be found again. It was as though loneliness divided him. He became two people, the one who was and the one who watched. The latter saw every foible, every falseness, and muttered continuous contempt.

Listening to the voice, which sometimes had the sound of Doc, sometimes of Dog Eye, Doc watched the rain streak the light in the stopping house's parchment window. He imagined a family gathered around that light, and a man whose job was to take Doc in and pretend to like him. He watched by the wet and lonely hour and did not move.

FORT MACLEOD

July 1882

AT THE SOUTHERNMOST POINT of the Porcupine Hills, it looked like it had never rained, and the wind came roaring from the west. Doc could almost see it coming out of the wedge that cradled the Old Man River. There was still lots of grass for the wind to comb, so it was not dusty, at least not until Doc neared the town. Where the flooding Old Man River had chewed the banks and bared the rocks, loose sand and gravel started to lick up. Grit and towering dust were his companions and heralds as he and his horses faced the boiling river across from Fort Macleod. In the river, both horses had to fight hard not to be knocked over by the galloping current. Doc himself was wet to the head and frightened by the time the horses dragged themselves out the other side.

The main difference between Fort Macleod now and the previous fall was that the river was high enough to flood the channel that made it an island. It was also high enough to squeeze over the banks, so all the lowest-lying shacks had their bottom logs in the soup. Backhouse holes were filled and spilling. Main street achieved the rare feat of being dusty and awash at the same time.

But even as they slopped down the street, Doc's panic lessened. It was amazing, even to him, that such a barren-looking town, such a windy bitch, could improve his mood, but all at once his hurry was replaced by method and he was calm. Through crowds of appraising Indians, Doc took his horses to the livery barn. The proprietor peeled off Pete's saddle and bundle, exposing the matted wet. Doc begged a brush and applied it liberally, breaking up the patches of sweat and dust on both horses. He took the two geldings to the river to drink, and an Indian followed. The man wanted money and tried to earn it by pointing out the swelling in Louie's leg. Even after the ice-cold crossing, the leg was puffed. Doc massaged it and splashed it while the horses drank. Back in the liveryman's corral, Doc told Pete and Louie what good horses they were, then let them loose. After watching them roll and dust, he shouldered his wet bedroll and crossed to the hotel.

The Macleod Hotel didn't appear changed inside. The benches at the two dining tables were occupied, one with eaters, the other with card players. Flies wheeled in the dusty glow above the lamps. The shattering sound of billiards balls made Doc jump, for he had not been aware that a room here was devoted to that play. He poked his head in to verify that the humps playing were men and not Pearly.

Inside this building, the thing Doc was most aware of was stink: that combination of sweat, boiled meat, liquor, cigar, cow shit, horse shit, dust, and mouse that together expresses "town." The longer Doc had been in pure air, the stronger and more revolting he found the town smell, the harder it was to stand his ground before it.

Outside, it was still light and cool. Here, it was dark and putridly hot. The men who lined the dining benches wore heavy clothes. Their faces were red and streaming sweat. Doc's strongest urge was to run off, get his horses, and ride away. But it was too soon to have forgotten the fearful nights, the keen-edged sorrow and loneliness that had driven him here.

As Doc stood within the hotel entrance, his wet bedroll over one shoulder, the Englishman who owned the place came out of his kitchen carrying a metal pot sloshing inside with something brown. He crossed the room and clumped it on the eaters' table. A river of steam ran up the lintel of his kitchen doorway. Beyond that door was a cabinet, one door open and a padlock hanging on the latch. It was full of bottles.

Kamoose had pretended not to see Doc when he went by to the table. Coming back, he grinned like a dog.

"My cowboy friend! Greetings!"

A baptism in the falseness of town. Doc didn't doubt the feat of memory, but resented being called friend on the strength of one egg breakfast. Friends were people whose leaving and dying grieved you.

"Would you be needing a bed?"

"I need to eat. Bed depends on the price."

"One price. Two dollars. First come, first serve. That's my principle. At the moment, you're in luck. A place near the stove."

"Who would need a stove?"

The price seemed a lot compared to out of doors. It would help remind Doc not to stay too long.

"Price includes a dinner of stew, my friend. Could I get you some? And raisin cider?"

Doc had it on his tongue to say *Stop calling me friend*. But at the mention of food, he was hungry. He said yes.

"You might want to read my rules, while you're waiting." The Englishman winked at Doc and butted his head at a handwritten sign on the wall.

Doc needed to get his bedroll drying, so he took it to the sleeping room and opened it on the hard pan between straw mattresses. He lifted out the wrapper that contained the books and was relieved to see they were only damp. He set them aside, the pages fanned. Then, because he could not resist anything written, he went back out to the sign.

Spiked boots and spurs must be removed before retiring.
Towels changed weekly. Insect powder available at the bar.
Two or more people must sleep in one bed when requested.
In case of FIRE *the guests are requested to escape without*
    unnecessary delay.
Assaults on the cook are strictly prohibited.

All boarders who get killed will not be allowed to remain.
All guests must rise at 6 AM as the sheets are needed for
tablecloths.
Indians and niggers will be charged double.

Doc might have laughed at some of it, but the Englishman, who was by now ladling stew, kept peeking at him and grinning.

Doc sat down at the table with a few men who were leaned over, gobbling their food. The most sociable one looked up and waggled his eyebrows as he fed. Soon Kamoose was back with a murky cup.

"Did you read my rules? Indians and niggers, eh?" The Englishman forced himself to laugh.

"Amusing," Doc said.

Seeing that Doc was a tough nut to crack, Kamoose stayed. First he got Doc to take a drink of the cider and asked him what he thought. Doc said it was fine.

"Then I'd advise you to stick with it and not drink any of that hop beer that Fred Pace is advertising across the street. I had some of Fred's hop beer and look what happened."

Kamoose gathered up his apron at the front and turned, showed Doc the ass of his overalls. The centre was patched in two directions, in different colours of cloth. He laughed furiously, as if he were the one hearing the joke for the first time.

Doc finished his stew, mopped out the bowl with a biscuit, downed the cider, and returned to the sleeping room. He raised one of the straw mattresses and thumped it down, watched and listened for movement. He held his hand on it and studied his arm for fleas. He picked up the damp book of poems and lay down on his back with it on his chest. He closed his eyes and opened the book at random, like he'd seen southern men do with their Bibles.

> *O camarado close! O you and me at last, and us two only.*
> *O a word to clear one's path ahead endlessly!*
> *O something ecstatic and demonstrable! O music wild!*
> *O now I triumph—and you shall also;*

O hand in hand—O wholesome pleasure—O one more
desirer and lover!
O to haste firm holding—to haste, haste on with me.

Doc read it twice and became unsettled. It sounded like Whitman
wanted Doc to turn some man into more than a friend. Then it came
to Doc that the "camarado close" wasn't necessarily the same person
as the "desirer and lover." In that case the oracle was fine. He would
find a friend with whom to travel, and somewhere up ahead, a woman
who would desire him. Doc became drowsy and, in his drowse, forgot
that Whitman's words were just a game. He looked forward to these
new people in his life. The sadness of the last two days blew off him
like dust.

The sound of a raised voice erupting in the kitchen woke him. His
joyful pleasure shattered when a blow smacked flesh.

"You drunken bummer! What do you mean getting into my cup-
board? I'll horsewhip you where you stand!"

Doc wondered who the hotelier talked to and used that way, like a
Sioux woman addresses and kicks her travois dog.

Very soon after, the Englishman entered Doc's sleeping chamber,
his grin looming yellow. He had his hands clutched in the apron again.
He lowered his patched ass onto the nearest cot.

"I'm afraid I don't know your name, Mr. . . . ."

"You never heard it. I'm Doc Windham. And you're Kamoose."

"My real name is Harry Taylor. Kamoose is a Cree name given me
in my trading days."

"Meaning?"

"Squaw thief!"

He bellowed another of his laughs. A laugh that smelled like a fart.

"Okay, Mr. Kamoose, you didn't come to introduce yourself."

"No. I just wanted to warn you that you're in for a shock. When
you were here in the fall, you asked about a young man of Ontario."

"Jim Adams."

"You had no more than left when, lo and behold, I met the young lad."

"Why is that shocking?"

"Thing is, this Adams worked for the Mounties at the start. Stable boy. The gentlemen in red punish the whisky very hard, you know, and Adams picked up their bad habits, if you get my meaning. Got the habit severely, in fact. Mounties fired him for it, and that's when he came to me. I took pity and gave him a job, though he's almost useless. Just now, I had to give him a hiding for breaking into my medicinal liquor cabinet and drinking half a bottle. I just thought it fair to warn you."

"What's medicinal liquor?"

"Whisky. All the liquor in Canada is medicinal. You get a permit from the government, place an order, and they send you your bottle. You have to be a male of age and white."

"How come you have so much?"

"Actually, I have none," Kamoose said, delighted by the irony. "All the liquor here is permitted to the gentlemen who visit me. They come to drink at my hotel so as to enjoy billiards or cards, and the community of other men while they take their medicine."

"So I can't have any."

Kamoose winked. "But you can."

He trotted back toward his cabinet. Doc heard the rattle of the padlock, then a roar of warning, presumably at Adams. Kamoose came back with a full bottle, along with a stopper and a cup.

"So there you have it." He leaned down and covered his mouth against untrustworthy listeners. "Dead man's bottle."

"What's that?"

"For gents like yourself, I keep a few bottles that are permitted, but to people who don't live in these parts, or don't live at all." He roared a laugh. "Hence, the name."

Doc sat with his bottle and his half-filled glass. His zeal for getting drunk was left on the trail, along with his panic. He sipped only enough to get the smell on him, like a wolf or a dog who rolls in a pile of dung. He kept looking at the kitchen door. Jim Adams kept not coming through it.

Then Adams did show. He staggered out of the kitchen, maybe by accident. He looked as if he were fighting a wind that had blown him there. Kamoose was standing bent over the card table, with his hands laced behind his back, and did not see his servant at first. Adams had not been thick in flesh when he and Doc had shared the calf wagon seat. He was down to bone now. Along with weight, he had lost the look of a man. He was scruffy-haired, with the patchy beard a boy grows. His head stood on its skinny neck like a sunflower on its stalk.

When Kamoose turned and saw him, the yellow grin yanked into a grimace.

"Get back in the kitchen, you bleeding sore! My company does not wish to look at you!" He chased Adams through the door, shouted at him, scuffled with him. When Kamoose returned, he came to Doc's table and sat beside him on the bench. The heat of his damp body felt swampy on Doc's arm.

"I wonder if you would help me, Mr. Windham." He nodded toward the sleeping chamber. Kamoose got up and walked into that room. Doc followed. They stood in the near dark.

"Mr. Windham, I've been thinking about Jim Adams. The boy needs more than employment. Now that you've seen him, you must agree. He needs a friend. If you want to take him with you, I won't prevent it."

The room was close. Doc went to the back where there was a door to open. He stood in the frame breathing the luxuriant night air. The wind was down and it was no longer dusty.

"What I think," Doc said, "is that you've been paying that boy in whisky. You've about destroyed him and you're afraid he'll die. Even that didn't bother you until I showed up. Now that there's someone in the world concerned, you're afraid you might get blamed."

"That's a damnable thing to say, sir." Kamoose puffed up.

"If I'm wrong, how much do you owe Adams right now, in wages?"

Kamoose pretended to calculate. "Ten American dollars."

"Make it twenty. Give me my meal of stew, the bottle of whisky, and the cider for nothing, and I'll help you."

"You're not helping me. I won't accept that view."

"Then don't. If you agree to my terms, I'll go to the livery barn right now and pay out my horses. Then I'll come back and get Adams drunk."

"He's drunk already."

"I'll get him drunker. When he's passed out, you're going to help me get him on a horse."

"Where will you take him?"

"What's it to you?"

"Nothing, of course."

"Then let's get at it. When I'm back, you send me Adams. And if you so much as pinch his arm, I'll bust your head."

"You talk big for a small man."

"You talk honest for a crooked one."

DOC TACKED UP AND LOADED the horses. He paid the liveryman for the bit of hay they'd eaten. He tied them to the hitching rail in front of the hotel and returned inside, to his place at the table and his bottle. Kamoose pushed Adams out of the kitchen, and he came staggering. He blinked at the light, surveyed the room slowly.

"Jim!"

Following the sound of his name like a blind man, Adams made it to the table. He thumped down on the other side. Doc told him to stay put, got up, and went to the kitchen. He came back with a second cup, which he poured half full of whisky.

"Have a drink, Jim. Careful you don't throw it on yourself."

Jim took the cup, then brought his other hand up from under the table to brace it. He lowered his face to the cup, drank in sips, then gulps. Steadier now, he looked at Doc.

"What do you want?"

"Nice to see you too, Jim."

"Something I'm supposed to tell you. Can't remember."

"Do you remember who said it?"

Jim tried but couldn't. When he shook his head, the gesture got out of control, became a shudder that twisted his whole body. He reached for the bottle, stopped his hand in mid-air, looked at Doc.

"Yeah, you can have more. But I'll do the pouring." Doc poured the cup nearer to the top. "Take it slow. You don't want to puke up your night's sleep."

"You're not drinking."

Doc took a sip. "There's drinking and there's drinking."

Jim blew out some air, made a noise that might have been a laugh, a slurred laugh.

"You're in one hell of a shape, Jim, if you don't mind my saying."

"Fine shape."

The whisky was hitting Adams like bare knuckles. Tough, he refused to go down. He drank the rest of the cup, asked for more. His eyes were mouse fuzz and piss holes. He looked at Doc for custom's sake, but Doc doubted he saw a thing. Doc poured him more.

Then Doc went to Kamoose's kitchen and asked to buy a second bottle, one they could take away. They were standing by Kamoose's liquor cabinet. Doc had his money out, but Kamoose refused it.

"What will you do with him?" the hotel man asked in a whisper.

"I can't figure out if you're asking because you think you ought to, or if you really want to know. If you really want to know, I wonder why."

The question flustered the Englishman. He waved his hands in the air. "No interest. I'm only talking."

"Jim's ready. My horses are outside."

Doc went to the sleeping room, put the full bottle in the bedroll, rolled everything back up to make his turkey. A voice in his head, maybe Dog Eye's, said something about getting people drunk and stealing them, if you couldn't get friends any other way. But Doc found that notion didn't bother him. If that's what he was doing, Adams wouldn't be any worse for it.

PORCUPINE HILLS/THE GAP

July 1882

WHEN JIM ADAMS CAME TO, he was on his stomach, hanging over the bare back of a yellow horse. His hands and feet were tied under the horse's belly and another rope kept him from sliding. He pulled his face away from the oily hair and a branch clawed him. He fell limp, let himself hang. Pain zig-zagged through his head. The forest floor crawled with snakes.

"I'm sick!" he yelled.

"That's right!" came a voice in front of him. He knew the voice but could not remember whose it was. He tried to remember the night before but that too was gone. He wanted a drink so the snakes would go away. He wished to return to blackness.

The horse stopped. A man stood in front of Jim's head, but Jim lacked the strength to look at him. The man untied his hands, went to the other side and untied his feet. He gave a pull and Jim shot backwards, flopped boneless to the ground. Rolling to his side, Jim saw harsh judgement in a horse's eye. Nausea bucked his whole body into his mouth.

JIM SAT UPRIGHT ON THE bare back of the yellow horse. His hands were tied in front of him, so he could grip the blond mane. Ahead was the back of the little cowboy, the one with whom he'd ridden on the seat of a wagon. That memory stood alone, as if it were his entire life history. The sun was behind them. They were in high country, among long-needle pines, and the trail was still rising. Once in awhile, a bend would reveal a black crown of trees against the blue.

His thirst was immense, maddening. When he looked ahead, he could see a canteen tied on his captor's saddle. He hated that he had not been offered water. A thin needle bored into the side of his brain. Even the empty sky writhed if he looked at it long enough.

THEY RODE THE HILLS all that day until they came to the edge of an escarpment looking west. They dismounted, and while the horses grazed, they sat in a sea of purple shooting stars and stared down into a fawn-coloured gulf. The slope descended to an oxbow stream that ploughed the valley's thick alluvium, then rose the other way into a bullock's ass of rock-spined hills. Above that stood the mountains. They were not individual but a wall, a rampart, the seeming terminus of the world.

"Where is this?" Jim asked, struggling to hold his perch on the unmoving ground.

"We crossed the Porcupine Hills. This is their western edge. I believe that down there is the Walrond lease."

The mention of the Porcupine Hills spiked a longing in Jim's chest. He tried to remember what he knew about the place. The effort started making him sick and he let it go. In the morning cold, he'd been sweating. Now, in the hot afternoon sun, his shoulders wrenched with chill.

"I have to get back to work. Untie me and let me go."

Doc went to Louie and dug in his saddlebag. He came back with the bottle Jim had mostly killed last night.

"If that was your job, you can work for me."

Doc sat down and wedged the bottle into Jim's tied hands. He pulled the cork. Jim lifted it to his mouth and started to pour. Doc let the apple in Jim's neck bob twice before he pulled it away.

"If you don't plague me, you can have more later."

"Why not give it all to me now?"

"Because I'm trying to cure you, not kill you."

THEY DESCENDED THROUGH the trees along a wet coulee. The evergreens gave way to aspens, then the aspens to tussocks of grass that ran down the slope. Doc and Louie led at a walk and Jim bobbed on Pete like a rag doll. There were cattle, and they ran away from them, wild as deer.

The early evening sun was a furnace on the tawny grass. Water drops coaxed out of Jim's flesh. When the sun winked behind the rampart, they came to a big river that fell from sill to sill. Doc dragged Jim off his horse and untied his hands.

"Take your clothes off and have a swim. It'll improve you."

About to curse Doc for his advice, Jim was overcome by longing for the cold water. Fighting out of his pant legs, he fell. He struggled on the rocky ground and was defeated. Laughing, Doc grabbed his boots and pulled them off, then his trousers.

Jim slid down a smooth sill into the icy water. His breath caught as the water rolled him. He turned his head and let the cold pulse through his hot sour mouth.

Later, there was a fire. Doc retied Jim's hands behind his back, took the long end of the rope and tied it to his own wrist. He told Jim to lie down on the unrolled bedding. Then he lay down too, and drew the blanket over both of them.

"Where would I go?" said Jim.

"If I knew that, I wouldn't tie you."

NEXT DAY, JIM WAS allowed to ride Pete with a bridle. His hands were again tied in front. Doc said the big river he had swum in was the same one that ran through Fort Macleod. Now they rode along it west. The mountains still appeared as a solid wall and how the water got through was a mystery. Farther on, the angle changed and a cleft appeared.

They crossed the river near the mouth of this gap, a sideways veer behind a rock wall. Doc entered first on Louie. When they were out of sight, Jim sawed the bit in the yellow horse's mouth, gummed the flanks with his naked boot heels. He gathered the reins and whipped them side to side. The gelding dropped his shoulder and shot away.

Jim landed on stones. His ribs and one shoulder took the blow and felt broken. In the rocks and rose thorns, he struggled to rise, could hear Doc laughing above.

"Don't laugh at me!"

"If you want Pete to leave his best friend," said Doc, "you're going to have to be nicer to him than that."

THEY CROSSED THROUGH the mountain along the Z-shaped gap, narrow and booming. The distance across was surprisingly short, and they emerged into a flat green meadow. Inside the mountains, the season seemed earlier than on the outer slope.

At a fork where two streams met, they took the southern one. Where this stream curved and some aspens grew with the spruce, Doc stopped and said it was good enough. He dug and cribbed a firepit, gathered and cracked an armload of deadfall. The chill came quickly after the sun was eclipsed by a mountain.

With the dark and the cold came a shaking and twisting in Jim. The canteen flew from his hands when he tried to drink. He crawled to the river, tried to hold himself over the water, but his elbows rattled and failed. He rolled onto his side so his nose and mouth cleared the water, his teeth crashing against each other. Doc peeled fast on a branch of green willow.

"What's happening to me?" Jim hollered, for his whole body was taking up the vibration of his jaws.

"You got the jim-jams. They're no joke."

Jim climbed from the river, fell backwards, went rigid. Doc poked the slender willow stick at the hinge of his mouth, pried open the jaws, set it like a wooden bit. He pushed a finger in behind the stick and fished Jim's tongue out of his throat. The boy's eyes were staring into the top of his head.

THEN IT WAS BLACK DARK, and the wolves were howling so close it raised the hair all over Jim's body. All night, he longed to sleep, to close out the weird sounds. He dreamt of sleep, hallucinated sleep, even thought he was asleep, but he never was. He was awake and dreaming hellishly. A grizzly came and chewed his head ragged. An Indian stood above him and fired a stone arrow that nailed him to the ground. In black woods, a burning horse ran in and out of silhouette trees. These were not imagined things. They were happening.

Several times, Jim tried to rise but the arrow held him. His cloven heart hammered as best it could.

"Easy, boy. It's all right, boy."

The wind was coming hard out of the west, stirring every aspen leaf and spruce branch to noise. Jim could not stand the sound. Too much like the burning horse in the trees. He held his ears and whimpered.

In the dawn light, he heard a gun fire and felt the bullet enter him. He could see his shattered heart thrashing in the middle of a surging red sea.

Jim-jam. Jim-jam. Jim-jam.

Doc came with a deer over his shoulder, its velvet antlers scraping the ground, blood streaming from its cut throat. The smell made Jim vomit, so Doc took it downwind to gut and butcher.

ONE NIGHT, JIM BEGAN to talk. "I don't need you," he told Doc. "I don't care if I die. I just want a drink. Why shouldn't I? You think I was sad, but I was happy. We made lots of jokes. 'Do you see that fella over there with one crossed eye named James?' 'What's the name of his other eye?' That's what you're supposed to say. What's the name of his other eye if the crossed one's name is James. You probably don't understand. 'Where's this trail go?' 'It doesn't go anywhere. It stays right here.' You probably don't get that either."

"You're right. I'm not much of one for jokes," said Doc. "If you've got to be talking, why don't you tell me where you come from? What's your father do?"

"My father doesn't do anything. He's dead. I was at the agricultural college in Guelph, doing really well. I was learning about cattle. My father gambled the farm right out from under me and my sister, Penny. Our old bitch of a mother blames me because my father left her poor. I remember it all."

His mind was out of control, speeding and sparking in the dark.

"I was on a train. Hanging on the outside. Right over the St. Clair River. I had a long pole. If a cow went down, I punched her with it, made her stand up. Cow puncher, get it? I worked for Mr. Anton. We were bringing shorthorns west."

Doc watched the liquored mind come unfogged. It was a balancing act. He had to give him whisky, because he'd heard of ones who jim-jammed themselves to death. He didn't know how long Adams had been drinking for his sustenance, how weakened he might be. So he gave him liquor, a measured amount, trying to slow his mind, his heart. He placed slivers of venison between his lips, and no matter how little, it came boiling back as if Adams's insides were horrified by the sight of food. They were tuned to whisky and nothing but whisky.

Doc boiled tea Indian-strong. The tea stayed down and seemed to bring on Adams's talking jags. This one had come in the middle of the night when the wolves were howling, when Doc would rather have been sleeping, but he was afraid Jim might fall into another fit and swallow his tongue.

"So you brought your cows into the States by train?"

"Chicago stockyards was like a city. All night long, the pigs were screaming. Give me some whisky please, Mr. Windham. Just a little. It stops me shaking."

"Have more tea."

"The hell with tea! I want whisky, you mean son of a bitch! Who asked you to help me? If I want to die of drink, who gives you the right to say no?"

"Drink the tea and quit aggravating me. I'll make you a smoke. So what place did you come to when you got off the train?"

"You think you can fool me, make me think of something else. We got off at Fargo. Loaded the cattle onto barges, went down the Red River to Winnipeg. Halfbreeds ran them. Give me that smoke then."

Before the Bull Durham cigarette was smoked, Adams was jimming and jamming again, still talking, but nonsense. Jibbering while he pushed his face along the ground. Doc dared not give him more whisky. It had to last to the end.

IT WAS COMING DAWN and Doc was asleep. Jim felt a wet cold down his front and legs and knew he'd pissed himself again. The fire was out and not even smoking. The mountain dawn was cold and still.

The small animals that scurried inside his body weren't running as fast as they had been. His heart did not slosh or feel cloven. What Jim felt most was a heavy sadness, a grief less bearable than the rest. Most of the other feelings were physical or about terror. This was shame and it ploughed deep.

Jim's feet were not tied, and with care not to wake Doc, he stood and walked around the firepit to where Doc's saddle stood on its horn. A canvas was over the saddle and Doc's things were inside, as if in a tent. Jim kneeled and worked his tied hands inside, until he was tickling the stock of the Winchester.

"Won't do you any good. I've got the bullets in my pocket."

Jim scrambled up, ran to the river, threw himself onto the rocks, dropped his paining face into the cold water, drank. He pushed his head deeper until the current gurgled in his ears. He opened his mouth and breathed.

Doc grabbed his feet and hauled him back into the air.

JIM SLEPT A LONG TIME. He had bad dreams about fleshy, webby things that filled the air. His legs and arms were sacks of blood that dragged when he moved. When he woke, he had no pants on, not even underwear. He looked around and saw his clothing, wet and draped on a bush. Farther in the same direction, strips of meat hung over a pole above a smoky fire. Doc appeared from the bushes, buckling his belt.

"I bet you haven't had a decent crap in a month," he said. "I recommend it."

In the smoky fire, a stick was wedged at an angle between rocks. A chunk of meat was speared, dripping fat and turning black.

"Damn! I overcooked your breakfast."

Jim's normal response to food was nausea. It came and went. Behind it crowded hunger. He looked at the meat with begging eyes.

Doc used a second stick to pry the meat off onto a flat rock. He took his skinning knife and sawed it in half. Then, holding the knife still, he considered something.

"Hold still."

He slid the blade between Jim's hands and sliced the leather by which they were bound.

"I guess I'm tired of feeding you. Hey, get back out of there! That's hot!"

"How do you know how to do this?" asked Jim, licking the fingers he had just burned on the meat.

"What? Cook meat on a fire?"

"What to do with me."

Doc used the point of his knife to flip the pieces of meat on the cold stone twice more.

"One of the first things I ever learned was about drunks. Back in Texas, my uncle Jack would come to sober my father up. We kids used to hide during the day, but the house was just one room so we had to be there at night. The old man blasphemed God. Cursed his brother, his wife, his children. He was always threatening to kill us in colourful ways. He'd try it too, if he got his hands on anything heavy or pointed."

"I wasn't going to kill you."

"This ain't over, Jim. Just so you know. It won't go on forever, but it ain't over."

"Is he alive? Your father?"

"No. Another drunk shot him."

Doc leaned and picked up the meat in his fingers, nibbled a corner. Jim dove on his and worried it with his loose teeth. Seeing the problem, Doc handed him the skinning knife, butt end first.

"Was your father a drunk?" Doc asked.

"No," said Jim, cutting the meat fine, chewing and chewing, his teeth rocking and bleeding in their gums.

"I assumed he was. It runs in families. I'd be a drunk myself, if I could be. Before and after Pearly pulled out—she was the love of my life—I drank like a fool. But I'd get this kind of headache that laid me out for days. See spots. Everything a whirly-gig. I even got after the opium pipe in St. Louis. I could tolerate that much better. But then I left for the cow country and had no more opportunity."

"I'm lying," said Jim. "My father was a drunk. Finally it hardened his liver, poisoned his blood. When he started to be really sick from it, he died quite suddenly."

Then Jim was crying, on his knees, bending up and down. He fell over onto the blanket and covered his face.

When he stopped crying, Doc was holding a rolled cigarette out to him.

"I have a theory," Doc said. "When you're young, you look around yourself and ask, what can I be? I saw Uncle Jack, who was a cowboy and a good man. It was like my home and family were a fence around me, and the only gate was Jack. But though I never considered it, my father was a gate too. So I became a cowboy in imitation of Jack, but when I got low down, the drunkard's gate was right there waiting. 'Cept, as I say, I was no good at it."

"My father was a stockman. But he drank. When he was drunk, he gambled."

"Well, there you are. Like Uncle Jack and my father in one flesh. You started out to be a stockman, something happened, and you went through the second gate and became a drunk. And I have to say, you did it with alacrity. Takes an average man much longer to reach your depths."

Jim got to his feet and washed his face in the river. He felt his clothing on the bush. His underwear was dry enough to put on.

"Why aren't you disgusted?"

"About what?"

"That I cried."

"Oh hell. I like a good cry myself. Not far from it right now. Get me talking about Pearly and Uncle Jack in the same hour, I'll cry like a baby."

"You don't feel cowardly?"

"If we were fighting Indians, and all I did was cry, I think that would be cowardly. But that's not the kind of crying we're talking about."

"No."

IN THE AFTERNOON OF THE fifth day, the sun vanished behind a sky like boiling mud. Lightning forked the nearest mountains and a slashing rain began.

Jim and Doc sat shoulder to shoulder on Doc's soogin, with the canvas tented over their heads. It leaked a little, but kept off most of the wet. In the close confines, Doc could feel Jim coiled as stiff as a wagon spring. His eyes drilled forward into the downpour. Doc thought to entertain him with stories.

Doc told how he'd seen the St. Elmo's fire dancing on the ears of his horse right across a high plateau near Walla Walla. And the time when, in the middle of a sheepers' conflict, a whole herd of woollies crowded on a hilltop were killed in one blow, as if God had weighed in on the side of beef. Then of course there was poor Tex Appleby.

Doc had several more but saw in the rigidity of his partner's face that he'd better stop.

"You don't like lightning. Not that any normal man does."

Two forces in heaven collided. Lightning turned the river white. Doc dove out and splashed to the horses. Louie had pulled free, but Pete had crossed his rope so the slip-knot was bound. The yellow horse was rearing against it, bending and twisting the grey willow that anchored him. Doc talked soothingly, drew the horse close so the rope could be uncrossed and slipped. Doc called Louie and took hold of his rope as well. In the continued lightning, he led the horses back and forth. When another bolt hit close enough to concuss the air, the horses almost pulled his arms out before he could let go. The horses ran together up the river's shoreline and Doc ran after. Half the time, he couldn't see for the amount of water splashing in his face.

In about an hour, the rain tapered and the lightning show pulled off toward the gap. It was still sparking on top of that split mountain when he got hold of the horses again. They had come quite a distance. The river had swollen until it was pushing through the trees, shortcutting across its turns.

When Doc and the horses got back to camp, the firepit was brimming. One corner of the canvas Jim and he had been sheltering under was lapping in the river. Adams was gone.

Doc yelled but got no answer. Forced to fatalism, he reasoned that Adams was either drowned or safe. Either way, he was what he was and Doc's abandoning his own gear to the elements would not help it. He ran the pieces up a slight rise and under a big spruce tree, piled it beneath the widest branches and around the trunk. In the process, he discovered his Winchester gone.

He kept calling while he worked, the answering silence becoming more doomful each time. He shut his mind and began searching in arcs, cutting for sign. A sound under another spruce brought him to a stop. On his hands and knees, he started in.

"Adams, I'm coming in where you are. Just me and I'm unarmed. I'm harmless to you, so you better be harmless to me."

He could see Adams in the black shadow of the branches, jim-jamming as bad as ever. His back was against the tree trunk, heels grinding in the needle muck. He was pointing the Winchester at Doc, his eyes blank, his humanity unravelling.

"Jim Adams! You listen now. You are not dead or about to die. So give me that rifle, if you please, right now."

The problem was Doc had lied about the bullets. He wasn't about to face mountain lions, mountain humans, and bears unarmed. He had no way to tell if Jim had a bullet levered into the breach.

"Christ, Jim!" Doc pointed a shaking finger past Jim's shoulder. World's oldest trick, and Jim looked just long enough for Doc to get on top of him. Proof of the gun's being ready to fire, it did. Up through the branches, and little pieces fell. Doc got the rifle free and threw it as far as he could, then clamped Adams from behind. He bear-hugged him so tight he could feel his hammering heart.

"Jim, you listen now. You think of something nice. Think of a loping ride under a blue sky on green grass. A good horse is carrying you to meet an old friend you haven't seen in a long time. All the dead are risen and at play. Children are laughing. Your father, before his troubles, has you by the hand. He's leading you to a bull sale."

It took a long time for the hammering to settle. There was not a drop of whisky left, but Jim subsided anyway. When the curl came out of him, so did tears. He wept as if he could keep at it for days. Like a baby, he cried himself to sleep.

Doc went to the stockpile tree and left the rifle there with his other gear. He took the tarp and the only blanket approaching dry. When he checked on the horses, they were also asleep, three-footed. Back with Jim, he lay the tarp down on the spruce needles, rolled Jim onto it, pulled the blanket over both of them. Doc went to sleeping wondering what else lightning had done to Jim Adams.

BY MORNING, THE WEATHER had changed again and it had even snowed a little, enough to white the ground. Snow in the mountains comes when it feels like. Louie's leg was worse from the exertion of running from the lightning. Doc spent a good part of the day cooling it with the fast-melting snow. Doc had felt the area so often he was sure no bone was cracked or broken. The swelling was along the tendons, which meant it was from too damn much distance and hard ground. What Louie needed wasn't a day's rest, but months of doing nothing but grazing.

Come evening, and as Doc thought he might, Jim Adams began to talk. He sat staring into the smoky fire, and the words came without any emotion you could see.

His story started on the east edge of the prairie, with his boss, Mr. Anton, and the two hundred shorthorn cows. There was also a Halfbreed who had hired on with them from the Red River barges. They had chased their cows parallel to the Canadian railroad tracks as far as those went, then had taken older kinds of trails. They travelled through clouds of mosquitoes that drove them and their cattle crazy.

It was muggy weather, and near the Assiniboine River, a lightning bolt struck beside the herd and sent them running. The French Half-breed, whose name was Baptiste, told Jim to follow and they chased and passed the herd, got them into a mill. Baptiste and Jim did it alone, and not a cow or a calf was lost or hurt. Jim had felt exhilarated, accomplished, strong.

Halfway between the Assiniboine and the next important river, the Qu'Appelle, they camped near some carters who were on their way northwest. They were all Red River Halfbreeds, and Baptiste, being of that people, went to visit them. In the night, Baptiste woke Jim. He was drunk. He wanted Jim to help him catch a sickly calf, so they could kill it. He had promised the carters beef. Jim refused and Baptiste cursed him and went after the calf alone.

Next day, Jim told Mr. Anton what had happened. He told Anton he should fire Baptiste. Mr. Anton was troubled because they were only three, and Baptiste was the one who knew the way. Jim was fearless and told his boss that right was still right, and Baptiste was wrong. Besides, Jim was confident they could find another Halfbreed guide at the settlement of Fort Qu'Appelle. Baptiste was paid off and turned out.

They were almost to the Qu'Appelle Valley when another storm caught them. It came like a freight train through the sky and turned the forenoon into night. Soon, the horses were flicking their ears at the electricity in the air. Because they couldn't hope to hold the cattle if they ran, and because the cattle were thirsty, Jim convinced Mr. Anton not to stop, not to take shelter. Maybe if they continued, the cattle would be distracted enough by the smell of the coming river not to run.

Out of all that black cloud, only one bolt of lightning struck. It hit Mr. Anton's wagon and smashed it in half right behind him. Some bedding in the box caught fire. Jim had been riding close and the force drove him off his horse and through the air. The blast knocked him out, for how long he did not know.

When he woke up, he was alone. Only the back half of the wagon remained to remind him what had happened. He stood, his legs shook, his head split with pain. He looked in every direction and there was nothing. He walked in a big circle until he found where the cattle had gone. On top of their tracks was a crazy double scratch, the trail of the broken wagon.

Not one drop of rain had fallen, and all that remained of the storm were occasional sheets of lightning and a veil of rain to the north. On foot, Jim followed the cattle tracks and the snake-shaped drag.

It wasn't far to where the tracks entered a coulee, the beginning of the long descent into the Qu'Appelle Valley. There was no wagon trail here, only an old path worn across the hill flank and down to water. Where the hill's slant was steepest, the wagon had flipped and twisted the oxen over. They had rolled and slid to the bottom, into a dry brushy crease. There the oxen lay tangled in their harness, roaring and kicking.

Scrambling down, Jim almost overlooked Mr. Anton. He lay on the slope with his long coat fanned under him. He looked unharmed, there on his side, but his eyes were glass. Jim rolled him and saw how his head was caved. The whole embankment was studded with cobbles, so it hadn't been extraordinary bad luck, just the ordinary kind.

Jim wrenched the coat out from under his boss and laid it overtop. He went to the wagon and cut the oxen out of their harness. They walked, shaking their heads, then ran to where the valley bottomed out. They stopped at the river's edge and roared at it.

Jim followed until he could see across the valley. On the far side of the river, above a cutbank, stood most of the cows. Many were bellering and chasing about, frantic to find their calves. Many of the calves who had survived were suckling, bunting and slurping as if their brush with death had starved them.

Returning to Mr. Anton, Jim knew he should scoop out a grave and bury his boss. He had no excuse for what he did instead, which was pull Anton's wallet from an inside pocket of his coat and count his wages. Seeing how much money was left, Jim took more.

After that, he climbed to the top of the coulee and called his mare. Finally, he saw her, standing still in the heat shimmers. Rabbit was her name. Rabbit's saddle had slipped to her side. She had stepped on one rein and sliced it short. When he was close enough to see, she was quivering all over. He took a very long time to approach her, talking in a soothing way. Finally, she let him touch her. She had one china eye and, in it, he saw something chaotic that hadn't been there before.

Jim rode her southwest through the blasted and broken country, looking for the Missouri. Mr. Anton had promised Jim that the land in this direction was full of rustlers, bootleggers, wolfers, and the last hostile Indians on earth, but he saw no one, not until he came to the big river and found a steamboat trapped on a bar.

The passengers and crew were unloading freight and pulling on lines, and Jim joined in the work all that day until the boat came free. He argued with the captain that his labour had earned a passage for himself and his horse, but Rabbit, tied in the willows, was quivering again and acting strange. She thrashed and kicked, and tried to rear.

"Fifty dollars for you," said the captain. "I wouldn't have that knot-head on my boat for any money."

A shaggy man dressed in wolf furs despite the heat had sat his horse all day and watched. He chewed tobacco, spat, and made no offer to help. Now, he came forward. With a brown grin, he offered Jim twenty dollars for his horse. Jim asked what he wanted the horse for, and the man said he'd pack her with wolf skins. If she was no good for that, he'd probably eat her. Jim pushed by and drew his Colt. Looking Rabbit in her china eye, he shot her. While the body still shook, he stripped the saddle and boarded the *Nellie Peck* for Fort Benton.

When the story reached that point, Jim stopped. He kept his eyes on the fire and did not signify in any way that it was over, but it was. Doc thought he had never seen an emptier man.

THAT NIGHT, LONG AFTER DOC believed Jim Adams bereft of words, he spoke again. Sitting like a dead man propped, bathed in evergreen smoke and the smell of wet clay, he said, "I remember now."

Doc was halfway down the well into sleep. The words jerked him up.

"When you came to Macleod and gave me a drink, I was trying to remember something. What I was supposed to tell you. I know now."

Doc waited. It took some time for Adams to continue.

"He came to the hotel. Kamoose knew him. He asked for whisky but it was me he'd come for."

"Who are you talking about?"

"He said his name was Overby. He said he was prospecting in the Porcupine Hills because a farmer named Nelson had found gold in a cow's stomach. I couldn't see his eyes because the brim of his hat was too low. But he had the scar on his neck and ear."

"Overcross?"

"Yes."

"Were you drunk?"

"Oh yes."

"What did he say?"

"I only remember the part about the girl and something about fishing."

"Jesus, Jim. Do better, please."

"I asked him if he was going to kill me, and he said no, because I was just the bait. He said I was to tell you he had information about the girl with the scarred face. I told him it was no use because I wouldn't see Doc Windham. He said, 'Yes, you will.'"

Doc began to fill with fury, that old emotion long untapped. The idea that Overcross knew anything about Pearly was having the effect Overcross wanted it to have.

Seeing the change, Jim said, "I'm sorry. I know it's important and I wish I'd remembered earlier."

Doc jumped up and began to pack the camp. Adams did not ask why or help until Doc told him to.

"Kamoose is either in Overcross's pay or just afraid of him. What saved us in Macleod was that I wouldn't tell him where we were headed. And because we left fast and at night. We'll do the same again. We'll keep jumping and stay a jump ahead."

"Maybe he's here," said Jim, gesturing to the dark.

"We'd know if he was."

THE WORST OF THE NIGHT ride was the early part. In the gap, a thousand echoes chattered at them. The horses were nervy, shying and bunching at all the sounds. Doc imagined a rifle opening up. How would you ever know, unless you saw the flash, where to shoot back?

But nothing happened and soon they were out of the rocks and back on grass under a half moon. Doc led them southwest over big hills, following patterns of pale through the greater dark of bush and trees. In the highest places, the brows of outcrop glowered and tortured silhouettes of limber pine were skylit against iron blue. The rocky tops were long rugged spines, ancient animals asleep all round them. Doc worried about Louie, imagined he felt hesitation in the injured quarter of his gait.

They came out into a wide south-trending valley. By then the moon was halfway across the sky. The black shoulders of the Porcupine Hills were on their left, the last few foothills in front of the mountains were on their right. The valley was mostly treeless and it was easy riding.

By morning's light, when the sky beyond the Porcupines turned to wild rose, Doc judged they had gone twenty miles or more, but weren't yet where they needed to be. Now, the falter in Louie's step was obvious, but Doc did not dismount to look. He pushed on.

When the sun was rising in the sky, a great mouth opened into the mountains, as though some American Moses had touched the rock mass and the sea of stone had parted. Doc guessed it was the pass he was looking for. A sizeable river poured out.

"Where are we?" Jim asked.

"Crow's Nest Pass. At the mouth of it."

"Can we stop?"

"Yes."

Before the trail began to drop into the valley, Doc dismounted and pulled the saddle off Louie. Jim had ridden bareback, and the insides of his pant legs were dark with Pete's grease. Louie's leg was puffed around its back and sides. He didn't want it touched. After the gelding rolled and went to graze, he walked three-legged, hanging the sore one.

Doc and Jim made their beds on the slope. The sun was almost too hot on their legs and bellies to sleep. Before Doc placed his hat over his face, he took a last look both ways and saw for the first time some specks that must be cattle, to the southeast.

Lowering the hat, he breathed the pleasing aroma of himself. "We need a job, Jim," he said through the hat, "and it can't be far. Louie's got to rest or I'm on foot."

Jim said nothing, but Doc believed he was awake and listening.

"Somewhere near here, there might be a ranch run by a couple named Prieston. They were at the Cochrane Ranch at Christmas and I ate with them. They said they were looking for a lease outside the Crow's Nest Pass. Unless I'm lost, that's where we are. It doesn't mean they got that lease, or that they'll hire us, but it's a thought."

Doc took the hat off his face and studied Jim closely. Physically, he was steadier, even better for the night of riding. But his eyes still had all the fear and pain in them.

"What do you think?" Doc asked. "You ready for public life?"

"I won't go back to Fort Macleod."

"No one's asking you to."

"I guess I'll come."

Everything Doc looked at started to swim, sleep's prelude. He fought it because he recognized this moment. It was like the moment after Dog Eye's fever broke and they were back at the line camp, when, rather than argue, Doc had joined Dog Eye in his silence. Given where that led, he must do something different now with Jim.

Doc reared to the sitting position. Jim jumped and braced. His eyes opened, full of fear.

"Listen here, Jim. I know you're probably not keen to hear my advice. All the same, I need to give you some."

Jim didn't move or make a sound, but as Doc took air to speak, he said, "You saved my life." It implied that Doc was permitted to be as boresome as he pleased.

"For better or worse, that's the question."

Jim was looking away across the valley. "There is something," he said.

"Something?"

"Don't say what happened to me isn't important, or that you've heard worse."

"Fine, I won't. I wasn't anyway." Doc wrenched his shoulders back and forth, squirmed. He decided he was ready. "I may be an infidel, but I do try to understand religion. It seems to me that God is what people came up with to try and understand weather, especially after weather killed someone. Lightning strikes a man dead. What can you make of that? At least with God, you could say, God did that for some reason beyond man's reckoning."

Jim looked puzzled.

"Most of the time, except for in my worst lows, I like myself," Doc continued. "I haven't met anybody I'd rather be. But at my absolutely most prideful, I have never thought that I cause the lightning and the rain."

Seeing where Doc was headed, Jim was both angry and disappointed. Doc saw a wave of it wash over him.

"If you think I'm wrong, speak up."

"I never said I caused the lightning. But I made Mr. Anton be out in it. And I was right beside Tex Appleby."

"Hold on, Jim. You're not thinking this thing through at all. Your Mr. Anton could have been killed as easy sitting beside or under his wagon. And if he had been, you'd be saying, 'If only I'd kept him riding.' You seem to want the blame. Even down to thinking Tex Appleby died because he rode too close to you."

Jim turned his body so it was pointed away. "I've failed at everything I've done out here," he said. "I told my sister, Penny, I'd be somebody's ranch manager within a year. I said I'd bring her out. I wasn't even a decent stable hand. Just a common drunk."

"You didn't know a thing about what was out here, did you?"

"That's true," Jim said mildly. As long as a statement about himself was negative, he would accept it.

"Who do you think does?" Doc asked. "It's only logical in a new country that nobody does. There's plenty to confound and kill you here. Lightning's only the most gaudy. I've seen a thousand cows stampede over a man who sneezed in broad daylight. I've seen an experienced man ride into a river and drown."

"So what are you saying? Because we're out west, nothing's anyone's fault?"

"You think your Mr. Craig, if he gets here, won't have problems?"

"If he does, he'll deal with them sensibly."

"You remember Major James Walker?"

"Of course."

"You think he's a good man?"

"Yes. Are you going to tell me he's not?"

"I bet the Major didn't make many mistakes before he came west. I even bet he led his men well when he was a Mountie. But I tell you for a fact that Major Walker made lots of mistakes as manager of the Cochrane Ranch. He bought his cattle too late, trailed them too fast, wouldn't let them go where they needed when it stormed. More than a thousand cows died in a winter that shouldn't have killed a hundred. Then, come spring, he branded cattle that weren't his and cost his ranch respect. All through that, Major James Walker never stopped being one of the finest men I ever met." Doc lay back down. "You lost a boss and you lost self-respect. That's important. The money isn't important. I'd forget the money if I were you. But if you go on blaming yourself for everything, you'll turn into a drunk again just to escape it."

"Why do you care what I do?" asked Jim.

"When I found you in Macleod, I was damn lonesome with nothing in my future. In a better mood, with better company, I might have left you be. And if I had, I wouldn't have thought much about you afterwards. So there."

Doc placed his hat back over his face, breathed deep, and closed his eyes.

THE MIDDLE FORK

July 1882

WHEN DOC HAD BEEN WITH the Cochrane drive, and they had crossed the wets above Fort Macleod, Frank Strong had told him how the rivers up here worked. The Old Man, which Jim and Doc had crossed yesterday, was the north fork of three that formed the river that ran past Fort Macleod. The Crow's Nest River, above which they'd camped, was the middle fork. Somewhere up ahead, the south fork ran in. When the three joined and went as one, they took the Old Man River name.

When the day got started, Jim and Doc descended to the Crow's Nest River and started along its north shore, heading east. Doc walked and led Louie for as long as his own feet could take it. When Doc's feet were chafed and raw, he rode, but slowly. The south side of the river was mainly cliffs, but their side had flats and meadows and aspen bluffs in the river bottom. When they finally came among the cattle, they were blooded Herefords with bright white faces and curly red backs, all newly branded.

Not far from the cattle, a smoke rose from some trees. A wagon track from the east turned in. Thinking it might be the Prieston Ranch, Jim stopped. "Will this Prieston be good to work for?" he asked.

Doc was caught in something like a lie. "You ever hear the one about the Englishman who died of thirst beside a river because he didn't have a cup? That might have been Prieston. What makes me want to go there, besides that it's close, isn't him. It's his wife. Though I don't commonly covet other men's wives, I covet Esther Prieston. I'm not aiming to get us killed about it, I just want to see the lady, at whatever distance."

"You'd do better without me," said Jim.

"That's not true. If I show up alone, it will look like I came all the way from the Cochrane Ranch to see her. Two saddle tramps is different. We been hunting in the mountains and got sick of Indian life. That could be our story. The hunting didn't go well and we want back on some rancher's grub pile. It's also possible that I'm so sneaky I dragged you here just to be my sidekick in this story."

"I don't care. I mean, I wouldn't care if you did."

Jim followed after Doc until the trees revealed a two-storey house with a rounded verandah. The house and the fences, even the bunkhouse, were recently painted. The buildings were red, the fences and railings white. There was a pile of orange sawdust where a saw had been. Though the day was hot, the bunkhouse chimney was smoking.

A horse alone in its corral raced back and forth. Two bristling hounds slunk up, baying and murderous. Doc loud-hailed until the bunkhouse door scraped open and a curly-headed man holding a

bunched towel stood framed. He wore trousers but no shirt. A sus-
pender was over one shoulder of his long underwear. He squinted
one eye at the noonday sun. There was the smell of trout frying.

"Sorry to interrupt your meal," Doc said, "but would this be the
Prieston place?"

"You're at Mr. Godson's. Prieston's beyond." The man was English.
When he said beyond, he pointed his towel west.

"We just come from there. How'd we miss it?"

"It's in the river bottom not far below the falls. On the river's south
side. Very hard to see."

Suddenly the trout smell was burnt and the man hustled in. An
iron pan scraped a stove lid. When he came back out, he said, "The
Priestons aren't home, just their carpenter. They're with Mr. Godson
at a horse race on the Pincher Creek."

"Where's the Pincher Creek?"

"Follow the wagon trail east and that's where it leads."

"What kind of horse race?"

"Captain Stewart's horse against an Indian pony. The racetrack's on
a flat the other side of the Pincher Creek. You'll find it easy enough,
but I doubt you'll get there in time on that lame horse."

They walked the horses away from the house. When the baying
hounds finally turned back, Doc dismounted and Jim did likewise.

"I wouldn't mind seeing that horse race," Doc said. "It would be a
good chance to talk to Prieston and his wife about a job."

"Go if you want."

"How's Pete?"

"He's strong. I'll stay here with Louie and rest his leg."

They went on until the wagon road met the river ford. Jim led
Louie into some poplar shade. Even lame, the buckskin didn't like it
when Pete went off without him.

Soon Pete was fighting the river, which was running high with
snowmelt. He bucked and plunged through the worst of it. Pete was a
shorter horse than Louie, and Doc got wet. They climbed out of the
river and then out of the valley, and followed the wagon road east
along the upland.

Through the day, torn cloud had risen from behind the mountains. Now that they were in the open, the wind hit them hard from the rear. Doc boosted Pete into a lope, and still the wind was faster. Doc's ears were full of roar, and when he turned to look back once, a pea-sized stone hit him above the eye.

After some up and down, they entered a flat that contained a cluster of Halfbreed shacks. A boy with a fishing pole stopped beside the trail to watch Doc go by. He must have been headed for the south fork, which Doc and Pete met over the next rise. The wind had dried them since crossing the middle fork. Now the booming south fork wet them all over again.

When they climbed the far escarpment and over the break of land, they could see their destination as a black meandering line in the sloping landscape. Beyond this creek was a flat stretching east like the man in the bunkhouse said. Pete had lots of run, and Doc let him go as fast he wanted.

Another half mile and Doc could make out a smudge across the valley. Closer still, the smudge separated into horses, buggies, and humans. A flag flapped from a peeled-pine pole above it all, and Doc thought it must be the finish line.

But first the Pincher Creek had to be crossed. Even though it was narrow, the creek was high and full of floating debris, and Doc was nervous of it. Doc went to where he could see upstream a distance and timed it so they crossed with nothing large in the water.

Once across, they were close enough to see what kind of people were at the race. There were more Indians than Doc had seen since being attacked by the Sioux on the Bozeman. Old and young; whole families. The rest were whites and Halfbreeds, about evenly divided. Their horses made up a series of little cavvys that postured and socialized apart from the people.

The crowd was bunched around the race oval, thickest near the peeled pole and its wind-frenzied Union Jack. The place was open to the wind, and those with hats were holding them on. A pall of east-moving dust passed above, and the sun shone through it as silver as money.

Doc hit the ground running, left Pete, and ran for the thickest knot of people, reasoning that's where the bookie must be. While he squashed in toward the centre, he looked for the contesting horses. The white man's horse was easy to find, a big gelded charcoal over sixteen hands. A bunch of white men were admiring it. The Indian horse, being no classical specimen, was harder to locate. Only by the fuss around him could Doc pick out the poor-assed cayuse. He was a weak colour, like treacle, and was probably a stallion. Already on his back was a hefty half-naked Indian with a bun at the back of his head shot through with an eagle quill. He walked the nervous horse back and forth.

Close now to the bookie who was licking his pencil and writing bets, and to the other man who was shoving the money in his pockets, Doc took one last look at the white man's horse. The owner of the charcoal gelding was a well-groomed gent in a brown tweed cap, slim and lively. His jockey was older, about Doc's age and size. The main difference between the jockey and Doc was that the jockey was fuller in the chest and shoulders, like a prizefighter from a low weight class.

It looked obvious enough. Doc put an American double eagle on the nose.

Doc went looking for a spot from which to watch the race. Fighting in near the finish line, he found the Englishmen. The key was sighting Victor Prieston, who towered above the rest. He wore a brown, round hat which Doc knew from his magazines was called a bowler. Beside Prieston was a shorter gent wearing a tall beaver and a monocle. He held the single lens by squinting against its edges with his eye socket. There was a bloom of red around them, for they stood with the Mounties.

Captain Stewart tossed his jockey on, and in about another minute a gun fired. The big gelding reared a little, then pounded forward. He was a real war horse, a thing to strike fear into puny infantry. By the time the race passed them, the white man's horse had opened a big lead. The big Indian was still having trouble getting his to run straight. The Indians, so eager before the race, were quiet and sullen now. Another defeat in the making.

Doc pushed farther up the line and deeper into the crowd that embraced the English contingent. His heart gave a lurch when, beyond the knot of men, he spotted two white women. Doc all but forgot the race as he moved to where he could make out their profiles, one round, one pointed. The pointed one was Esther. She wore a black riding hat. Her black-gloved hands were clutched tight under her chin. A pink of excitement in her cheeks.

Doc was brought back to the race by Victor's sudden yell of "Blast!"

Doc turned in time to see the two horses come by the pole the first time. They were neck and neck. The big Indian on the cayuse had leaned forward, snapping a bead-handled quirt on his horse's hip, more in rhythm than in earnest. The charcoal gelding was game, but his head and neck had started to pump. The cayuse's head was steady.

They went around another time, but it was no contest. The treacle cayuse scampered home under the burden of the big Indian, winning by twenty yards or more.

Moving closer to the ranchers and Mounties, it was not hard for Doc to guess which horse they'd bet on. They were cursing and kicking the ground. Victor Prieston proclaimed loudly that the race could not have been honest. That offended one of the Mounties, a big fellow with mutton-chop whiskers.

"I'll have you know Captain Stewart is a friend of mine, and so is his jockey Mr. Herron. I don't care for the result, but damned if I'll . . ."

While everyone tensed and watched to see if they'd fight, Esther ignored them. With a delighted look, she was bouncing on her toes, trying to see across to where the winning horse and rider were mobbed. The Indians were war-whooping, and it gave Doc the old tickle to hear it.

Doc stepped out onto the track to put himself in Esther's line of view. It was hard because it forced him to imagine his own appearance. More than a week of stubble, clothes dirty and wet. He could now see the whole of her, her jacket buttons done up tight to the neck, a long riding skirt below. She was even taller and more beautiful than he remembered.

For a time she stared through him. If she saw him at all, it was probably to wonder why this dirty little cowboy was daring to study her.

Then recognition. She smiled and walked toward him, her gloved hand lifted.

"Mr. Windham," she said.

Doc had no idea what to do with her hand. He knew enough not to kiss it, but there must be a different style for shaking the hand of such a woman. As he delayed, she reached and gave his hand a sturdy pump.

"Mrs. Prieston."

"I heard Major Walker was on his way to Montana. Weren't you to go with him?"

"I don't work for the Major now."

Her eyebrows went up. It took Doc an effort not to explain.

"We did take a lease in this country, finally," she said. "West of here, near the falls on the Crow's Nest River. You must visit."

In all the excitement of the race and Esther, Doc had forgotten about Jim. Now, he imagined him and Louie back at the ford.

"You know, Mrs. Prieston, I had in mind more than a visit. I've partnered up with a young Ontario man named Jim Adams. We are both looking for jobs."

Esther registered this, then looked at her husband, who appeared to be apologizing at some length to the Mountie whose friend he'd called a cheat.

"Victor does need help, but now might not be a good time to ask. Why don't you come back with us? I'll tell him I've invited you—and Jim, is it?—to look at the ranch and have dinner with us."

"You don't seem as disappointed in the race as the others."

She covered her mouth and grinned. "I bet on the Indian horse, just to irritate them. Victor, Mr. Godson, and three Mounties gave me five to one. Did you lose much?"

Doc winked. "Didn't get the odds you did, but no complaints."

"I was just doing it as a joke. Why did you?"

"Indians love to gamble, but they don't like to lose any more than whites. Actually they mind losing more because they can afford it less. If I had a horse in a race and was worried about losing, I'd put the lightest boy I could find on his back. If I was confident, I'd put up a big man so more people would bet for the other side." Then Doc wanted to seem humbler than this was sounding. "Mind you, I've lost on horses more than I care to admit."

"I should go back and let you collect your winnings."

Doc watched her go. There was a slight suggestion that he might be lying. He went and stood in the line of Indians and Halfbreeds before the bookie. It appeared no other whites had bet the race correctly.

When he'd finally had his turn with the bookie, and his pocket was bulging with money, Doc looked for Esther. She was still waiting for Victor to finish the same or another speech of apology. Finally, she drew him down and said her news into his ear. He made a face and the two of them withdrew. It looked like hard dealing.

ON THE RIDE WEST, Victor Prieston and Mr. Godson, the gent with the monocle, rode ahead and relived the race. For all his apologies, Victor was still contending it was fixed or bungled by Stewart and his jockey. Doc rode behind with Esther.

They talked about their respective winters, with Doc circling wide around exactly why he no longer worked for the Cochrane Ranch. Perhaps because of that, he recognized that Esther was steering clear of a few topics of her own. What she did say was that they'd lived with Mr. Godson until their own house was roofed. Their home was still far from finished but they could live in it while the carpenters continued.

Remembering the wildness of the south fork, Doc was wondering how Esther would get across. She rode a giddy Arab that Doc did not trust. When they came to the ford, Victor didn't even look back at his wife, just plunged in with his big dark bay. The horse was strong as an ox but had to contend with Victor yanking its head, righting his own balance by hauling on the reins. Godson had a giant chestnut that practically walked across. Then went Esther on the prancy Arab, and the horse, being light and short, lifted and started to carry with the current. Doc started downstream, so he could get in ahead of the Arab and push it through the hard centre current, but Esther sat the horse and urged it until it was across and found bottom again. Her long riding skirt poured water as they climbed out. She acted as though nothing of importance had occurred.

Where the wagon road branched north and dropped off, Victor stopped his bay and backed its big ass between Esther and Doc. Ignoring Doc, he said, "I'll see you later then, darling." Still not looking, he said, "Windham," and spurred off after Godson. Esther stared at the flapping tail of her husband's coat, with a not very pleasant expression.

"I've got to go that way too," said Doc, "just to the river. That's where Jim is with our other horse."

Esther nodded. "Pardon my husband's rudeness. He claims to have serious business to discuss with Mr. Godson and won't be joining us for dinner. The good news is that you and Jim are hired at a dollar a day, at least to the end of round-up. Now go ahead and fetch your friend. I'll wait here."

MOUNT EAGLE RANCHE

August 1882

DOC'S GOOD LUCK WAS to see Mount Eagle Ranche for the first time with Esther and not Victor. As Godson's man had said, their place was down beside the river on its south side and hard to see. It was at the bottom of a steep switchback road broken by sandstone sills. The cascade said to be above it wasn't visible from the road, but the view into the Crow's Nest was pretty.

Esther said the site had been chosen by Victor because of an improbable oxbow the river made at this point, squeezing a thin pendant between its curves. The name came from his having seen a white-headed eagle the first time they came here. At the base of this jut was the ranch house, a two-storey with a west-facing verandah, much the same as Godson's but unpainted.

Behind the house, on a narrow strip of ground, were two small outbuildings and some fence. A stable and a pig pen, Doc made out as he got closer. The horse corral at the far end was a thin triangle because the ground squeezed out to a point. Beyond that point, a cliff rose straight up from the river's edge.

Doc observed to Esther that they must have spent some part of winter marooned down here. She allowed that they had.

When they reached the house, they sat their horses in front of the verandah steps, on a circular track where the grass had been peeled back. At the circle's centre was a flagpole. Union Jack. What Doc saw last was the bunkhouse. Spruce and balsam poplar lined the foot of the hill and the cowboys' residence was built up a skinny path between them.

The Priestons had a pretty place, but a voice in Doc grumbled. If the mountains were full of snow some spring and it got hot or rained, he imagined a torrent biting off this oxbow, bowling that fancy house into the river. Doc had seen the remnants of that possibility on the sod rooftops at Fort Macleod.

Esther dismounted and said she must go inside and see about dinner. Doc and Jim could stay in the bunkhouse and put their horses in the corral. She asked if they'd mind seeing to her Arab, whose name was Nile. She warned Doc to put the horse in the stable's *left* stall. If put on the right, he would throw a fit.

Jim and Doc tacked down all three horses, watered them at the river, then found a brush and a comb in the two-horse stable. Esther's Arab jumped every time Doc touched him, until he finally put him away ungroomed. Their own horses were glad of the brush and more glad to be freed in the corral to roll and dust. Three cayuses stood in the fence's triangle point, as far from the newcomers as they could get.

While Doc waited to see what the mix of horses would do, he looked into the page-wire pen at the porkers. Yearlings, he thought, twenty-four. Most were remodelling the landscape with their noses, while a few flopped in the lean-to pen.

By now, a ruckus had started in the corral. Louie and a big grey mare, the boss of the peck, were sizing each other up to fight. Doc winced at the thought of Louie getting kicked in his bad leg. Jim agreed there was no sense risking it. They pulled their horses out and led them past the house to the flagpole, where there was plenty of un-grazed grass. Doc trusted Louie not to go anywhere, and Pete wouldn't go without Louie.

At the bunkhouse, a young Halfbreed, maybe sixteen, opened the door for them. Inside were another young fellow and a long-bearded white man. The man introduced himself as William Gladstone, "Old Glad" if they cared to call him what others did. He was the carpenter. This Old Glad was maybe ten years older than Doc.

The boys were Gladstone's son, Billy, and his grandson, Alex. Doc had seen it before where, in a big family, the youngest children and the oldest grandchildren could turn out the same age. There were only three beds, so it was a full house. Doc and Jim unspooled their bedrolls at the back.

There was water heated on the stove. Doc took some in a basin and shaved. It was a fight but he came away smooth and not too bloody. Inspired by the change, Jim borrowed the razor and did the same, parting ways with his scrawny beard. A finer-looking person emerged, albeit even more hollow in the face.

The only uncomfortable moment was when Old Glad said he rec-ognized Jim from Fort Macleod, where he had a little house and car-penter shop. Doc could tell the idea of the old carpenter having memories of him bothered Jim badly.

Esther had said for them to come when ready. Doc chose the front door because it was closest. A Chinese cook answered, looking stiff with outrage. He might even have blocked their way but Esther was coming down the stairs and backed him off.

"That's Woo Tom," she said of the man disappearing down the hall. "He's angry because he made a roast beef, and it's ruined by our lateness."

"Ruined's how I like my beef," said Doc, doubting that was the source of Woo Tom's temper.

The cook had just put on the potatoes to boil, so at least they would be done properly. That left an interval, and Esther offered a tour. She led them upstairs and, with no embarrassment, showed off the house's most private quarters: two rooms containing her and Victor's beds, and a smaller enclosure with a toilet and bathtub. Jim was familiar with toilets. Doc had only experienced the one in the Denver hotel, and it was down the hall. It had never occurred to him you could have one of your own. Esther assumed he'd never seen one and invited him to pull the chain and see it flush. He did so, feigning amazement.

The rooms were rooms in idea only, spaces separated by two-by-four studs. What interested Doc was the fact that Esther and Victor had a room each, so apparently slept apart. Her room was neat and the bed made. Victor's was strewn with tack and smoking gear. The bedding was a rumpled tower.

Esther took them downstairs next and showed them a fine stone fireplace and a many-paned window that looked out at the mountains. What took Doc's fancy were two side rooms filled to the ceiling with "Victor's first shipment from England." Mostly unpacked and waiting for the house to be finished, the objects were novelties you might pay money to see in a St. Louis museum. Doc went in and touched the seamed hide and little ivory toenails of a thing he could scarcely believe.

"That's a footstool worthy of the name," he said, for it and its identical partner were made from an elephant's feet, cut off flat at the knee.

Taken from higher on the elephant was a pair of tusks. One stood in a corner with its point near the ceiling. The other was sideways and glued to a mount. When he looked closer, Doc saw little turbaned humans, some carrying fat old waddies on portable beds, carved inside the latter tusk. There were even little elephants inside that elephant tusk.

Doc also studied two round leather shields and spears with matching feather decorations. Esther encouraged him and Jim to try the shields on. They slid their arms in the leather slings, and Doc took a spear and held it shoulder high. He whooped and poked at Jim, but Adams was too shy to play.

"I never saw an Indian with the likes of these," Doc said. "What tribe are they?"

"Zulu. From South Africa."

The second room contained mounted animal heads. The mounted part was no novelty, but Doc had never seen the animals.

Little pint-sized buffalos with dangly beards. Antelope with horns that spiralled as they went up. There was even a lion's head, stuffed in full roar.

The guns that might have brought down these animals leaned in a corner, looking well oiled, polished, and very expensive. Doc had read an article in a magazine at the Major's about English women who hunt. The thought made him ask if Esther had killed any of these beasts.

"I prefer animals alive," she said.

Finally Woo Tom was ready and they started eating. Doc did his best not to gobble, though he was starved. As he suspected, the ruination of the roast was to his liking. Doc noticed that Adams was eating as much as he was. Whenever Doc's father had dried out, a sudden appetite signalled the worst was over. He would fatten, almost before your eyes.

Doc thought the supper conversation might be something unusual, when led by a woman of distinction, but maybe to humour them, Esther started in about cows. She was concerned that theirs hadn't been looked at for some time. When Victor returned, she would suggest that Jim and Doc be made free to do so.

Doc asked what the cattle were, meaning breed. Esther seemed embarrassed by the question. "They are many things."

"Do they wear a brand?"

"Most of them have a P. It has a dish under it."

"Half circle pointing up or down?"

"Up."

"That's a Rocking P. That's a nice brand."

Esther blushed. "It's not ours. None of the cattle currently have our brand. Victor plans to do it during the fall round-up."

Doc was used to ranch operations as orderly as a high mass. The idea of branding a whole herd during fall round-up was shocking. Esther was embarrassed enough already so he didn't say. Still, it was a hell of a note: cows running around identifiable only by a previous brand, calves slick-sided so any fool could blamelessly steal them. During this upcoming round-up, Victor Prieston would have to find his animals by default. The ones left over.

"How many?" Doc asked, sticking to safer questions.

One hundred and forty, she said, bought early this summer in the Choteau area of Montana. The man who sold them was so anxious to leave he rode away in the same hour as he got his cheque. Because of the mixture of brands and breeds, the Mounties on the Milk River had held Victor's cowboys and cattle for a week.

"That's part of why our last cowboys quit."

"But why'd your husband buy those particular cows?"

The cold-eyed look overtook Esther. Doc found her anger exciting, as long as it was directed at somebody else.

"Victor heard a story about a man who came west and called himself a rancher without owning cattle. The man was made fun of. Victor was determined it wouldn't happen to him. Next spring, he intends to buy better stock."

"Where are they, then? The cows you have now?"

"Over the hill to the southeast. At least that's where they were last time I saw them."

They had eaten their fill by now. Esther called for a pot of tea. Woo Tom brought it with even greater hostility. He hated feeding cowboys at the master's table, was what Doc thought. That they should linger over tea was worse.

Then it was not Woo Tom's worry any more. The master himself was making a loud racket of arrival at the front door.

"Esther! What in blazes are those horses doing on the lawn?"

She was already up and moving. Around the front door was a bit of framing for a porch. It was possible he hadn't seen the cowboys in his dining room. When he entered and did see them, he expressed mock surprise the way a clown might in a music hall.

"What's this? You chaps unable to find the bunkhouse?"

Esther said, "Victor," in a tone sharp as a needle. It stopped him from more rudeness, or rudeness of that kind at least.

"Fine, then. As we have company, let's drink."

He went to the sideboard, opened the little doors on the front so a forest of bottles showed. Pulling out a glittering jar with a glass stopper and some glasses, he began to pour.

"Not for me, thank you," said Jim.

Victor swung around, affecting his grin. He set a chiselled glass in front of Doc. The first whiff shocked and nauseated him. Brandy, which Doc had not smelled since Smith Banks's billiards room.

"Did your business with Mr. Godson go well?" Esther asked.

"I'm furious with Gladstone, that's what."

"Mr. Gladstone angered you when he was here and you were there?"

"Thing is, darling, I was commenting on how Godson's house doesn't echo. In the front room, like. And he said that's because they put seaweed in the walls."

For the benefit of Jim and Doc, Esther said, "Mr. Gladstone built Mr. Godson's house before starting ours."

"Exactly! And not a word from Old Glad to me about seaweed."

"Maybe we don't need it."

"'Course we do. Can't have the place echoing."

"I suppose that means a further delay in putting up the walls."

"That's the thing. I won't know until I send a messenger to Fort Macleod. Then they'll have to send a message somewhere else. West coast, I guess. Wherever you get seaweed around here. Nuisance."

He looked at Doc. His face was a high red in the cheeks and nose.

"Now what about those horses, gentlemen? I don't much care for their being on my lawn."

"Oh, Victor, it's not a lawn."

"I don't want piles of horse manure where my guests park their buggies."

Doc took a sip and pushed the drink away. He told Victor that the horses would have to stay there the night. "The Gladstone horses and ours don't get along. I don't suppose they want their horses kicked and bit any more than we do."

"Fine," said Victor. "Problem's over tomorrow morning anyway. I'm sending Glad's boys to Macleod on the seaweed errand. The bossy mare belongs to Billy. Old Glad's nag is a total coward. You chaps can help Gladstone after the boys leave."

Doc rose and thanked Esther for dinner. He started for the door, with Jim following.

"No, no, Adams, Windham. Front door's for guests."

THE CARPENTRY WORK Doc and Jim started next day was to make holes through the framing with a wood-handled brace. They were to drill big holes through the studs, one after another in a row. When all the holes were done, they would start inserting lengths of little tube that connected the way a stovepipe does. The tubes would carry sound through the house. Esther would speak in one end and Victor could answer wherever in the house he might be.

Later on, Old Glad told them, they would be drilling a second row of holes a few inches under the first, but using the smallest bit in the box. Through the smaller holes, they would thread wires, which would attach to a couple of bells in Woo Tom's kitchen and bedroom. From anywhere in the house, Esther and Victor could fetch Woo Tom by pulling on a sash.

The only problem was that the nickel-plated speaking horns with plugs in their ends had not arrived yet. As a result, when they finished hooking up all the tubes, the system would stand wide open.

After a week of work, they were ready to connect the first set of tubes from upstairs to downstairs. As Doc and Jim walked up to the house that morning with Gladstone, he gave them some advice. "Whatever you do, boys, don't complain about the boss today, and don't fart."

That would have been good advice for Victor, who either didn't understand what the connected tubes with their open ends meant or didn't care. He made a variety of rude noises in his room and said whatever came to mind, both when Esther was with him and when he was alone.

"Godson tells me Hugh Arnott is on about my bull again. What's the bloody point of an open range if a man has to follow his bull around making sure he doesn't breed the neighbour's cow?"

There were also arguments, most of which were about a big party Victor had planned to celebrate the end of round-up. He'd had this notion so long he'd ordered wine for it all the way from San Francisco.

"I don't feel I have to ask your permission, Esther."

"It's silly ostentation."

"No, my darling girl, it's culture. If we turn our backs on the tiny bit that one can exercise here, we will rapidly go the way of the great apes."

"I may not have your broad experience of wine, Victor, but by the time it's been over the mountains and on the road from Fort Macleod, you might as well finish it off in a butter churn."

What existed in Britain and didn't in Canada was another topic that raised Esther's ire. After a loud bout of complaint from Victor about what Canada lacked, Esther shouted, "You cannot find *that* in England!" She must have been pointing out the upstairs window at a mountain. "Ben Nevis would fit in that four times!"

"Oh, I don't think *four*, darling. Definitely not four."

After the Ben Nevis exchange, Esther came bounding down the stairs in her riding get-up: a skirt sewn up the middle, in which she rode astride. She stopped near where Doc was working.

"Would someone please saddle my horse? If I don't get away from here, I'm going to lose my mind."

She was still angry at the stable, marching back and forth, slapping her riding crop in the palm of her gloved hand. Doc saw this in quick glances as he dealt with Nile. As usual, the Arab tried to bite and kick him while he got the English pad saddle on. Doc disliked everything about this horse: its prancy walk, its arched neck, its erratic temper. Character in a horse was one thing; vanity, something else.

Then came the joy of feeling Esther's weight on his hands and her leg sliding up his shoulder as she rose and swung over into the saddle.

"Thank you, Doc. You're sweet."

He had a feeling, watching Esther ride away, that she wished he was riding beside her.

WORKING WITH WILLIAM GLADSTONE was a history lesson on top of a carpentry one. With his hand clamped over the nearest tube, the old fellow answered Doc's questions about his life in this country. He had arrived in the 1840s, when he was not much more than a boy. He had come west from Montreal in a Hudson's Bay Company canoe. Having learned that he hated rowing and pulling boats, he apprenticed to build them instead. That was on the North Saskatchewan River, a river far north of here.

They say if you can build a boat you can build anything. On that principle, Glad quit the HBC after a few contracts and fed his family by building mission churches for the Methodists, gold rush saloons in Fort Benton, and whisky forts here in the British Possessions. These ranch houses were his latest boon, and he confessed he was out on a thin branch much of the time. There weren't too many curved veran- dahs and speaking tubes in a whisky fort, just loopholes to point guns through and iron works to hold the gates. About every two days, Victor came up with something new he remembered from a house in London or had found in a magazine. Then it would be up to Glad to figure out how to build it.

Releasing the speaking tube after one of these stories, Glad would say something comical like, "Well done, gents. You're really getting the hang of things. Let's move on."

But finally there was nothing to move on to. The connection of the speaking tubes and the completion of the wire apparatus marked the end, at least until the missing parts showed up and they could cover over the inside walls. Glad decided he would take his horse come morn- ing and ride to Fort Macleod. Most of his family were living in a place southwest of here called Mountain Mill, but he wanted to check on Alex and Billy and the status of the speaking horns and seaweed.

Hearing that Gladstone was going, Esther invited him to dinner that evening, along with Jim and Doc. The three arrived at the back door just as the sun was setting and turning the mountains black. Doc's clothes were clean, having been washed thoroughly in the river, and he had just shaved for the second time that day. When Woo Tom opened the door and the smell of roasting pig wafted past them, Doc was dis- appointed. He was hoping for more ruined beef. In the hierarchy of meat, he rated pork below buffalo, beef, and venison. It was about on a par with chicken.

They were barely inside when Victor ran at them down the hall. He had on a snowy boiled shirt and a black suit. The way his hair was slicked back and comb grooved made him look like a gambler in a *Police Gazette* story about graft in San Francisco.

"Hold on!" he cried, as though they were about to fall in a hole. He grabbed a wool jacket off a peg and held it up in front of Jim and Doc. The jacket was huge and only Gladstone might have fit it, but apparently the rumpled one Gladstone wore, saturated in sawdust and sweat, passed muster. Victor gave the jacket to Doc.

"Just a moment," said Victor and he sprinted away again.

With the jacket on, Doc pulled about a foot of sleeve up inside each arm. There was nothing he could do about the slumping shoulders or the length to his knees. When Victor came back, he had a white jacket for Jim.

"I imagine you fellows think dressing for dinner is a matter of English fussiness," he said as he led them toward the front, "but if you had lived as we have, you'd see it's a matter of not reverting. Savagery may be too strong a word . . ."

In the dining room, the wood shavings had been swept into a corner. The big table was covered in a white cloth. Silver and cut glass reflected the light from several delicate lamps. Esther stood to greet them, wearing the dress Doc remembered from Christmas.

"Is Victor defending civilization again?" she asked. "What's uncivilized is making fine-looking men wear clothes that don't fit them. Jim, Doc, give me those jackets. Victor, silence."

After she returned from upstairs, they took their places at the table. Woo Tom served them sweet liquor in tiny glasses, except for Jim who handed his back. Next came bowls of greens. Doc observed that Esther poured oil on hers, and he did the same. It helped to get it down.

Victor started the dinner conversation, and again it was about cows. He singled out Jim, who turned out to know a lot about shorthorns. That's what his family had raised back in Ontario. Victor kept trying to get Jim to say that English shorthorns were better than Ontario ones but he wouldn't. Jim was able to recall exact sales and prices where English buyers had bought Ontario shorthorns to take back to England to improve their herds. It was a pleasure to see Prieston so completely defeated in argument.

Old Glad had leaned into this shorthorn conversation, and Doc and Esther were left to themselves.

"He's practically deaf when he talks about England," she said. "I could say anything."

It made Doc blush, as if she were suggesting they do something indecent.

"What would it be if you did?"

"Did what?"

"Say anything."

"I might say how terribly upset he is that some English cricketers were beaten this summer by an Australian side."

Prieston wasn't that deaf. "Awful thing," he bellowed up the table. "First time ever on British soil. Australians! Convicts! And with Murdoch himself in our lineup." Then it was back to cows.

Esther's eyes were laughing. "I might say that you're fun to talk to, and that I don't have much fun these days."

"What's that, darling?" said Prieston. "Fun?"

"I said it was fun at the horse race."

"Well, I suppose some of us had fun. Some of us lost money. I still don't believe Stewart's horse was sound. The race should have been called off."

Prieston jumped up and went to the sideboard. He yanked the cork out of a wine bottle. He started gushing it into glasses until Woo Tom ran in and took it away from him. Jim put his hand over his glass.

"Doc," said Victor, as he sat down, "Esther thinks you and Jim should look at the cows, now that you're done with Glad. Personally, I think it could wait until round-up, but . . ."

"It's a good idea," said Doc. "Things happen to cattle in summer. Foot-rot, mange, warbles. Up here close to the mountains, a bitch wolf might have a litter of pups to feed. I once found a calf with a moose pelvis wedged over her head. She couldn't eat and was almost starved. Another time . . ."

"Yes, well, I guess we don't need the entire litany. Has Esther mentioned that the cattle don't currently wear our brand?"

"Yes. But I don't know what your brand is."

"Double Z. Two bolts of lightning."

"Which rib?"

"Beg your pardon?"

"Which side of the cow?"

"Right, of course."

Doc might have laughed or lectured, but he kept it to himself. Z was a stupid brand. Lightning or no, it would smear in the corners. Right rib meant you couldn't see it in a mill. Cows mill clockwise. Only the left shows.

"The brand most of them wear is a P with a sort of cup under it."

"Rocking P," said Doc.

"So you know the brand?"

"No. That's just what you call a P with a half circle under it."

Woo Tom brought in the pig, a big greasy lump with a pile of slices on one end. It was pink inside. Esther saw how Doc was looking at the meat and put her fingers to her lips to hide a smile.

"Something funny, darling?" Victor had hold of the bottle and was going around again. He tried hard to get some past Jim's hand.

Doc decided it was time. "Jim here don't like to talk about it but alcohol causes him dangerous trouble in the stomach. A doctor back east said he might have to have a chunk chopped out if he isn't careful. Sorry, Jim. Just thought the Priestons ought to know so they don't offer you more."

"We certainly won't," said Esther, with a meaningful look at Victor. He was staring in horror, as if a man fated not to drink might as well hang himself.

While he gaped, Esther spoke. "I'm interested in the people I meet in the West. They often have more exciting lives than people in England."

Victor looked at the ceiling, then faked his smile.

"I've had the pleasure of Mr. Gladstone's story," she continued, "but perhaps Jim and Doc would like to hear it."

"I've bored them already, ma'am," said Glad.

"I'm wondering if you would tell us your story then, Doc. When you've finished eating."

"I'm finished," he said, pushing his plate. He couldn't get any more raw pig past his breast bone.

While the others continued to pick, Doc started talking. He made short work of his childhood in Texas and didn't slow down until he was following Uncle Jack and Nelson Story north with Story's longhorns. He told how the blockaders turned them, how they wound up on the Bozeman Trail with hostile Sioux all around them.

He did not bloat himself. The person he described was the scared-to-death boy he had been, narrowly missing pulverization by a rock hammer in the hands of a Sioux brave. He told of Eric Schauerte holding that arrow in his shoulder, as if it would plunge deeper if he relaxed, and the sorry sight of the scalped Frenchman and boy who Doc and Jack had to bury near the Powder River.

He was in full gust now, and it was lovely to see how closely Esther attended. She had her elbow up on the cloth and her neat chin resting on the back of her wrist.

Doc brought the story to a conclusion on the morning he had found Uncle Jack swinging from the arch over the corral gate at Virginia City. Then, neatly avoiding all mention of Pearly, Freemasons, and Ivan Overcross, he said, "And that's pretty well it. I cowboyed in Montana from then until coming here last fall."

Esther applauded. The others joined in. Doc looked down sheepishly at the cloth in his lap. When he raised his eyes, he happened to be looking at Victor. The teeth were showing but the eyes had no humour. Right then, Doc knew he wasn't quite the fool he appeared to be. He was a jealous husband, with all the danger that implies.

NEXT MORNING, OLD GLAD was ready to leave same time Jim and Doc were, so all three horses climbed the snaky road together. About a mile along the upland, cattle showed to the south, and it was time to divide. Glad had become a friend over the past week, and Jim and Doc shook his hand with feeling.

"What do you think, Glad?" asked Doc. "Will Jim and I be here when you get back?"

"Victor would fire you yesterday, if his wife would let him." Then Glad winked at Jim. "As for Jimmy, now that he's so sick and can't drink, he might get fired too."

After an awkward silence, Jim burst out laughing and couldn't stop.

The last thing Old Glad said was that, if he did miss them when he returned to finish the house, they should come and visit his stopping house at Mountain Mill. He pointed south-southwest into the mountains where it was. He said for them to come and spend a week, so they could have some fun that wasn't interrupted by hammering.

Once they were on their own, Doc and Jim travelled south along the naked ridge. Flanking them on the west was a broad sloping valley held in on the other side by mountain foothills. In all that space, the horses were full of spunk and it was hard to keep them from running.

When they came to a better view of the cattle, they saw that the half with the Rocking P were roans and sprockle-faced. The rest were Herefords and wore a fresher brand. As they came up on the cattle, an old brindle bull was forked over a nice Hereford heifer. Two young Hereford bulls were grazing close by, pretending not to care. The old stag had no doubt punished them into this attitude.

Doc said, "If that was my cow, and not my bull, I'd be perturbed. I once worked for a man in Montana who would shoot a bull that ugly. Just draw his rifle and shoot him dead. Didn't matter if it wasn't his. He said he'd shoot an ugly bull sooner than he'd shoot a wolf. His reason was that a wolf will get your weak ones, but an ugly bull could breed your best."

A few hours later when they were finished checking and counting the cattle, Doc and Jim returned to the ranch house. Victor had the chocolate bay out of the stable and was brushing him. Victor wore his fancy riding clothes.

"Found your cattle," Doc told him.

"How many?"

"One hundred and thirty-seven cows. Eighty-nine this year's calves."

"You missed several, then. Should be one hundred and forty-four cows and exactly one hundred calves."

Doc went to Louie and untied something from the back of the saddle. He threw it on the ground beside Prieston and kicked it out flat. It was a rectangle cut from a green cow hide. It stank of death and released a cloud of flies. Victor's horse spooked at the smell, and Victor covered his mouth with his handkerchief.

"God, man! That stinks!"

"This is one cow you can cross off your tally book." Doc pointed to the Rocking P brand crawling with flies. "The whole hide and bones were in a bluff. Ravens pointed us to it. Whoever killed it was good enough to shoot it close to the brand, so we only had to bring this little bit."

"Those damned Indians!"

"Ground was damp inside the bluff. Boot heel marks all round. Guess an Indian can wear boots, but you don't see it often."

"You're suggesting what?"

"Don't know that I'm suggesting anything. Just saying somebody killed this one, probably stole her calf. Bunch of others are missing." Doc shrugged.

Prieston had saddled the bay while they were talking and now he pulled a watch out of a vest pocket by its fob.

"What should I do?"

"Take this hide to the Mounties, for starters."

Victor reached his toe toward the iron stirrup. He sprang aboard and stared down at Doc.

"Are you finished?" he asked.

"You don't need to be part of any general round-up. If we had two more horses and men to ride them, we could cut your herd from the one they're mixed with, bring them back, and brand them."

Victor eyed him angrily. "I *will* participate in the round-up. It's my duty as a local rancher. Right now, I'm late for a meeting to plan it." He stood up in his stirrups.

"There's a couple more things," said Doc.

"Well, hurry up."

"You should corral that old brindle bull."

"I prefer to let nature take its course."

"Your neighbours feel the same?"

"I have no time to debate you, Windham. If you can think of some way to contain him, be my guest."

"I'm not your guest. I'm your hired man. And my horse is not your horse. Since you got no remuda, you should pay for both our horses."

"Are you welching?"

"No. Are you?"

"Fine then. Have another dollar a day for your damn horses. That's one dollar for two horses. Frankly, Windham, I wouldn't count on your working here for the winter. On the other hand, I *would* like to retain young Jim. Perhaps you could tell him." Prieston drove his English spurs into his horse's flanks and galloped around the house.

As soon as Victor was gone, Doc went straight to the back door. Woo Tom met him, and Doc asked to speak to Mrs. Prieston. Soon, Doc and Esther were sitting opposite at the table. Doc said he was there to thank her for supper the night before.

"No, you're not," she said. "You're here because my husband left, which is fine as long as we both understand that I'm a married woman."

"You don't beat around the bush."

"No."

Doc told her what Jim and he had seen on their ride this morning. It made her angry.

"So seven of our cows and maybe eleven calves have been killed or stolen."

"I'd say so."

She got up. "Can we—Jim, you, and I—cut our cattle away from the others and bring them home?"

"I doubt we can with just three. Will that Arab of yours look at a cow?"

"I don't understand."

"Some horses chase a cow by instinct. Others look at them as they would a deer or a dog."

"Let's find out."

They saddled up again and rode back to the sloping valley. After two hours of hot work, it was clear they would not get the herds separated by dark—or probably ever. Prieston's crossbreds and the Herefords didn't feel as divided as they looked and struggled to stay together. Pete was a fine cutting horse and did most of the work of peeling the Prieston cattle out of the larger herd. Esther on her Arab and Doc on Louie tried to keep them apart, and that's where the problem was. Louie's leg meant he couldn't do much, and Esther's Arab wouldn't work at all.

A white moon rose in the late afternoon. When the blue started to darken around it, Doc let the cattle spill back. It was no use.

They dismounted, loosed the cinches, and let the horses graze. The three of them sat on the wiry grass, with a few grasshoppers still zipping. The last summer flowers, horse mint and goldenrod, were dying off. Esther was sunburned and her hair was pulled loose from its pins. She was exhilarated, laughing.

"We should stay overnight," she said. "Continue tomorrow."

Doc didn't contradict her. They were without food and water and even less likely to succeed another day. Probably she knew all that and meant she was having fun and didn't want it to stop.

They leaned back on the cool ground and talked more. Esther was fascinated by what Pete could do. Though the best cutters were often mares, Pete had mare-like tenacity. He would bite a cow before he would let her by him.

Even when he had been healthy, Louie was too reasonable to be a great cutting horse. But he could still cut circles around the brainless Arab. Nile had fallen far in Esther's eyes. She said she would get a real cow horse soon and save the Arab for "state occasions."

Hungry as they were, no one moved during the full transformation of evening. The long rays turned the horse mint to amethyst, the tired grass to gold. Then the sun was devoured by a jagged mouth. The gold, pink, then purple washes of sunset. Finally, the moon was an egg yolk in a purple sky.

Esther flapped her skirt and stood. "Take me home, gentlemen, before my tatty reputation is destroyed."

Even the ride home was pretty, the pothole lakes shining ice blue in the black land.

The Prieston house showed light only in Woo Tom's kitchen. He was probably reading Chinese newspapers, which he did given any respite. Doc walked beside Esther from the stable to the front door, stepped with her inside. Standing in the frame that shaped the entry, they fell silent. Woo Tom's elbow on the table down the hall kept them apart. Esther seemed frustrated to be in the house at all, a trap she sprung each time she stepped across its threshold.

"You got any magazines you don't want?"

Doc knew there were any number lying around. He also knew the question would smash the moment so they could move on. She smiled at his methods.

"Why?"

"I like to read and I have only two books. Also, it's getting cold at night."

"How would reading magazines help with the cold?"

"You paste the pages over the cracks. Add layers until the wind is caught."

"I suppose pictures of women in their underwear work best."

"Those and pictures of gunplay and horses."

"I'm afraid all we have are stuffy English magazines. Lots of horses. Not much else."

"As long as the pages are thick, Jim and I will make do."

Esther returned with an armload. There was a newspaper on top. She nodded to it during the exchange. "You might enjoy this. It's the first ever *Fort Macleod Gazette*. July 1, 1882. Don't paste it to the wall. I'm saving it."

Doc left with the Macleod paper, the British magazines, a can of paste, and a tingle on one cheek. Just before he left, Esther had pulled him out of sight and kissed him in thanks for the wonderful day.

By the time Doc got to the bunkhouse, Jim had the lamp lit. Jim started going through the magazines, selecting the pictures he liked for the top layer. Doc sat down on his bed with the *Gazette*.

The newspaper started off with a poem in the top left corner.

> *If you were a lily and I were Oscar Wilde,*
> *Our souls would intermingle with intensity ajingle.*

It was probably English but Doc chose to read it as a cowboy poem, maybe addressed to a lady like Esther who had come west. Oscar Wilde was a cowboy whose big Mexican spurs were ajingling.

> *Our aesthetic chests would flutter*
> *like two butterflies in glue.*

Doc read that part aloud for Jim, who was now swabbing glue on magazine pages.

Deeper into the paper, there was a report about a war the English were having with the Arabs, the Crusades all over again. Doc wasn't expecting anything in a Canadian paper about the fate of President Garfield's murderer, but there it was. Charles Guiteau had been found guilty some time ago and had been hanged in June. Though the cracked-brain defence had evidently failed, Guiteau kept on enacting craziness on the gallows. The paper said he stood up there reciting a poem of his own invention. He said, "I am going to the Lordy, I am so glad," over and over until they hanged him.

Then came an illumination. For the first time, Doc thought of the cracked-brain defence and Walt Whitman's poem about evil side by side. In a glowing instant, both seemed sensible, one made so by the other. Truly, it did seem like a mistake to call a cowardly act of murder like Guiteau's, or even the excesses of Overcross, evil. Maybe that was what Whitman was getting at when he said there was no evil: that it was wrong to dress up the kinds of men who did these things in horns and tails. Maybe their actions were just sparks from the sky or harness buckles that break halfway down a hill. In Overcross and maybe in Guiteau, the faulty buckles were in the brain.

As for whether that should save them from the gallows or other violent death, Doc thought it depended. He looked at Jim and remembered the night of the lightning show, when the boy came very close to shooting Doc with his own Winchester. If Doc could be both victim and member of the jury that tried him, he knew he would argue to set Jim free. For, in his craziness, that wasn't Jim. Overcross was different. For all his play-acting, he only had one self and you would have to kill him to stop him. Guiteau had departed this vale a mystery. Maybe murdering the president was the only violent act in him. Maybe he had been no crazier than Jim. But maybe he was the beginning of Overcross.

Jim broke the spell of Doc's thoughts by asking if there was news of local interest. Doc read on and found a mention of a spring trip Mr. Godson had made to Winnipeg. Then he spotted Captain Stewart's name, the man who owned the charcoal race horse. Stewart had brought eight thoroughbred bulls into the country.

Turning the page, Doc read: "Inspector Francis Dickens, son of the famous British novelist, Charles Dickens, took part in a full dress parade at Fort Macleod and, while at the charge, was bucked off his horse."

Doc could barely believe his eyes. Was it really possible that a son of the author of *Great Expectations* was falling off horses fifty miles from here? Doc asked Jim what he thought, and Jim said it was no mistake. Francis Dickens was Charles Dickens's son and a Mountie, and currently posted at Fort Macleod. Jim had seen him several times, most often drunk. The other Mounties made fun of him.

When Doc finally looked up from the paper, Jim was applying the outer layer of pictures to the west wall. It was a far cry from the lewd depictions Doc had lived with elsewhere. What he was looking at were prize pigs, cows, and horses. But the wall wasn't totally devoid of women. Jim had found some ink drawings of English matrons. One was reading a story to her curly-headed children while a storm lashed the window. Another was walking down a street with an umbrella that barely cleared her giant hat. Though amply clothed, the women were a welcome relief from the livestock.

Then, all at once, both men were beat. Each flopped on his bed. Doc rolled cigarettes, and they smoked and stared at Jim's handiwork in silence. The lamp was turned low so its light flickered over the pictures. The wind had started up and was roaring in the treetops. Doc was thinking of Esther. As it happened, so was Jim.

"Do you wonder how Esther and Victor got together?" Jim asked.

"Not much. No more than every five minutes. I think he stole her off a train. How do you picture it?"

Jim watched the tobacco smoke drift in lazy clouds.

"Maybe her family went to London for a summer tour. They might have had some sort of letter of introduction to a social circle that included Victor's family. Maybe they met in the City of Bath or walking a Roman wall. Or at a horse show."

"Holy cow, Jim! That's got me beat all hollow. I got as far as a horse show, but didn't know where to put it down."

"But that doesn't explain it," said Jim.

Doc knew what he meant. "No, it doesn't. Not even if he's rich and related to the queen. I can see Esther's family being excited about that, but not her."

"Maybe he changed."

"I bet he didn't."

"Maybe she did."

With the wind roaring and a few pages flapping loose, the two tried to imagine a younger, sillier Esther meeting Victor, taking him on as a diversion, a rebellion, then proceeding through a dozen innocent-seeming steps to getting stuck with him.

"Oh," said Doc, "I forgot. Victor told me to tell you he wants you to work for him after round-up."

"What about you?"

"He told me that, come the end of round-up, I can go to hell and fornicate with mules for eternity. By the way, I told him to pay me for the use of my horses. He howled like a stuck pig."

Jim sat up, spun his legs off the bed. He stubbed his cigarette in a coffee-tin lid.

"What will you do?"

"I guess when I am fired, I'll go."

"And forget Esther?"

"I don't expect to forget Esther."

"But forget about doing anything?"

"I never was planning on doing anything. All this changes is I won't be seeing her while I don't."

Doc had risen on an elbow to say these things. Now he fell back and stared into the rafters. Veils of cobweb were dancing with the smoke.

"But I won't like it," he said.

"It seems a waste," said Jim after awhile.

"You're right. But she's a married woman. There is no opening."

"No."

"Unless I shoot him." Doc raised his arm and pointed at the Colt Dragoon weighing down its holster off a nail in the wall. "Sometimes I miss Montana," he continued. "Down there, Victor'd open his big mouth and tell everybody how much better England is than America.

At very least, someone would threaten to kill him. You get a lot of bad behaviour down there, way worse than here, but at least it don't go unchallenged."

Jim blew a thin stream of smoke. "That's a lot to put up with, just to keep Victor quiet."

That made Doc laugh. He laughed, raised his knees, pulled them back, farted.

"Ah, hell, Jim. You're right. That's a good one. Sorry for the farting. I blame it on that bowl of grass last night, and how they didn't quite kill the pig we ate."

"Where will you go?" Jim asked.

"When I met you, I was down to one desire. That led me here. Now I'm stumped. Don't seem to want anything. How about you?"

"I don't know either," said Jim. "I guess I'll stay for awhile anyway."

"Your choice, partner. Just don't get stuck."

"Or like you say, we could shoot him," said Jim. "We could forget this is Canada, forget about the Mounties, and shoot him anyway. Then you can marry Esther and take over as rancher, and make me your foreman. Maybe Esther has a cousin like herself who would come to visit from Ontario . . ."

"Oh, damn it, Jimmy. You made me fart again. I'm bad as a horse tonight. If Esther could hear me, that would be the end of the romance anyway. Not that Victor deserves to die any less for that."

MOUNT EAGLE RANCHE

September 1882

WHEN AUGUST TURNED TO SEPTEMBER, Victor became excited. Round-up loomed. His party would be immediately afterwards. Every time Victor saw Woo Tom, he gave the Chinese cook another order. A three-year-old steer must be butchered, spit-roasted over an open fire. Cured aspen wood. A high mountain blueberry had been reported, called a huckleberry. Some must be acquired and a condiment for the pork made from it. A shooting contest would be an interesting novelty. Targets. Targets must be drawn.

In a private moment between them, Esther told Doc the party infuriated her, was nothing but foolishness.

"I'm not a house-proud woman, but even I think people should have walls inside before they entertain."

She said Victor's response to that was that the house's incompleteness added to its rustic charm. "We are new to the country, darling. The walls are the symbol."

Victor's idea of a concession to Esther on this point was to call Jim inside for half a day of hanging animal heads all over the rough lumber.

Finally Esther gave up trying to stop the party. Instead, she pressed her demand for a horse with cow sense. She intended to ride in the round-up, and Nile would not do. With a week to go, Victor stormed out of the house one morning in a noisy sulk, declaring he would "get the damn horse then" if it would put an end to her reminders. Late that night, he arrived back leading not one horse but two. He had a sorrel mare for Esther and a second bay gelding for himself, both purchased from one of the ex-Mounties who ranched along the Pincher Creek. Victor was liquored bright and seemed to have forgotten his resentment.

When Doc studied the sorrel's eye by morning light, he saw trouble. He asked to ride her first, but Esther preferred to try herself. Doc saddled the horse, and the mare stood for it. She also let Doc boost Esther into the saddle without moving. After a few steps around the corral, she threw a twist in her back and bucked. Esther bailed off, landing on her knees but unhurt. Slapping dust out of her skirt, she apologized to Doc for her stubbornness and asked if he would try to gentle the mare. Worried suddenly, Victor asked Doc to iron out any wrinkles he found in the little bay while he was at it.

A time or two on the bay was enough. He was a sweet tempered pet that any child could ride. Doc named him Little Bill, though Victor had applied some more dignified handle.

But the mare was tricky. She looked like a good animal and probably was, but Doc had known good horses who would buck every morning of their lives, just to warm up. Tulip, as Esther had named the mare, seemed to be one of those. Doc ventured aboard Tulip every morning for a week and took what she had to offer. A pleasant aspect was that Esther felt responsible and insisted on being there to watch. She applauded when Doc stuck, sympathized when he got planted.

In the end, Doc was credited with solving the mare, but hadn't really. What he noticed was that the sorrel's eye softened whenever Esther spoke. Doc encouraged Esther to spend time with the mare but not to ride her. In the afternoons, after the bucking contests, Esther brushed the mare, fed her, lifted her feet, led her. Doc would have prescribed a lot of talking, but Esther was doing that anyway. After a few days, Esther tried riding the mare again and Tulip was fine.

"You're wonderful," Esther told Doc from Tulip's back. He ducked his head, trying to feel deserving. He had solved the problem only in a sense, because the horse was sure to buck still if any rider but Esther mounted. Hopefully, Victor would give Tulip a try during round-up, with all the ranchers from the three forks watching.

In Doc and Esther's unobserved moments, something was going on. She touched him more than was ordinary, especially when he hit the hardpan, courtesy of Tulip. She rested her hand on his shoulder when she asked if he was all right. She brushed dirt off his shirt slowly, like a caress.

He touched her back too. Nothing rude or too personal, but he would touch just her elbow when he came up beside her, or would touch her hand with just the point of his finger before he went away. Those little touches sent puffs of excited feeling through him, and he hoped through her.

It really was the damnedest thing, and soon it would be over. Round-up would come and go, taking a few weeks at most as there weren't many cattle in this country yet. Then, without doubt, Victor Prieston would run him off, and Doc would be alone again. Not just alone the way he had been before he found Jim, but alone without Esther too. That would feel worse.

The day before they left for round-up, Victor rode off on some urgent mission. Doc and Jim were shoeing horses, and Esther came out and stood near. There wasn't a forge, so Doc was fanning a coal fire built on rocks. Two shoes were slowly turning red. There was an anvil and, when Jim judged the iron heated, he picked off the hottest one with his tongs and started hammering. While he was clanging away, Esther signalled Doc to come and led him to the river side of the stable.

"Where will you go?" she asked. The look on her face was hard to decipher. Doc thought he saw both anger and hurt.

"I don't know," he said.

"Back to Montana?"

Doc had been avoiding this subject, even in his own mind. Now, in a matter of seconds, he decided.

"I like it here."

"You mean in Canada?"

"The West anyway."

"Why?"

"You."

"Besides me."

"There aren't too many people yet. I can ride as I please and be pretty sure no one's going to shoot me or hang me. If Uncle Jack had come here instead of Virginia City, we might still have his company."

There was something wrong about this statement, given that Doc might be killed by Ivan Overcross at any time. His reasoning was that Overcross wasn't Canadian trouble so much as Montana trouble spilt over. Canada should not be blamed for him. If Doc shot Overcross, what he said about Canada could be true.

"You'll stay then?"

"If I can find a ranch that'll have me. If not, Fort Macleod doesn't appeal much as a town to winter in, so I might go south."

"Maybe you'll meet a new employer during the round-up."

"Maybe so."

She reached and touched his cheek, stroked down the bristled surface. It caused a high white anguish in Doc.

"I'll miss you," she said.

"I'll miss you too."

Then the back door slapped and they stepped apart. It was Woo Tom, yelling that Victor was back. The wagon full of wines had arrived and everyone was to drop what they were doing and help.

An old spring wagon stood in front of the house by the flagpole, dripping red from its tailgate. Victor was flapping his arms, and the driver was apologizing. He'd been careful as he knew how, he said, but the trail down was steep and had many ledges.

They took turns carrying the whole bottles to the door of the cellar. Woo Tom received them and disappeared into the dark. Doc and Jim were left with the broken glass to pick up afterwards.

The wagon driver had brought something else, besides the wine. When Glad's boys left for Fort Macleod, Doc had asked them to send any mail for him or for Jim with any driver or rider coming this way. He had repeated the request to Glad. Now there were letters.

Jim and Doc waited until that night in the bunkhouse to read them. Pretending to read his one letter, Doc watched Jim with his three. Jim read as if it was punishment. When he finished, he sat with his head hanging and the pages draped over his thigh. Sick and pale all over again.

Doc's letter was from Lowell Ferris. Lowell was at the Canadian Circle Ranch and gave directions for getting there. He said if Doc came sooner, he could hire him for round-up. Later, he could still try, but it wouldn't be easy. There was nothing in the letter about Pearly or Overcross, but there was sad news from Dillon. Len Spikes had died.

Lowell also had news about Major Walker. The Major had been in Dillon and was about to close the deal on Poindexter and Orr's four thousand cows when a messenger from Senator Cochrane tracked him down, saying the deal was off. The eastern bosses were negotiating with the I.G. Baker Ranch. Dealing together, they reckoned they could get a better price than the P&O was offering.

The Major had backtracked to Fort Benton and run into another telegram there. Now the I.G. Baker deal was off and he was supposed to return to Dillon and go ahead as planned with Poindexter and Orr. By the time the Major got back to the Beaverhead, Poindexter and Orr were still willing to deal, but the price had gone up twenty-five thousand dollars.

That had been the final straw. The Major made the deal and hired Poindexter and Orr to drive the cattle up. Then, according to the rumour, he had resigned.

Doc read Jim that part, but the news failed to move him. He sat on his bed forlorn.

"All right, Jim, I have to ask. Bad news?"

"No," came the surprising answer. He jammed the letters back into their envelopes, then lay on his bed with his boots over the end. Doc was about to give up on any explanation when Jim started talking.

"Two were from my sister. Last time Penny wrote, our mother had taken her out of school. Now Mother has fired the old servant, saying it's because I don't send money any more. She's forcing Penny to do all the servant's work. Penny's too young to change it or run away. I should never have bragged that I could bring her out here."

"Do you write your sister back?"

"No."

"You listen here, Jim. You write that girl. She isn't asking you for a detailed explanation of your life or for a thousand dollars. She only wants to hear if her brother's alive."

Jim made no reply.

"What about the other letter?" Doc asked finally. "Mr. Craig?"

"It was posted in Fort Macleod. His lease is north of there. He's building at the Leavings of the Willow Creek."

"He still want you to work?"

"Yes."

"I may be simple-minded, but that sounds like good news."

"He asked me about Fort Macleod."

"I don't follow."

Jim pulled the letter back out of its envelope, held a page, read aloud. "I've heard some disturbing information. It is so far-fetched, I will wait to hear from you. I am most concerned that you seem to have disappeared from here, but I hope this letter will reach you and you will apprise me of the truth directly. Having seen Fort Macleod, I can understand that winter here can't have been easy." Jim dropped the hand with the page in it.

"He sounds all right, your Mr. Craig."

"He's a good man."

"What did he like about you, back when you met him?"

"It was at the agricultural college in Guelph. He said I reminded him of himself at twenty. That's why he asked if I would be interested in working for him out west."

"So what's the problem now?"

Jim was angry at Doc for making him say it. "It's obvious. Somebody told him I was a drunk. If I see him, he'll ask if it's true. When I tell him it is, that will be the end of it."

"Why?"

Jim stuffed the letter in its envelope. He lay back and rolled away.

"He wanted to hire you because you remind him of him," Doc kept on. "Because you've briefly been a drunkard, you think he won't want you around?"

"Of course he won't!"

"You're assuming his younger self was the same as his older self."

"Shut up, please. It does no good to twist things. John Craig would never have done what I did. Saying he could have is just stupid."

Doc got up off his bed and walked. He was more fascinated than offended at being told to shut up and that his thoughts were stupid. He could have said a lot more about what the younger Craig might or might not have faced in his time. It was doubtful he'd ever been lonesome in a town as drunk as Fort Macleod. But he knew all that would only make Jim madder.

It had become dark. Doc went to light the lamp. The lens was fogged with carbon, and Doc crumpled a page left over from the wallpapering to wipe it. The lens came so clean, and the light so luminous when the lens was replaced, that it gave Doc some hope.

"Don't criticize Mr. Craig either," Jim grumbled.

"Well, Jimmy, since you've gone on ahead of me, maybe you could do the talking."

"You'll say it's lightning. You'll say Mr. Craig hasn't dealt with lightning yet."

Doc sat back down and rolled a smoke. His tobacco pouch was hanging slack. He tossed it and the papers onto Jim's bed. Seeing how empty the pouch was had a softening effect on the younger man. He sat cross-legged and poured the last crumbs into a vale of paper.

"Where do you think Overcross is right now?" Jim asked.

Doc accepted the change of topic. He closed his eyes tight and imagined the ugly bastard. In his head, he made a shape the massive crooked shoulders could fit inside. He remembered the exact colour of the scarred neck and ear, the corded strength of the arms. He tried to feel the place on his shoulder where his tickle ran.

"I don't think he's close," he said finally. "But I don't imagine he gave up either. Since he didn't come for us in the mountains, maybe he has another plan. I think he might be waiting for me to come out of here alone."

"Do you think Esther will leave with you?"

"No. Strong as it feels, I think we're just dallying. Maybe she'll wake one morning and it will be over like a dream. If it isn't over, then we're stuck. Sort of like how you are stuck."

As if the word "stuck" itself could stick them, the conversation stopped. Doc read magazines until he was seeing words but not hearing them any more. He got up and snuffed the lamp. Jim had already crawled into his blankets, and his back was round like something drifted over.

PINCHER CREEK ROUND-UP

September 1882

THE MORNING OF ROUND-UP, they left the ranch in the dark, and the golden eye of dawn rose enormous before them. When they passed a bluff, all its leaves were the same pale yellow. The wind smelled of fall and came cold from the north.

Victor rode ahead, quirting his horse for no reason. By a long rope he led the young bay, which was carrying a load that included the clumsy double-Z branding iron. If there was one thing worse than a Z in a brand, it was two Zs on one iron. The thing weighed like an anvil and was even more likely to slip and smear on that account.

Esther rode Tulip behind the little bay. She seemed to want to be alone and Doc obeyed. He rode Louie in the drag with Jim and Pete. Jim was looking better than he'd been the night before.

When they topped the hill and entered the big sheet of grass to the naked ridge, Doc asked Jim how *he* was, and Jim said fine. Then he asked Doc how he was, implying that Doc did not look good.

And no wonder. All night long, as if it were her last chance and she was going to use every trick and power, Pearly had been at him in his head. She scolded, said terrible things, threatened to unman him with a dull blade. Inside the dream and even when he woke from it, he was arguing against the notion that she had any claim on him.

"This isn't right, Pearly. You left me fifteen years ago and have made no effort to find me. You left a letter saying you were permanently gone and not to look for you. You suggested I find another woman."

He managed to get back to sleep and had a dream that they were in a saloon tent. Pearly was shooting billiards. She played in a fury, smashing each shot even though they were bouncing out of the pockets and off the table. Doc kept asking her what was wrong and she kept not saying. Then Esther walked in and brushed by Pearly. She came straight up to him and started undoing the bone buttons on a shirt he hadn't owned in years. He enjoyed this but whispered that they had to be careful that Pearly didn't see. Then Pearly's face began to bleed along the scar, dripping on the billiards green.

There was no sleeping after that.

THE RENDEZVOUS WAS NEAR a ford on the Pincher Creek, at a ranch owned by an Irish ex-Mountie named O'Driscoll. O'Driscoll wore a big brush moustache and mutton chops, which Jim had earlier explained to Doc was what the Mounties grew because they weren't allowed beards. O'Driscoll was mustered out with a land grant and could grow what he pleased but kept his naked chin maybe out of nostalgia.

O'Driscoll met them at his gate and hustled Victor into the house for a meeting. Victor dropped the rope attached to Little Bill instead of handing it off to anyone. Startled by the freedom, the little bay promptly ran off. As a result, the first thing Doc and Jim rounded up on this round-up was their own horse. Esther had gone inside too, by a different door.

Jim and Doc loosed the cinches and led the horses to the Pincher Creek to drink. The creek was much tamer than a month ago. The horses sucked back water by the gallon. The valley was shallow at this point and well crowded with poplars. Lots of yellow leaves were floating on the stream. After the horses were taken care of, Doc and Jim joined the cluster of cowboys at the bunkhouse. Some helped the cooks load chuckwagons. Others leaned, chewed, smoked, spat. It was a reunion for Jim and Doc because the Gladstone boys, Billy and Alex, were there, looking good in new woolly chaps. As Old Glad could do no more on the Prieston house for now, he had given them leave to take jobs with this round-up.

Counting all the men and horses, Doc concluded they had too much of everything. It would slow them down just to feed so many. By the look of it, Doc was the only American in the mix. The stories going around included news of big cow herds moving north. The Cochrane's four thousand and another two thousand for Fred Stimson on the Highwood. That's where the experienced hands were, and most of those would be Americans. Everybody here was dressed not enough like a cowboy or too much like one—except for Old Glad's boys, who looked the way they should.

The ranchers in the big house would be deciding on a round-up captain, and Doc hoped aloud to Jim that someone with know-how existed for the job. If Doc was the most seasoned hand on the crew, that was not good.

When the bosses spilled out finally, smelling of liquor, only one had cowboy in him that Doc could see. That was a Mr. Lee from the south fork. But he wasn't the captain. Doc gleaned that Charlie Sharples was the chosen one. Sharples was Captain Winder's manager, a man from Quebec who had been loaned to this round-up. Sharples had a fine horse at least, and knew how to ride it. That was a start. Mr. Arnott was the boss of the south fork wagon, to which the Priestons, Doc, and Jim belonged. Mr. Lee was their segundo.

What came clear soon enough was that Doc, Jim, and Esther had made a long ride for nothing. Arnott lived near Godson. Lee's range was to the southwest. To begin gathering the south fork, they rode back to where they'd started.

When they got to that night's camping place, it was still light, and Victor loudly declared that, though he was close to home, he would sleep under the stars with the other cowboys for the sake of camaraderie and adventure. Esther said nothing but turned her horse for home. When she was well gone, Doc asked Victor if he and Jim could go too, and sleep in the bunkhouse at the ranch. Victor showed by his look that he didn't like it, but as it was a reasonable request and a public one, he acquiesced.

Back at the ranch, Doc made a noisy entrance to the yard in hopes that Esther might invite them for supper. Instead, Woo Tom brought a plate of grub out to the bunkhouse. Woo Tom had spent the day chopping firewood and had made a pile of it by their stove. Doc and Jim went to sleep warm, to the sound of wood snapping.

The first day of gathering, the riders went up the south fork. A couple of riders working for Mr. Lee met them with most of his herd. They spent the rest of the day sweeping north until a good-sized herd was moving between the naked ridge and the treed foothills.

Doc got a kick out of how the English ranchers worked. Except for Lee, who rode well and played his part, the others gathered cattle the way generals fight wars. They stayed close to the wagon and took frequent nips from pocket flasks that glinted like signal mirrors in the cool sunlight. Every once in a while they would dart gamely up a draw and look for a cow.

Esther came out to ride that day but stayed well away from both Victor and Doc. She chose Jim to ride with, and for a while Doc let himself be jealous of that. Such a childish thought kept him from the harder one: that she didn't want to be with Doc simply because it was painful. If they were soon to part, why not begin the pining now? Get it over with.

By late afternoon, they were about three miles south of the middle fork and twice that from the south fork. The cattle were bellering, and the bulls were getting snorty with each other. It was decided they would camp for the night by a little trickle of stream.

After the cattle had watered and the cowboys were starting to bunch them on the bed ground, Doc rode up on Hugh Arnott. The Englishman wore a jacket that Doc would have worn to a wedding and wool trousers with balloon sides. But he was a good horseman with some sense about cows. Louie and Arnott's gelding scrutinized one another in a respectful way.

"Mr. Arnott? I work for the Priestons. I am Doc Windham. While it may sound like braggery, I've rounded up a good many cattle in Texas and southwest Montana."

"If you wish to give me advice, Mr. Windham, I'll listen."

"I'm pretty sure there's no more than a handful of cows in this thousand that don't belong to you, Prieston, Godson, or Lee."

"That should be the case."

"All we really have to do is fan through these cattle and choose the ones you and the other owners want to sell. The beef herd and a few pilgrims are the only ones that should cross the south fork. The rest should stay here." Then Doc remembered Prieston's double-Z branding iron. "I guess Mr. Prieston wants to do his branding. If you already had these thoughts, I apologize for putting my two cents in."

"Actually, it's roughly the same advice I've been given by Mr. Lee. I was arguing with him, but the force of the two arguments together has convinced me."

That evening over supper, Arnott explained to the others why they should stop most of the cattle on this side and take only a beef herd to the other side. When Arnott publicly thanked Lee and Doc for the inspiration, it was too much for Victor. He hardly said a word or looked at anyone through supper and coffee afterwards.

The others were talking about which animals they would cut out and sell. Godson had some threes this side of the river that he thought the Mounties would buy for Indian rations. Arnott had yearling steers and poor heifers he didn't want to winter. Even if Victor was willing to talk, he'd have had nothing to offer. He had only cows and bulls and this year's calves.

"What about my branding?" Victor finally asked, grinning around a fresh cigar.

No one answered him or looked at him. You could hear the wind clicking the curled wolf willow leaves. A cow or two was still calling. Victor laughed into the uncomfortable lack of talk and made his beaver teeth shine.

"Some problem then?"

"The others and I have had a talk," said Arnott. "Thing is this, Prieston. Branding your calves and cows would take a day, maybe two. Without that chore, this crew could be across the river helping with the rest of the round-up. It's the difference between our wagon forging ahead or lagging behind."

"What happened to cooperation among neighbours?"

"You are not our only neighbour. Once the round-up is finished, some of these men could certainly go back to your place and help brand. Your cattle have gone unbranded this long. What's the harm in a bit longer? Does anyone see anything wrong with that?"

Arnott looked around, his face glowing and damp from the heat of the fire. Prieston looked around too, principally at his friend Godson, who raised his shaggy eyebrows and let them drop.

"Oh, very well." Prieston forced a smile. "I suppose I have my own opinion, but I'm not going to be difficult." He made a big show of untangling his long legs and getting to his feet. He went to his pile of gear and brought back two bottles. "Let's drink brandy to warm ourselves then, shall we?" he said, plunking himself down.

Esther had watched all this from the edge of the light. Now she got up, smoothed her riding skirt, and spoke. She thanked them for an enjoyable day, for letting her be part of the round-up. She would be going home now.

"Oh, come on, Esther. Don't spoil things."

"As a rule, women are said to spoil things by staying."

That got a laugh. When it stopped, Victor made another pantomime of untangling his limbs. "Oh, very well then," he said.

"No," she responded. It was sharp and stopped him. "I'm not asking for an escort. I would appreciate help saddling my horse, though. Doc, would you mind?"

As Doc started after her into the dark, Victor called to both of them.

"Esther, I won't have you riding home alone. Doc, go with her. You can take a shift of night watch or whatever you call it when you get back."

CLOUDS HAD BLOWN IN from the north, and the moon was well smothered. The ground was barely visible in front of the horses' feet. It was very cold. Esther's mare occasionally shied when the brush rustled, but Doc could hear how easily and calmly she ironed out these eruptions.

Doc was muzzled by the strangeness of Victor's suggestion. It wasn't the same as when Jim and Doc had ridden back after Esther last night. Victor's having ordered it stole the pleasure.

Finally, that's what came out of Doc's mouth. "Why did your husband do that?"

"Strange, isn't it? Like a test."

They rode on, thinking. Finally Esther said, "It can't be a test. Victor's not that subtle."

For a not-subtle man, Victor had managed the incredible. Here they were together, with the whole country and the whole night to themselves, and they were thinking not about each other but about him. Doc tried to concentrate on how Victor did think, and what he could possibly gain from this. Then it came to him.

"Do you think Victor told me to go with you to show the others he could make me obey an order?"

"That does sound like him," she said. "That's good then. We understand it. Let's not think about him for another second tonight."

The sentence stirred Doc, for it contained every possibility.

AT THE RANCH, Esther led the way down the hill. Not even Woo Tom's light was lit. The dark house was like a place abandoned, silent except for the north wind. They unsaddled the horses, and not yet sure of Esther's mare, Doc went to the stable and found a picket pin and hammer.

As if it had been discussed and agreed upon, Doc walked the trail into the forest darkness and Esther followed. The bunkhouse door made its cranky sound, and Doc left it open while he struck a match and found the lamp. He turned the wick up to light it, then down before setting the lens. He closed the door behind Esther. There was wood still, and Doc built a fire in the stove. For the first time, Esther admitted she was freezing.

"There's a way to warm up that's better than others," said Doc, then wished he hadn't. Meant as flirtation, it made him think of lying down naked beside half-dead Dog Eye. Esther seemed to waver in the same instant. Doc forced himself to move, to throw open the front plate of the pot-belly stove so the heat came out, to bring Esther near and begin to undress her. She wore simple clothes and was soon naked to the lamp and the stove glow. The lean pale beauty of her, hands folded. The soft plume of her coiled hair, her legs slightly apart.

She was shivering, and Doc undressed fast as he could. He turned back the soogin, conscious of how it was no more than patches sewn to other patches. "I washed this in the river the other day. It's going to be cold as a piece of tin, though."

They lay together very still. She seemed so smooth and he so hairy and rough, so gouged and scarred. He started believing what Victor would have him believe: that he was not quality enough. Like Victor's spotty old bull.

Esther touched her finger to his lips. Said, "Hush."

Doc reached to the floor and groped until he found his boot, held it by the shaft and used the toe to slam the stove's grate. The lamp was guttering and the jumpy light moved all over the matrons and the livestock menagerie.

Esther did not wait for warmth or for Doc. She rolled on top of him, gripped him in a rider's embrace. She put him inside her. She rode him hungrily and shuddered top to toe when she came. He was so deeply lost he could not say how or when he finished.

"You warm now?" Doc asked, not meaning to be funny. But it was funny, and Esther laughed. She rubbed her hand in the slippery warmth, brought her fingers up shining to the light, anointed his face and her own as in some ceremony.

"Don't go," she said, even though he had not got that far in his thinking. "Jim will do whatever you're supposed to."

"You know that?"

"He wants to help. We have until dawn."

So they started up again. The coyotes and wolves might have gathered outside in appreciation of their wildness before they were quiet again.

After that, Esther was suddenly asleep. Doc found he could not follow her there. For a long time, he lay awake and happy, Esther warm and clammy at his side, her mouth open and wet against his furry chest. He burrowed so his face was under the blanket's edge. Past the soogin's own flavour, he breathed their steamy aroma.

Though it was still coal dark and far from dawn, and though he believed what she said about Jim, Doc began to get up. He wanted it to seem that he had vanished from her embrace, like a good dream that left her sleeping peacefully. He eased off the bed and with the same snail slowness drew on his clothes. Even his boots he put on slowly. He was standing in the dark, trying to figure out how to get through the squawking door, when she said, "Good night."

Then the wet air flooded cold upon him, and Louie murmured in the dark ahead.

WHEN DOC AND LOUIE reached the cattle, not one cow or calf was standing. There was the sound of cud and groaning and the grinding of teeth. By the light that wasn't yet light, Doc saw the jaws revolving and the pulsing white of frozen breath.

He walked Louie until he found the first night herder, an Irishman singing prettily. He touched his hat and continued. The next rider was Jim. Pete's yellow was a dull lamp in the remaining dark. Jim had his coat collar up and was scrunched down in it. He had taken a blanket from the chuckwagon and wrapped it around himself inside his coat. One corner was pulled up into a kind of scarf.

"You need to draw your wages and buy some clothes."

"You're right. I'm frozen."

"You been at it long?"

"Since midnight. Quiet, though. I guess I'll turn in."

"You go ahead."

"You'll be tired tomorrow," said Jim through a yawn, and Doc paused to realize he'd never felt less tired.

"Thanks, Jim. You're a good friend."

Jim rode off, and Doc climbed down from Louie. There wasn't much night left and he thought he would walk rather than ride to give Louie a break. Even at that, Louie was telling him in small ways that he was unhappy to be working still at this hour. Doc started singing his few songs and imagined Esther stepping out of his bedroll in the dusty first light, stretching naked by the stove. Then he imagined her inside her own house, tip-toeing up the stairs, and Woo Tom awake in his room, listening to the green wood complain. Doc imagined the cascade above the Prieston ranch, its whiteness like frost on fur. The water hitting and scouring and coming muddy, then coming clear again about the time it tumbled by Esther's window in the morning.

THE FIRST THING MR. ARNOTT saw by the morning light was Victor Prieston's spotty bull running on its back legs, clutching a fine Arnott heifer. With one look at Prieston, still asleep and snoring with an empty brandy bottle close to his hand, Arnott ordered his cowboys to rope the bull front and rear.

Roping such a strong bull was a tall order for green hands, and the boy going for the horns caught them but the boy roping the heels missed. Now the head roper had to gallop to stay off the horns of the charging bull.

This was the scene as Doc came off night shift. He put his spurs to Louie and unlimbered his rope as he came. His throw was less than perfect, but the brindle bull obligingly swung his hip and jumped both feet into the loop. The two horses stretched him out and dropped him hard on the shitted grass. The brindle's change of fortune was so abrupt his pizzle had not fully resheathed.

Arnott came running, dropped his knee into the bull's flank, tested his knife for edge against his thumb.

That was when Mr. Godson woke up Victor. Godson may have agreed with Arnott's action, but not with the idea of doing it while the owner slept. Victor's bloodshot eyes popped round, and through the shards of a brandy headache, he saw Arnott lifting a severed ball the size of a bread loaf and tossing it toward him. If that was the first thing

Victor saw, the second was Doc Windham with his rope tied to the bull's back legs, while Arnott delved in the blood.

"What the hell are you doing?" screamed Victor, finding his feet. Rising up, he shied the horses and gave the bull enough slack to thrash. Arnott rode the billow, kept his hand to the wrist in the bloody scrotum and came out with the second ball.

"I'm doing what you should have done yourself."

He severed the cord and threw the big nut aside. He stood and wiped his knife across his trouser leg.

"You damn well should have asked!" screamed Victor.

"I did. You ignored me."

Victor's face was bright red. He pressed close to Arnott, and Arnott didn't like it. He shoved hard, and Victor staggered back.

"Damn you!" Victor yelled.

Arnott was calm. He closed his knife and pocketed it. All the cowboys were gathering slowly. Most fights brought them running, cheering and trying to bet, but these were bosses, gentlemen, and that was different. You watched cautiously and in silence.

"Your speckled bull has put its last calf into a cow of mine. I'll pay for the damn bull if you like, but the ranchers of this round-up will decide its worth."

Doc could almost see Victor's thoughts forming. Hysterical and livid, he still understood he was beat. The way of retreat stood open. He took it.

"Fine then." Victor straightened his rumpled coat, pushed his long lank hair back behind his ears. "But I'm damned if I will participate in this round-up any longer. Not with people who do not understand the rights and prerogatives of property or the ways of a gentleman. Since my men are waiting on you already," he pointed at Doc, in case it wasn't obvious who he meant, "they can stay and work until my cattle are separated. Then they can bring them home."

Victor marched to the chuckwagon, gathered his things—including the big branding iron—rolled them up. He went to the cavvy to get the young bay. Frightened by his manner, the young horse let him grab the halter ring, but Victor could no more get the parcel on the horse's back than fly. Finally, he punched the little gelding in the neck. Little Bill pulled out of his grasp and ran.

While this went on, Jim had been calmly saddling Victor's big horse. He led him over. Victor grabbed the reins and swung aboard, rode heavily away. The whole episode was embarrassing, and no one talked about it after he was gone.

WITH LITTLE BILL TO RIDE, Doc gave Louie his overdue liberty. Besides giving Louie a rest, his second goal was to show Little Bill that not all humans are assholes.

Without Victor around, the cutting was pleasant work, though at times clumsily done by men who were only learning and horses who didn't know much more. Cutting on Pete, Jim knew a day of elegance and admiration, for he and Pete were the keystone, the only way the job got done.

After they quit for the day, the task was to keep the beef herds from mixing back. It took about a third of the men, while the rest lounged in camp. They spent the evening in a spirit of cordiality, as though Victor had given them a reason to like each other. The only bad part was the north wind, coming harder and colder all the time.

The question in Doc's mind was if Prieston would fire him on the spot when he and Jim got back or if he'd wait until the cows and calves were branded. Doc would have fired himself straight away, but Victor was a lazy man, perhaps enough to opt for the latter course. Either way, it would make only a day or two's difference in when Doc and Esther parted company forever.

When everyone was talked out and tired, and the cattle had bedded, Mr. Arnott came to where Doc sat by the fire. He paid Doc some compliments about his know-how and skills. Jim was still awake and present, and Arnott made a fuss over him too, for his handling of the good cutting horse.

Finally, Arnott got to his point. "Things don't seem cordial between you and Victor Prieston," he said to Doc.

"He's told me I'm fired. I expect he means the day we get back with his cattle."

"Jim too?"

"He likes Jim."

"What I came to say is that we could use your help across the river. It's no secret that we're short of competent cowboys. I don't want to hire you away from another man, but should Prieston and you part company, there's a job if you want it." He remembered Jim. "And you too, Jim."

Doc thanked him. If he was fired, as he expected to be, he would return and help them finish their round-up. Arnott took the cue and left. Doc and Jim suddenly realized they were without soogins, having left them at the ranch on the assumption they would return there for the night. Doc had left Esther naked in his. The thought derailed him for a while.

"Well, hell," said Doc, when finally he could speak. "We'll have to crawl in with some old hairy ass and get a bad name for ourselves."

One of the men heard this and laughed. "Cook's got extra blankets in the wagon in case of snow."

"Snow. Now there's a cheerful Canadian thought."

IT TOOK A DAY TO REACH the place where the south and middle forks joined, and another day to split out the ranchers' beef herds. Just after dawn on the third day, they swam the beef herds and the pilgrims across the south fork. The rest of the cattle stayed put on the west side. Some of the riders came back and helped separate the Prieston roans from the Godson, Arnott, and Lee cattle, then helped Doc and Jim start the Prieston cattle west. When these boys split off and rode whooping for the river, Jim and Doc were left on their own. They took their time drifting the cattle west, Doc riding Little Bill and Louie following at his own speed.

Eventually, they were on the cliff above the Mount Eagle Ranche. The drive home had been so peaceful the cattle were next to silent. It was late evening.

Halfway down the zig-zag trail, Doc knew what awaited him. He sensed Victor and all his bitterness below.

For a brief second after knocking on the front door, Doc wished he had his Colt in the back of his pants. He had briefly imagined Victor in possession of the whole truth and coming to the other side of the door with one of his expensive rifles. But, though it was Victor who opened the door, he was unarmed. He came out in his shirt sleeves and gave himself a stretch that looked artificial. Then he asked Doc and Jim where his cattle were.

Doc pointed to the top of the hill, where a couple were skylined. Victor reached into his shirt pocket and tweezed out a folded piece of paper. "Here's a draft on a bank in Fort Benton. The I.G. Baker store in Fort Macleod will honour it."

Doc looked at the numbers on the slip. It was more than he expected.

"It's to the end of the month. Esther insisted."

"I don't want to seem hard to deal with," said Doc, "but I am paid in cash."

"How much cash do you think I keep around?" said Victor, instantly hostile.

"More than this."

Victor spun and entered the house. He came back in a few minutes, cash in hand. Doc refolded the money and put it in his pocket.

"What about me?" said Jim.

"Didn't he tell you that I wish to keep you on?"

"He did. You didn't."

"I'm telling you now. I might be able to see my way to a small raise. I'll continue to pay for your horse."

Jim looked at Doc though he spoke to Victor. "The horse isn't mine. Doc has to take Pete. Louie has a hurt leg. I'm okay with the little bay."

"It's not much of a horse," said Victor.

"He's horse enough," Jim answered.

Doc didn't like what he saw. Something was oozing out of Jim.

Esther came through the door behind Victor. She stepped up beside her husband. "If you're done with these men, Victor, I would like to talk to them."

Victor shrugged and went inside. Jim took a step away, thinking Doc and Esther wanted to be alone. Esther stopped him with her hand.

"There's something I want to tell both of you. Victor is going ahead with his party. On September eighteenth. I have agreed to that arrangement on condition you are both invited. Will you come back, Doc?"

"I will if you want me to."

"Thank you. I'll let you two say your farewells. I'll wait over there."

When Jim and Doc were alone, they stepped off the verandah and stood with the horses.

"I wish I could leave Pete for you, but you're right about Louie," Doc said.

"I like Little Bill. If I'm riding him, Victor will leave him alone."

"You sure you don't want to come and finish the round-up?"

"I'm sorry."

Jim was staring at the ground, ashamed not to be able to go.

"I can't believe he's having that party," said Doc. "If Arnott comes, there'll be a dust-up."

"Maybe Mr. Arnott will kill him," said Jim, trying for the old joke, but not finding it funny.

Doc laughed anyway. "Well, Jim, don't take any shit from that rascal. Squeeze his head hard to get it if you do. I'll see you in ten days."

Esther at the foot of the bunkhouse path was almost more than Doc could bear. She stood with her head bowed and her fist pressed in the palm of her other hand. Sad but resolute. Doc had left nothing behind in the bunkhouse, so when he reached her with the two horses, they walked together to the wagon road. They were still in sight of Victor if he was watching.

"Do you have a plan of some sort?" said Doc.

"It may not be what you think."

"I feel pretty good for a fired man, but by the time I get to the top of that hill, I'll be low as a squirrel."

"What will you do now?"

"Go back and finish the round-up. They like me over there."

"I'll miss you too. But you will come back for the party?"

"You asked me, so I'll be there. Eighteenth of September. I wish I could kiss you goodbye."

"You can't. So you better go."

Doc was in a dip when he tried to mount. He bounced for the stirrup and missed.

"Here." Esther knit her hands and set them on her thigh. Doc stepped as lightly as he could. From the saddle seat, he saw there was mud on her hands and wet in her eyes. He touched Pete with his spur.

Seeing the other two horses leaving, Little Bill came to life. He whinnied and jerked the reins from Jim's hand, ran for the wagon road. When Esther called his name, Little Bill stopped. He went to her and stood with his nose to her elbow, held by a rope invisible.

MOUNT EAGLE RANCHE

September 16, 1882

EIGHT DAYS LATER, upon completion of the Pincher Creek round-up, Doc returned to Mount Eagle Ranche with Alex and Billy Glastone in tow. Hugh Arnott and some other ranchers had decided to take their beef herds east to the Canadian railroad construction camps and had asked Doc to be their trail boss. Doc agreed but said he was not available until September 20.

"Besides," he'd told Arnott and the Irishman O'Driscoll, "this north wind's telling you something and you don't know what. It's best to wait and see."

As for the Gladstone boys, the Prieston place was their next meet-up with Old Glad, who was still hoping to put seaweed in the walls and ends on the talking tubes before winter. They thought they might as well come with Doc and help brand cattle.

When the three sat their horses in front of the Prieston house, the place looked deserted. Shingles had blown off in the recent wind. Several panes in the big west window had shaken in their putty until they cracked. When no one came out to greet them, they went to the bunkhouse and found Jim sleeping. When the door squalled and woke him, he was sheepish. It was afternoon and his excuse was that Victor had gone away and there was nothing for him to do between morning and evening.

"Where'd Victor go?"

"North. To find new guests for his party."

Doc asked Jim to explain.

"He decided he was too mad at the local ranchers to invite them to his party. He thought it would snub them best if he invited somebody else. So he rode up to the Highwood where he says he can find more civilized people."

"Esther?"

"She's here."

Doc went to the house and knocked on the front door. While he waited, he stared at a pile of half green, half yellow leaves drifted against the railing. The north wind was still strong enough to lift his hat. It wasn't Esther but Woo Tom who answered. Esther was riding, said the cook. Then he closed the door in Doc's face. Doc didn't blame him. Woo Tom believed Doc was trouble for the household, and he was.

Doc asked Jim where the double-Z branding iron was. After giving the horses an hour to sleep and graze, Doc and Jim caught Little Bill and led him to the hitching post. The little bay was everybody's friend. He rubbed his head up and down Doc's shoulder until Doc made him stop.

"Sorry to turn you into a mule," Doc told the horse as he started to load him. Jim would ride Pete and Doc would go on Louie, who he hadn't ridden during the last days of round-up. Later, Doc and Jim would share Pete as needed. On Little Bill, they packed the branding iron and as much of Woo Tom's wood as would fit. They took a coal-oil lantern for the oil, lots of matches, and made sure they had a sharp knife.

Since Doc and Jim had last moved them, the Prieston cows had drifted southeast. They were about where they'd been before round-up started, except now they had the big sloping range to themselves. There were a few bluffs dotted on that prairie and Doc led his crew to the biggest. They tied their horses on the leeward edge, and Doc squatted on his heels and drew his plan with a stick. Here behind the aspens they would build their fire. On Pete, Doc would heel-rope calves. The Gladstones would rope the cows. Four cowboys was barely enough so they would work slow. If the cows went off too far, or if the wood ran out, they would stop and do what was needed. No one was in a hurry.

Doc put Jim in charge of the fire, and he soon had the wood pyred and soaked in coal oil. It would be Jim's job to heat the bulky iron and slap it on. Aboard Pete, Doc caught a bull calf by the heels and dragged him back to the fire at a walk. The calf's mother came roaring alongside. The Gladstone boys followed her to the shaking dome of trees before they snapped their ropes on and dropped her.

The iron was hot and Jim plastered the stupid brand on the right ribs of both cow and calf. He brushed out a fire in the cow's woolly hair with his glove.

The smell of hide and hair burning, and the bawling of the mothers after their dragging calves, caused the herd to move. After a dozen cow-calf pairs were done, the riders had to get around the rest and bring them back. They rebuilt the fire and burned another twenty before the cows left a second time.

By then, they were out of wood and had to return to the ranch. At Woo Tom's wood pile, they took turns chopping through the logs that Victor had skidded in, probably for his party. Woo Tom stood on the back porch and cursed them in Chinese.

Then Esther came around the house, riding Tulip. Her hat was tied but some hair had come loose and blown wild. Tulip's lungs were working hard. Esther jumped down, unfastened the cinch, and pulled the saddle off. The horse's back was wet in the shape of the saddle pad and steamed when the cold hit it.

"You're early," she said to Doc. There was nothing glad in her tone.

"For the party. Not for branding."

They stood and looked at each other. She was red-cheeked from the wind. Her breath came white. She studied Doc with a look of pain.

"I'm sorry," she said. "I'm alarming you. I'm not prepared to see you yet, that's all."

"We'll be gone soon. Could Woo Tom feed us?"

She went inside. Soon, the cook came out. He slung a platter of meat and bread at them, which they took to the bunkhouse and ate out of the wind. Doc studied the matron on the wall who was most like Esther.

They ran out of wood again near dark and returned to the bunkhouse for the night. Doc did not see Esther that evening, or Victor when he came home. The first they knew Victor was home was when he barged out of the house next morning, as they were chopping more wood and packing Little Bill. Victor had his pipe fired and trailing sparks. He crowded Doc as he had Hugh Arnott, the morning of the bull castration.

"What the hell do you think you're doing?" he yelled. No false grin this time. "Can't you understand that you've been fired?"

Doc touched the chest that was only inches from his face and pushed Victor back.

"I'd appreciate you didn't yell in my face. You'll remember that Mr. Arnott said he would send men to brand your cattle after round-up. Alex and Billy and me are those men."

"So, on the strength of what Arnott says, you come here, take my horse, and my man, and mark my cattle without my consent?" He was still yelling and longing to come closer so he could tower.

"I would have told Mrs. Prieston but she wasn't here either."

"Mrs. Prieston is not in charge of this ranch! Did it not occur to you to wait?"

"I'm wanted back on the Pincher Creek in a couple of days. We had to start or we wouldn't finish."

Victor chewed the stem of his pipe. He flapped his arms. "It is hopeless to argue with you. Finish it then."

What did he think, Doc wondered, that they would thank him for the opportunity to do his work?

Victor had turned and was walking away when Doc called his name. He froze and, like a raven, bunched his shoulders around his ears.

"The boys and me are not working for free. Neither are our horses. Are you agreeable to five dollars a day per man? Another dollar a day for each horse?"

"No!"

"All right. Boys, unpack Little Bill."

"Oh, for God's sake, you'll get your damned money!"

BY DARK THAT NIGHT, they were done. Jim, who had the best night eyes, pushed through the cattle from various directions, said he could not see any that weren't branded. While they packed the gear and kicked dirt over the fire, each man complained of hunger. But back at the bunkhouse, they were almost too tired to chew the food Jim brought from Woo Tom's kitchen. Besides tired, they were chilled. They took to their beds with the last chew of meat in their mouths. Billy Gladstone was snoring before the lamp snuffed.

Although the wind pounded the walls, Doc slept a dark exhausted sleep, at least until a dream of Pearly woke him. It was the one where her face was split and bleeding. He was kept awake by a feeling that the coming day would be one he would not forget. Whether success or failure, joy or sadness, would be the cause, he did not know. All thoughts of Esther were haloed by an aching fear.

Staring at red and gold spiders in the dark, he waited. Good or bad, sad or glad, he wanted the damn day to begin.

When the grey light finally inched indoors, Doc rose and built a fire. Only Jim woke to the noise. He rose on his elbow and stared at the north wall, through which icy pencils of cold were penetrating. Unusual for him, Jim's first words were amusing.

"If Woo Tom's supposed to roast a pig today, he'd better put the spit south of the fire."

Doc tried to think of a funny response, but his mind was flat. Too much worry and not enough sleep had wrung the humour out of him.

Doc chunked wood into the stove, and still the Gladstones didn't wake. But when Woo Tom brought the smell of bacon and coffee to the door, they jumped straight up. Besides setting down the plate and a coffee can, Woo Tom told them Victor wanted every man in the yard as soon as they had eaten.

Chewing dough-gods and bacon, Doc filled with indignation.

"Ignorant Englishman," he said. "End of round-up's a day off. Any fool knows that or should be able to figure it out." He chewed and swallowed. "We don't even work for him. No damn manners."

Jim ate fastest and started dressing for the cold.

"Day off," Doc entreated him.

"I still work for him," said Jim. He put on his old grey hat and tied it down with a leather stampede string. He exited into shadow and then crossed into striped sunlight. The north wind was still blowing strong out of a dirty gauze to the north, but the upper sky to the east was broken cloud with some sun getting through. Doc was holding the door open a crack, watching.

He was still watching when Victor came into the yard from the west. He had his big-assed bay hauling another poplar log. Victor seemed to have a hundred hats, and Doc recognized today's from a magazine article on mountain guides in Switzerland. A snow-white scarf was tied over the roof to hold it on. He looked falsely burly in a buffalo coat.

Because of the direction of the wind, Doc heard what he was yelling at Jim.

"Throw the rope off! Make a fire circle! Big stones! Big circumference! Chop the log into three-foot lengths! Where the hell are the others?"

Something in the tone jerked Doc through the door. Hatless and coatless, he walked down the path. Victor didn't see him coming. The bay horse was moving back and forth because of how Victor gouged him and sawed the bit in his mouth. Fool couldn't ride worth beans.

When the horse backed crooked, Doc came in sight. Victor yelled, "There you are, finally. Where are the Gladstones? Time's wasting."

"Our contract with you ended last night. Any outfit I've worked on, day after round-up is a day of rest and liberty."

"I'll judge that."

"We are free men. We'll judge for ourselves."

"You always speak with such authority, Windham. As if you really were anybody in this world." Victor was still gouging and yanking.

"The Gladstones accept me as their segundo. That's my authority for speaking for them. I don't need anybody's permission to speak for myself."

"And you don't think you have a lot of nerve to speak to me as you customarily do?"

"This ain't even a scratch on my nerve."

Victor's revolver was stuck in a holster at his side. The buffalo coat was bunched overtop its grip. It was blue and looked new from the store. Doc watched the hand nearest it, in case Victor lost his mind. But just then, the Englishman let off the gelding's mouth. Because he was still poking with his spurs, the horse shot forward. Victor directed it around the side of the house toward the stable and pens.

Jim was gathering rocks for his fire circle at the river. When a shot rang out from behind the house, Jim dropped the rock and ran. Doc followed. When they got to the house's far side, Victor was on his horse by the pig pen. The new revolver was in his hand, barrel up. On the ground where he was staring, a pig lay on its side, twitching. A blossom of red was growing between its eye and its ear. The other pigs were scrabbling in the farthest corner, pushing and climbing, squealing like banshees.

Victor raised the pistol higher, moved the barrel in a circle as if stirring the sky.

"Fetch Woo Tom! This pig must be butchered immediately!"

Finally Doc and the Gladstones couldn't watch Jim and Woo Tom do this work alone. They helped hoist the pig, bleed it, gut it, scald it, all of which were heavy jobs. Woo Tom had already built a frame above Jim's firepit. Now they helped Jim peel a pine pole, point it, and run it through the pig, mouth to ass. Meanwhile, Woo Tom got his fire burnt down so the bottom was a pile of coals.

Toward the end of this work, Doc studied the metal washtub they'd used for scalding. He filled two buckets at the pump and started them heating on the downwind edge of the fire. He rinsed the washtub at the pump and took it to the bunkhouse. While the buckets heated, he sat at the bunkhouse table with two handfuls of wood splinters, cutting them into chips and sorting them into piles.

When Alex Gladstone and Doc went to fetch the buckets, they came upon the sorry sight of Jim still working through logs with an axe. Victor had brought more for him to split. The north wind had snow in it now. Jim was sweated through and had his flimsy coat off.

"Boiled owl, Jim. Take 'er easy."

Jim smiled but did not stop. Alex took both buckets and started up the trail. Doc went closer, close enough that Jim couldn't swing his axe.

"Heating yourself up in this cold wind will give you chills and bad lungs every time. You could fever up and die. Why don't I tell Victor you've stopped for the day. Then come up and have a bath."

"I can tell him myself."

"But you won't."

"Then I won't."

"You're stubborn."

Jim picked up the axe again. Doc stayed in the way. He pulled out his tobacco pouch, which he had refilled through various borrowings in the round-up camp. He put his back to the wind and started rolling tight to his belly.

"Don't tell me you don't want a smoke." Doc finished rolling and held it out. Jim set down the axe and took it.

"Rolling's too hard in this wind. I'm going to the bunkhouse. Come with or the wind's going to smoke that smoke before you do."

When Doc finally got Jim inside, the Gladstones were sitting on their beds, staring at the buckets.

"You boys are polite to a fault. Get yourselves in that tub. It took an hour to heat and you're letting it cool."

"You should go first," said Billy.

"Why? Because I'm old? Anyway, I'm smoking."

Still the boys were reluctant. They looked at each other awhile before they poured the water into the tub. The room filled with steam. They flipped a coin, and it was Alex who got in first. Billy laughed at his skinny nakedness. Alex threw water at him, some hitting and sizzling on the stove.

Under cover of their noise, Doc asked Jim how he'd been.

"You mean how has Esther been?"

"Don't be miserable. I asked about you."

Jim got up and went to his bed. He came back with an envelope. He sat, holding it by its corners. It was sealed and written on.

"To your sister?"

"It took a long time."

"You got it done, though."

Pale and tired from the work and the cold, Jim looked not much different than he had in the mountains, drying out. It bothered Doc that Jim could keep going forward, getting better, but still not outrun what was chasing him.

"What happens when the letter gets there?"

Jim stared at it and shrugged. He took the letter back and slid it between the layers of his soogin.

After a time, Jim was convinced to bathe along with the rest of them. There was plenty enough wood for Woo Tom to finish roasting his pig, which was dribbling rivers of fat into the fire already. The water was more or less like mud when all of them finished, but everyone was shaved and looked clean.

After bathing and dressing, Doc sat at the table with all the wood chips and proclaimed, "Five hundred."

"Five hundred what?" asked Billy.

"Poker chips. We're four of us and four into five hundred is one twenty-five. Five to a penny. Let's play."

Billy complained that it would be no fun gambling for so little.

"You wait and see, young Glad. Jim here told me the Mounties at Macleod would play for socks when their money was gone. See if you aren't hollering in a few minutes, as if your whole summer wages was on the line."

So they played, and it was good fun as the chip piles got bigger and smaller. Jim lost first and went to the door to see what was happening in the yard. He said Victor was on his horse again, riding around with his pistol, that Woo Tom had sliced into the pig to test it.

Told that, Doc cursed pork in general and undercooked pork in particular. "Though I'm liking Canada for the most part," he said, "here we are finished a beef round-up and about to eat pig. That's barbarity."

Billy was out of chips next, and it wasn't any fun to play with two. Doc took his pile, which was about the same size as Alex's. He gathered the chips in two hands, carried them to the door, flung them out. The wind caught them and threw them back, some inside, some against the wall.

"You can all buy me a drink some day when you're old enough."

Alex did the same with his chips, and said the same, which made them laugh, since he was the youngest.

THE BUGGIES AND WAGONS started rolling into the yard an hour before sunset. The first two, spring wagons, were driven by men in buffalo coats, one alone, one with a white woman. The third outfit, a delicate open carriage, didn't look tough enough to make the grade but had. It carried three people packed tight on a springy seat. The driver of this buggy wore his buffalo coat open over a tuxedo. The person in the middle was a white woman. The man beside her was dressed more plainly than the driver and he wore a monocle.

The pair of horses pulling this rig were matched dapple greys. Their knee action was high and strange. It reminded Doc of a crazy Italian he'd read about who'd forced a horse to learn to gallop backwards. If Doc had that sonofabitch in his sights, he'd pull the trigger without hesitation.

When the group got down from their buggy seat, the woman slipped down on one knee. She climbed the steps crookedly, motioning for one of the men to give her his arm. He ignored her, and she appeared to be cussing him.

All four bunkhouse cowboys were by now wrapped in blankets, staring out the open door. Doc asked if anyone knew the last three people who'd gone in the house. Nobody did, but Billy wondered if the man and woman who were arguing might be the ones his father had refused to build a house for. If so, they were remittance people from near Fort Calgary. Remittance meant getting paid regular from England. The couple were putting up in the Macleod Hotel and sent word to Glad's carpentry shop that he should come discuss building their new home. Glad went and they were drinking in Kamoose's dining room at midday. Despite their being drunk, all went well until the man suggested a big window facing east and the woman laughed at him. To Old Glad's astonishment, the man reached across and hit his wife with a closed fist.

"I like the sunrise," he said.

"You've never seen one, you lazy bastard," she replied, rubbing her jaw.

He hit her again. She ran into Kamoose's kitchen and returned with a cleaver, which she pegged, coming closer to Old Glad than to her husband. Glad left then, saying they'd have to find another carpenter.

Billy did not know if this was the same couple, but maybe it was.

Later, four men arrived in two more wagons. Doc was surprised that Mr. Godson was not among the guests. Apparently, Victor had burned all his bridges, even the one closest to home.

Proving that the guest list was complete, Woo Tom came out with a big platter and started slicing meat. The boys decided to go out and watch at close range. While the pink flesh came flopping off, Victor bounded from the house with a cigar in his mouth. He crossed the yard in huge strides.

"Gentlemen, you're welcome to eat. Woo Tom, get some plates and cutlery so they can serve themselves. Oh yes, and there's a keg of beer. You'll have to tap it yourselves. I'd appreciate if you didn't come into the house tonight."

As Victor leapt back up the steps and into the house, the cowboys were silent. Not even Doc, who was a connoisseur of bad manners, had considered he might be invited to this party, then kept out of it.

"Well, boys," he said into the awkward silence, "at least we're clean. Let's get that beer."

Woo Tom was back in the house. At the rear door, he acted too busy to help them. And he was busy, with umpteen pots bubbling on the stove and the kitchen hot as a pistol. "Don't be hard to deal with, Woo Tom. How much time does it take to point at a keg?"

The keg was in the cellar, where the wine had gone. Woo Tom went into the darkness and came back first with a hammer and a spigot. Then he waved them down into the rooty cave. The keg was cold to the touch and Doc asked the boys to hoist it carefully. Back at the bunkhouse, they set it down in the empty washtub and discussed what to do next. Doc had the idea you hammered the bung through, then tightened the spigot into its place. No one else having an idea, that's what they went for. Even with the keg cool and carefully handled, the hammering pressured it up so a geyser of beer fired when the bung went in. With the tap slugged in place, nothing would pour but foam. They kept pouring and dumping until a little yellow started. It was good-tasting beer when they finally got to it.

While the rest drank, Jim had nothing. Doc went to the house again and pestered Woo Tom until the cellar produced three bottles of ginger beer. From the kitchen, Doc heard a shrill scream barely recognizable as laughter. He tried to hear or see some sign of Esther but could not.

After they had the beer keg working, the cowboys sliced pink pork onto tin plates. Doc was thinking potatoes and was heading to the big house to get some when Esther came out the front door with a serving plate piled with them, also carrots and biscuits. She walked fast to keep centred under the load and Doc ran to relieve her.

"Would you have some beer with us?" he asked. "At the bunkhouse? It's foamy, but cool."

She followed. It was strange to have a woman in their sleeping shack, and everyone was shy at first. No one spoke or moved until it was pointed out that Esther had no cup. When she said she'd use the one hanging on the pump, all four men tried to get out the door at once.

When the cup was fetched, Doc turned the spigot and filled it. Jim's bed was the only one made and Esther sat beside him there. She raised her cup.

"I would like to thank all of you for helping me. Here's wishing you a good winter and many good summers."

The toast made them all feel better. They could remember this September as the month they worked for Esther Prieston. They could forget Victor. That would make it a story worth telling.

Woo Tom had left one too many plates and an extra fork. Doc went back to the pig and sliced some for Esther. She took a few bites.

"Tastes better than in the house," she said.

As the boys became less shy, their tongues loosened.

"Is it true," said Alex, "that you've got a pig's head on the wall in your house?"

"It's a wild boar. From Germany."

Billy elbowed Alex, as if to say he'd told him so.

"But that's across the ocean," Alex persisted.

"In Europe. That's right."

"You put a pig's head on a boat and crossed an ocean?"

"I didn't personally. If you think it's idiotic, I agree with you."

Alex flushed crimson, as if he had called Mr. Prieston an idiot to his face.

Then Victor himself banged on the door. When Doc opened it, Victor did not come in but stood in the frame, a cigar in one hand, a brandy snifter in the other. He swirled the brandy, and his hips weaved a circle. It was snowing again and some blew in past him.

"So there you are, darling, regaling the troops. Our guests were worried. They thought these chaps had absconded with you."

"These chaps are my guests and I have spent no time with them until now."

"Yes, well. We're about to start the shooting competition in the yard. If we don't hurry it will be dark."

"What will you shoot?" she asked.

"We've emptied a few bottles." He laughed. "Thought we'd shoot them off chairs. Will you shoot, darling?"

"No."

Victor turned away, then back. He had a look of mischief.

"We're having a wager. Would you like in on it, Doc? I could give you an advance on your branding wages."

"Wouldn't be much of an advance. Tomorrow, I'll be wanting it all."

"Does that mean you want to shoot, or not?"

It was a trap, the assumption being that Doc couldn't shoot as well as the gentlemen. Drunk as they were, he imagined it wouldn't take an expert. But mainly he didn't want to leave Esther and the boys' company.

"No, thank you. But I don't speak for these boys."

"The invitation wasn't for them."

"Then I'll turn you down on two counts instead of one."

Victor shifted his view from Doc to Esther. "Don't worry, darling, they're only chairs."

Esther took a drink of beer. "I don't care what you do, Victor. Have your guests shoot the bottles off your head if you'd find that more exciting."

Again, Victor's false laugh, into which he replanted the cigar. Then he left.

As soon as the shooting began, the five in the bunkhouse rose without discussion. They put on their coats and walked down the path. The snow was falling thickly, swirling around the house, sticking in the grass. The guests, most dressed in buffalo coats, were lined up in front of the verandah to shoot. The line of chairs was between the river and the roasting pig.

The woman who had slipped on the steps took the first turn. Every time she tried to aim, she buckled at the waist and laughed. She fired twice, then shrieked. Apparently she had shot the pig.

Doc was beside Esther. He said, "I thought you didn't shoot."

"I said I didn't hunt."

The first of the men took the top off a bottle with his third shot.

Esther said, "Could we go back in? Would you teach me poker?"

At the bunkhouse, they gathered the wood chips that Alex and Doc had thrown away earlier. They were soon around the table, playing. Outside it was too snowy for a sunset, just a gradual dying of the light. It didn't seem like they had played long before the firing stopped, the shootists having called their game for darkness or lack of bottles left to destroy. Inside, Jim lit the lamp.

They played cards for maybe an hour, and Doc loved how bright and pleased Esther looked. There was pride all around. If the night was a contest against the nabobs in the house, the cowboys must've been winning because they had the prettiest woman with them. When the beer started to run through, the boys excused themselves to pee.

Finally, looking flushed, Esther rose and brushed her dress.

"I have to go," she said.

"You don't, do you?" said Alex.

"I have to pee, and I'm going to the house to do so. I have a feeling I won't get out again. Thanks very much for having me as company and teaching me poker."

Doc went with her to the door and asked if he could walk her. They went as far as the last tree and stopped. Esther's home was lit up like an opera house, the snow making streaks across the light. Neither of them seemed able to speak. Doc looked at the carriages, and the horses that had been left out in the wind. There was one more buggy than there had been earlier, a little rig with a stout black in the traces.

Doc gave Esther a kiss.

"Don't worry," she said. "I'll see you tomorrow before you go." Then she kissed him back and they didn't stop until they were both shivering.

"Goodbye, Doc," she said, and Doc's eyes swam. Though they might say goodbye again tomorrow, this was likely the only private time.

Inside, the boys were still playing poker and drinking beer when Doc returned. They were quiet and distracted now that Esther had gone. They took turns saying how nice she was. They were all a little in love with her tonight.

Billy went out to piss away more beer and came back wearing a cap of snow on his black hair.

"They're coming out," he said. "Looks like all of them."

They put their coats and hats on again. The wind had slacked, and it was not so cold. The stand of spruce and poplar was like a room, the floor dark with needles, while beyond, the snow had deep-ened above the tramped grass so the ground glowed dully.

The dinner guests came out of the house like meat from the face of a grinder, pushing, stopping, pushing again. Most were wearing coats. Esther wasn't there. Victor's bare head stuck up above the rest. He had no coat. He held up his arms, pistol in hand, and advanced through the crowd with a swimming action.

Woo Tom was the last one out, his low-crowned hat and black cape making him look like a missionary. He carried a glass lamp high in both hands. It traced light along the faces he passed. Some were looking up into the falling snow like children.

From the shadows, the cowboys could see it all and not be seen.

When Woo Tom got to Victor, he shone the light on his boss's face. Aglow, Victor talked but it did not carry. He had the cylinder of his gun popped out and was feeling in his pants for bullets.

"They all got their pistols again," said Billy.

Followed closely by Woo Tom, Victor started down the steps, his springy stride bouncing in and out of the oblong light. The others jerked into motion behind him. A man slipped on the stairs. His leg shooting out tripped the drunken woman, who threw her bottle as she caught herself. The bottle didn't break but lay coughing liquor in the snow. She went and retrieved it, brandished it in one hand, her pistol in the other. I'm not done yet, the gesture said, an attempt at pluck.

The parade came toward the cowboys. When Victor next spoke, they could hear him.

"Don't, for God's sake, shoot yourselves. *Or me.*"

A man the shape of a newel post thanked him to keep his advice to himself.

For a second it seemed they were marching on the bunkhouse, but then the parade bent and made for the stable and pens. Victor in the lead was overstepping his gait in an attempt to be jaunty and natural.

Jim jabbed Doc in the ribs. "We have to get the horses out."

They ran toward the fresh path in the snow. As they crossed it, the first shot rang out. They could see the Arab's pale hip through the stable opening. The gelding crouched, then drove ahead. Out of sight beside him, the chocolate bay kicked the wall so hard it shook.

Doc dove through the stable door, beside the dancing Arab.

"Quiet, Nile, you brainless lily."

He asked Jim if he was there and Jim answered from the far side of the chocolate bay. "This horse is wobbly. I think he reared into the roof."

Outside, the guns kept firing. The horses tightened and jerked each time. Above the gunfire, the pigs were screaming.

They backed the horses out and led them to the Gladstone boys, who stood where the paths scissored in the snow. Nile pulled back and reared. Doc handed him over to Billy and gave the boy the halter rope. "Give Alex the bay, Jim. We'll go for the others."

Walking to the horse corral, they saw Woo Tom holding the lantern high, pointing light into the pig pen. The guests lined the page wire, each with a pistol trained. They squeezed off shot after shot. It was smoky above them. Victor was trying to reload, dropping bullets in his hurry.

The drunken woman fired and shrieked, "I hit one! I did!"

"Like hell," her husband growled. He was levelling his own pistol from the shoulder like a duellist of old.

Inside the fence, the snow was tramped black. The closest pig bodies floated like white lilies on a dark pond. Most were jammed in the far corner, the dead and the living. The few survivors bounced on their back legs, clawed wildly with their trotters, their voices ripping the night.

"Steady now," yelled Victor, as if his troops were losing heart, as if they might break and run except for his bravery and resolve. At the end of his long arm, he poised his pistol. It jumped, barked light. Other guns exploded after his. The voices of the last pigs died inside them.

In the final silence, Doc's ears sang. There was nothing else to hear until the drunken woman began a magpie laugh. With it was a clicking sound. She was pointing her gun, thumbing the hammer, pulling the trigger.

"God's sake, Ethel," said her husband. He grabbed her roughly, taking the empty gun away.

Doc and Jim passed behind them, opened the gate. The horses in the corral ran as one to the farthest corner, turned and pointed their ears at the strangeness. Doc spoke earnestly to the horses. Then he turned to see what Victor would do next.

Halfway over the fence, Victor had snagged himself on a poke of wire. He cursed and ripped free, then stepped in the pig mire to the ankle of his boots.

"Knife!" he yelled at Woo Tom.

Woo Tom produced a blade from under his cape. Victor took it and went to the nearest pig, knelt on its hip, and stabbed below the ribs, a spray of blood answering. He poked around with the knife, reached in with his bare hand, cursed, and asked for better light.

"Let the Chinaman do it, Victor. He'll know where the liver is."

Victor stood and beckoned. Woo Tom handed off the lamp. He climbed the fence at a post and jumped. He took the knife from Victor, knelt, and neatly sorted through the gore. He lifted the knife with a flap of dark flesh trapped between his thumb and the blade.

"Damn, this is complicated," said Victor. "Now we need a plate or a bowl or something."

The white woman who was not drunk started for the house to get one. Victor took back the knife from Woo Tom so he could at least stab the next pig, before giving way.

"Exciting, isn't it?" he called to the others. His face was bloody in the lamp light. "I can almost taste them."

Doc and Jim led the horses out, and no one seemed to notice. Each horse shied around the arc of light on the ground. Halfway to the house, they heard the back door slam. Esther was there, dressed to ride, wearing extra for the cold. When Doc met her, the house light was behind her. Her expression was in shadow.

"Get me away from here," she said.

The Gladstones were tying the horses in the trees. They heard Esther's request and started saddling Tulip and Pete. Doc got what they would need from the bunkhouse. While everyone worked, a sound started inside the house. Deep and loud, it was a man singing.

They all stopped to listen. The words of the song were in another language. German, Doc thought.

"Our opera singer," Esther said, sarcastically. "He came to the door tonight. Said he'd been told Victor was looking for cultured music. Listen to him. Charlatan."

The wind had risen and was full of snow again, snow hardened by the cold into stinging pellets.

When Doc and Esther had mounted the horses, Esther led. Instead of to the wagon road, she passed the buggies in the direction of the river. The horses should have hated it but were so glad to escape the gunfire and strangeness, they entered the inky water without complaint. Pete was unmoved by Louie's calling. Doc looked back once and saw Jim standing beside the buggy that had come last, beside the black horse that must belong to the singer. Then snow blurred the picture, erased all but the house's glow.

BELOW THE WATERFALL, Esther and Doc led the horses under a cliff. Willing until now, the horses balked at the crashing sound. Doc coaxed them to the corner where they could see the white cascade and feel its spray. Back in the protected lee, they relaxed enough that Doc and Esther could safely strip off the bridles and saddles. There were some shafts of grass poking out of the rocks and snow, enough to interest them for awhile.

Doc had tied a tarp behind his saddle. He spread it on the rocky ground. He and Esther sat, with the horses' legs close enough to touch.

There had been no attempt at talk while riding. When they spoke now, it was taut and to the point. Esther said the business with the pigs was the end. She could bear Victor no longer.

"It's not easy to get out of a marriage," she said. "My family is difficult, but they're the only ones who will help me now."

There was nothing in Esther's talk about Doc or the two of them riding off and being a couple. Doc didn't resent it, just believed it.

"What will Victor do?"

"He isn't dangerous. Except to animals. He's a boy, really. He'll play it to the hilt with his friends, pretend to be wounded. But he'll be thinking how much fun it will be to come and go as he pleases."

Doc didn't know why, but his mind was drifting to the big herds of cattle that were coming north—Poindexter and Orr with the Cochrane's four thousand, and the two thousand for Fred Stimson at High River. Doc saw them pushing north into this wind. With all their hearts they would want to turn and drift. He felt the sting like salt on their tender noses, heard the ringing of the ice in their hair.

Esther pushed her bare hand up his coat sleeve, pressed with icy fingers into the meat of his forearm.

"What will you do now?"

He almost said he would wait for her but caught himself in time. Freed from one man, she wouldn't want to hear that she was the subject of another's sacrifice. So he said that part to himself where the news was familiar. Might as well wait for two women as one.

"The ranchers across the south fork asked me to trail a beef herd to the railroad camps. I'll do that if the snow lets me."

"After that?"

"I'll have enough money to pick and choose. Might go to a wedding up north. Might go work for Lowell Ferris on the Circle Ranch. Or I might go to Fort Benton. There's a brand new hotel there called the Grand Union. I like a fancy hotel."

"You loved someone very much, didn't you?"

This shocked him. He had never mentioned Pearly.

"The other night, you seemed a little sad. If love-making makes you sad, it must mean you miss someone."

"She was long ago, and she wasn't near as nice as you. I apologize it showed. It's a flaw in me."

"I treasure that night. I just find it touching that you still think of her. There's not much love in the world."

"She didn't want what I had. She run off." Doc didn't like the whining sound of what he'd said. "She had her reasons." Doc took hold of Esther's ice-cold hand, rubbed his thumb over the back of it. "You're the first woman ever made me forget Pearly. Even for awhile. I'm grateful."

"I'm grateful too."

She kissed his mouth. He imagined they would stop there and go back to the house soon.

"Do you think the horses would let us make love?" she asked.

"Don't suppose they'd mind."

MOUNT EAGLE RANCHE

September 18–19, 1882

WHEN THE DINNER GUESTS returned to the house through the snow, Victor Prieston led them, carrying the platter full of livers above one shoulder like a headwaiter. Inside the house, the opera singer did not stop his song or even pause to receive them. The singing moved from room to room, floor to floor, and always seemed to be the same song.

For a time, they were giddy and louder than they had been before. Silhouette heads moved behind the glass, like the characters in a Punch and Judy show. For a time, Punch danced slow with Judy to the opera man's song.

The Gladstones and Jim pulled Doc's bed around between the stove and the door. With their back to the heat and the door open, they sat on the bed and watched the play through the falling snow. They took turns telling each other it was time to sleep, took turns ignoring the advice. Even when the singing stopped and the other sounds tapered away, they were still staring at the light in the blank windows.

"Why don't they blow out their lamps?" asked Alex, irritably, as if that was what was keeping him awake.

"Everybody's passed out, I guess," said Billy.

"Bet Woo Tom isn't."

Woo Tom's was the only dark part of the house.

Jim told the other two that he feared a fire, and that was his reason for going. The boys didn't question it or why he dug his old pistol out of his turkey, loaded it, and took it with.

At the door, Jim did not knock. He pushed it open quiet as he could. As many lamps as the Prieston's owned were burning, some guttering as their fuel became low. Jim moved slowly through the party's unconscious guests and mess. Glasses on the floor, one broken and the shards unswept. Plates of food. Bottles.

On the swollen floral couch that fronted the fireplace, the man like a newel post lay sprawled, his belly a bloat between the open jacket halves. A pink hand, swollen and freckled, rode the belly's rise and fall. His head was thrown back, his mouth wide open with a surprising silence escaping. One foot was planted on the floor, the knee squared, as if the leg and foot understood their duty and carried on while the master lay senseless. His wife was curled small and neat under her coat in the remaining space, composed and innocent.

Of the others, two drew Jim's eye. The drunken woman's husband appeared to have removed the platter of livers from the dining table to the floor, then pushed himself through the rest of the glassware and cutlery until he was lying there, face down. Another guest had rolled himself tight in a thick carpet from the storage room.

Missing among the rest were Victor, the drunken woman, and the opera singer.

There was light at the head of the stairs and no way to hide the sound as Jim mounted. The squeal of the steps made Jim remember a school lesson in Guelph taught by an Englishman who had been to Japan. He told them of a Japanese lord so fearful of assassination he built his castle with floors that squealed all around the chamber where he slept. Jim thumbed back the loose hammer on his Colt, continued to climb.

When his head rose above the level of the upstairs floor, the lack of walls ended most of the suspense. Through the empty doorway, Jim saw Victor on his bed, the clump of his trousers down to the knee and flopped over his riding boots. The long white shirt covered his buttocks, leaving only a small span of leg visible. His suit jacket was still on above that. Victor's ragged breathing was the only sound, though he was not alone. Beyond him, her back spooned to his front, lay the drunk woman. Coming to the top step, Jim could see her naked flank past Victor's shirt, between the paraphernalia of stays, straps, cloth. Her face was invisible beneath a curtain of coarse hair dotted with something. It took a moment to understand it was vomit, specks of which were still around Victor's mouth.

The bed in the other framed room, Esther's, was neat and uncreased. Jim went there and sat on the bed's end, facing down the stairs. The old gun dangled from his hand over the sill of his knee. He rubbed the back of his neck, suddenly very tired. The bed was soft. He imagined flopping back and sleeping. Afraid he might actually do it, he tried to get up, but a knife was at his throat.

"So, little bait, here you are."

The knife edge scratched up and down, giving Jim a crude shave. A hand came past his side, closed over his gun, lifted it from his hand. He couldn't see more, but felt hot breath on his neck. The voice was deep, the accent German.

"We'll go for a ride in the snow."

"I won't go."

"Then die here like one more butchered pig."

"Maybe I don't have that much to live for."

"What are you? Twenty-two? What do you know of the future?"

Jim laughed.

"What is funny?"

"I know about you, Overcross, Overby, whoever you are. Your giving me a speech about the value of life is funny."

Overcross moved the knife, appeared to be taking it away, then

poked it into Jim's neck from the side. The point pierced the skin between cords of muscle, a pain sharp and strange that jumped to his ear.

"I am anxious to go, before Windham returns."

Jim took a deeper breath, intending to shout, but the knife jammed,
the pain blinding, then a trickle of blood into his collar.

"If you don't do as I wish, not only you will die. I'll begin with the
two Halfbreeds in the bunkhouse. Then Windham and whoever else
gets in my way."

The bed squashed as Overcross rose. He passed in front of Jim and
through the frame door to the far side of Victor's bed. He put the knife
blade against the drunken woman's throat.

"Even to save the lives of these two, who would not lift a finger in
your place, you will do as I say."

Jim rose to his feet. Overcross lifted Victor's buffalo coat off a nail
and tossed it at him through the studs.

Downstairs, the opera singer found his own buffalo coat and put
it on. He collected slices of pig roast off one plate, then pig livers
from the platter, wrapped them in cloth napkins and stuffed them in
one pocket. Into the other coat pocket, he slid a bottle of brandy.
While doing these things, he held the knife in his teeth. Then he slid
the dagger into his boot. Jim's gun was already wedged in his belt at
the front.

"Put your collar up and cover your wound," he said to Jim at the
door. Then he looked back wistfully at the sleepers in the yellowing
light. "Failed monsters. There's nothing more pathetic. It grieves me to
leave them alive."

He opened the door a crack, then stopped.

"Your friends at the bunkhouse may come down and want to know
why you're going. Be careful what you say."

BILLY AND ALEX WERE UP when Doc returned to the bunkhouse at
first light. Jim had left with the opera singer, they told him, in the middle of the night, in the stranger's buggy. He had on somebody's buffalo
coat, and none of it seemed right to them. They had gone out and held
the rig up, but Jim only laughed at their concern. He said the opera

man had a horse in his camp as good as the one in the traces and was willing to sell. A horse that good doesn't come along every day, he told them, laughing again as the buggy pulled out.

"You didn't believe it," said Doc.

"Jimmy don't laugh that much," said Alex.

Doc knew the singer was Overcross, had known from the start. It was the role from the silly play in Helena, and he was pretending it was his life. Now Jim had gone off into the blizzard with the man. But Doc said none of this to the Gladstones. He did what Jim had done, smiled and yawned, said he wasn't even going to think about it more until he'd had some sleep. When the boys saw their segundo in his soogin, they too felt sleepy. Doc waited until he was sure the sound he heard was both boys snoring, then he left.

AFTER RIDING FOR AN HOUR, the light was still no more than you would see inside a jar of milk. The only good part was that he was going south, with the blizzard at his back. By now, Doc was on the upland, maybe a mile into it, with Louie trudging tough snow and Pete trailing behind. Pete wore a halter but wasn't on a rope.

Back at the ranch, Doc had considered leaving Louie, but the big gelding snorted and stamped as soon as Doc walked with the saddle in the direction of Pete. He could also have brought Louie but let him trail. But there are times when you go with your best, even risk your best. Pete had superior sense and ability for cows, but they weren't after cows now. Louie had longer legs for breaking trail, and most important, Doc could shoot off him.

Since they'd topped the cliff side of the valley and started south, nothing suggested the direction Overcross and Jim had taken. Any trail was long drifted under. For a time in this opaque place, this milky room, Doc had despaired. How would he find them? Then he rebuked himself with the idea that Overcross had not held a grudge for fifteen years to kill a proxy in the end. Bait and fish. If Doc had a finding problem, Overcross had a fishing one. Overcross couldn't do what he wanted unless he helped Doc find him.

Believing that, Doc continued, but his faith was tested. He had chosen to go south, because it was the easiest and because the span of grass led to hills and trees. The hills were the foothills of the mountains, and there were trees on and between them. It was probable that Overcross had a camp to which he was returning, and those sheltered valleys were strong contenders for where that camp would be. Another piece of evidence was the butchered cow Doc and Jim had found. That had also been in one of these side valleys. Having shown up here, Overcross seemed a likely suspect for the killing of Prieston's cattle.

When Louie finally made it to the first foothill and the treed edge, the aspens were plastered on their north sides and the branches weighed down with snow. Moving along the edge from one hill to another and finding nothing to help him, Doc began to doubt his theory and to wonder if indeed Overcross was getting away, if he really had taken Jim to kill him in some nasty fashion. Thinking like that, Doc almost missed the first message: a little aspen growing separate from the rest, with the knifed-off edge of Jim's grey hat pulled over its biggest branch.

From then on, Overcross and Doc worked more closely. Doc crossed two more valley mouths and the bare insteps of the intervening hills. Then came a valley with a much broader opening, across which Doc could not see. He stopped to think if he needed to follow it in, then saw an aspen to his left chopped off and planted upside-down in a drift. Follow here, it said, don't waste time in that pinched-off valley. Doc aimed Louie into the whiteness and soon they found the base of a new hill to follow.

The next marker was the buggy itself, abandoned and mostly drifted over. Doc imagined Overcross riding his harness black, and Jim floundering after, maybe at the end of a rope. Doc could see nothing of the black horse's trail, but Louie found it under the snow, a broken way where the travelling was easier. The big buckskin sped up, against Doc's attempt to slow him down. Louie seemed to believe finding the trail meant they were close to where they were going.

Even now, Doc had no plan. Overcross was leading him to a place favourable to himself, where he could have built any kind of blind or trap. But Doc could think of no other action than to follow. He took off his holster and put it in his saddlebag. He pushed the pistol into his pants at the back, under his coat. He pulled the Winchester from the scabbard and rode with it at the ready.

On the treeless instep of another hill, Louie started to favour his good leg. In the wooded vale that followed, Doc found a chopped evergreen, cut-end up, in their path, then a second one closer to the trees. The two together pointed into a snowy gap.

On his own, Louie had stopped at the first marker. He turned and started toward the second. Doc held him up. He slid to the ground and went ahead into knee-deep snow, finding for himself the difference between trail and not-trail. He knotted Louie's reins behind the saddle horn and set the gelding free to follow with Pete.

Where the trail entered trees and bush, Doc stopped. Ahead was a camp, his enemy concealed, an innocent man in danger. Doc's death might be up there too. Paused like that, Doc found his life tasted pretty sweet. Esther's skin. Knowing you are stone-cold sane compared to the kinds of people you're up against. Pearly.

It was a nice moment and a shame to leave it. But Jim's life was the thing that meant Doc should go on, for it was not yet sweet enough to leave.

The horses were yearning and pricking their ears. Louie nudged Doc in the back. He knew there was a horse up ahead and wanted to see it. Doc moved with the rifle poised, looking on both sides as well as to the front. Nothing moved except for the odd clump of snow falling from a branch.

It wasn't long before the storm took a breath and revealed the camp, its fire a gauzy yellow through the pale tree trunks. It looked as if Overcross had been hollowing out the bluff he lived in. Coming nearer, Doc could see that one tall aspen had been left standing in the centre, the way Indians leave a centre pole in their sun-dance lodges. An erratic pattern on the ground was the stumps of felled trees. The back of the space looked solid because of two big spruce that grew there.

When Doc stepped into the open, the horses behind him nickered at the one ahead. The black was tied in the spruce. Overcross stood beside the centre tree and Jim was beside him, three feet off the ground. On a sideways branch, Jim balanced. His weight bowed the branch, and that tightened the noose around his neck. The rope from the noose went to a higher, heavier branch. Jim's hands were tied behind and of no use. He did his balancing by the rope that choked him. Jim and Doc studied each other, and Jim's expression was more sad than fearful.

Overcross had his buffalo coat draped over his shoulders, sleeves empty. Only his left hand showed. It was folded around the handle of a double axe, the bottom blade of which rested on the bark between Jim's worn boots.

Doc took it in, felt the weight of his own rifle across his hands. He imagined shooting the rope between Jim's head and the branch. He tried again, imagining that if he shot Overcross, it would propel the man and his axe away from the branch and Jim. What deprived him of resolve was thinking that Overcross had to have imagined these things, must have set a trap by which the obvious would fail.

As Doc thought this, the big man turned to him. His coat opened and showed the mouth of a pointed pistol in his other hand. He laughed at Doc.

"What a pair you are," he said in his German voice. "Adams could have stayed away from me and saved himself. You too. Now, I give you a clear shot at me, and you don't take it. The two of you, so dedicated to one another's survival, will almost certainly die."

He opened his mouth wide, laughed like a cry of pain. He pushed the pistol farther into view.

"No trap, Windham. You could have shot me dead. But it's not so simple now. If you shoot me, I will shoot you. Gravity will take care of Mr. Adams."

"You're not in a play any more, Overcross. You don't have to be a German for my benefit."

"You know nothing, Windham. It was Overcross you saw, so it is Overcross you believe. You are too stupid to see the logical fallacy in that."

"If you're trying to tell me that's a real German accent, why not put on a paper beak and tell me you're a duck?"

Overcross raised the axe a foot and chopped. The branch jumped lower. Jim danced, relying for balance on the rope that choked him. Doc raised the Winchester. Overcross pointed the pistol. Nothing happened.

"You're a prize, Overcross. Trust you to make a plan nobody can survive."

"You are no chess player, are you, Windham? Do you really think there are no moves left? If it's my turn, could I not give the branch another tap and hang Adams? While he died, could I not point my gun at your head and test your own desire to die? If it's your turn, you could hand over all your weapons on the promise that I would let Adams go. Then you and I could settle the score between us."

"You think I'd find your promise a reliable bond?"

"Why not? What promise to you have I ever broken? I promised in writing to find and kill you. Here I am, fifteen years later, about to make good."

Doc tightened his finger on the trigger. Suddenly, Overcross changed aim, was pointing at Jim.

"Different again, see? Something else you didn't think of, *doctor*. If this gets boring, which it is a little, I can bring it to a close by counting. On the count of five, I will shoot Adams, unless you surrender your two guns. The Winchester and that old Civil War pistol in the back of your trousers." Overcross lifted his eyebrows, made his eyes round. "That got a rise, didn't it, Adams? Does Doctor Windham think I chased him all these years and learned nothing?"

With his free hand, Overcross started making Mason signs, a burlesque of them. He giggled while he did.

"See how much I know? But don't expect the craft to help you today."

Doc did not know his thought until it came out his mouth. "You were the one beat up Dog Eye French in Fort Benton."

"Is that what he told you?"

"He told me nothing."

"Good soldier, your friend. Though drunk, he had the courage to stay silent. And I urged him, shall we say. My how I urged him. You're wrong. That's not how I know your secrets."

Doc couldn't help himself. He was becoming angry with Overcross, even though he worried it might cause him to make a mistake. The man wanted Doc to ask about Pearly. He was trying to make Doc think he had got it all from her.

In the seconds of that anger and then the anger subsiding, something else became clear. If Doc did take the bait and ask about Pearly, Overcross would tell him he had found her, raped her, tortured her, killed her. He would say all of that whether he had seen Pearly again after the Cheyenne billiards tent or not. The one thing Doc would never know from the mouth of Ivan Overcross was any reliable truth regarding Pearly.

"I want to ask you something," Doc said.

Overcross smiled. "Of course, Mr. Windham."

"If Jim and me owe our invitation to what I did to your head, maybe you could explain what happened."

Overcross took the gun off Jim and pointed it at Doc. Colour rose from his coat collar, up his neck and along his scar. The scar's terminus, so like a boil, turned black.

"You claim not to know?" Overcross set the axe's head on the ground, leaned the handle on Jim's branch, and took a half step toward Doc.

"I honestly don't know. I thought I'd killed you. You were about to kill me, and I had my pistol in my hand. I put it to your head and fired. I was the most surprised man in Colorado when the vigilantes told me you were alive."

Overcross stripped off his hat and threw it to the ground. He gripped his fingers in his thick, coarse hair and pulled. The hair on one side was rooted but, on the other, it pulled away. He let the hair drop, a clump matted with paste. The bare half of his scalp was like ground covered in mouse runnels. There was a sag to which they led.

"Your handiwork. Are you proud?" His voice was self-pitying, aggrieved. "The bullet went up the side, this way." He brushed his hand up his neck and the side of his head. "It tore a furrow up my neck, almost severed the ear, blew off half my skull, creased my brain. When I awoke, the pain was in my neck and scalp. Oddly the brain does not feel pain in the sense that other parts do. Instead of painful sensation, you have painful delusions, terror."

Doc tried to look mildly inquisitive. "I guess a skull don't grow back either. You must be able to reach up there and tickle your brain."

Overcross was angry now, and it made Doc quiet and sad. Tears started forming in his eyes, because he did not want to die. At the same time, he knew death was close. He could see it in Overcross's enraged eyes, then moving in a wave to the muscle of his shoulder and down the arm to the fingers. Doc tensed, put the sights of the rifle directly in the middle of Overcross's chest, instructed himself to squeeze no matter what.

As he braced for the bullet, he saw a motion behind Overcross, like a bird flying past the corner of his eye. When he risked a glance, he saw Jim balancing by his neck again, but with one foot raised. He lifted his old boot, turned the toe up, pointed the last square edge of the worn heel. He drove it down into the hollow on Overcross's head.

Overcross stiffened and his arms flung out like a man on a cross invisible. Doc's fortune was that his enemy's hand gripped and fired the pistol not in the first instant but a fraction later. Instead of passing through Doc's head or heart, the bullet went through his right arm.

A shower of something frozen poured over Doc. Darkness washed his sight, followed by a strange brightness. In the light, he saw Overcross face down in the snow at his feet, the pulped head lodged against the erupted bark of a stump. The man's body bucked like a broken machine.

Doc was aware of his sleeve filling with blood, then one of Jim's boots plopped in the snow. He looked up and saw Jim's feet kicking in the air.

Doc dove for Jim and corralled his legs with the arm that worked. He lifted. The kicking kept on, so he took a lower grip and lifted again until the kicking stopped. He screwed his neck enough to see past Jim's body. The boy's face was dark with blood and strain. While he watched, the corded neck muscle pushed the knot a fraction open. Jim sucked air with a piping sound.

Jim's face became less blue. Then Jim gathered the power to yank one leg out of Doc's grasp and to set that knee on Doc's shoulder. Then the other leg and the other shoulder. The weight on Doc was Jim's whole weight, and Doc was weakening. Blood was dripping out his coat sleeve and dotting the snow.

Doc tried to think, tried not to watch Overcross jerking in the snow. Then Jim's voice came like a rasp.

"Shoot between my hands."

Doc understood. He reached behind for his Colt and brought it up outside of Jim's legs. He couldn't see what he was aiming at, so he drew the gun closer to his own face and pushed it between Jim's thighs. He bent himself back until he could see the tied hands: a dark shape against the sky's flannel. The hands were a single thing, no light between them.

"You got to force them apart."

"I can't feel them."

"Do what you'd do if you could feel them."

Nothing happened for a while. Then the hands rose off the shelf of Jim's ass, and a little sliver of light appeared between the pads of muscle on the thumbs. Doc wished Jim could spread them farther. He wished he hadn't been shot in the arm of his shooting hand and that he had a newer gun. And he shot. Somewhere in the explosion, he heard Jim's cry.

FORT MACLEOD

October 1882

BESIDES THE FACT THAT blizzards kill livestock and sometimes people, and take a gut-breaking amount of work to clean up after, they can also be a holiday of sorts. Like a big heavy blanket, a blizzard settles on the world and forces it still. The odd man who doesn't know how to stop nibbles at the white ocean with a shovel and proves himself insane, but most retire to the stove. Doc was definitely the stove type. He had not yet plumbed his capacity for idleness. In the aftermath of the September blizzard, he was studying its dimensions in Kamoose Taylor's Macleod Hotel.

By now, Doc had digested all the *Fort Macleod Gazettes* there were: one every two weeks since the flagship issue he'd read at the Prieston ranch. Not far away in his newspaper building, Mr. Wood, the editor and publisher of the *Gazette*, was writing and setting print for a new issue that would tell about the blizzard, as well as the amazing chinook that followed and was still going on. Doc had made Mr. Wood's acquaintance and told him twice how Jim and he were almost killed by Overcross, until Jim risked his neck to kick the villain's head in and saved them both. He told him quite a bit of the rest: about the days of waiting out the blizzard, of eating rustled beef and pouring brandy into his arm wound. When the snow had melted enough, they went out into the dazzling white brilliance and were found by Alex and Billy Gladstone.

Doc was doing everything he could to get their story in the paper. He had never seen his name in one and longed to.

Of course, there was a lot more to the story than what he told Wood. He had lost a lot of blood, and most of the work of surviving had been left to Jim. He was the one who found Overcross's cache of rustled beef. Jim was also the one who built the two travois that Pete and Overcross's black were pulling when the Gladstones found them, the two groups coming together in an immensity of white so brilliant it was only light. Doc was in the cradle of one stinking green hide behind Pete, while Overcross, still unconscious, was in another behind his black. Louie, on the limp, was following.

By the time the group of four men and five horses got back to the intersection of trails along the Crow's Nest River, Doc was feeling strong enough to escape his stinky cradle. He boarded Overcross's black and resumed his station of segundo. He decided what they would do next.

His instructions to Billy and Alex were to return to the Prieston ranch and tell Esther that Doc and Jim were safe. Then the boys should stay and help her pack and leave, if that was still her intention. The Gladstones should also take Louie the short distance to the ranch and corral him there. He was not fit to continue with Jim and Doc.

"Protect Louie from Victor, and take him with you when you leave."

Then Doc and Jim pointed themselves down the trail to the east, intent on dragging Overcross to the Mounties at Fort Macleod.

It turned out that Victor was not behind them but ahead. He was part of a crew of ranchers, ranch hands, and Indians applying themselves to digging out a trail from Pincher Creek to Fort Macleod. Jim and Doc followed that trail, waded rivers and meltwater lakes, and saw the trail crew briefly. A few miles short of Macleod, the trail diggers were camped where their chore had run out, where the chinook itself had taken over. They came to look at Overcross in the travois and to listen to him rant and curse, for he had come angrily alive during the previous night. Victor was the only one who stood back, saying nothing for a change.

BESIDES READING, THE ROUTINE of Doc's life in Fort Macleod was to rise from his mattress in front of the stove in Kamoose's sleeping room and to get the Englishman to make him an egg breakfast. While Doc ate, it was Kamoose's job to give him coffee and all the news.

"Com'mon, Kamoose. A man like you, with spies in every corner, and men running out to the hills to pass on information to known killers—you must have more than what you're telling me."

A mention like that per day and Kamoose was kept servile. To keep the old whisky trader on edge, Doc left every day after breakfast and headed for the Mountie barracks. Once there, he would check for mail, visit with the orderly room constable, then look in on Overcross.

Ivan Overcross, alias Overby, alias Jan Uberkreuz, was in the barracks guardroom now, chained hand and foot. His long one-sided mane had been chopped off by the Mountie surgeon so he could better treat his wound. Bald, he was even uglier than haired. During each visit, Doc entertained the constable standing guard with a list of Overcross's nasty deeds, saying that if the boy didn't want to wind up as supper, he'd best stay back from the bars at all times.

Overcross stared at Doc with fathomless hatred that, under the circumstances, Doc found thrilling.

Then one day Overcross pretended charm and beckoned Doc. He was being his German self that day.

"Come, Mr. Windham, come talk. I am lonely for intelligent conversation. There's no need for us to be enemies. Not any longer, is there?"

Doc told him to talk then, if that was his ardent wish.

"Closer, please," he said, the picture of pathos. "Since my head wound, my hearing is not good."

"I'll talk louder," said Doc, staying put. "What's your choice of topic?"

"I thought you might want to know about my last meeting with your girlfriend. Pearly was her name."

Even knowing what he knew, Pearly's name in this man's mouth caused Doc to scratch with bad sensation.

"Actually, Overcross, I have no interest in that lady. We parted a long time ago. All is forgotten."

"Since she so cruelly left you, maybe you would enjoy hearing how I punished her."

"Nope. No, thank you. I was hoping we might talk about something more literary. You ever read Walt Whitman?"

"Of course. He's not my favourite."

"He's one of mine. Just before you were going to kill me and Jim kicked your head in, I was about to quote you a passage. It goes: *I am myself just as much evil as good, and my nation is—and I say there is in fact no evil.* What do you make of that?"

"Trust me, Windham. There is evil." He said it with a wet grin.

"That's exactly what I expected you to say. But you know, I don't think there is."

"Let me tell you about your Pearly. Then you will."

"What I think Walt Whitman was getting at was that it's all cracked-brain stuff. Sort of like a headless chicken running in a circle. Evil's too fancy a word for that. If there is no evil, a person who dedicates himself to it must be nothing too."

Overcross let all his ugliness show. "Go ahead, Mr. Windham, exult. Things are far from over between us."

"Soon, though." Doc slapped his hat on his knee and rose.

"It's a lovely day, Constable," he said to the ashen boy clutching his rifle by the door. "I think I'll go right out and be a free man in the sunshine."

But in truth Doc went to St. Martin's Hall. He wanted to look at the bowling set-up the young constable had built before he got transferred to Fort Calgary. It wasn't open but Doc persisted with argument and bribes until it was. Then, while a herd of local idlers watched, Doc went through his repertoire of tricks. Cutters and slow curves. He bowled a bit with his left hand, which drew applause. All the while, Overcross sat in chains at the edge of Doc's imagination. After every good shot, Doc would tip his hat.

DOC HAD HIRED A HALFBREED boy named Paul to watch the road. He left instructions to watch for two things: a young cowboy with bandaged hands riding a yellow horse, and a wagon with a trunk in the back and a white lady sharing the driving seat with one of the Gladstone boys. There should be a tall buckskin following after.

For a long time the boy watched in vain, and what finally came of Jim Adams was not the horseman himself but a letter.

Dear Doc,

I told Mr. Craig my story and, lucky for me, there was an English visitor present fresh from Macleod who knew it too and vouched for its being the truth. Mr. Craig was disappointed that I had taken to drink, but in the light of this new information, has agreed to give me a chance. So I have my job and we are busy building barns and corrals. My hands have healed enough to work.

Mr. Craig and Mr. Hill had an adventure with the blizzard too. Mr. Hill is one of the English owners of our ranch, which is called the New Oxley. The blizzard trapped them by some lakes on the far side of the Porcupines. They were stuck tight and caught fish and shot ducks for their living. Mr. Hill blazed a tree and carved their story. That's how close he thought they were to not getting out.

When I left you at Macleod, I thought I was coming straight back. I didn't say what I should have said which is thank you for my life, especially now that it looks worth living. If not for you,

I'd either be drunk or dead. The shame often drove me close to killing myself.

This is not a farewell letter as I'm sure we'll see one another again. For one thing, I have Pete and you're not likely to leave without him. And whenever the magistrate comes to Macleod, there will be a trial. I want to testify against Overcross. Make sure they don't forget me.

After that is over, I will go back east for Penny. Mr. Craig said he would employ her as a cook. If you happen to be chasing your beef herd to the railroad camps around then, I hope to ride with you at least part way.

Have you seen Esther yet? I hope so. I hope you have reconsidered doing nothing about her. My only regret is that we never shot Victor. Oh well.

Your friend,

Jim

A few days later, Paul got to earn his money. He ran into Kamoose's hotel greatly excited. The white lady with the trunk and the Gladstones and the lame buckskin had all arrived together. Doc got up and went to the granite basin. The water in the bucket wasn't too foul and he risked shaving.

The wagon was in front of the livery barn when Doc got there. Billy Gladstone was taking harness off their horses, while Alex sat on the wagon seat regaling young friends with his adventures. Esther stood on a nearby boardwalk, having her hands pressed by two ladies in bonnets. She watched Doc come but did not make any move in his direction.

Doc greeted the Gladstones, shaking their left hands because his right was still in a sling, then he went to the back of the wagon and visited Louie and Tulip, both of whom were tied there. Louie's leg was bad again, and Doc promised him solemnly that he wouldn't have to go anywhere for a long time, that Doc would buy him a long rest, either here at the livery corral or on somebody's ranch. In his head, he knew that he might never ride Louie again and was resigned to it. Then Doc noticed that Alex had stopped in his story when his segundo showed up.

"Go on, Alex. I won't interrupt, not unless you portray me badly."

So Alex started again and Doc listened, with one eye on Esther.

Finally, she excused herself from the women and came to him. Her face was smudged with campfire ash. There were burned spots on her riding skirt. She was freckled by the sun.

She took off her hat, shook out her hair, put her arms around him. Careful of his arm, she set her head on his shoulder.

"I passed Victor on the road," she said. "I told him I was on my way. I'll go to Fort Benton with a freighter or the mail driver. From there, I'll take a stagecoach to the nearest train. It's at Butte, I think."

Doc was looking through a coil of her hair at the two women. Shock and surprise didn't begin to cover it.

"Maybe there's another way," he said.

"What?"

"This snow's going fast. Soon I'll take that beef herd to the railroad camps. I'll hire Billy and Alex if they'll come, and maybe Jim. You could join us. Then you can tell folks back home you were on a cattle drive and rode Canada's new train."

"I love you, Doc. You are the freest person I have ever known."

He was about to say his piece about not feeling so free when she got on the train, but kept it to himself.

She lifted her head and stood away. "Mrs. Austin has offered me a bath and a bed." Then she looked in his eyes and her own began to glitter and swim. "I thought you were dead."

"Overcross did his best. Jim saved us. Now Overcross is in irons and Jim's working on a ranch. I'm mainly drinking coffee and medicinal liquor and reading newspapers. I wish you'd stop crying so I don't start."

Esther dabbed her eyes with a sleeve. One crystal eye winked at him. "I'll see you," she said, and turned to the women.

After the horses and the wagon were taken care of, Doc took the Gladstone boys across to the hotel. Kamoose came out of his kitchen at the sound of his door. Doc was standing by the famous list of rules, with his finger on the number about Niggers and Indians paying double.

"This here's Billy and Alex Gladstone. They will stay here and pay the same as I do. Otherwise, I guess we'd have to go sleep in the Mounties' stable and see what stories we can think up for our keep."

Kamoose moved his hands as if he were unscrewing a jar.

"These gentlemen are as welcome in my hotel as you are."

Doc laughed. "That may be the only true statement I ever heard you say. How about some tea, boys? I can hear Mr. Kamoose's kettle ajingling."

Doc could have asked for medicinal liquor, but he didn't want anything to muddle the moment. It was as rich and satisfying and clean a moment as he could remember. For years, he had believed such moments were behind him, but here he was inside of one. Jimmy was off with Mr. Craig. Esther was in a tub of steaming water. Overcross was in irons hand and foot. Alex and Billy were laughing about what Doc had just told Kamoose. Louie was in the livery corral with a bale of hay.

Up on the Cochrane lease, Lippy might be getting married to Olaf's daughter, with big Dwight standing up for him. Maybe Lippy's wife had their first baby inside her, Doc's first grandchild of a kind.

And Dog Eye French was underneath the ground where he had chosen to be, rather than be alone and crippled all his days.

As for Pearly, Doc could not guess where she was, but felt she was somewhere. If she could give one of the richest men in Denver the slip, and her lover too, it was doubtful Overcross ever found her.

Maybe Pearly was taking a walk with her husband and some curly-haired kids. Maybe she was climbing on a billiards table, nursing a shot to the amazement of some willing fool.

Wherever she was, Doc hoped Pearly was happy. He hoped she was as happy as he was.

THE END

ACKNOWLEDGEMENTS

THANKS TO Pamela Banting for giving this novel a very important reading. Her enthusiasm for the book, and for the West itself, buoyed me over many doubts and difficulties.

Support for my previous novel *The Trade* was essential to the creation of *Lightning*. For their interest in publishing both, I thank Patsy Aldana and Scott McIntyre. Thanks as well to Patsy and to Jennifer Glossop for their guidance when the big chunks of this story were still falling off and shifting around.

I am sad that friend Cathy McKay, owner of Pages Books and Magazines in Calgary, will never see this novel, but I would like to acknowledge the great support she gave *The Trade*. When she passed away, she was gearing up to do the same for *Lightning*. Canada's book world is much poorer for her passing.

In terms of research, I thank all those who have preserved the history of the open-range ranch era in Alberta and the story of the Canadian cowboy. Making a list will leave many good people out, but I will make one anyway: L.V. Kelly, Edward Brado, Andy Russell, and Hugh Dempsey.

As for the American side of the story, it is a pleasure to acknowledge as a source Teddy "Blue" Abbott's *We Pointed Them North*. Without this true and unashamed memoir, we would know a whole lot less about the nineteenth-century American cowboy.

Many thanks to Richard Gardner, Historian of the Golden Landmarks Association, for his detailed help in picturing Golden City, Colorado, in 1867. Mr. Gardner was very generous to this Canadian stranger with his time and his knowledge.

Fred Stenson